TEMPTATION AFTER DARK

GANSETT ISLAND SERIES, BOOK 24

MARIE FORCE

Temptation After Dark
Gansett Island Series, Book 24

By: Marie Force
Published by HTJB, Inc.

Cover Design: Diane Luger
Print Layout by E-book Formatting Fairies
ISBN: 978-1952793783

View the McCarthy Family Tree *marieforce.com/gansett/familytree/*

View the list of Who's Who on Gansett Island here *marieforce.com/whoswhogansett/*

View a map of Gansett Island *marieforce.com/mapofgansett/*

The Gansett Island Series

Book 1: Maid for Love *(Mac & Maddie)*
Book 2: Fool for Love *(Joe & Janey)*
Book 3: Ready for Love *(Luke & Sydney)*
Book 4: Falling for Love *(Grant & Stephanie)*
Book 5: Hoping for Love *(Evan & Grace)*
Book 6: Season for Love *(Owen & Laura)*
Book 7: Longing for Love *(Blaine & Tiffany)*
Book 8: Waiting for Love *(Adam & Abby)*
Book 9: Time for Love *(David & Daisy)*
Book 10: Meant for Love *(Jenny & Alex)*
Book 10.5: Chance for Love, *A Gansett Island Novella (Jared & Lizzie)*
Book 11: Gansett After Dark *(Owen & Laura)*
Book 12: Kisses After Dark *(Shane & Katie)*
Book 13: Love After Dark *(Paul & Hope)*
Book 14: Celebration After Dark *(Big Mac & Linda)*
Book 15: Desire After Dark *(Slim & Erin)*
Book 16: Light After Dark *(Mallory & Quinn)*
Book 17: Victoria & Shannon (Episode 1)
Book 18: Kevin & Chelsea (Episode 2)
A Gansett Island Christmas Novella
Book 19: Mine After Dark *(Riley & Nikki)*
Book 20: Yours After Dark *(Finn McCarthy)*
Book 21: Trouble After Dark *(Deacon & Julia)*
Book 22: Rescue After Dark (*Mason & Jordan*)
Book 23: Blackout After Dark *(Full Cast)*
Book 24: Temptation After Dark *(Gigi & Cooper)*
Book 25: Resilience After Dark *(Jace & Cindy)*

More new books are always in the works. For the most up-to-date list of what's available from the Gansett Island Series as well as series extras, go to *marieforce.com/gansett*

CHAPTER 1

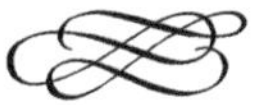

Cooper James had had a *lot* of girlfriends. So many, his mom had stopped bothering to get to know them because, as she said, they were never around long enough to make it worth the investment of time. His sisters called him the Honey Pot. Girls had been the bees, buzzing around him from the time he was old enough to realize girls were the secret to eternal happiness. When Cooper was fifteen, Mindy Farthing's father caught them having sex in their barn and threatened to shoot Cooper's balls off if he ever went near Mindy again. No one had wanted to hear that Mindy had been the one to suggest they have sex, not Cooper.

His mother had marched Cooper to the parish priest for a stern lecture about sins of the flesh.

Poor Fr. Patrick had tried to put the fear of God into young Cooper.

It hadn't taken.

The girls kept buzzing around, and he kept letting them catch him, temporarily, of course. As a make-love-not-war kind of guy, he knew just when to invoke his patented exit strategy to get himself out of a situation before it turned ugly. As a result, most of the women he'd dated in the past were still his friends, regularly checking in via text to see how he was doing.

He was doing just fine, thank you very much.

Cooper loved everything about women—their soft skin, the way they always smelled so good and how they had curves in all the right places. He liked them tall and short, thin and plump. He loved the tomboys as much as the princesses, and more than anything, he loved how freaking brilliant they were. They kept him constantly intrigued as he sought to understand what made them tick. Figuring out the unique characteristics that each new woman brought to the game had become a hobby of his.

He took his responsibility to show them a good time seriously and was always a gentleman in his dealings with them. At the outset of every new "relationship," Cooper made sure the lady of the moment knew he wasn't looking for anything serious, and if she happened to be looking for a husband, he quickly made sure she knew that wasn't going to be him. He believed in honesty and was straightforward about what he was and wasn't offering.

A good time? Absolutely. A ring on her finger? *Hell no.*

Why would any guy want to settle down with one woman when he could dine at the smorgasbord?

That said, after spending time with his brother Jared and his wife, Lizzie, Cooper saw that Jared had found something special with his wife. If someone like Lizzie came along, Cooper might be tempted to give up his serial-dating ways to settle down. But thus far, he hadn't met anyone who'd made him want to change his life that dramatically.

That was until he'd come across the goddess of all goddesses swimming in Jared's pool on Gansett Island.

Gigi Gibson.

He still couldn't believe his Hollywood crush *lived in his brother's Gansett Island garage apartment* and was *swimming in his pool.*

In a white bikini.

Dear God, the woman was so smoking hot that Cooper had been tongue-tied around a female for the first time in his life. Also, for the first time, one of the "bees" had been somewhat underwhelmed by Cooper's honey. She'd played along with his flirtatious banter (another of his trademarked skills), but he had a feeling she'd be fine if she never saw him again.

Whereas he was counting the minutes until their date that night. With the island contending with a power failure and a heat wave, he wasn't sure what would be open, but he was determined to show her a good time anyway.

He, Cooper James, was going out, on a *date*, with *Gigi Gibson*. Best day of his life, and it was just getting started. Before he did anything else, he had to find Jared and convince him he needed to let Coop borrow the Porsche. A woman like Gigi had certain expectations, and Cooper was determined to meet them by not asking if she could drive.

Things were tense around the house right now. Jared had told Cooper that their latest attempt at IVF had failed, and they weren't sure what they were going to do. A pervasive feeling of sadness had overtaken them, so he needed to tread lightly on his frivolous request to borrow Jared's prized Porsche—the first splurge Jared had made after he started making money. He was incredibly sentimental about that car.

Cooper's heart ached for Jared and Lizzie, who were so stupidly in love, it wasn't even funny. They were also filthy rich thanks to Jared's astounding success as a stockbroker. They were proof, however, that there were some things money couldn't buy. After Jared told him what they were going through, Cooper had wondered if he maybe ought to head back to New York to give them some privacy. But both Jared and Lizzie had asked him to stay. They said he was an entertaining distraction that they could use right now. So, he was staying until he wore out his welcome.

He found his brother by the pool, reading *The Wall Street Journal* and puffing on the once-in-a-while cigar Lizzie allowed him—as long as he smoked it outside. Since Jared's house had a generator, they weren't suffering through the blackout the same way much of the rest of the island was, but it was stuffy in the house with the AC running on low.

"Hey, Coop. What's up?"

Cooper stretched out on the lounge next to Jared. "You've been keeping secrets from me, brother."

Jared looked over at him. "What secrets?"

"Hello? *Gigi Gibson is living in your garage apartment?*"

"So?"

"I already knew you were older than dirt, but do you honestly have no idea who and what she is?"

"She's on some show with Mason's girlfriend, Jordan."

Cooper laughed. "Some show. It's only the number one show on TV."

"Is it?"

"Duh. Honestly, Jared, how can you not know this?"

"And you watch it?"

"*Everyone* watches it. It's the funniest fucking thing you've ever seen. Two beautiful women who are *hilarious* together, living their best lives."

"I'll have to check it out."

Cooper rolled his eyes. "If you got your nose out of *The Wall Street Journal* for ten minutes a day, you might find there's more to life than growing your fortune."

"I already knew that, thank you very much. Just because I don't watch much TV doesn't mean I don't have a life."

"I know you do, but you need to watch their show. It's awesome."

"I'll do that. If you're a fan of the show, you must've heard she and Jordan are filming out here."

"I did hear something about that, but no one told me she's living at my brother's place."

"I didn't know you'd care."

"I care."

"Did you come out here hoping to run into her?"

"I came to see my brother and sister-in-law and attend my other brother's wedding," Cooper said with feigned indignation.

"You must've flipped a nut when you found her right here with us," Jared said, laughing.

"I did! She was in the pool in a white bikini, and I almost swallowed my tongue."

"I have to admit I love the idea of a woman like Gigi looking down her nose at you."

"She's so far out of my league as to be laughable."

"No, she isn't. She's a nice person. Lizzie and I like her a lot."

"I have a feeling I could like her a lot, too."

"This is very interesting," Jared said.

"Don't go blabbing to the girls about this," Cooper said. "The last thing I need is the sisters knowing about Gigi."

"I'll see if I can refrain from spreading this very juicy gossip."

"You do that. Where's Lizzie?"

"Inside with Jessie and the baby."

"How's that going?"

"Who knows? I have no idea what we're doing with a newborn staying with us, especially right now." Cooper couldn't miss the edge in Jared's tone, which was highly unusual when speaking of his beloved wife. "I don't want her doing this, but you know Lizzie. When she hears of someone in need, she can't help herself, even if it's at her own expense."

"Are you mad?" That would be unprecedented, as far as Cooper knew.

"I can't be mad with her and her big heart. It's just sometimes I wish she'd put herself first. She took the latest IVF failure hard. Hell, we both did. She's barely had ten minutes to process that news, and now she's brought home a new mom and an infant? That's not in Lizzie's best interest."

"Probably not."

"Even if it breaks her heart, she'll help Jessie with whatever she needs."

"She's probably the best person I know."

"She's the best person any of us has ever known. We should all aspire to be more like her, but I hate to see her hurt."

"What can I do?"

"It helps to talk about it, so thanks for listening to me rant."

"I'm always happy to listen. I might be the stupid younger brother, but I feel for you guys."

"You're not stupid, Coop. You just graduated with honors from NYU business school."

"That was a fluke."

"No, it wasn't. I read your proposal last night."

Cooper's heart skipped a beat. He couldn't recall the last time he'd wanted something as much as he wanted Jared's approval of the business plan he'd crafted during the MBA program at NYU. "You did? And?"

"It's brilliant."

"You think so?"

"I really do. It's a great idea to create a business to support the growing wedding industry on the island. Booze cruise bachelorette and bachelor parties will be a huge hit. I have one major concern, though."

"What's that?"

"Liability. Putting drunks on boats is a huge risk."

"I thought of that and built in a robust insurance plan as well as a three-drink limit on the boats. In addition to that, we'll breathalyze them on the way in."

"That's a good idea. The last thing you need is drunk people falling overboard."

"We workshopped that scenario in my business law class. The professor thought it was a meaty issue for the class to take on, and they helped me perfect the plan."

"I'm impressed, Coop. For real."

"Thank you." Jared's approval had always meant the world to Cooper, but never more so than now as he stood on the cusp of starting his own business.

"I assume you're looking for investors."

"Only if it sounds like a good idea to you. I've got a plan to move forward on my own if you're not interested." Cooper had made up his mind to start this business on his own—or as much on his own as he could with the money Jared had shared with each of his family members. "I have some money of my own from the investments I've made. They're doing surprisingly well."

"Good for you."

"Got to keep up the James reputation, after all."

Jared laughed. "You're well on your way. It's a sound idea, and it seems like you've done your homework. I'm happy to invest some start-up capital if that would help."

"That'd be amazing, Jared. Thank you."

"What else can I do to help?"

"Two things. I could use an introduction to Kara Ballard—"

"Torrington now. She and Dan got married."

"Right. I heard that."

"What do you need with her?"

"I want to buy my boats from Ballard Boatworks. I thought she might be able to facilitate that."

"What's the second thing?"

"A business introduction to the McCarthys. I'd like to operate out of their marina if they'll have me."

"I can do that. They're good people. Soon to be Quinn's in-laws."

"I'm looking forward to getting to know them better. And while I have you, there is one more favor I'd like to ask."

"What's that?"

"As I said, I met Gigi earlier. Through some miracle, I got her to agree to go out with me."

"I thought you didn't ask out women as a rule?"

Mortified to hear Jared say that so bluntly, he said, "Usually, I don't have to. *They* ask *me* before I can get around to asking them. But in this case, I did the asking."

"And she said yes?"

"Don't act so surprised."

Jared cracked up. "Does she have any idea what she's getting herself into with you?"

For the first time in his entire life, Cooper felt a twinge of discomfort over his track record with women. "No, and she'd better not hear it from you."

"She won't, Honey Pot."

"Shut up with that."

Jared lost it laughing. He laughed so hard, he had tears in his eyes. "You and Gigi Gibson. She'll eat you up and swallow you whole."

Cooper went immediately hard at the thought of such a thing. "I can only hope so."

"Ewww, that's not what I meant."

Cooper waggled his brows at Jared. "But what a picture you painted."

"You're disgusting."

"Nothing disgusting about it, brother. If you find it so disgusting, maybe I could give you some pointers."

"Save your pointers," Jared said disdainfully. "What's the favor?"

"Can I *please* borrow the Porsche tonight?" He felt like an idiot little kid begging to borrow his big brother's car, but as a resident of New York City, he didn't own a car, and since he was there on vacation, his options were limited.

"Absolutely not."

"Oh, come on, Jared! Lizzie told you to let me use it, and I won't let anything happen to it. I can't go out with a woman like Gigi and ask her to drive."

"Why not? She's a woman of the new millennium. She won't mind driving."

"Please, Jared? I want to do this right."

Jared lowered his aviator sunglasses for a closer look at Cooper. "What's gotten into you?"

"Nothing. It's just that she's *Gigi Gibson*."

"Yes, I'm aware of that."

"You're not. You've never seen the show. She's a fucking *goddess*. Every hetero man in America would kill to go out with her, and she's *going out with me*. I can't ask her to drive or to take her car."

"If I let you borrow the Porsche, you have to promise nothing will happen to it, because I'd hate to have to kill you."

"I promise. Nothing will happen to it."

"When I say, 'kill you,' I hope you know I mean it."

Grinning, Cooper said, "You'd never kill me. You need me around for comic relief."

Jared rolled his eyes. "If you hurt my baby, I *will* kill you."

CHAPTER 2

Jared was going to kill him. He was a total idiot for trying to get a selfie with Gigi and the car at the bluffs. And now the car was hanging off the edge of a cliff, and he'd about crippled himself trying to stop it from going over. Only a rotted log stood between him and certain disaster.

Gigi was on the phone with the fire department dispatcher. In the distance, he could hear the trucks coming.

They weren't going to arrive in time.

He couldn't hold on much longer. He'd have to let go of the car or go over with it. Going with it might be preferable to dealing with Jared if his precious car ended up at the bottom of a cliff.

In trying to stop the car from going off the edge, Cooper had smashed his ribs by slamming against the log. He wasn't sure what he'd done to his face, but it hurt like a mother-effer. That probably happened when he lunged for the car as it started to roll toward the edge.

Gigi had screamed and run for more stable ground while he waged war with gravity—a war gravity was about to win. He had one, maybe two minutes before the car would be a total loss.

"Cooper, let go!" Gigi screamed at him. "It's not worth risking your life! Jared wouldn't want you to do that!"

Jared *would* want him to do that, and Cooper wasn't letting go until he absolutely had to. If it felt like his fingers were about to separate from his hands, well, then, so be it. The sirens were getting closer. If he could just hang on for another minute, he could save the car and his own life. Pain radiated from his hands and arms through his entire body. Every muscle was engaged in the effort to hold on.

"Cooper, *please*! Let it go!" Gigi sounded like she was crying now, and he hated that. He'd wanted this to be such a fun night for them, and it'd turned into a disaster.

The sirens were close enough now that their volume hurt his ears. That was a good sign, right?

He was at the end of his rope in every possible way by the time a firefighter appeared next to him with a chain that he wrapped around the car's bumper. "You can let go now."

Cooper's arms and hands were so strained that he couldn't get them to comply with the firefighter's directive.

Gigi appeared at his side.

"Get back," the firefighter said to her. "This ground isn't stable."

She pried Cooper's hands from the car's bumper and half dragged him to safety. "Jesus H. Shitballs," she muttered when the two of them landed on the grass. "You scared the *fuck* out of me."

"Sorry."

A paramedic approached them. "Are you hurt?"

"I, uh, I think I might be." The pain coming from his chest was too intense to be ignored.

"He landed against the log when he lunged for the car, hit his face and chest," Gigi said.

Cooper could only recall realizing the car was going off the bluff and that he had seconds to stop it.

"His hands are messed up, too," Gigi said.

"We'll take him to the clinic and have them check him over," the paramedic said.

"Gigi, are you okay?" another guy asked. He had to be at least six and a half feet tall and wore a white shirt, whereas the other firefighters were in blue shirts.

"Oh, hey, Mason. I'm fine. My friend Cooper just kept his brother's car from going off the bluffs."

"Holy shit," Mason said. "You're lucky you're not dead."

"Believe me," Coop said, "I know."

"Cooper, meet Gansett Fire Chief Mason Johns. Mason, this is Cooper James."

"Thought I recognized the Porsche. Your brother is Jared?"

"Yeah."

"You want me to notify him?" Mason asked.

"God, no. I don't want him to ever know this happened."

"Ah, okay. Good luck with that on this island where everyone knows everything."

Cooper groaned. Jared would kill him for the near miss, not to mention whatever damage the chain around the bumper would do as the firefighters cranked the car back to solid ground.

"How'd the car get that close to the edge?" Mason asked.

"He wanted a selfie with me, the car and the sunset," Gigi said.

"Somehow, I knew you were going to say the word 'selfie,'" Mason said. "If you knew how many people have fallen off these bluffs in recent years, you wouldn't have driven around the barriers."

Cooper wanted to tell the guy to take off with his lectures. Yes, they'd done something stupid. Yes, they shouldn't have done it. Yes, they'd learned their lesson. Did he honestly think they hadn't gotten the message when the car started rolling toward the edge of the cliff? And he'd been so certain he'd left it in gear when he got out.

He was spared further lecturing when the paramedics loaded him—painfully—onto a gurney and rolled him across bumpy ground to the ambulance. "You can take the car home," he said to Gigi.

"I'm not going home. I'll follow you to the clinic."

"You don't have to do that. This isn't what you signed on for when I asked you to go out with me."

"This is the most exciting night I've had since I came to Gansett Island."

"That can't possibly be true."

"It's true, and I'm not going to ditch you." She gave him a saucy wink. "Not yet, anyway."

After Gigi headed for the car to follow the ambulance, the younger of the two paramedics stared at Cooper, his eyes wide. "Holy shit, was that *Gigi Gibson?*"

"The one and only."

"And you were *on a date* with her?"

"I was. Not sure what you'd call it now." *Disaster* was a good word.

"*Dude...*"

"Believe me, I know."

"I heard a show was filming here, but no one said it was them."

"I think that might've been deliberate. They wanted to surprise their viewers."

"Color me surprised. How'd you meet her?"

"She's a friend of a friend."

"Quit bugging him and give him something for the pain," an older female paramedic said.

"Don't give me anything that'll knock me out. I have to drive later."

"You're not doing any more driving tonight, sport," she said. "And you should take the meds before they examine you at the clinic."

"Fine," Cooper said with a sigh. "But don't knock me out. I don't need this guy moving in on Gigi while I'm out of it."

"Haha, as if," the young man said. "She wouldn't look twice at me."

Cooper would've laughed if the pain hadn't required his full attention. After this, Gigi would never look at him again either. She was just being nice going to the clinic. Sighing, Cooper closed his eyes and tried not to think about the pain coming from his ribs, face, arms and hands. Whatever the paramedic had given him had dulled the pain somewhat, making him feel like he was floating.

Until the ambulance hit a bump.

Cooper bit his lip so he wouldn't scream from the pain. Shit, this fucking *sucked*. He'd had a date with the woman of his dreams, and he'd had to ruin it by being a fool with the car and the selfie. He had no one to blame but himself for the disaster this night had turned into. How long would it take for Jared to hear about this?

GIGI HAD KICKED off her heels to drive the car, giving thanks to the high school friend who'd taught her how to drive a stick. Since she hadn't done it in years, the car stalled when she shifted it into gear, until she realized the clutch released lower than she was accustomed to and needed more gas to keep from stalling.

As she followed the ambulance into town, she hoped Jared didn't see her driving his car and wonder what the hell had happened to Cooper.

When he'd lunged toward the cliff to grab the car, her heart had nearly stopped. And while they waited the endless minutes it took for help to arrive, she'd been certain every second that Cooper was about to plunge to his death, all to save a stupid car.

"Sorry," she said to the car. "I know you're a very expensive, very pretty car, but he shouldn't have risked his neck to save you."

In response to her comment, the car stalled at the next stop sign.

Gigi restarted the car, and as she released the clutch, it lurched forward. The car was probably in more danger with her driving it than it had been while teetering on the edge of disaster. After she pulled into the clinic parking lot and shut off the engine, she breathed a sigh of relief.

What was she even doing here? She'd just met Cooper that morning and was under no obligation to sit by his bedside. Except he'd been sweet and funny and charming before the car started rolling toward the edge of the bluffs.

"It's all your fault," she said to the car. "This was turning out to be a rather nice evening before you ruined everything."

When was the last time she'd been out on a traditional date in which the guy showed up at her door with handpicked wildflowers and told her how happy he was to be spending time with her? Um, never?

The wildflowers had been a nice touch, especially since Cooper came from staggering wealth and could've gotten her the most elaborate floral arrangement the island had to offer. She vastly preferred his handpicked wildflowers to elaborate bouquets that were a dime a dozen, not to mention he was ridiculously handsome.

She'd noticed that at first glance from the pool that morning, and when he'd arrived at her door, dressed for an evening out, he'd taken her breath away. He'd worn khaki shorts and a white cotton button-down rolled up to reveal sexy forearms, with a chunky silver watch on his left wrist. The white shirt offset his deep tan and the dirty-blond hair that was effortlessly messy, as was the scruff on his jaw. He was God's gift to women, but the funny thing was, he didn't seem to know it. Before disaster struck, he'd been sweet, nervous and funny.

She'd laughed more in the hour before the car started to roll than she had with any guy in longer than she could remember. Men had become tedious to her. They were all the same as they bent themselves into contortions trying to impress her with their endless bullshit.

Cooper was refreshing. He hadn't tried to be anything other than himself, and even though he'd scared the shit out of her by trying to save the car, she gave him credit for the effort. His brother was one of the world's richest men and could buy the Porsche a thousand times over. But Cooper had still risked his own life to save the car, and she had to give him big points for that, even if she'd died a thousand deaths waiting for the firefighters to arrive.

Speaking of firefighters, she hadn't mentioned to Jordan that she was going out with Cooper. Mason would tell her, as they told each other everything. They were so crazy in love as to be nauseating.

"Oh, shut up," she said as she found her cell in her purse. "You're just jealous."

Watching Jordan fall madly in love with Mason had been jarring, to say the least. After Jordan's disastrous marriage to rapper Zane ended in dramatic fashion, Gigi had expected her best friend to stay single for a while. But then she'd met Mason when he saved her life, and Jordan had been a goner for him almost from the get-go.

Gigi would never understand why people wanted to shackle themselves to one person for the rest of their lives. Monogamy made no sense to her. She'd never seen it work long term. Her ex-mother was married for the third time, her ex-father for the fourth, and from what she heard from people at home, both marriages were failing.

She'd stopped bothering to get to know her various stepparents, because the marriages never lasted. Hell, she barely heard from the parents who'd adopted her and then forgot about her until she took them to court to emancipate when she was sixteen.

Jordan and her twin sister, Nikki, had been through one of the worst custody battles Gigi had ever witnessed after their parents split. Yet they were madly in love with Mason Johns and Riley McCarthy. Love was in the air on Gansett Island. Riley's brother, Finn, had fallen hard for Chloe Dennis, and even Riley and Finn's dad, Kevin, had found new love with Chelsea after his thirty-year marriage ended.

Why did people put themselves through it? Gigi would never understand that, even if she had to admit that she'd never seen Jordan happier than she was with Mason. They each glowed when the other was around, and Jordan smiled all the time, even when Mason wasn't there.

She composed a text to Jordan. *Before you hear it from Mason, I went out with Cooper James (Jared's brother) tonight.*

Jordan wrote right back, probably because Mason was on duty, and she was home alone. If Mason was off, it could take twelve hours for Jordan to respond to a text. That was another remarkable change in her always-connected friend since the freakishly tall fire chief had come into her life. *Where'd you see Mason?*

Of course Jordan would rather know where she'd seen Mason than what Gigi was doing with Cooper. *Ran into a little problem at the bluffs, and the firefighters came.*

OMG! You didn't fall off, did you?

No, but Jared's Porsche almost did. Cooper somehow stopped it from going over. Very scary.

HOLY SHIT, G. Are you ok?

I'm fine, but Coop is banged up. We're at the clinic. Or, well, he is. I'm sitting outside wondering what I'm doing here.

The phone rang, and Gigi took the call from Jordan. "Hey."

"What the hell, G?"

"I know! I have no idea what's happening."

"Tell me the whole thing. How'd you end up going out with him?"

"I was swimming in Jared's pool, and Cooper came out. We started talking, he asked me to go out, and I thought he was cute, so I said yes."

"You said *yes*? You never say yes the first time a guy asks you out."

That was true. Before she agreed to go out with any guy, she usually made them ask three or four times to make sure they were legit. Cooper had asked only once. "He seemed nice, and I'm bored with you and your sister being all domesticated. It was something to do." As she said those words, she felt disloyal to Cooper, which was weird. She'd known him for twelve hours. Why would she feel disloyal to him?

It was those damned wildflowers.

"Is Cooper okay?" Jordan asked.

"I think so. He hurt his ribs and his face and probably his hands and arms."

"That must've been really scary."

"It was crazy. I kept screaming at him to let go, but he wouldn't. There was this rotted log, and he had his feet hooked behind the log as he held on to the car for dear life. I don't even know how it all happened. One minute, we were messing around taking sunset pictures with the car, and the next minute, he was lunging and bleeding."

"Yikes. Sounds like a close call."

"It was. My hands are still shaking, and I have no idea why I'm sitting outside the clinic worrying about a guy I barely know."

"If Cooper is anything like Jared, I bet he's hot."

"He's not ugly."

Jordan cracked up. "I'm still trying to get past you saying yes to him the first time he asked."

"Don't make a thing of it. I told you. I'm bored, sweaty and sick of this power failure and heat wave."

"Right."

If there was one person she could never lie to, it was Jordan, who knew her better than anyone else on earth.

"Maybe he's your one."

"Oh my God. Will you listen to yourself? My *one*? I have no interest in having a *one*, and you know that."

"Don't knock it till you've tried it," Jordan said in that sexy, suggestive tone that had come along after she started getting busy with Mason.

"Not happening, so you can quit with all your blissed-out bullshit. I went out with Cooper because it was something to do. That's it."

"So, you're not going inside to check on him?"

"I'll do that because I'm not a monster, but then I'm going home."

"I want you to do something for me."

"What?"

"Give this guy a chance. If he's anything like his brother, he's a really good guy."

"He's an *infant*. I think he's barely twenty-five."

"So what?"

"Come on, J. Get real, will you? This is me we're talking about. You know how I am."

"I know how you've *been*. That doesn't mean things can't change."

"Things can only change when you want them to. I'm happy just the way I am."

"Are you, though?"

Gigi laughed. "You're killing me with this. You're all freshly fucked twenty-four seven these days, so you think everyone wants what you have."

"First of all, it's not twenty-four seven."

"Okay, twenty-three six, then."

"Very funny. You'll have to forgive me if I want my best friend to know what it's like to be in love."

"I'm good. Thanks, though."

"How can you know that when you've never gone there?"

"I know it because I've seen where going there gets people, and I'm not interested."

"You think Mason is going to break my heart, or Riley is going to break Nikki's?"

"I haven't given that much thought, to be honest. They both seem like nice guys, and I'm happy for you two. I honestly am. But that lifestyle isn't for me. Why are we even having this conversation? I went out on a date. Big whoop. People do that all the time. Dates are something to do when you're sick of doing nothing. They don't necessarily lead to happily ever after."

"They can."

Exasperated, Gigi said, "Just because you've been bitten by the love bug doesn't mean I want to be. That's the last thing I want. I like my life just the way it is, thank you very much. I've got to run and check on Cooper and get home. I've got client work to do." Somehow, she'd managed to keep up with her law practice and the needs of most of her LA clients while marooned on Gansett Island for the summer.

"Text me later and let me know how he is."

"I will."

Gigi ended the call with a feeling of relief that she'd shut down Jordan's nonsense. Soon enough, she'd be back in LA where she belonged, and her summer on Gansett would be a distant memory. Couldn't happen soon enough for her.

CHAPTER 3

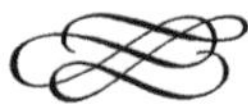

Where was she? She'd said she was coming to the clinic, so what was keeping her? Had she wrecked Jared's Porsche on the way? Ugh, wouldn't that be the ultimate irony? After Cooper had nearly killed himself saving the car, she crashed it. And if that'd happened, was she okay?

She'd come to the door earlier in a yellow floral dress that barely covered all the most important parts, sky-high wedge sandals and her blonde hair falling in waves down her back.

As long as he lived, he'd never forget how gorgeous she'd looked standing in her doorway with the sun shining down on her or how her brown eyes had lit up with delight when she saw the wildflowers he'd brought her.

They'd been a nice touch, if he said so himself.

Ugh, where was Gigi, and where was the doctor? He'd been waiting almost thirty minutes since the rescue brought him in. Cooper was apt to die of the heat that had overtaken the clinic, even with a generator keeping the lights on. A nurse had told him the doctor was with another patient and would be with him shortly. He ought to take it as a good sign that they weren't worried about him dying or anything.

Things might've turned out differently earlier if the car had gone off the cliff and taken him with it. The thought of that had him breaking into a cold sweat. He could've been killed. A degree of slope here or there, and this story could've ended very badly. It was his own fault for forgetting to deploy the emergency brake when he parked outside the logs that had been placed to keep drivers from doing exactly what Cooper had done.

So stupid.

And so freaking lucky.

He took a deep breath and instantly regretted it when pain lanced through his chest.

"I'm so sorry to keep you waiting," the dark-haired doctor said when he came into Cooper's cubicle and did a double take. "Oh, hey, Cooper. I'm Dr. David Lawrence. We met a while ago when I used to live at Jared's place."

"Yes, I remember. I'd say it's nice to see you again, but..."

"What happened?"

Cooper relayed the story of the car and the bluffs and the near miss with catastrophe.

"Holy crap, so you kept it from rolling off the edge?"

"Somehow."

"Jared loves that car."

"Believe me, I know."

Dr. Lawrence consulted the computer. "The nurse says you've got pain in your ribs, and obviously your face is a mess."

"Worst pain I've ever had right here," Cooper said, pointing to the ribs on his right side.

"We'll take X-rays to see if anything is broken." He leaned in for a closer look at Cooper's face. "What happened here?"

"I dove for the car and connected with rotted wood on the ground."

The doctor took a closer look. "You've got splinters in there that're going to have to come out."

Cooper choked back the bile that rose to his throat at the thought of having splinters picked out of his injured face. It already hurt bad enough. What was that going to feel like?

"We'll numb you up before we do it," the doctor said, patting Cooper's shoulder. "When was your last tetanus shot?"

"I have no idea."

"We'll take care of that for you, too. I'll be back in a minute."

He'd no sooner left the cubicle than Gigi appeared, looking as fresh and pretty and put together as she had when they left the house. But then again, she hadn't dived on the ground to grab a rolling car. "Hey," he said. "You made it."

"I made it, and so did the car."

"That's good," Cooper said, relieved to hear she and the car were okay.

"What're they saying about you?"

"The doc was just in. They're going to take X-rays and pick the splinters out of my face. Can't wait for that."

"Ouch."

"No kidding. He said they'd numb me up, but does that mean shots in the face?"

"I don't even want to know."

"Sorry this night turned into such a shitshow. That wasn't what I had planned."

Gigi came in and took a seat next to the bed. "What did you have planned?"

"After we watched the sunset at the bluffs, we were going find some dinner and go to the Beachcomber to listen to music. I hear there's a guy there who plays the guitar, and he's really good."

"That would've been fun."

"Can I have a rain check?"

She shrugged. "We'll see."

That wasn't what Coop wanted to hear, but he could hardly blame her after the mess he'd made of their first date. "You don't need to hang out. Take the car and go home if you want. I'll grab a cab when I'm done here."

"I don't mind waiting."

"Are you sure?"

"I'm sure, but I'm not watching them pick splinters out of your face."

"Can't say I blame you. That's not high on my to-do list either."

"What is? High on your to-do list, I mean."

He got the feeling she was making conversation to keep his mind off the splinters in his face. "I'm working on starting a business."

"What kind of business?"

He told her about his idea for booze cruises for bachelor and bachelorette parties. "The wedding industry has gotten big on the island. I figured there might be a space for supporting services."

"That's an interesting idea."

"I'm glad you think so."

"If you need a lawyer to look over the particulars for you, let me know. I'm not licensed in Rhode Island, but I could give you nonbinding advice."

Cooper stared at her in disbelief. "You're a *lawyer*?"

"I am."

"I thought I knew everything there was to know about you from watching the show."

Gigi scoffed. "We show you what we want you to see—two silly women doing silly stuff and having fun."

"How come you don't talk about being a lawyer?"

"Because that's boring and doesn't make for good TV."

"I can't believe this."

"Why? Because I seem too silly to be an attorney?"

"God, no. Not at all. Anyone who watches the show can see how smart you both are. That's what makes it so fun to watch. Well, that and the fact that the two of you are hot as fuck."

"Are we?"

Now he scoffed. "As if you don't know that."

"We've heard that a few times, but we're both about more than how we look."

"I knew that before you told me you're an attorney."

"Is that right?"

"Hell yes. The stuff you guys do for underprivileged kids in LA is amazing."

"That started when one of our producers told us about a family in her kids' school who didn't have the money for school supplies. We said that's something we can help with. Jordan and I got that family what they needed, and then we started to think about how we could help other families who had the same problem. It kind of took off from there, and now we do drives in all fifty states."

"It's very impressive."

"Thanks. Knowing we're doing some good makes us feel less ridiculous about how silly the show is."

"The show isn't silly."

"Yes, it really is, but it's fun, and people seem to enjoy it. It'll be weird not doing it anymore."

"Wait, so this is the last season?"

"I think so. Jordan hasn't said for sure, but she's happy as a pig in shit with her giant firefighter. I don't see her wanting to leave here any time soon. And there's no way I'm staying after we finish shooting."

"You're not digging Gansett, huh?"

"It's not that. The island is beautiful, and I've met so many great people here."

"But it's not home."

"Right. And of course a days' long power failure during a heat wave isn't helping to make Gansett look good to me."

"I guess not. Home is LA?"

"Always has been, but I don't know. I may relocate."

"To where?"

"I don't know yet. Just somewhere I can be left alone."

"Why do you look sad when you say that?"

"Do I?"

"Yeah, you do."

Before he could further pursue that line of questioning, the doctor returned with a pretty, dark-haired woman.

"This is Victoria Stevens, one of our nurse practitioners. She'll be taking you for X-rays, and then we'll clean up your face wounds."

"Can't wait," Cooper said dryly. He looked up at Gigi. "You really don't have to wait. I'm sure you have better things to do than hang out here."

"It's fine. I don't mind waiting. You'll need a ride home afterward."

"I can call a cab."

"I'll wait."

AFTER THEY WHEELED COOPER OUT of the cubicle for X-rays, Gigi returned to her seat in his visitor's chair. Again, she wondered what she was doing there. She hadn't even known him this time yesterday. Why was she waiting around to drive him home when he'd told her to leave? Maybe it was because he was fun and funny and cuter than any man had a right to be, even with half his face looking like ground beef.

She liked him.

And that was weird. She hardly liked anyone. Most of the people she'd chosen to trust had disappointed her at one point or another. As a result, she tended to allow very few people to get close to her. Cooper wasn't going to be an exception to that rule, but the fact that she liked him intrigued her.

Gigi prided herself on having an internal radar when it came to people. Within a matter of minutes, she could tell whether someone was full of shit. She hadn't gotten that kind of reading on Cooper. She wasn't entirely sure yet what the reading on him would turn out to be, but it wasn't a full-of-shit reading. That was why she was still here, in the clinic on a warm late-summer night, waiting to give him a ride home.

GETTING THE X-RAYS SUCKED. They twisted and turned him until Cooper was sweating and nauseated from the pain radiating from his right side.

"So sorry," Victoria said. "I know it hurts. We're almost done."

After they took the last image, Cooper took a series of deep breaths that he immediately regretted. He'd had no idea that injured ribs could hurt so badly. *Fuck.* This was not how he'd hoped to spend this evening with the woman of his dreams. She was a trouper for sticking it out, even though he wouldn't have blamed her if she'd cut and run.

He felt like such a fool for the incident at the bluffs. He'd behaved like every other tongue-tied dickwad she'd ever dated by wanting a selfie with her and the car and the sunset. As if he might have to someday prove to someone that he'd once had a date with the captivating Gigi Gibson.

They wheeled him back into the exam room.

Gigi popped up from the chair when she saw him coming. "Why are you all pale and pasty?"

"Turns out that getting X-rays of injured ribs isn't as much fun as you might think."

She smiled, which made her eyes light up with mischief. "I wouldn't have thought that'd be fun."

"I can give you something a little stronger for the pain," Victoria said.

"That's okay," Coop replied. He needed to keep his wits about him for the time he had remaining with Gigi. Not that he had a chance in hell of a second date after the disaster this evening had become. But a guy could hope.

"Take it, Cooper," Gigi said. "I'll get you home."

"I don't want to be knocked out. I'd rather look at you than sleep."

Her sweet smile made him glad to be alive, as he was fully aware this evening could've turned tragic. It'd been stupid to try to save the car. He knew that. But he hated to disappoint the older brother he'd idolized all his life. That was what had motivated him to not let Jared's beloved car roll off a cliff.

Jared would be pissed when he heard what Cooper had done. His older brother had adored Cooper from the time he was born when Jared was twelve. They'd always shared a special bond, and with everything Jared and Lizzie were dealing with, the last thing Cooper wanted to do was cause further heartache for his brother by letting his prized Porsche roll off a cliff.

The doctor returned with a tray of tools that Cooper refused to study too closely, sensing he was better off not knowing what was coming.

Gigi surprised him when she took hold of his hand. "Look at me."

"Happy to." Looking at her was no hardship.

She met his gaze and held it as the doctor explained that he'd first be numbing the area with some injections.

Cooper had to struggle not to cry like a baby from the pain of the first shot.

Gigi tightened her hold on his hand, her gaze never wavering as two more shots were delivered.

Thankfully, the first one had kicked in, making the second and third ones slightly less excruciating.

Tears spilled down his cheeks.

Gigi wiped them away with a tissue as if it was no big deal to tend to him that way.

His heart felt light in his chest, which he attributed to the medication. But it wasn't just that. It was her, too. He'd had this idea of what she might be like in person, but the reality of her was so much more than what he'd imagined.

The splinter search took about thirty minutes. Cooper was thankful he couldn't feel anything, but suspected it would hurt like a bitch after the numbness wore off.

Gigi held his hand and his gaze, giving him something to focus on other than the pulling and tugging of his skin.

Victoria came into the room. "X-rays show two hairline fractures, and you're going to have some serious bruising."

"What do we do about that?" Cooper asked.

"We'll wrap them and encourage you to take it easy for a few weeks while they heal. But they'll be quite painful for a week or two."

Some vacation this was turning out to be.

"We'll make sure he doesn't do too much," Gigi said.

We will, will we? Did that mean she planned to nurse him back to health? He had to immediately shut down the train of thought that led to her in a naughty-nurse getup before he sported wood in front of everyone.

As it turned out, having broken ribs "wrapped" was no fun either.

Cooper walked out of the clinic on rubbery legs, supported by Gigi's arm around him. Having her touching him was the best part of being injured, but he'd much rather have had that happen organically. They'd given him pain pills to hold him until the pharmacy opened in the morning and antibiotic ointment for his facial injuries.

"Hang on a sec." He withdrew his phone from his pocket and turned on the flashlight to check the bumper on the Porsche. "Is it possible that they managed to pull the car back without damaging the bumper, or am I seeing things?"

Gigi leaned in for a closer look. "I don't see anything."

"Thank God for that. Jared will be checking it with a magnifying glass tomorrow."

"He will not!"

"Yes, he will."

Gigi opened the passenger door for him. "Do you need help getting in?"

"I think I've got it." Easing himself into the passenger seat of the low-slung car was almost as painful as the X-rays had been. After he landed, he put his head back against the seat and tried to breathe through the pain.

Shit, this totally sucked!

"Are you okay?" Gigi asked after she got into the driver's seat.

"Never been better."

"Right."

"I promised you dinner. You want to grab something on the way home? My treat."

"I could eat. What about you?"

He didn't think he could eat, but wanted her to feel comfortable about stopping for food. "Sure, sounds good. Want to call in an order to Mario's? I think they're open during the blackout."

"I love their house salad. What do you want?"

"A small supreme pizza cooked well-done. Unless you want some, too. If so, get a large."

"That sounds good, but I'll stick to salad until we're done shooting. I swear every pound shows up as ten on film."

"You don't need to worry about that."

"Yes, I do."

"Don't."

"Do."

She called in the order for a house salad and a small supreme pizza cooked well-done. When she started the car, it lurched forward and stalled.

Cooper had to bite his lip to keep from screaming in pain.

"Sorry. This clutch is psychotic."

"S'okay," Cooper said through clenched teeth. "Takes a second to get a feel for it." Jared would kill him for letting her drive the car, but what choice did he have? There was no way he could drive with who-knew-what drugs in his system. "Let it out slowly. That's your best bet."

She did as he directed, and the car moved smoothly forward and out of the clinic parking lot.

Cooper was glad to see the last of that place, at least for now. They'd promised to call tomorrow to see how he was doing. He could hardly wait.

CHAPTER 4

Gigi drove them slowly and carefully through town to Mario's, located behind the Beachcomber.

"We were supposed to end up there." Cooper pointed to the iconic white hotel that anchored the Gansett downtown. "Sorry to mess up our night."

"It would've been an even bigger mess if you and/or the car had gone off that cliff, so thanks for not letting that happen."

"Ha," Cooper said with a grunt of laughter. "That's the truth."

"Can I have a rain check on the Beachcomber?"

"Of course you can," Cooper said, immediately feeling a thousand times better to know they'd have a do-over.

"And how about we take my car next time?"

"Sounds good," he said, smiling.

"It's an automatic, so no clutch to worry about."

"I'm an idiot for wanting to impress you with my brother's car," Cooper said, sighing.

"You impressed me with the wildflowers and the way you risked your own safety to save something that means a lot to your brother."

Cooper wished he felt well enough to celebrate those victories. "I know it seems silly that I risked myself for something Jared could buy a thousand of and never feel the hit. But the car was the first thing he bought for himself when he struck it rich. He set us all up for life, paid off my parents' house, my grandparents' reverse mortgage, the mortgages of all our aunts and uncles, set up college funds for all our cousins. And only after all that was done did he do something for himself." Cooper looked over at her. "I couldn't let that car go off the cliff."

"That's amazing," Gigi said, "how he did those things for your family."

"He's super generous, sometimes to a fault. A few people in our family and his group of friends have tried to take advantage by treating him like a bank."

"That's so lame."

"It is, but he tries not to let it get to him. He says his conscience is clear after what he did for everyone."

"So, you're set for life, huh?"

"Yes and no. Jared put most of what he gave me in a trust until I'm thirty so I wouldn't end up useless, as he put it."

Gigi laughed. "I love that."

"I was pissed about it at the time, but he was right. If I'd had access to that when I was younger, I would've gotten into trouble. Jared gave me just enough to pay for college and grad school and let me live in his New York apartment while I was in school. And he set me up with an investment account that I've used to learn the market. He's a great teacher. I've managed to grow that account significantly."

"He's a good brother."

"He's the best. We've always been close."

"What's the age difference between you guys?"

"Twelve years. He was good to me when I was a pesky kid, always had time for me, took me places. I'd do anything for him."

"That's sweet. I don't know him and Lizzie as well as you do, but they've seemed off lately."

"If I tell you why, do you promise not to repeat it to anyone?"

"Of course."

"They've been trying to have a baby for a long time, and another round of IVF failed recently."

"Oh no. That's terrible. They'd be such great parents."

"They would. It's been so hard for them."

"It's weird how we all spend so much effort when we're younger trying not to make babies," Gigi said, "and then when we want them, some people have such an awful time."

"I know."

"And it's proof there are some things all the money in the world can't buy."

"True. Jared is worried about Lizzie getting involved with the new mom and baby."

"I can see why. Lizzie is the sweetest person I've ever met. At first, I wondered if she was for real."

"She is," Cooper said. "She's exactly how she seems. There's nothing she wouldn't do for anyone."

"I wish I was more like her."

"We all need to be more like her. Jared is always after her to be as good to herself as she is to others, and he says how she loves to spend his money on her causes—never on herself. He learned early on not to try to give her extravagant gifts. Once, he gave her a Louis Vuitton purse. She made him take it back and give her the money he spent on it, which she donated to a food bank."

Gigi reached for the purse she'd propped between the seats and put it down on the floor. "I'll be consigning this and my luggage when I get back to LA and donating the proceeds to a food bank."

Cooper laughed. "Lizzie would be proud of you."

Gigi pulled the car into the parking lot at Mario's and brought it to a smooth stop before the car stalled, lurching forward.

Cooper grunted through the pain.

"Sorry."

"No problem."

"I suck at driving a stick. I always have."

"Now you tell me," Cooper said with a laugh. "It's fine. Better you than me all doped up."

"I'll just run in and pick up the order."

Before he could tell her to wait for him to get his credit card from his wallet, she was out of the car and on her way into the restaurant, teetering on crazy heels that did wondrous things for her sexy legs.

Could this night become any more of a disaster? Now, she was paying for dinner, too. His only goal in life would be making amends for letting this night turn into such a train wreck. No other date in his extensive dating history had ever gone so wrong. Figured it had to happen with his dream woman.

She returned with a pizza box and brown bag that she handed to him to hold for the ride home.

"That was supposed to be my treat."

"Don't sweat it."

"I'm sweating it. This has to be the worst date you've ever been on."

"Haha, nowhere close to the worst. This one will be memorable. That's for sure."

Cooper wished it had been memorable for better reasons than a near catastrophe that involved EMS and a trip to the clinic, not to mention she was driving and had paid for dinner.

Thankfully, she managed to back the car out of the parking space and drive it out of the lot without stalling.

"So what's the worst date you've ever had?"

She glanced at him as if deciding if she should be truthful. "I dated this guy for a month before I realized he was a celebrity stalker who I'd let into my house and my life. I had to get a restraining order to get him away from me, and I have to testify against him when I get home."

"Damn, Gigi. That's horrible."

"People suck. That's kind of why I'm dreading going home. He's out on bail awaiting the trial."

"Do you have security?"

"Yeah, I have to have it when I'm there. He's got an ankle monitor that keeps him from leaving the area, so I'm safe here." She let out a nervous-sounding laugh. "The downside of pseudo-celebrity."

"You're hardly a pseudo-celebrity. You're the real deal."

"If you say so."

"I say so."

As they headed for Jared's, she drove slowly along the dark, winding island roads that led out of town. The sun had finished setting during their time at the clinic, and with the power out, everything was dark.

"This place could do with some streetlights," Gigi said.

Cooper laughed. "I was just thinking the same thing."

"It's dark as fuck out here."

"That it is."

"The first few weeks I was here, I was afraid to drive at night because the road home is so crazy dark. Where I come from, it's lit up like daylight at night."

"Same in New York."

"Gansett is like a foreign country. No streetlights, no stoplights, sketchy internet, basic cable, no AC in some places, power failures that last for days. I could go on."

"It's a different world, for sure."

"What's interesting, though, is I've never felt more relaxed than I do here. There's nothing to do, so that forces you to just chill and smell the roses as Evelyn says. She's Jordan and Nikki's grandmother."

"That's why Jared loved it so much the first time he came here for a wedding. He called it his decompression zone before he moved here year-round."

"I can't imagine spending a winter here."

"I bet it's fun."

"I bet it's not."

"Jared and Lizzie seem to love it, and my other brother, Quinn, and his fiancée, Mallory, love it, too."

"That's because they're all stupid in love and have each other to keep them entertained."

Cooper cracked up laughing and immediately regretted it. "Ugh, don't make me laugh."

"Sorry you're hurting."

"It's my own fault. I never should've driven around that one log to get a selfie. What was I thinking?"

"You weren't thinking," Gigi said. "We all do dumb things in the pursuit of the perfect selfie."

"I'm done with selfies after this."

"We'll see if that sticks."

Gigi took a right-hand turn into Jared's driveway and parked the car. She turned it off and removed the keys, handing them to him. "Phew. That's a relief. The car is home in one piece. Jared will never know how close he came to losing it—and his brother."

"You think we can keep that secret on this island? I bet he already knows about what happened."

Sure enough, his brother came out of his house and walked over to the driveway. Floodlights illuminated him as he came toward them with purpose in his stride.

"Yep, he already knows," Cooper said.

Jared opened the driver's door. "Are you okay?" he asked Gigi.

"I'm fine. Him? Not so much."

"What the hell happened?"

"It's kind of a long story," Cooper said.

"I've got time."

"We haven't eaten yet. Can I tell you the whole sordid tale tomorrow?"

"I guess." Jared stood to his full height and stepped back to let Gigi out of the car. "Just tell me what happened to you?"

"Two broken ribs and a banged-up face. Nothing to worry about."

"Jesus, Coop."

"The car is fine."

"I don't give a shit about the car!"

"Now you tell me."

Gigi giggled as she extended a hand to help Cooper.

He braced himself. This was going to hurt like hell. Crap, he nearly passed out from the pain of getting himself out of the car.

Gigi put an arm around him, which was the only thing that kept him from falling over.

Jared rushed around to the passenger side of the car. "Oh my God, Cooper! Your face! What the hell?"

"I'm okay. I swear."

"You're not okay. You're sweating and breathing funny."

The sound of a baby crying came from Jared's house.

"Is there, uh, anything we can do?" Cooper asked.

"No, but thanks for asking. We're going to try to find them somewhere else to stay tomorrow. I'll let you guys have dinner. Let me know if you need anything, Coop. And I do want to hear your version of the story."

"Does that mean you've already heard other versions?"

Jared had started to walk away. Over his shoulder, he said, "Maybe. Maybe not."

"Great."

Gigi laughed. "You're so busted."

"I guess so. This freaking island. Nothing stays secret here."

"Nope. Can you do the stairs to my place?"

"I hope so."

"Take it slow."

Gigi held his arm with one hand and the pizza box with the bag on top of it with the other hand.

Cooper made his way slowly and painfully up the stairs. By the time he got to the top, he was winded and sweating. He'd never been this seriously injured and hoped he never was again.

"Are you okay?"

"Yeah, sure."

"Liar. Come in and get comfy."

"I think it's going to be a while before I'm comfy."

"Let's see what we can do."

Inside, she led him to the sofa and helped him get settled with throw pillows under his right arm for support. Thanks to Jared's whole-home generator, she had power in the apartment. "How's that?"

"Not bad. Thanks." Truth be told, he was afraid he might pass out from the pain, but she didn't need to know that.

Gigi went to the kitchen and returned with a glass of ice water. "Have some of this."

Cooper took the glass from her and downed a swallow of cold water. "Thanks."

"You need to stay hydrated."

"How long until I can have more pain meds?"

"Three hours."

"I'll die before then."

"No, you won't."

"I might."

"Do you think you could eat something?"

"Maybe."

Gigi went to the kitchen and returned with plates and silverware. She put a slice of pizza on a plate and handed it to him.

"Thanks."

She took the ice water and put it on the table. "Let me know when you need more water."

"I'm really sorry you're having to tend to me like this. That's not how I wanted this evening to go."

She raised a saucy eyebrow. "You didn't hope I'd end up tending to you?"

Cooper grimaced as he held back a laugh. "I told you not to do that."

"Sorry, I can't help it."

"Try."

While she ate her salad, he took tentative bites of pizza. He wasn't sure his stomach would be hospitable to food, and the last freaking thing he needed was to puke. That would surely kill him.

"Mario's has one of the best house salads anywhere in the world," Gigi declared.

"What sets it apart?"

"The shaved Parmesan, the croutons, the house Italian dressing. So good."

"See? Gansett has her charms."

"I never said she didn't. She just has fewer charms than other places."

"Is that such a bad thing?" he asked.

"Not at all. There are some things about LA I definitely don't miss."

"Like what?"

"Traffic. It's the worst in the country."

"I've heard that. What else?"

"People."

"There are people on Gansett."

"Millions fewer than in LA. You wait in line for *everything* there. It's not unusual to spend thirty minutes waiting for coffee in the morning. We waste *so much time* waiting."

"That's true in New York, too. Drives me crazy."

"And some people are worse than others, such as the aforementioned ones who like to stalk celebrities."

Cooper paused midbite. "You have other stalkers?"

"A few of them."

"For real?"

"Yeah, it's become a problem since the show got popular."

"Shit, Gigi. Having security in LA must suck."

"It does, but it beats the alternative."

Cooper needed a minute to process what she'd told him. "And the cops are aware of this?"

"They are, and they've done what they can by arresting the one guy who crossed every line before I realized he was dangerous. More than anything, it's affected my ability to come and go freely, which is inconvenient. I resisted security for a long time until one of the stalkers got a little too close for comfort."

"What happened?"

"He was, um, in the back seat of my car when I came out of a coffee shop. He said he was in love with me and wanted us to be married and have children together."

"Holy shit. What did you do?"

"I showed him my pepper spray and told him I wasn't afraid to use it."

"Did he go away?"

"It took a few minutes, but he got the message. By then, we'd attracted a crowd that included a police officer. He had a talk with him and gave him a warning."

"He should've arrested him."

"He hadn't really done anything more than trespass, though."

"Still, he made you feel unsafe, and that shouldn't be allowed."

"I know how to take care of myself. In addition to my pepper spray, I also have a handheld Taser."

"Is that legal?"

"Ish."

Cooper smiled at the way she said that. "Whatever it takes to stay safe."

"Exactly. As you can imagine, Gansett has been a nice reprieve from all that."

"Are you safe here without security?"

"Other than Jordan's crazy ex-husband showing up and taking her grandmother and sister hostage, we haven't had any issues here. People leave us alone on Gansett."

"Zane took Jordan's grandmother and sister *hostage*?"

"Yep."

"How come I didn't hear about that?"

"They kept it quiet. The last thing Jordan wants is any more publicity tying her to him. He agreed to give her the divorce and leave her alone and to tell his fans to leave her alone, in exchange for them not pressing charges."

"Wow. He's an example of someone who had it all and let it go to shit."

"Indeed. We're all glad she's free of him. Their marriage was a nightmare for her and those of us who love her."

"Sounds like it."

"What you've seen reported about him in the media is a fraction of the reality. He's got major addiction and mental health issues that he's refused to take seriously until this happened. As part of the agreement, he was ordered to seek in-patient treatment. Again."

"Addiction is a bitch. I had some friends in college who let the partying get out of hand, and they've had problems ever since. A few have ended up in rehab. Some more than once."

"I've had friends who struggled with it, too. Drugs are way too easy to get in LA. I had friends in high school who were hooked on cocaine."

"That's young. I didn't see it until college."

"I never touched that shit. I was afraid I'd be the one person it killed the first time I tried it."

"Me, too. My dad used to tell us it only takes one time to stop your heart if you got bad shit. That scared me enough to steer clear. A little pot now and then is more my jam."

"Right there with you. But not lately. I think I've outgrown it."

"Well, you're *much* older than me. I haven't outgrown it yet."

"Watch it, mister. I'm not that much older than you."

"You're a senior citizen compared to me. A regular Mrs. Robinson."

"What do you know about Mrs. Robinson?"

"We watched *The Graduate* in grad school."

"What kind of grad school did you go to that you watched movies?"

"NYU grad school, MBA program. I took a Business of Film class, and that was one of the movies we watched."

"Huh, we never watched movies in law school. Maybe I should've gotten an MBA instead."

"Where'd you go to law school?"

"UCLA."

"I'm very impressed that you're a lawyer."

"Because I don't seem smart enough?"

"No! God, no. I just think it's interesting that you don't work the fact that you're an attorney into the show."

"That's not what the show is about. Before we started, we talked about how much of our real lives we wanted to share. For Jordan, her difficult childhood was off-limits. She and her sister were the subject of a custody battle that dragged on for years. The last thing she wanted to do was relive that nightmare in front of millions of people."

"What was off-limits for you?"

"My two ex-fiancés and my legal career."

"You have *two* ex-fiancés?"

"Yep, and that's something I don't like to talk about. I was young and dumb and thought I was in love. I dumped the second one when I was in law school, and I've learned that love and marriage aren't for me."

For some reason, hearing that made him feel sad for her—and himself. "You've lived an entire life before you're thirty."

"I don't recommend it."

Cooper had never enjoyed a conversation more than this one, but it was all he could do to stay awake. Whatever they'd given him at the clinic was about to knock him out. "I hate to say it, but I think I should head next door before I fall asleep on your sofa."

"It's okay if you want to stay put."

"And start a scandal at the James estate after our first date?"

"Pretty safe to say you've already done that."

"Probably so." Cooper started to get up, but the pain had other ideas. "I had no clue how painful injured ribs could be."

"I've heard it's a bitch."

"I can confirm you've heard correctly. Would you mind giving me a hand up?"

"No problem." She stood and extended both hands to him and then pulled him gently to his feet.

He almost passed out from the pain. When he'd recovered enough to speak, he reached out to tuck a strand of hair behind her ear. He was operating on pure adrenaline powered by pain meds. "I'm really sorry this evening turned into such a mess. Other than the car nearly rolling off the bluffs and the banged-up ribs, I had a great time."

"You forgot the splinters in your face," she said, smiling.

"How could I forget that?"

"You're going to remember when the numbness wears off."

"Can hardly wait for that. Anyway, maybe we can have a do-over some night soon?"

"Sure."

"Thanks for sticking with me through the clinic and driving me home."

"It was no problem for me. The car might say otherwise."

"The car has lived to see another day."

She shocked the shit out of him when she placed a hand on his chest. "Despite the injuries, it was pretty cool how you managed to stop the car from rolling off the cliff. There was a certain Superman-ish element to it."

"Is that right?"

"Uh-huh." She shocked him even more when she went up on tiptoes to kiss him.

The soft peck on the lips was over before it began, but Gigi Gibson had *kissed him*. He could die happy now.

But it would be much more interesting to stick around to see if she might do it again sometime soon.

CHAPTER 5

Jared woke from a deep sleep to the sound of a baby crying. At first, he thought he was dreaming, because why would a baby be crying in their house? They couldn't have babies. He reached for Lizzie, but her side of the bed was cold.

And then he remembered the mother and baby Lizzie had brought home from the clinic. This was their second night in residence, and Lizzie was up with the baby again.

Son of a bitch.

It was so rare for him to be unhappy with Lizzie, he had no idea how to handle feeling that way. He loved her madly, and under normal circumstances, he supported her in everything she did. But this… This was too much. They hadn't begun to deal with the heartbreak of learning that another round of IVF had failed, and she'd brought a newborn into their home?

He was angry with her and self-aware enough to know he needed to get that under control before he said or did something that couldn't be undone.

For a long time, he lay in bed, staring up at the ceiling as he listened to the baby cry. When he could no longer take not knowing what was going on, he got out of bed, put on gym shorts and went to find his wife.

He found her in the family room, walking the crying baby from one end to the other of the big room.

The baby cried so hard that Jared wondered how she could breathe.

"Where's Jessie?" Jared asked, looking around for the child's mother.

"She's so exhausted after being up with her all night that I told her I'd take a turn."

They had to speak loudly to be heard over the baby's cries.

"What's wrong with her?"

"I don't know. I've tried everything. I fed her, changed her, burped her, but nothing I do calms her."

Jared didn't intend to reach for the baby, but he wanted her to stop crying. He snuggled her into his arms, and she immediately went quiet, looking up at him with big gray eyes.

"How'd you do that?" Lizzie asked, sounding amazed.

"I have no idea." As he gazed down at the adorable little face, he was filled with an overwhelming feeling that this was not something he ought to be doing. He shouldn't be holding this baby who didn't belong to them. And Lizzie shouldn't be holding her either. Every instinct he had told him this wouldn't end well for them. "We can't do this, Lizzie. We just can't continue to help this way."

"I don't know what else to do. I can't let her go to the Beachcomber employee housing with a newborn, and she won't take our money. I mentioned the Chesterfield apartment to her, but she said she can't live that far from work."

"Tomorrow, she has to go somewhere else. I don't care where they go. Anywhere but here."

"I'll try to figure something out for them."

"*Jessie* needs to figure something out for them. This isn't our problem."

"I know it isn't, but how do I turn them out when they have nowhere to go?"

"Jessie must have family or friends somewhere that she can turn to for help. We'll give her money to get whatever she needs."

"She doesn't want charity."

"That's all well and good, but if she doesn't have any other options, she has to accept help."

"I'll talk to her in the morning."

"You know I try to support you in everything that's important to you."

"Yes, you do."

"This is too much for me. After everything that's happened… I can't do this, Lizzie. And you shouldn't do it either."

Her pretty eyes swam with tears, and her chin quivered.

Those tears wrecked him, but he couldn't back down when he saw them headed for catastrophe. The baby was adorable. If she stayed for even one more day, they would get attached to her, and their hearts would be broken all over again when she left.

"Please tell me you understand how I feel," he said softly, not wanting to disturb the baby, who was on her way to sleep.

"I do. I'm sorry. I never should've brought them home."

"You did what you thought was right, but tomorrow, we're relocating them."

"Okay."

"Can we take her to her mother now that she's asleep?"

"Yes, I set her up with a makeshift bassinet."

"Lead the way."

They tiptoed into the guest room where Jessie was sleeping and got the baby settled. Jared realized Lizzie had used the baby carriage they'd bought for the baby they'd hoped to have as the bassinet.

He took Lizzie by the hand and walked out of the room, leaving the door open in case Jessie needed anything. They had to get through this one night, and then they'd figure out another plan for the mother and baby.

Back in their room, Lizzie got in bed on her side and turned away from Jared.

That, too, was unusual.

"Come here, honey."

She didn't move.

That's when he realized she was crying.

Damn it.

"Lizzie."

"It's not fair."

"What isn't?"

"That she can have a baby she doesn't even want, and we can't have one we desperately want."

"How do you know she doesn't want her?"

"I can just tell. Jessie is very detached. Like she wishes she was anywhere but with the baby."

Great. This just got better and better. "I know you want to help her, but she has to figure this out for herself, Lizzie."

"I know, and that's what's so unfair. I'd give anything to have that baby, and she'd give anything *not* to have her."

Jared slid across the bed until his body was pressed up against Lizzie's and put an arm around her. "You're right that it's not fair. None of this is fair. But we have to take a step back and let Jessie deal with this situation. We can offer her any kind of help she needs, except shelter in our home."

"I'll talk to her in the morning."

"I'm sorry your heart is hurting, sweet Lizzie."

"I'm sorry yours is hurting."

"We're going to find a way to be parents. I promise you."

"I don't think I can do any more fertility treatments."

"Then we won't do that. Maybe it's time to hire a surrogate."

"Maybe," she said with a sigh. She'd resisted that avenue up until now, preferring to continue the fertility treatments in the hope of carrying her own child.

"It'll happen. We just have to be patient, and we need to protect ourselves from more hurt."

"I know."

"Try to get some rest. We've got Quinn's wedding coming and lots of happy things to look forward to."

"I'll be okay."

"That's the only thing that matters to me—that you're okay and not hurting. Having the baby here is hurting us both."

"I wish we could keep her."

"Lizzie..."

"I know we can't. But I wish we could."

Jared wished with all his heart that he could give her the baby she wanted so badly, but it wasn't going to be Jessie's baby. They needed to get that baby out of their house before a bad situation got worse.

COOPER DIDN'T SEE Gigi the day after their date, or the day after that. He'd heard from Jared that she sometimes disappeared for days at a time when they were filming the show. The first two days with broken ribs had totally sucked, but after that, Cooper started to feel better. His mother used to marvel at how quickly he bounced back from illness and injuries, and he was thankful for that trait now.

While he was hoping for another chance to see Gigi, his brother Quinn married his love, Mallory, in a gorgeous ceremony at the Chesterfield, a home that Jared and Lizzie had turned into an elegant wedding venue. The festivities had been interrupted when Maddie McCarthy went into labor and had her twin baby girls in the helicopter on the way to a Providence hospital. But that hadn't been the most dramatic development at the wedding.

Nope. That'd happened when Jessie brought the baby to Lizzie at the Chesterfield in the middle of the wedding and then *left*. She'd been staying at Jared and Lizzie's for a couple of days by then, and they'd all helped out with the baby as needed. Even Cooper had taken a few turns holding the baby girl. Since Jessie had mentioned finding somewhere else for her and the baby to live, none of them could've imagined she would bring the baby to Lizzie during the wedding and then take off.

Jared had asked Cooper to go after her, to track her down at the Beachcomber, but there'd been no sign of her there or at Jared's house, or anywhere else, for that matter.

He'd returned to the Chesterfield, aching from all the activity, to figure out what he could do to help Jared and Lizzie, who were stunned by the day's events.

"I checked everywhere I could think of," Cooper said. "I even went by the clinic in case she was there."

"Thanks for trying," Jared said. "The police chief has people looking for her."

He was as stressed as Cooper had ever seen him.

"What's going on, you guys?" Quinn asked when he came upon them gathered in the foyer. "And whose baby is that with Lizzie?"

"The baby belongs to a woman named Jessie, who Lizzie was helping after she gave birth," Jared said. "She dumped the baby with Lizzie and took off. We're trying to find her, but we think she might've left on the six o'clock ferry."

"Holy shit," Quinn said. "What can I do?"

"Go back to enjoying your big day," Jared said. "We're doing what we can."

"Are you sure? I can help if you need it."

"No need, but thanks, Q. We'll be back in when we can. I'm sorry this is happening on your big day."

"Don't sweat it. Do what you need to. Nothing could ruin this day for Mallory and me."

After Quinn had walked away, Jared glanced toward Lizzie and the baby before his gaze shifted to Cooper. "We have to find her. Maybe she didn't get on the boat. Will you go to the Beachcomber and ask around to see if you can find someone who knew her? Talk to Libby, the manager, and see what she can tell you."

"I'll get on it."

"Thanks."

As he drove back into town, Cooper took a closer look at everyone he passed. He went right to the Beachcomber and found Libby in the manager's office. "Hi there, I'm Cooper James. You might know my brother Jared?"

"Of course. What can I do for you?"

"I'm trying to find one of your employees. Jessie Morgan?"

"I'm trying to find her, too. She's blown off work the last few days, and no one has heard from her."

"She had her baby."

Libby blinked several times. "She was *pregnant?*"

How had her boss not known that? "Uh, yeah?"

She took a second, seeming to think. "She started wearing larger tops, but it never occurred to me that she was pregnant. Goodness gracious."

"My sister-in-law Lizzie was asked to help her. Lizzie brought Jessie and the baby home, and now Jessie has left the baby with Lizzie and taken off. We're desperate to find her, to say the least. We think it's possible she took the six o'clock boat to the mainland, but we wondered if anyone here has seen or heard from her."

"I checked with the entire staff earlier, and no one has heard from her in days. They haven't seen her in the staff housing either."

"Would it be possible to check to see if she packed up her things?"

"Yes, let me just grab the keys. I'll be right back."

While he waited for her, Cooper texted Jared. *I'm at the Beachcomber, talking to Libby. No one has seen Jessie since the day before she had the baby. We're going to check her room to see if she took her stuff.*

Thanks, Coop. Keep me posted on what you find out.

Will do.

Libby returned with a ring of keys. "The housing is out back if you want to come with me."

"Sure. Lead the way."

As they walked out the hotel's back door, Libby glanced at him. "That's a pretty mean-looking wound on your face."

"Doesn't feel too good."

"I'll bet it doesn't. Are you the one who stopped the Porsche from going off the bluffs the other night?"

"That'd be me."

"No one at the fire department can believe you were able to hang on to it."

"My ribs, face, shoulders, arms and hands are feeling it."

"You're lucky you weren't hurt more seriously."

"I know." He followed her up an outdoor set of stairs to the second floor of a white building. In the yard were bikes, a cornhole game, overflowing trash cans and recycling bins full of empty bottles. It was obvious that some serious partying went on there, and he could see why Lizzie hadn't wanted Jessie to bring the baby to the employee housing.

At room eighteen, Libby used a key in the door. "Wow," Libby said. "I guess she really did leave."

Upon a quick glance, Cooper could see the room was empty other than an unmade bed. Now that he knew that Jessie had come here before the Chesterfield, he texted the update to Jared.

His brother responded almost immediately. *Son of a bitch.*

Do you want me to confirm with the ferry people that she got on the boat?

We probably can assume that. Crap. What do we do now?

I'll see if I can get a mainland address from Libby and will talk to people here to see if anyone knows where she might've gone.

Thanks for trying.

Try not to worry. We'll find her.

As they went back down the stairs, a police officer approached with the name tag Taylor on his shirt. "I'm Cooper James. Are you looking for Jessie Morgan?"

"Deacon Taylor." He extended a hand that Cooper shook. "And yes, we are."

"Her room here has been cleaned out, and we're operating on the assumption that she took the six o'clock boat to the mainland," Cooper told Deacon.

"I was able to confirm she bought a ticket on that boat," Deacon said. "I showed them a photo from her Facebook profile, and the ticket agent recognized her. I've called the Narragansett police and asked them to stop her coming off."

"My brother and his wife… They don't want the baby to end up in foster care."

"I understand. We'll do what we can."

"Thank you."

"Where will they be later today?"

"Back at their house after my other brother's wedding at the Chesterfield."

"Okay, we'll find them when we know more."

"Thanks for the help."

"Of course."

After Deacon walked away, Cooper thanked Libby for her help and sent another update to Jared with the info Deacon had shared. Dejected and worried about how this situation would resolve itself, Cooper walked back to the parking lot. His phone rang as he got into the Porsche. He took the call as he put down the window.

"Hey, it's Gigi."

The sound of her voice was all it took for his mood to vastly improve. "Hey."

"I'm so sorry I haven't checked on you before now. We've been filming twelve hours a day."

"I heard that's where you were. How's it going?"

"Fine, but I didn't call to talk about me. How are you?"

"I'm better. The ribs hurt less than they did at first, and my face is a gigantic scab."

"Such a crime to have that pretty face messed up."

She thought his face was pretty? "Hopefully, it won't leave a scar."

"Why do you sound weird? Are you still feeling crappy?"

"No, I was at my brother Quinn's wedding—"

"Oh my God, that's right! I totally forgot that was today. I heard Maddie McCarthy went into labor at a wedding."

"That was the first crazy thing that happened. The second is that Jessie Morgan, the new mom Lizzie was helping, brought the baby to her at the Chesterfield and then took off."

"What? Where'd she go?"

"We think she took the high-speed ferry back to the mainland."

"Holy shit. Lizzie and Jared must be losing it."

"They're pretty upset. The police are trying to find Jessie, and Lizzie is concerned about the baby ending up in the system. It's a mess."

"What can I do for you guys?"

"I can't think of anything, but thanks for asking."

"I'll be around later if you want to hang out."

"That'd be good. I'm not sure what time we'll be back at the house."

"No worries. I'm going to sit by the pool and chill. It's been a crazy few days."

"Okay, I'll see you later, then."

"Yes, you will."

Suddenly, Cooper couldn't wait until later. He drove back to the Chesterfield, wishing he'd found Jessie. What if the Narragansett police couldn't find her? The ferries were super crowded this time of year. She could easily blend in and get by them without much effort.

At the Chesterfield, he found Jared and Lizzie with the sleeping baby in a sitting room off the main lobby. The music from the wedding reception could be heard in the background.

"Any news?" Cooper asked them.

Jared shook his head. "We're just waiting to hear whether the Narragansett police were able to stop her coming off the boat."

"They couldn't find her," the Gansett Island police chief, Blaine Taylor, said as he came into the room.

"Seriously?" Jared cried. "How could they miss her?"

"I spoke to two of their officers. They said the ferry landing is swarming with people, and they tried to check every person coming off the ferry, but they didn't see her. I asked if she'd possibly stayed on the boat so she wouldn't get caught. They checked the boat, too. No sign of her."

"What're we going to do?" Lizzie asked, her eyes big.

"We can get social services involved," Blaine said.

"No," Lizzie said. "Jessie might come back when she realizes she's made a mistake. She'll come back for her."

"Lizzie..." Jared's beseeching tone made Cooper ache for his brother and for Lizzie.

"Let's give them a minute," he said to Blaine.

He followed the police chief out of the room and shut the door to give Jared and Lizzie some privacy. "We have to find her," Cooper said.

"I'm working with the Rhode Island State Police. We'll do our best to find her."

"God, I hope so."

CHAPTER 6

After the wedding ended, they said their goodbyes to the happy couple, who were leaving the island in the morning for a honeymoon in Ireland. Because Jared had hit the bottle when they couldn't find Jessie, Cooper drove his brother, Lizzie and the baby home. They'd borrowed an infant car seat from Mallory's sister, Janey Cantrell, who'd sent her husband home to get it when word got out about what'd happened.

Jared and Lizzie didn't say a word to each other the entire way home, and the silence between them put Cooper on edge. Jared didn't agree with keeping the baby for even one more night, but Lizzie wasn't backing down.

Thus, the silence.

Cooper probably ought to go back to New York and leave them to work this out in private.

It was too late to leave tonight, but maybe he'd go tomorrow.

He parked Lizzie's car in the driveway and got out to help her with the baby's seat. "Is there anything I can do?" he asked her.

"No, thank you for helping earlier."

"If you need me, I'm right here."

"Thanks, Coop." She sounded exhausted as she walked inside, carrying the car seat with the baby in it.

Jared hung back, so Cooper waited to see if his brother wanted to talk.

"This is the most fucked-up thing ever," Jared said after Lizzie had gone inside.

"Ever."

"What if she never comes back? What the hell are we going to do?"

"You need legal advice and a private investigator to try to find her," Cooper said.

Jared looked up at him. "You're right. I'll call Dan Torrington in the morning, and I've got a guy in New York that I can put on finding her."

"Do what you do, Jared. Handle it like a business challenge."

"I will. Thanks for the advice, little brother."

"You want me to get out of here? I can go back to New York."

"No, don't go. I might need more clearheaded advice before this is over."

Jared would never know what it meant to Cooper to be treated like a peer by the older brother he worshiped.

Since he was on a roll, Cooper decided to say the other thing that was on his mind. "I know it's really hard to keep your emotions out of this, especially considering what you guys have been through lately. But try to be kind to Lizzie. You can't just love that big heart of hers when she's doing things you approve of. You have to love it all the time."

"I know," Jared said with a deep sigh. "I love her more than anything. But how do I sit by and let her do something that I know is going to devastate her?"

"She knows that as well as you do, and she's doing it anyway. Follow her lead."

Jared blew out a shaky-sounding deep breath. "It's going to devastate me, too. That baby is adorable."

"She is. Did Jessie give her a name?"

"Not that I've heard." He glanced at Cooper. "If you ask me, she's not coming back. Jessie told Lizzie she never wanted the baby, that she was the result of 'one mistake' and that Jessie was afraid she might harm the baby."

"God, that's some heavy shit."

"It is. More than anything, I resent how she took advantage of Lizzie's kindness by doing this to us."

"Remember, she doesn't know what you guys have been through with the IVF and all that. If she did, she might've made different choices."

"Yeah, I guess that's true. The only thing I know for sure is we've got a newborn living with us for God knows how long, and when we're forced to give her up, it's gonna get ugly around here."

"I'm sorry, Jared. I wish there was something I could do for you guys."

"It helps to have you here. Don't go anywhere, all right?"

"I won't. But if you want me out of here, just say so."

Jared squeezed his arm. "I want you to stay for as long as you want to. If there's any good news today, it's that the freaking power finally came back on."

"That is good news for sure. I'm going up to see Gigi. Text me if you need me. I can go get diapers or whatever you need."

"Thanks, Coop. One thing I can say about this day is we'll never forget Q's wedding."

"That's a fact," Cooper said with a laugh.

"He and Mallory managed to have a great day despite all the craziness. Twins being born in a helicopter and another baby being abandoned by her mother. What a day."

"I've never seen Q as happy as he was today."

"I know. Me either."

"This is going to work out, Jared. It's intense right now, but it'll be okay. Just keep breathing."

"I'll try. See you in the morning."

"See you then. Text me if you need anything. And I'll retrieve the Porsche from the Chesterfield in the morning."

"I will and thanks, Coop."

Cooper watched his brother walk away and waited until he was inside before he went up the stairs to knock on Gigi's door.

When she opened the door, he immediately noticed she was wearing a crop top that left her flat abdomen bare and boy shorts.

Holy smoke show.

Maybe Jared had been right when he said she was too much woman for him.

"Cooper? Is everything all right?"

He shook his head.

"What's wrong?"

Cooper wasn't sure what came over him, or if he was even welcome to put an arm around her and draw her in tight against his instantly aroused body. He had no idea if she wanted him to kiss her until he did it, and she responded by curling her arms around his neck and opening her mouth to his tongue.

In his extensive history of kissing, he'd never had one go from zero to two hundred the way this one did, in a flash of heat and desire so hot, it was a wonder they didn't burn the place down.

He wished he could lift her and take her to the sofa to continue this conversation, but with his ribs still aching like a bitch, he didn't dare attempt anything like that. Rather, he kicked the door closed and walked her backward toward the sofa without breaking the kiss. He leaned her backward, hoping she'd take him with her onto the sofa.

But his ribs had other ideas.

Gasping, he broke the kiss.

"Oh shit, your ribs," she said. "Are you okay?"

"I was very much okay until I tried to be smooth."

She smiled, and he went stupid in the head. God, she was gorgeous in a completely natural way. Her face was free of makeup, her lashes long and lush, her lips damp and swollen from their kisses.

"Whatcha staring at?"

"The prettiest girl I've ever seen."

"No way."

"Way."

"Marilyn Monroe was prettier."

He shook his head. "She had nothing on you."

"Right."

"Seriously. She would've liked to have been you."

"You're funny." She sat on the sofa and reached out a hand to help him sit next to her.

His body ached from the long day, and by the time he was settled next to her, he'd broken into a cold sweat. "Broken ribs *suck*, in case you ever wondered."

"Can you take anything?"

"I have painkillers at the house, but I didn't take them because I wanted to be able to have a beer or two at my brother's wedding."

"That was stupid."

"I know that now."

"I have some Motrin. Would that help?"

"Might take the edge off."

"I'll get it."

He stopped her from getting up. "I didn't want to stop kissing you."

"I didn't want you to stop."

The sultry look she gave him made him instantly hard. He wasn't going to survive this woman.

WASN'T Cooper James full of surprises? As Gigi went into the bathroom off her bedroom to find the medication, she relived the way he'd looked at her when she answered the door and how he'd smoothly put his arm around her and kissed her. He hadn't asked permission the way so many guys did. While she appreciated courtesy from men, asking permission first tended to take the spontaneity out of a romantic moment.

Whereas before he'd come to her door, she'd been mildly interested in him, after kissing him, she was much more intrigued. Not that she had the time to be intrigued by any man on Gansett Island, especially when she'd be going home to LA in about ten days. But that didn't mean she couldn't have some fun with handsome, sexy Cooper, who kissed like a man who'd had a lot of practice, which made her wonder what else he might be good at. The last fourteen months had been the longest dry spell of her life, following the end of a relationship that'd turned toxic toward the end. That one had come after the stalker. She was on a roll lately.

But that crap was the last thing she wanted to think about when she had a sweet, sexy new guy around who kissed like a dream. Cooper might be a fun candidate to end her dry spell and help her kill some time before she could get back to her real life.

She delivered the pills along with a glass of water that she handed to him.

"Thank you." He downed the pills and half the water. "Sorry to kill the mood with busted ribs."

"My mood is fine. How's yours?"

"Better now." He reached for her hand and held on after she sat next to him on the sofa. "The shit today with Jessie abandoning her baby with

Lizzie was intense. The timing is tough considering their recent challenges."

"Yeah, that's got to be a lot on top of all that."

"Jared is really upset. He's trying not to be, but he can't help it."

"I don't blame him. You know they're going to get attached to the baby in no time."

"That's what he's afraid of."

"I feel for the mom, too. If she doesn't have what it takes, at least she left the baby with someone who'd care for her rather than harming her."

"There is that," Cooper said.

"A girl I knew in high school had a baby in the bathroom and didn't tell anyone. By the time they found it, the baby had died."

"Ah, that's so sad. Why didn't she tell someone?"

"People were really upset about it for a long time. I guess she was embarrassed and freaking out about people knowing she'd had a baby."

"Did she get in trouble?"

"I think so. She left school and didn't come back."

"That gives me a different perspective on what Jessie did. Like you said, at least she left her with someone responsible. And she had no idea what they're dealing with right now."

"Whatever happens next, that baby is lucky to have someone like Lizzie looking out for her. She'll make sure the baby is safe and well cared for."

"Yes, she will. But enough about them. Talk to me about you."

What guy ever said *that*? They were usually too busy talking about themselves to ask about her. "What about me?"

"Anything you want to tell me. How was the shooting this week?"

"Long. But I think we got some good stuff. The show runner is happy. If she's happy, we're happy." When was the last time she'd held hands with a guy who didn't immediately try to make that into more? She couldn't recall. They always wanted more—as much as they could get as fast as they could get it. "Jordan is having a dinner party tomorrow night. She said I can bring a plus-one if I want to."

"Oh yeah? You got anyone in mind?"

"Not really."

He made a hurt face that had her laughing. "Ouch."

"You want to go?"

"I'd love to go, as long as Jared and Lizzie don't need me for anything."

Cooper's concern for his brother and sister-in-law also set him apart from other men she'd dated, who almost always cared more about themselves and scoring with her than they did about anything else. She hadn't known him long, but she already knew he'd put his family first, even if that meant missing a chance to be with her. Perhaps it made her weird, but she liked that about him. "It's sweet that you're so worried about them."

"Jared has been really good to me. Like really, *really* good. And Lizzie is just the best person you'll ever meet. I hate to see them upset like they were earlier."

"It's an upsetting situation."

"It is, and they don't agree on how to handle it. Jared wanted to turn the baby right over to the authorities, but Lizzie wasn't having that."

"Because she doesn't want her to end up in the system. Trust me, she's doing the right thing."

He tipped his head, eyeing her with curiosity. "Are you speaking from experience?"

"Maybe." Gigi cursed herself for being so comfortable with him that she mentioned something she never talked about. "It can be rough for kids to grow up that way."

"I imagine so."

She could tell he wanted to ask her about it, but to his credit, he didn't.

Gigi took advantage of the lull in the conversation to change the subject from painful things that were better left in the past. She leaned in to kiss him, expecting more of the fire and passion. But this time, she got soft sweetness.

She could handle the fiery passion, but tenderness was another story altogether. That was a risk she wasn't quite as willing to take. "I, um, have an early morning. Our call time is at seven."

"Will it be another long day?"

"Only a half day. Jordan wanted time to get ready for the dinner party."

"You want to hit the beach in the afternoon?"

"Sure, that sounds good."

"I'll pick up lunch. Any special requests?"

"You can surprise me—as long as it's not fried."

"Got it. Will do." He leaned in for another of those soft, sweet kisses that made her feel off-balance and light-headed.

She had no time to be off-balance or light-headed, which meant she needed to be careful around Cooper James. Getting overly attached to a handsome, sweet, sexy guy who lived three thousand miles from her wouldn't be a good idea.

COOPER WAS MORE intrigued than ever as he made his way—slowly—across the yard. His ribs were on fire after the long day, and the pills Gigi had given him hadn't put much of a dent in the pain.

As he walked through the sliding door from the patio into the kitchen at Jared's, the first thing he heard was the baby crying.

Jared came into the kitchen, looking stressed.

"Is she okay?"

"We don't know what's wrong. We've tried everything—bottle, diaper change, rocking. She's inconsolable."

"I wonder if it's possible that she somehow knows what happened today."

Jared paused to consider that. "I hate to think she knows that. The poor thing."

All at once, the baby went silent.

The brothers stood perfectly still, listening to the silence.

"I'm going to check on them," Jared whispered. "See you in the morning?"

"If I can help..."

"Thanks, Coop."

After Jared left the room, Cooper poured himself a glass of water, forgoing the ice so he wouldn't wake the baby with the noise, and tiptoed to the guest room. The first thing he did was take one of the prescription pain pills. Goddamn, he hurt. Tomorrow, he'd take it easy to recover from his brother's wedding day.

Stretched out on the bed, he breathed a sigh of relief at being horizontal. He'd never had an injury that hurt like his ribs did. And his face didn't feel much better. As predicted, once the numbness wore off, it'd hurt like hell.

His thoughts wandered to Gigi and the revealing thing she'd said about growing up in foster care. He'd read a lot about her in the press over the years, but he'd never seen anything about her being in the system as a child. Though he was tempted to get on his phone and see what he could find out, he resisted that temptation. He wanted her to tell him about her life—her real life, not the one that played out in public.

Kissing her had been amazing, but he'd known it would be.

And now he had an afternoon at the beach with her to look forward to. He couldn't wait to spend more time with her, to get to know her, to kiss her and maybe...

No, he couldn't let his mind go there. Not yet, anyway.

His mind might not be ready to go there, but the rest of him certainly was.

"Down, boy," he said out loud, as if his cock listened to him.

He was wandering into uncharted territory where she was concerned. Usually, he didn't spend much time overthinking his interactions with women. They happened somewhat organically. But being with Gigi required thought and intention. Except when it came to kissing her. He hadn't planned to do that, but when she came to the door looking like a goddess in her crop top and boy shorts, he'd acted without thinking.

Thankfully, she hadn't minded and had responded in a way that accounted for his current agitated state.

His phone was full of texts from "friends" in the city who were wondering when he'd be back in town, and he'd had a bunch of Tinder matches from women on the island. But he wasn't interested in pursuing any of them. Not when he had the alluring goddess known as Gigi Gibson to keep him entertained.

He couldn't wait until tomorrow afternoon.

CHAPTER 7

Quinn and Mallory stayed at their reception until all the guests had departed, except for her father and stepmother, Big Mac and Linda McCarthy.

"I'm sure you kids want to get on with the wedding night," Big Mac said, grimacing.

Mallory laughed. "What I'd love more than anything is a glass of sparkling cider with my parents on the porch before we say good night."

Big Mac smiled at his daughter. "We can certainly make that happen. We'll get the cider and meet you out there."

After he and Linda had walked away to speak to the bartender, Mallory looked up at her handsome husband. "I hope you don't mind."

"Of course I don't."

"I wanted a minute with them to thank them again for this amazing day. I wouldn't have thought I wanted the big production, but this was..."

"It was magical."

She put her arms around his waist, inside his suit coat, and rested her head on his chest. "Yes, it was."

"My bride was the most beautiful bride in the history of beautiful brides."

She laughed again. She did that a lot with him. "And you're not the slightest bit biased, right?"

"Not at all. It's just true."

"Thank you for this beautiful second chance. After Ryan died, I honestly believed that part of my life was over until I met you and found a whole new love." Her first husband had died suddenly at twenty-seven, a lifetime ago.

"You don't have to thank me, sweetheart. I was a wreck of a man until I met you the day we came upon that accident and found out we had so much in common."

"That feels like a million years ago when you consider what's happened since then."

As they talked, they swayed to the instrumental music the cleanup crew had playing.

"Best year of my life, hands down," he said.

"Me, too."

"Did you check on Jared and Lizzie?" Mallory asked.

"I texted with him. They took the baby home with them tonight, and he's calling in an investigator to find the mom tomorrow."

"What an awful situation, especially after what they've been through recently."

"I know. I'm glad Coop is there to support them. My baby brother is all grown up."

"He's a sweetheart."

Big Mac returned with a bottle of cider and four glasses. "Ready for a nightcap?"

"We're ready," Mallory said, taking Quinn's hand to follow Big Mac and Linda to the back porch.

Big Mac popped the cork and filled the four glasses, handing one to each of them. "A toast to my daughter and son-in-law. I hope you're as happy every day as you were today."

"I'll drink to that," Quinn said as they all touched glasses and took a sip of bubbly.

"A toast to my dad and extra mom," Mallory said. "Thank you so much for this beautiful day, for convincing me to upgrade my wedding plans and for giving me the family I've never had but always wanted. The best thing I ever did was come to find my dad on Gansett Island."

Her father blinked back tears as he touched his glass to hers. "After I recovered from the shock of finding out I had a daughter I never knew about, that became one of the seven best days of my life—one for my wedding day and one for each of my six kids."

She loved being one of his six kids, even if she hadn't met him until she was in her late thirties. They'd done their best ever since to make up for the time they'd lost.

"A toast to my spare daughter," Linda said, "and new son-in-law. If you'd asked me before we met you, Mallory, if our family was complete, I would've said yes, it was. But you've completed us so beautifully, and we love you very much."

"Thank you," Mallory said over a huge lump in her throat. "You're the key to it all, Linda. If you hadn't supported both of us the way you did, things could've turned out very differently."

"My Lin is the best of the best," Big Mac said. "And with that, we're going to let you newlyweds have some time to yourselves." He put down his glass and held out his arms to her.

Mallory went to him as if she'd been doing it all her life. Tears filled her eyes as her dad wrapped his arms around her and hugged her tightly. "Love you so much," she whispered. In her wildest dreams about her missing father, she never could've imagined the reality of Big Mac McCarthy, the kindest, sweetest, funniest, most loving dad there ever was.

"Love you more," he said.

She hugged Linda while Quinn hugged Big Mac, and then they delivered their bottle and glasses to one of the trays waiting for cleanup and walked to the foyer.

"I meant to ask if you've heard any more from Mac and Maddie," Mallory said.

"I talked to him an hour ago, and mother and babies are doing well," Big Mac said. "They're going to keep the babies for a few days to monitor their breathing. Hopefully, they'll be home within a week or two."

"I can't wait to see them when we get back from our trip," Mallory said. "What a day for the McCarthy family."

"Indeed," Big Mac said. "It's not every day that we acquire three new members."

"Thank goodness for that," Linda said. "My blood pressure couldn't handle it."

They shared a laugh before Big Mac put his arm around Linda. "Take me home to bed, my love."

Mallory realized he was more than a little tipsy, but happier than she'd ever seen him—and that was saying something. He was the happiest person she'd ever met.

"I'm making breakfast in the morning for everyone," Linda said over her shoulder. "Come by before you leave if you'd like."

"We will," Mallory said.

They waved them off as Linda drove Big Mac's truck down the driveway.

"Ready to check out the honeymoon suite?" Quinn asked, extending a hand to Mallory.

"So ready."

He tucked her hand into the crook of his elbow and escorted her up the stairs to the third-floor suite that Lizzie kept off-limits to brides and grooms until after the wedding. As a result, they had no idea what to expect when they stepped into the candlelit room.

"Oh, wow," Mallory said, taking in the beautiful room with the king-size bed. White curtains fluttered in the ocean breeze, and a table had been set with a late-night snack of cheese, crackers, grapes, chocolate-covered strawberries and more sparkling cider.

Mallory had never had more cider in a single day than she'd had that day. Years after giving up alcohol, she didn't miss it at all—or the way it made her feel sick the next day.

"This is great," Quinn said of the room.

As he stepped toward the table for a closer look at the snacks, she noticed a slight limp from being on his feet most of the day. Most of the time, it was easy to forget he was an amputee, until he did too much and paid the price.

"Is your leg hurting?"

"A little. Nothing I can't handle."

"What do you say we get out of these clothes and make ourselves comfortable?"

"I say that sounds like a very good idea."

"I thought you might approve." She turned her back to him. "Can you unzip me?"

"I'd be happy to, although I'm sad that I'll never again see you in this amazing dress."

"It's my favorite dress ever," she said of the off-the-shoulder silk dress that had made her feel young and sexy.

From behind her, he kissed her shoulder and neck. "At least we'll have pictures."

"Yes, we will."

He unzipped her slowly and nudged the dress off her shoulders, letting it fall into a cloud of silk at her feet. Extending his hand, he held hers while she stepped free of the dress, his eyes going wide at the sight of the getup Tiffany Taylor had talked her into for under the dress.

"What the..."

"You like?" she asked of the bustier, garter belt and stockings that had made her giggle earlier when she put them on, anticipating this very moment.

"Holy hell. Can I take a picture of this?"

"No!"

"Please? I promise no one will ever see it but me."

"Famous last words."

"I mean it. I want to remember the way you look right now for the rest of my life."

How could she say no to that? "All right. As long as you promise it's only for you."

"I wouldn't share you with anyone."

Mallory felt ridiculous as she struck a pose for her new husband, who took a quick photo and then tossed his phone aside. He'd just reached for her when the phone rang. Groaning, he said, "I need to check that in case it's Jared. I told him to call me if they needed anything with the baby."

"No problem."

He glanced at the phone. "It's my parents. I'll be quick."

"Take your time."

"Hey," he said. "Yes, it was a great day. Glad you were able to watch the ceremony. How's Italy?" After a long pause, he said, "Don't feel bad. You were here in spirit." To Mallory, he said, "They say happy birthday to both of us."

"Tell them thanks from me."

"She says thanks. We'll do that. Call me when you get home, and we'll make some plans. Love you, too." He ended the call and put the phone on a table. "They said they are so sorry they missed the big day and want to come visit when they get back from Italy."

"That would be fun."

"Enough of everyone who isn't my gorgeous wife." He put his arms around her and stared down at her for the longest time.

"What?"

"Just looking at what's mine. I feel so lucky to have you and us and this."

"I feel just as lucky. I thought I was done being in love and getting married and all that, and then there you were to show me otherwise."

"In case you're wondering, this was the absolute best day of my entire life. And I know this day is tied with another for you."

"No, it's not," Mallory said, choosing her words carefully. "*This* was the best day of my life, too, because it's proof that life goes on, even when you think it won't. I don't mean to take anything away from my wedding day with Ryan, because that was right up there as one of the best days. But this one means even more to me after everything I went through to get here. What we both went through."

"Well said, love. I know Ryan will always be part of you and part of us."

"Thank you for honoring him that way."

"Thank you for marrying me," he said, smiling.

"Best thing I ever did." She went up on tiptoes to kiss him. "I've been thinking about changing my name."

"Have you?"

She nodded. They hadn't discussed that before the wedding. "I'd like it to be Mallory Vaughn McCarthy James. What do you think?"

"I love that, and your dad will, too."

"Mallory James. I like the sound of that."

"I do, too."

As he kissed her and held her close to him, Mallory experienced a feeling of peace that she'd finally ended up right where she belonged following so many years of spinning after her first husband's sudden death. Finding her father and family on Gansett Island had led her to Dr. Quinn James and a second chance at forever love.

IN PROVIDENCE, Mac and Maddie McCarthy were in the neonatal intensive care unit, visiting Evelyn and Emma. He still couldn't believe that they'd been born in a helicopter during his sister's wedding. Leave it to Maddie to make every other chaotic birth look tame by comparison.

"What are you thinking?" his wife asked from the wheelchair he'd pushed from the OB unit to the NICU.

She was still unsteady on her feet after giving birth to the twins, and her nurse had insisted on the wheelchair. The girls' lungs weren't quite ready for life outside the womb, but the doctors expected them to be there for only a week. Two at the most. They'd been told the extra time in the NICU was perfectly normal for twins born almost a month early.

"I'm still trying to process everything that happened today," Maddie said as she gazed at the babies.

"Me, too."

"It's a good thing they're our last ones, or you'd be putting a moratorium on any more babies."

"I would indeed. A *helicopter*, Madeline," he said for the tenth time. "*Honestly*."

She laughed as she shrugged. "I'd say I'm sorry, but it'll make for one heck of a story for the girls to tell someday."

"I never thought I'd say that I can't wait to get a vasectomy."

"I never thought I'd hear you say those words either. Your precious junk and all that."

"My junk is very precious, but I can't handle any more pregnancies, births or babies."

"*You* can't handle it," she said with disdain. "I'm so sick of being pregnant, it's not even funny. I feel like I've been pregnant the entire time we've been married."

"Not the entire time, but pretty close."

"Enough is enough, my friend. Snip, snip."

"You don't need to sound so vicious about it."

"If I were being vicious, I would've gotten out the kitchen scissors a while ago."

He covered his package. "I can't believe you'd even say that out loud."

"Desperate times."

"I've got the appointment for next month, so you can chill out with the kitchen scissors."

"Just so you know what's ahead if you fail to keep that appointment." She made a scissoring gesture with her fingers.

"You're mean after giving birth to twins."

"You'd be mean, too, if you'd had to push out *two* babies."

"Even when you're mean, you're still my hero. You make it look so easy."

She snorted with laughter. "Easy. *Right.*"

"I know it wasn't, but you're awfully good at making beautiful babies."

"They are rather beautiful, aren't they?"

"Along with their sister, Hailey, they're the most beautiful baby girls I've ever seen."

"I can't even begin to imagine what a squad the three of them will be someday."

"Don't put those ideas in my head. I'm going to need to be tranquilized for the teenage years."

"Thankfully, we don't need to think about that tonight," she said, yawning.

"Let's get you back to your room and tucked into bed."

"As much as I don't want to leave them, I can barely keep my eyes open."

"Your driver is ready whenever you are."

She leaned in for another look into the side-by-side incubators. "Good night, my sweet girls. Your mommy and daddy love you very much, and we can't wait to bring you home to meet your brothers and sister and the rest of your family."

Mac was trying not to think too much about the logistics of getting twin babies back to Gansett, but he didn't have to think about that today or even tomorrow. Since they'd arrived early and would be going home to a remote island, the doctor was proceeding with caution that Mac appreciated. The last thing he wanted was any more emergencies. He'd had enough of those to last him the rest of his life.

He wheeled Maddie back to her room, helped her to the bathroom and then tucked her into bed. She was pale and drained from the ordeal of giving birth to twins, not to mention the grueling pregnancy that'd preceded the births and the hours she'd spent earlier pumping breast milk to feed the babies. His wife was a warrior. "Do you want to give Thomas, Hailey and Mac a quick call before you sleep?"

"I'd love to."

He used his cell to call them via FaceTime on his mother's phone.

When she answered, Mac could see she was still dressed from the wedding.

"Hi there," she said. "How's everyone?"

"We're good. The girls are sleeping, and Maddie is headed for bed. How are the kids?"

"They're excited to meet their baby sisters and resisting bedtime. We just relieved Ned and Francine for the night, and Kelsey will be back in the morning. She's been a godsend." Mac had hired the au pair earlier in the summer when Maddie had been put on bedrest.

"Kelsey is amazing," Mac said. "We sure got lucky when we found her. And thank you for staying with the kids."

"We love staying with them, and we're happy to help. You look tired."

"I'm okay as long as Maddie and the kids are. How was the rest of the wedding?"

"It was lovely. Mallory and Quinn are so happy, but you won't believe what happened." She told him about the woman Lizzie and Jared had helped bringing the baby to the Chesterfield.

"She just *left* her baby with them?" Mac asked, incredulous.

"She did, and they're shocked and confused and trying to find the mother. Your dad heard they've been trying to have one of their own and not having any luck."

"Ugh, that's rough. I'm sorry to hear all that."

"It was quite a day at the Chesterfield. I have two little ones here who want to talk to Mommy and Daddy. Mac is the only one who went to bed like a good boy."

Thomas's and Hailey's little faces filled the screen, and with one quick glance, Mac could see they were wide awake.

"Dada, where's the babies?" Thomas asked.

"They're in special beds to keep them warm and snuggly. Did you see the pictures I sent?"

"Yeah, they're little."

"Very little. We have to be super gentle with them."

"I will, Dada."

"Da!" Hailey said. "Mama."

Mac handed the phone to Maddie, who lit up at the sight of their kids.

"Hi, guys. Are you being good?"

"So good," Thomas said.

"You need to go night-night so you can be well rested for when your sisters come home."

"I promised three stories to any kids who agree to go right to sleep after," Big Mac said. "And that's in addition to the three Grandpa Ned already read them."

"Scammers!" Mac said.

Thomas giggled.

"Can't wait to get home to see you guys," Maddie said. "I want to hear that you were the best boy and girl, and you helped to take care of baby Mac, too, okay?"

"Yes, Mama," Thomas said while Hailey nodded.

"Love you," Maddie and Mac said together.

"Love you."

"We'll talk to you in the morning," Linda said.

"Thanks again, Mom."

"Our pleasure." She blew a kiss before she ended the call.

"I already miss them so much," Maddie said. "And five minutes after we get home, I'm going to wonder why I missed them so much."

Mac laughed. "The dichotomy of parenthood in one sentence."

"Yep."

"We need to enjoy this little calm before the storm of *five* kids."

"Don't even think about trying to get lucky, mister. You've got six weeks and a snip before that's happening."

"Duh, I'm an expert. I know all about the six weeks."

"Remember how you came running home from work when I got the green light after Hailey was born?"

"I remember, but don't remind me too much about that when I'm on day one of the six-week wait."

"My poor baby," she said with a pout face. "So neglected."

"I'm glad you realize that."

Laughing, she held out a hand to him. "Come sleep with me."

"You're so sore, babe."

"I want you here with me."

She grimaced as she shifted toward the far side of the hospital bed to make room for him to stretch out next to her. She lifted her head, and he carefully put his arm under her so she could rest on his chest. "There," she said, exhaling. "That's what I needed."

"I'm always happy to provide anything you need, my love."

"I have everything I'll ever need—more than I ever dreamed possible before you knocked me off my bike," Maddie said.

"That was the best day ever, except for the blood and scabs."

"I love to remember that day and the days that followed when you moved in to take care of me and Thomas and then never left. Everything that's happened since then is like a beautiful dream, even the difficult parts."

He knew she particularly meant the loss of their third child, Connor, who'd died in utero. "I wouldn't trade a second with you for anything in this world."

"I wouldn't either. With you, that is."

"I can't wait to take the babies home and introduce them to their brothers and sister."

"I'm very excited to see them all together for the first time," she said.

"If only Connor could be there, too."

"That would be perfect."

"No one gets total perfection, but our family is as close to perfect as it gets."

"All thanks to you, my warrior woman."

"No more babies, Mac. I mean it."

"I hear you, love. I can't go through that again."

She poked his ribs, making him startle and then laugh.

"Really, though, Madeline. A *helicopter*?"

They laughed until they cried, and then he kissed her lips and eyelids. "Go to sleep, sweetheart. Our *five children* are going to need their mom to be well rested, or the inmates will take over the asylum."

"You won't let that happen."

"I gotcha covered, my love."

"Hey, Mac?"

"Hmm?"

"In case I forgot to mention it today, I love you."

"I love you, too, and our babies. Thank you for this beautiful life."

"Thank *you*. You're the one who made it happen by crashing into me on my bike."

"*You* crashed into *me*."

"Nope."

"Yup."

"Nope."

She pinched his lips shut, effectively ending their regular "argument."

He fell asleep smiling.

CHAPTER 8

They were going crabbing. Gigi hadn't signed on for that when she agreed to be Jordan's sidekick on the show. Then again, she hadn't signed on for a summer on Gansett Island either, but there she was. The things she did for her best friend. But *crabbing*? That might be going too far.

What did it even mean to *go crabbing*? Matilda, the show runner, had explained that it was something people loved to do on the island, and it would make for a fun segment for the show.

Gigi disagreed, but no one had consulted her.

Jordan, that perky, well-fucked bitch, was all smiles as they rode in one of the show vans to McCarthy's Gansett Island Marina, where they were shooting. They'd already endured an hour in hair and makeup that was intended to make them look "casual and sexy." Everything about the show was focused on the sexy, including the skimpy sundresses they wore over skimpier bikinis.

"Why are you so grumpy?" Jordan asked as she scanned her Instagram account.

"I'm not grumpy."

"Yes, you are."

"Anyone is grumpy next to you. How many times did you get lucky last night with that six-and-a-half-foot mother-effer with the ten-inch cock?"

Jordan laughed as she always did at the way Gigi described Mason. "Just once. It was a slow night."

"Ugh, you're *such* a bitch."

Jordan cracked up again. "Maybe if you got some, you wouldn't be such a grumpy beast."

"You bring me to this place for *an entire summer* while you're off humping like a randy rabbit, and you expect me to be as happy and perky as you are?"

"I am *not* a randy rabbit."

"You're fucking like one."

"I'm *in love*. You ought to try it sometime."

"Ew, no, thank you."

"Don't knock it until you try it."

"I'm good. You and your sister are enough to give me cavities with all the sweetness and sugar you've got going on."

"You could use some sweetness. What about that young thing you were out with the other night? If you got busy with him, maybe it would change your disposition."

"My disposition is going to stay *just like this* until I'm back in LA where I belong."

"So that's a no with Cooper?"

"I like Cooper."

"But?"

"No buts. I like him. He's fun and cute and funny."

"Then why not take him for a spin?"

Gigi shrugged. "What's the point? I'm leaving soon, and he's putting down roots here, starting a business."

"The point is to have some good sex to make everything look better, even crabbing."

"Nothing can make crabbing look better. What does that even mean, anyway?"

"We're going to catch crabs."

"So much I could say to that, including I don't *want* to catch crabs."

Jordan snorted at her double meaning. "I hear it's fun."

"How in the world can catching crabs be *fun*?"

"I guess we'll find out."

When they arrived at the marina, Big Mac McCarthy greeted them with a warm smile and a firm handshake. "Welcome to our humble marina," he said. "We're honored you chose us to be on your show."

"Thanks for having us, Mr. McCarthy," Jordan said. Her sister, Nikki, was engaged to Big Mac's nephew Riley.

"Call me Big Mac, honey. Everyone does. Come on in and have a bite of one of our famous sugar doughnuts."

Gigi's mouth watered at the words *sugar doughnuts*. She couldn't recall the last time she'd eaten anything in the doughnut or sugar families. The marina was well-kept and chock-full of boats. On the long wooden pier that extended into the Salt Pond, people were enjoying the late summer day on the water.

"Will your doughnuts sweeten up my partner in crime?" Jordan asked. "She's not feeling enthusiastic about the day's activity."

Gigi sent her a foul look that made Jordan smile like the blissed-out fool she was these days.

"Our doughnuts make everything better," Big Mac said.

They were led into a large building that opened right onto the pier. At the counter, Big Mac ordered two coffees and a half-dozen doughnuts.

"I hope you're eating some of them," Jordan said.

"We won't let them go to waste," he said. "Don't worry."

The young woman behind the counter was obviously trying to hold her shit together in the presence of Jordan and Gigi.

"Are you a fan of the show?" Jordan asked sweetly.

She was so sweet these days, but getting laid two or three times a day —on a usual day—would do that to a girl.

"I *love* your show. I watch it with my friends in the dorm at college."

"We'd be happy to sign something for you all."

The girl's eyes bugged out of her head. "I, uh, I'll be right back."

She disappeared behind the back wall and came back a minute later with a notepad and pen that she thrust at them.

They signed messages to Monica, Samantha, Emily and Tori.

"They're going to *lose their minds*," Monica said. "Thank you so much."

"How about a picture to go with it?" Jordan asked.

Gigi wanted to stab her, but she posed for the photo that Big Mac took of them with Monica.

"Thank you so much," Monica said, her eyes glistening. "You'll never know what this means to us."

"Thanks for watching," Jordan said, nudging Gigi.

"Yes, thanks for watching."

"We can't wait to see the show from Gansett. No one can believe that I work where you guys are filming."

"Let's give the ladies a minute to enjoy their coffee before they're needed." Big Mac smoothly guided them out of Monica's clutches and led them to a picnic table on the pier. "Although, I'm sure you're used to finding adoring fans everywhere you go."

"We're very fortunate that people seem to like the show," Jordan said.

"My wife and I love it."

"Seriously?" Gigi said. "You're not exactly our target demographic."

Jordan scowled at her.

"Sorry, no offense intended."

Big Mac laughed. "None taken. Watching two adorable, funny young women is certainly no hardship. We laugh our asses off at every episode."

"That's nice to hear." Jordan pointed to Gigi. "She's the funny one."

"You're both funny," Big Mac said.

When Gigi took the smallest possible bite of doughnut, just to be polite, the greasy sweetness exploded in her mouth. Holy mother of God, that was good. "You gotta try this." She broke off a piece of hers and handed it to Jordan, who popped it into her mouth.

"Damn, that's delicious. Gimme more."

They'd each eaten a full doughnut by the time Matilda came looking for them.

"We're ready for you, ladies."

"Duty calls," Jordan said.

"I've been hired to teach you how to fish for crabs," Big Mac said. "Let's have some fun."

"Can hardly wait," Gigi muttered, earning an elbow to the gut from her BFF. "Ow."

They followed Big Mac down a ramp to a floating dock that had smaller docks attached to it.

"Be nice," Jordan whispered. "My sister is marrying into his family."

"Duh. Thanks for reminding me. I might've forgotten that if you hadn't."

"I'm going to hire Cooper to sweeten you up."

"Stay away from Cooper. He's off-limits."

"Hmmm," Jordan said, flashing a mysterious grin that wasn't so mysterious.

Maybe Gigi shouldn't bring him to the dinner party if Jordan was in the mood to meddle. Before she could share that thought with Jordan, their attention was required to learn how to bait rusty hooks with raw, slimy hot dogs.

Disgusting. With the camera rolling, Gigi had to pretend she was deeply invested in this activity when she'd rather be anywhere else. She had no idea why she was in such a state today, but the dark moods came on her without warning and never for any good reason. Sometimes they were short-lived. Other times, they stuck around for a while.

"Crabs really like hot dogs?" Jordan asked Big Mac.

Was it Gigi's imagination or did Jordan suddenly look a little green as the smells of diesel fuel and rotting seaweed filled the air. *Huh, wonder what that's about,* Gigi thought.

"They love them. We've tried all kinds of other bait, but nothing gets their attention like a hot dog does." He made sure the piece of hot dog was firmly attached to the hook. "Now, the secret to catching crabs is patience."

Great. Gigi was fresh out of patience on a good day. But since she didn't want to have to reshoot the segment, she feigned interest and went along as she and Jordan baited the hooks with hot dogs while trying not to retch at the gross feel of the raw meat.

"Okay, now drop your lines into the water," Big Mac said.

Gigi looked down and was surprised to realize she could clearly see the bottom—and the crabs that were scurrying around like they were out doing their morning errands or something. As one of them approached her baited hook, she held her breath, waiting to see if he—or she, how did one know such things with crabs, anyway?—decided whether the bite of hot dog was worth the risk.

"I've got one," Jordan said with a screech of excitement.

"Raise it up slowly," Big Mac said. "Nice and easy. That's it."

Jordan's line cleared the water with a gigantic crab attached to it.

Gigi instinctively took a step back, and only Big Mac's hand on her back kept her from toppling off the other side of the skinny dock. "Keep that thing away from me!"

Big Mac took the crab by one of its claws and held it up for inspection. "That's a good one, Jordan. He'll be a competitor."

"A competitor in what?" Gigi asked.

"The crab race we'll have at the end."

"We're going to *race* crabs?" Gigi had never heard of anything crazier than that.

"Yep." Big Mac put Jordan's crab in a bucket of water. "That's the best part."

Gigi would have to take his word for that. As she looked down to check her hook, she saw a crab bigger than the one Jordan caught taking an interest in her bait. She held her breath, hoping it would come a little bit closer and then...

"Bring him up," Big Mac said. "That's a good one."

Gigi slowly wrapped her line around the spool, barely breathing as she waited to see if the ginormous crab would hang on long enough to break the surface. He did! Big Mac grabbed him and held him up.

"That's the granddaddy of crabs," he declared.

Gigi felt inordinately proud to have caught the granddaddy. "I want another one," she said, tossing her baited hook back in the water.

"I've got one!" Jordan said.

"This time, you have to take it off the hook," Big Mac said.

"I don't know about that," Jordan said hesitantly.

"You can do it. They don't eat much."

As she watched Jordan's intense concentration, Gigi had the most diabolical idea. She had to fight back the urge to howl with laughter. Not yet, she told herself. But soon. More determined than ever to catch another crab, she watched the activity below until she saw a crab approaching. "Don't they figure out what's going to happen when they see a hot dog suddenly appear down there?"

"They haven't gotten wise to us yet," Big Mac said.

"It's safe to say that crabs aren't the sharpest tools in the shed," Jordan said.

Big Mac laughed. "Their pincers are pretty sharp, but their smarts? Not so much."

Hearing that, Gigi briefly reconsidered her prank and decided it was a go. They were supposed to make good TV, and this would make for good TV.

As she slowly raised her line with a second crab, she was relieved to see it was much smaller than the first one. As Big Mac supervised, she removed the crab from the hook by grabbing one of the arms and avoiding the pincers that opened and closed. Jordan was going to kill her for this.

She walked toward the bucket as if to deposit her catch, but instead, she placed the crab on the top of Jordan's head and then pretended to be looking on with interest as Jordan watched the crab activity below.

Gigi was rocking with silent laughter by the time Jordan let out a bloodcurdling scream.

"You crazy bitch, get that thing off my head!" She screamed and clawed at her head, but the crab burrowed in deeper. *"It's biting me!"* Jordan danced around like a lunatic as she tried to get the crab off her head.

Yep, that would make for good TV.

Gigi was laughing so hard, she couldn't do a thing to help Jordan, not that she wanted to, anyway. This was what she got for flaunting her overactive sex life in Gigi's face all summer.

Big Mac took mercy on Jordan and removed the crab from her head, along with a few strands of hair.

Jordan shot daggers at Gigi. *"I can't believe you did that!"*

"You can't? Really?" Their show was all about ridiculous nonsense, and the audience ate it up.

Jordan poked Gigi in the chest. "Revenge is a bitch, my friend, and so am I."

"Tell me something I don't know."

"That was excellent, ladies," Matilda said. "Your face when you realized she'd put a crab on your head, Jordan…" Matilda lost it laughing. "Priceless."

"Not funny at all."

"Sorry," Matilda said. "I'm with Gigi on this one." She gave Gigi a high five.

Gigi responded to Jordan's glare with a smug smile. If nothing else, her mood had improved in the last few minutes.

"Let's catch some more crabs, and then we'll race them," Matilda said, signaling to the camera crew to get ready to film.

Over the next half hour, they filled the bucket with crabs.

"Wouldn't you think the word would get out down there?" Gigi asked. "They're kidnapping our friends. If it smells like processed pork food, don't bite!"

Jordan cracked up. "Or maybe it's a badge of honor, like the Olympics. I bit the hot dog and got to run in the race today! And everyone gathers around them and treats them like a returning hero."

"Do you think they give out prizes or medals?"

"They get extra algae for dinner for making the community proud," Gigi said.

"It's like a spaghetti dinner for the crab crowd."

A few minutes later, Matilda said they had enough footage of the crab catching and were ready to move on to the races.

"Can we eat something first?" Gigi asked. "I'm freaking famished."

"You're always freaking famished," Jordan said. "How you stay so thin when you eat like a football player is beyond me."

"Good metabolism, baby. Don't be jealous."

"I'm so jealous. I feel like everything I eat lands on my ass these days."

Gigi followed her up the ramp to the parking lot. "You're not knocked up, are you?"

Jordan spun around, a look of horror on her face. "What? No."

"Are you sure?"

"What? No."

Gigi bent in half, laughing. "You are *so* knocked up."

"I am not. I can't be!"

"Uh, I hate to tell you that when you have sex three times a day, it is, in fact, possible you're knocked up."

"Stop it. There's no way. We've been careful."

"No, you have not. Are you going to tell me there's no chance he slipped one by the goalie when he's shooting every ten minutes?"

"It's not every ten minutes, and shut up already, will you?"

Gigi cackled with laughter. "You are so preggo, it's not even funny."

To her dismay, Jordan began to cry. "I can't be pregnant. We're not ready for that."

When Gigi realized the cameras had been capturing their conversation, she put her arm around Jordan and led her into the bathroom. At the door, she turned to the cameraman and said, "Back off. And I'd better not see any of that on the show or anywhere else. I mean it." She slammed the door and slid the lock into place.

"They were *filming* that?"

"I'll talk to Matilda. Don't worry. It won't get out."

"Ugh, I'd better talk to Mason before someone on the crew talks."

"They won't say anything. They're under NDAs. I made sure of it."

"Sometimes having a best friend who's also a lawyer is very convenient."

Gigi pulled some paper towels from the dispenser, wet them and then wiped the tears and mascara from under Jordan's eyes. "If you're pregnant, Mason will be thrilled."

"What if he isn't? We've never even talked about having babies."

"Not once?"

"Just vaguely. It's not something that comes up on the regular."

"That's because his dick is too busy coming up on the regular, which is what caused this."

Jordan sputtered with laughter. "I can't believe the shit you say."

"You've known me how long?" Humor had been Gigi's go-to defense mechanism for as long as she could remember.

"What am I going to do, Geeg?"

"The second we finish today, we're going to buy a test and figure out if it's true."

"I can't walk into the pharmacy on this island and buy a pregnancy test. It'll be on Twitter in ten minutes."

"Then we'll get someone else to do it."

"Who?"

"Nikki?"

"She can't do it either, or the entire McCarthy family will think she and Riley are the pregnant ones."

"I've got it. We'll send your grandmother."

"Stop it! I can't send her."

"Why not? She'd do it for you." In Gigi's experience, there was nothing Evelyn Hopper wouldn't do for her granddaughters. "Just ask her." Gigi handed Jordan her cell phone. "Call her." Jordan never had her phone on her when they were filming, whereas Gigi refused to be separated from hers since she had clients other than Jordan who needed her from time to time.

Jordan took the phone from her and held it for a full minute before she punched in Gigi's code and made the call to her grandmother, putting it on speaker so Gigi could hear.

"Hi, Gigi," Evelyn said. "How's the filming going?"

"It's me, Gram. Jordan."

"Oh, hi, honey. Are you okay?"

"I, um…"

"She might be pregnant and needs you to pick up a test for her in town," Gigi said. "Would you mind doing it? If she does it, it'll be all over Twitter."

"No worries," Evelyn said, laughing. "I'll take care of it right away. Imagine the scandal that'll set off when I buy a pregnancy test."

That made Jordan smile for the first time since Gigi mentioned the words *knocked up*.

"Sorry to ask you to do this, Gram."

"Don't be sorry. I'm happy to do it, but I'm not so sure how I feel about being a great-grandmother. I'm way too young for that."

Jordan sniffled and swiped at tears.

"Aw, honey, are you upset?"

"I don't know what I am. It never occurred to me that I might be pregnant until Gigi said something."

"It's all my fault," Gigi said. "As if she and the giant fire chief haven't been—"

Jordan's hand over her mouth cut her off.

Evelyn laughed hysterically. "I take it my granddaughter didn't want you to finish that thought."

"She didn't, and it was going to be a good one."

"I can only imagine where you were going with that," Evelyn said.

"This is not funny!" Jordan said. "If I'm pregnant, we didn't plan it. What will Mason say?"

"He'll be delighted, sweetheart. That man loves you more than life itself. Try not to worry. I'll grab a test, and we'll get you some answers. Come by here after you're done filming?"

"We'll be there," Gigi said, earning another glare from her bestie.

"Thanks, Gram," Jordan said. "I hate to ask you to do this for me."

"Oh stop. It's no big deal. And I'll do my best to make sure it doesn't turn into a big Gansett Island scandal."

"That'd be good. If it's true, Mason and I need a minute to process it before the whole world finds out."

"Try not to worry. It'll all be fine, my sweet girl. We'll make sure of it."

"Thanks again, Gram. See you in an hour or two."

"I'll be here, and I'm on board to help with the setup for later, too."

"God, I forgot all about that. If that test is positive, how will I get through a whole dinner party before I can talk to Mason about it?"

"We'll get you through, sweetheart," Evelyn said. "One step at a time. Finish your day at work, and then come find me."

"I will. Thanks, Gram. As usual, I don't know what I'd do without you."

"You're stuck with me. I'll see you soon."

Jordan ended the call and handed the phone back to Gigi. "Evelyn to the rescue—again."

"She's the best of the best." Gigi had spent most of her adolescence wishing Evelyn could be her grandmother, too, until the day Evelyn had playfully suggested she "adopt" Gigi as her third granddaughter. Gigi had broken down into sobs that had alarmed the older woman. That had been one of the single best days of Gigi's young life, and her relationship with Evelyn was one of the most important to her. She talked to Evelyn almost as often as she did Jordan and Nikki. None of them had any idea how much they truly meant to her.

"Let's get this done so we can get out of here," Gigi said when Jordan was presentable again.

They were wearing sunglasses for outdoor shooting, so the damage to Jordan's makeup didn't matter.

"I can't think about anything else."

"Put it aside for an hour so we can race the crabs and go find out if it's true. You might be freaking out over something that isn't even an issue."

"Now I don't know if I want it to be true or not."

"You're a red-hot mess."

"I know!"

Since Jordan had rarely been a red-hot mess since she finally ended her disastrous marriage to the rapper known as Zane, Gigi had reason to suspect her hunch was true. They'd find out soon enough.

CHAPTER 9

"Thank you for joining us, ladies," Matilda said, sounding annoyed.

"We had an issue," Gigi replied. "It's been addressed. Where do you want us?"

Matilda gave a look that indicated she had more to say, but wisely held her tongue. Gigi was in no mood to go ten rounds with her, but she'd do it to protect Jordan, who was not only her best friend but also her client. "Over there." Matilda pointed to a spot on the main pier where the camera crew was set up.

Gigi and Jordan walked the short distance to join them next to a cutout in the main dock that ramped down into the water.

"This is your bucket of crabs," one of the crew said to Gigi. "And that one is Jordan's. The plan is to dump them on the ramp, and then each of you cheer for your team."

It sounded like the dumbest thing Gigi had ever heard, but if it would get them out of there sooner, she'd do it.

"Needless to say, we've got to get this in one take unless you guys want to catch another bucket of crabs." The director gave them pointers about where he wanted them positioned in the scene so they could capture the action. "Everyone ready?"

"Ready." Gigi glanced at Jordan, who was a million miles away and going through the motions. "Get your head in the game, girl. We don't want to have to redo this."

Jordan nodded. "I'm good."

When the director called for action, they slipped into character, squealing predictably at the buckets of crabs as they dumped them onto the ramp and then screamed at them to go faster.

Gigi was surprised to find herself more engaged in the race than she'd expected to be as the crabs scurried down the ramp and jumped in the water. "I win!"

"No way! Mine got there first!"

"You can't prove that."

"Let's go to the film."

"And *cut*," the director said. "That was perfect. We can do a slow-motion roll of the race that'll be funny."

"Are we good?" Gigi sensed that Jordan was on the verge of a complete meltdown.

"We're good," Matilda said. "See you tonight."

"See you then." Gigi took Jordan by the arm and directed her toward Gigi's car, which they'd dropped off earlier so they could leave as soon as they were finished filming. "Get in."

Gigi started her car and did a U-turn to head away from the marina. At the three-way stop sign, she took a right for Eastward Look, Evelyn's longtime summer home where Nikki and Riley lived. They'd talked Evelyn into spending the summer. Thank goodness for that, because having Evelyn around made everything better for all three girls.

Gigi knew it was weird to glom on to other people's grandmothers, but when you didn't have family of your own, you created one from the people who mattered most to you. Evelyn, Jordan and Nikki were the three most important people in Gigi's life. Without a doubt, she knew any of the three of them would be there if she needed them. She tried not to need them or anyone. Independence was her middle name, but she liked having a backup plan.

Just in case.

Of what? She had no clue. But life had gone sideways for her often enough that she tried to be ready for any possibility. "Say something."

"What should I say?" Jordan asked.

"Tell me what you're thinking?"

"My brain is spinning."

"You're not worried about what Mason will say, are you?"

"No."

"Then what?"

"It's just that we've only been together a few months, and if it's true, it's a lot to put on a new relationship."

"It'd be a lot with a twat like Brendan-slash-Zane," Gigi said of Jordan's ex-husband. "I used to hold my breath and pray you'd never get pregnant with him and be tied to him for life through a child."

"Thank God that never happened."

"Everything about your relationship with Mason is different."

"I know that."

"So don't worry. He'll be elated. He loves you so much, Jord."

Jordan sniffled and dabbed at her eyes. "I love him, too."

"Everything will be fine. If you're pregnant, you guys will have a baby, and that will make what's already great even better."

"I hope you're right."

"When have you ever known me not to be?"

Jordan laughed even as tears spilled down her cheeks.

Gigi couldn't bear to see her upset, even over something good. After everything she'd endured with her ex, Jordan deserved nothing but happiness. Gigi was determined to make sure nothing and no one ever hurt Jordan again. The time she'd spent with Brendan/Zane had been torture for the people who loved her. Gigi had had many a difficult conversation with Nikki about what they were going to do to get Jordan free of him. But when Jordan had gone back to him after he released a sex tape that featured her without her permission, Gigi had thrown up her hands and walked away.

She regretted that.

Jordan and Brendan's relationship had blown up in one violent night in Charlotte, North Carolina, landing Jordan in the hospital and Brendan in jail. The story didn't end there, but Gigi couldn't bear to think of the day Brendan had come to Gansett looking for Jordan and held Nikki and Evelyn hostage.

She shivered at the memory of being in LA with Jordan when she received that phone call. Her job that day had been to keep Jordan calm on the long flight to Gansett. But nothing and no one could've kept her calm as she tried to picture life without Nikki or Evelyn or, God forbid, both.

After that day, Gigi had taken a step back from the three of them. The fear of losing the only people she loved, and who loved her, took a toll. She'd been a mess for weeks after that and had started to feel better only when she joined the others on Gansett to begin filming their show on the island. Being here had been therapeutic for her, but she still couldn't stand to think of how close they'd come to losing Evelyn and Nikki.

She took a right into the long driveway that led to Eastward Look. For years, Jordan and Nikki had tried to convince Gigi to visit them at their grandmother's summer home. Gigi had never been interested in checking out a remote island off the coast of the smallest state. But after she'd spent a few months on Gansett, Eastward Look had begun to feel like a home away from home.

There she went again, glomming on to someone else's home and making assumptions about what she meant to these people. She'd learned the hard way not to do that. Putting her faith and affection into people who were under no obligation to return the sentiments hadn't worked out well for her in the past. Yes, Evelyn, Jordan and Nikki were different from everyone else in the world. Gigi honestly believed there was nothing the three of them wouldn't do for her, but she didn't want to count on that.

Rather, she'd prefer they count on her to be there for them. That's what she did. She took care of things for Jordan and her other clients. If she'd occasionally like to have someone take care of things for her, well, that wasn't how things worked in her life.

Evelyn walked out to greet them, hugging Jordan, who collapsed into her grandmother's embrace.

"I can't believe I sent you to buy a pregnancy test for me," Jordan said.

"Proving there's nothing I won't do for my girls." Evelyn released Jordan and hugged Gigi. "Hi, sweetie."

"Hey, Ev." Gigi would also never forget the day that Evelyn had told her to call her Evelyn and not Mrs. Hopper.

"How's our girl?" Evelyn asked.

"Rattled but holding it together. Barely."

"Let's get some answers, shall we?" Evelyn led them inside to the kitchen, where a bag from Ryan's Pharmacy sat on the counter.

Jordan eyed it with trepidation. "I've never taken a pregnancy test before."

"Ever?" Gigi asked, incredulous. She'd never forget the first time she'd thought she was pregnant and the desperation that had come with wondering how she'd ever care for a child when she could barely care for herself.

"I've never had so much as a scare."

"*Girl.* That's crazy!"

"I know! Is there any secret to it?"

"Nope," Gigi said. "Just try not to pee on your hand."

"Ew."

"Go." Gigi gave her a gentle push toward the main-floor bathroom. "When you're done, leave it on the vanity."

"Here goes nothing."

"Or everything," Evelyn said.

Jordan huffed out a deep breath and headed for the bathroom.

"I hate Brendan for making her uncertain about everything, even things she knows to be true," Evelyn said when she and Gigi were alone.

"I know. She has nothing to worry about where Mason is concerned. And she knows that, but still… The insecurities never let up."

"She's lucky to have you," Evelyn said. "We all are."

"Thank you." Gigi tried to hide her emotional reaction to Evelyn's kind words. "I'm lucky to have you guys, too."

"I love that you girls are as close as you were ten years ago."

"Me, too." Evelyn would never know how true that was for Gigi.

She recalled the weeks leading up to their high school graduation, when Gigi had feared they'd go their separate ways and never see each other again. Thank God that hadn't happened. If anything, they'd gotten closer as the years went by, until Zane had come along to wreck their groove.

Now he was gone, Jordan was back, and things were better for all of them. No way would any of them allow Jordan to have any kind of setback when she'd been doing so much better. Meeting Mason had been the best thing to ever happen to her, even if they'd met when he saved her from a fire at Eastward Look. What *could* have happened in that fire was another thing Gigi couldn't bear to think about.

"It's been good for her to be here with you and Nikki this summer,"

Evelyn said. "And Mason, of course. She seems more like herself than she has in years."

"Yes, she seems good."

As they waited for Jordan, it occurred to Gigi that a positive pregnancy test was going to change *her* life as much as Jordan's. If there was a baby, Jordan wouldn't go back to LA. She'd stay on Gansett with the man she loved, and the life she and Jordan had shared in LA would be over for good, probably along with the show.

Before she could fully wallow in that thought, her phone chimed with a text from Cooper. *Hope you're having a good day. Jared and Lizzie seem to be doing okay with the baby. If the invite is still good, I'd love to go to Jordan's party with you. If so, let me know what time, dress code and what I can bring.*

The phone immediately chimed with a second text. *Oh, and last night was fun. I want to kiss you some more. Still want to go to the beach?*

His texts made her smile.

"What's happening over there?" Evelyn asked, grinning at Gigi. "I haven't seen you light up like that in a long time."

"Just a friend."

"Hmmm. A friend or a *friend*?"

"I'm not sure yet, but he's adorable, sweet and makes me laugh." Gigi shrugged. "So far, it's nothing more than that."

"Those are three very important things."

"It's nothing. Just some late-summer fun before I go back to LA, and he heads home to New York." Even as she said the words, Gigi felt a pang of sadness at never again seeing Cooper or his gorgeous face, which was somehow still gorgeous even with half of it looking like ground beef. "How long does it take to find out if you're pregnant, anyway?"

Gigi's thoughts wandered back to how this news could change everything for her as well as Jordan. Although she'd known for months now that the likelihood of Jordan returning to LA after falling for Mason was low, Gigi had held out hope, nonetheless. She wanted things to go back to "normal," or what passed for normal since the show had become a huge hit, and the two of them had rocketed to the kind of fame that had to be experienced to be fully understood.

A sinking feeling overtook her at realizing she'd be heading back to LA alone. Nikki and Jordan would be staying here with the men they loved and starting new families with them.

Gigi swallowed the huge lump that lodged in her throat and made her eyes fill. Ugh, she would *not* cry. She couldn't recall the last time something upset her or moved her to the point of tears. She wasn't a woman who cried the way others did, and she refused to start now.

Jordan came out of the bathroom carrying the stick, a dopey smile on her face.

"Well?" Gigi asked.

"Positive."

Evelyn let out a shout of happiness and wrapped her granddaughter up in a big hug. "I can't believe you're going to do this to me! I'm too young to be a great-grandmother!"

Gigi watched the scene unfold with a surreal feeling of detachment. Yes, she was happy for Jordan, Mason, Evelyn, Nikki and everyone who'd be excited about the baby. But she was crushed for herself and felt like an ass for worrying about how it would affect her when she ought to be celebrating her friend's big news.

"Congrats," she said when she finally got the chance to hug Jordan.

"Thank you. I think."

"You're going to be a wonderful mother, honey," Evelyn said.

"You should call Mason," Gigi said.

"I was going to tell him after the party tonight."

"You'll be a wreck if you don't tell him before." Sometimes Gigi felt like she knew Jordan better than she knew herself. "Call him and ask him to come by so you can tell him now."

"He'll know something is up if I call him when he's on duty. I'll text him and ask him to come by." She sent the text and then glanced at the clock on the kitchen wall. "Thank goodness I took your advice to have the party catered, Gram. If I had to cook after this news, I'd make a mess of it."

"You'd make a mess of it even if you hadn't found out you were pregnant," Gigi said.

Evelyn pointed at Gigi with her thumb. "What she said."

"You two think you're so funny."

"Nope," Gigi said. "We just know that cooking isn't one of your talents."

"I'm going to have to learn. You guys. I'm having a *baby*." The look of wonder on Jordan's pretty face was adorable, and Gigi's heart swelled with love for the woman who, along with her twin sister, had been the best friend Gigi had ever had. They had no idea what they'd given her. No idea at all.

Though she'd planned to be long gone by the time Mason arrived, Gigi was still at Eastward Look when the tall-as-fuck fire chief came into the house, walking in like a member of the family. Which he was after the summer he'd spent with Jordan.

"Hey, babe." He zeroed right in on Jordan with the laser focus that made Gigi envious of her friend's relationship, not that she wanted that crap for herself. Not even kinda. But she couldn't help but be moved at the way Mason's face lit up with joy at the sight of Jordan, and he didn't even try to hide it.

That'd certainly never happened with Brendan or any of the other guys Jordan and Nikki had dated. Until they met Mason Johns and Riley McCarthy, and Gigi had gotten an up-close view of two relationships that set the gold standard.

"Could I, um, talk to you outside for a minute?" Jordan asked him.

"Everything okay?" Mason asked, peeling his glance off Jordan for a second to look to Evelyn and Gigi.

But they weren't giving anything away.

"Yes, everything is fine."

He held out his hand to her. "Lead the way." As he followed her like the besotted fool he was, he nodded to them. "Ladies."

The sliding door slid closed behind them.

Evelyn nudged Gigi toward the door to watch.

Jordan looked up at him, and a second later, he let out a loud whoop and lifted her right off her feet into a bear hug.

Safe to say Mason was happy.

"I'm going to go," Gigi said to Evelyn. "See you tonight?"

"I'll be there."

Gigi squeezed the older woman's arm.

"Hey, Gigi?"

She turned back. "Yes?"

"You're going to get your turn, too. I just know it."

"I don't want all that." She gestured toward the deck, where her best friend had just told her boyfriend their lives were about to change forever. "That's not for me."

"Don't be so sure."

"I'm very sure, but thanks for the kind words."

"Love you, kiddo."

It was all she could do not to completely lose it when Evelyn said that to her. "Love you, too." *More than you'll ever know.* Before she lost her composure in front of Evelyn, she hurried out the door and got into her car, appalled when tears filled her eyes. What the ever-loving fuck was her problem? Her best friend was deliriously happy after surviving a hideous marriage to a man who hadn't deserved one minute with Jordan, let alone years of her life.

So why did Gigi feel so completely lost?

CHAPTER 10

Jordan looked up at Mason, her mouth dry and her heart pounding. As well as she knew him, she wasn't completely sure how he would take the news of an unplanned pregnancy.

"What's the matter, honey? You're scaring me."

"Nothing's wrong. At least I don't think so."

He placed his hands on her shoulders. "Whatever it is, we'll figure it out."

"I, um, it seems that I'm, ah… pregnant."

Mason stared at her in complete shock for a second before he let out the loudest *whoop* in the history of whoops and swept her right off her feet into one of the hugs she'd become addicted to in the months they'd been together. He gave the best hugs. "Oh my God, babe. This is amazing!"

"Is it?"

"Hell yes, it is. We're going to have a *baby*!"

"I wasn't sure you'd be happy about it. Everything is so new, and we never talked about—"

He put her down and kissed her, nearly knocking her over with his enthusiasm. When he finally pulled back, she was touched to see tears in his eyes. "This is the best news ever."

"I have no idea how it happened."

"You don't? Really?"

She laughed at the silly face he made. "I mean, I'm on birth control, but somehow, we fell into that five or ten percent of whatever it is that get pregnant anyway."

"You're happy about this, right?"

"I'm stunned. I think I'll be happy after the shock wears off."

"How did you even know to check?"

"Gigi figured it out before I even suspected."

"Of course she did. She knows you better than anyone."

"Not better than you."

"Maybe a little better, but I'm catching up fast." He brushed the hair back from her face. "You're the best thing to ever happen to me, and I can't believe there's going to be even more. I'm going to be a dad!"

"Yes, you are," Jordan said, elated by his reaction.

"We'll get married."

"*Whoa.* What? We don't have to get married just because I'm pregnant."

"It's not just because of that. How can you even say that? I love you more than I've ever loved anyone in my entire life, and all I want is forever with you and our baby and any other babies we might have. Will you please marry me and make me the happiest guy who ever lived?"

"You swear this isn't just because of the baby?"

"I swear to God. I've been dreading the end of filming and you moving home."

"My home is wherever you are, Mason. You have to know that by now."

He hugged her again. "Are you going to answer my question?"

"Yes."

Pulling back, he gazed down at her. "Yes to what?"

"Yes, I'll marry you. And by the way, I love you more than I've ever loved anyone other than Nikki and my gram. Oh, and Gigi."

Mason's handsome face lit up with a big smile. Everything about him was *big*, especially the way he loved her. "I don't mind sharing you with them." He kissed her again. "How soon can we get married?"

"I'm not upstaging Nikki, so any time after November."

"I suppose I can wait a few months, as long as it's not longer than that."

"We'll see what we can do."

"I'll get you a ring as soon as I can."

"I don't care about that."

"I do." He continued to stare at her as if he couldn't quite believe she was there and bringing him this life-changing news. "We're going to have a baby—and we're getting married."

"Yes, we are."

"Best news *ever.*"

"I'm glad you think so."

"I hope you didn't worry for one second about what I might say."

"Maybe one or two."

Shaking his head, he said, "You never have to be afraid to tell me anything, Jordan. I'll always be happy about whatever you tell me."

"Even if I wreck the car or spend all our money?"

"Even then."

"You're crazy."

"About you." He pulled the portable radio off his hip. "Dermott, come in."

"Yeah, Chief. What's up?"

"You're in charge for the rest of the day. I've got to take care of something."

"On it. Hope everything is okay."

"Everything is just fine. Don't bother me unless something's on fire."

"Got it."

Mason returned the radio to the holster on his hip.

"What do you have to take care of?" Jordan asked, even though she already knew.

"My baby mama. Let's go home."

"I have to get ready for tonight."

"We'll do that. *Too.*"

As Jared ended a call with his investigator, it was all he could do not to throw the phone against the wall. No sign of her. The trail had gone cold. They could find no trace of a woman named Jessie Morgan or Jessica Morgan anywhere in Rhode Island. The investigator said he was expanding the search to include Massachusetts and Connecticut. He'd also said these things could take time, they needed to have patience, etcetera. Jared had no patience on this topic.

Every second that baby spent in their custody, Lizzie fell more deeply in love with a child they would eventually have to surrender.

Jared wanted to scream from the sheer injustice of this situation.

Cooper appeared in the doorway to Jared's office. "Is it safe to come in?"

"Yeah."

"Any news?"

"Nothing."

"Shit."

"Yep. What the hell are we going to do?"

Cooper came in and took a seat in the chair that he and Lizzie called their "meeting chair." She sat there whenever she came in to talk him into some new scheme that usually resulted in helping someone who needed it. "Have you thought about turning her over to Blaine and letting the system do what it does?"

"Hell yes, I've thought about it, but Lizzie won't go for that."

"What if Blaine said she has no choice? You guys aren't licensed foster parents, so won't they have to intervene eventually?"

"Blaine said this is a slightly different situation in that we know Jessie, and she asked us to watch the baby, so it's not quite as sticky as it would be if, say, we found the baby on our doorstep and had no idea who the mother was."

"Somehow, that makes it worse."

"I know. And every minute that goes by, Lizzie gets in deeper."

"But you don't?"

"I'm trying to stay removed, but that's easier said than done. She's awfully cute."

"She sure is." Cooper wanted to ask a question that he was almost afraid to pose. "So, um, what if you never find Jessie?"

"I don't know. I just don't know. I'm talking to Dan Torrington in an hour. I'm hoping he'll know what to do."

"Is there anything I can do for you guys?"

"Nah, but thanks for asking. It's good to have you here right now."

"Are you sure? I don't mind getting out of your hair if you want to be alone with your wife."

"For the first time ever, I'm afraid to be alone with my wife. I feel like I'm in the midst of an emotional battlefield that's full of land mines everywhere I step." He let out a deep sigh. "Lizzie wants a baby so badly, and nothing we've tried has worked. For someone to dump their newborn on her, of all people..."

"I know. It's awful."

"You can't tell her that. She's so blissed out and happy to be taking care of that little one. I've never seen her like this before. It's like she was born for this moment, or some shit like that."

Cooper's heart ached for Lizzie, the sweetest, most generous person he knew. "And all you want to do is protect her from the train wreck headed her way."

"Yeah. This isn't going to end well, Coop. I just know that, and there's not a damn thing I can do to keep it from blowing up in our faces."

"You're doing everything you can to keep that from happening. That's all you can do."

"It's not enough. Every hour that goes by, she gets in deeper."

"If there's anything at all I can do for either of you, just ask. There's nothing I wouldn't do for you, Jared. If you want me to go to the mainland and find this woman, I'll do it."

"I've got someone looking for her, and he's damned good. If he can't find her, it's because she doesn't want to be found."

"What about the clinic? Maybe they have some info on her?"

"We already tried that. Dead end. Privacy laws keep them from telling us anything. The Beachcomber requires a mainland address for all their employees, and hers was in Dartmouth, Massachusetts. That was the first place my guy went. The people there have no idea who she is, so she gave a fake address."

"Do you think she came out here looking for someone to take her baby?"

"Who knows what her plan was?"

The doorbell rang.

Cooper jumped up. "I'll get it." Wondering who'd be ringing the front doorbell when everyone came and went through the patio door, Cooper unlocked the door and opened it to a man he didn't recognize. "Help you?"

"I'm Oliver Watkins. I have a meeting with Jared James."

"Oh, um, sure." Cooper was fairly certain Jared had forgotten about their meeting. "Let me just grab him. I'm Cooper, by the way. Jared's brother."

Oliver shook his hand. "Good to meet you."

"You as well. Hang on just a second." Cooper went back to the office to find Jared right where he'd left him, staring off into space, probably hoping a solution to their quandary would magically appear. "Oliver Watkins is here for a meeting."

"Oh shit. I forgot about that."

"What's it about? Can I help?"

"I met him at a dinner the McCarthys had to introduce him and his wife to people on the island. They're the new lighthouse keepers. He's interested in getting into the market, and I offered to give him some pointers."

"You want me to have him come back another time?"

"No, it's fine. There's nothing else I can do about Jessie right now." Jared got up to go greet the man. "Stick around. You might learn something."

As Cooper laughed at Jared's comment, he was relieved that Jared could joke about anything, considering current events. Cooper sat in the chair he'd been in before he answered the door.

Jared returned a minute later with Oliver. "Can I get you anything?"

"No, thank you. It's such an honor to have a chance to meet with you."

"Have a seat." Jared went around the desk to return to his chair. "You met my brother Coop."

"I did."

"He's been doing some investing, too, and having great results."

"That's great. Congratulations." Oliver withdrew a pen and small notebook from his pocket. "I've been doing a ton of reading, but there's so much to learn."

"It's a lot at first," Jared said, "but like anything, the more you do it, the better you get at it."

"Do you have a background in finance?" Cooper asked.

"No, I worked for years in politics."

"What brought about the career change?" Cooper had no sooner asked the question than he regretted it due to the stricken expression that overtook the man's face.

Oliver quickly recovered, but his eyes conveyed a world of sadness. "My three-year-old son was killed in an accident. That sort of upended everything."

"I'm so sorry." How did anyone survive such a loss? Cooper's heart went out to the man.

"My wife and I are taking this year on Gansett to reinvent our lives, and I've decided I'd like to work for myself. I realize there're probably less-risky fields I could venture into than investing, but the market has always fascinated me. And when I met you, Jared, I figured that might be a sign."

"I'm happy to coach you," Jared said. "I enjoy teaching others what I've learned."

They spent the next forty minutes discussing some of the tricks that'd made Jared so successful as a stockbroker and trader, and sure enough, Cooper learned a few things he hadn't heard before. "Everyone has a different comfort level with risk," Jared said. "The one thing I want you to take away is not to risk anything you can't afford to lose. And start slow. Rome wasn't built in a day, and your portfolio won't be either."

"I appreciate this so much. My grandparents left me money that I've had invested for a while, and I'm planning to use that as my seed money for this new endeavor. I wouldn't be happy to lose it, but if I did, we'd still be okay. We sold our house and are living off the proceeds until we figure out our next steps. My wife is applying for a summer job at the Wayfarer, and living rent-free at the lighthouse buys us some time."

"Let's do a weekly meeting so I can take a look at things for you," Jared said.

Oliver stared at him, seeming stunned. "You'd do that?"

"I'd be happy to. I want this to work for you." Jared handed him a card. "That's got my cell number and email. Feel free to reach out any time. We'll get this business launched for you."

"I don't even know what to say. That's so incredibly generous of you."

Cooper was always proud of his brother—unreasonably so, if you asked his friends in the city who made fun of his hero worship for Jared. But seeing him extend himself to Oliver while in the midst of his own crisis only increased Cooper's admiration tenfold. After Jared walked Oliver out and returned to the office, Cooper told him so.

"It's no big deal. I'm happy to help him."

"It's a huge deal to him, Jared. Having you coach him will make all the difference."

"I want to see him succeed. He seems like a great guy, and I feel so bad for what he and his wife have been through."

"It's awful. I was wondering how anyone survives that."

"I have no idea."

"I was thinking about hitting the beach. You want to come?"

"I'd love to, but I'd better stick around here in case Lizzie needs me." He tossed his keys to Cooper. "Take the car."

The keys felt like a hot potato in Cooper's hand. "Are you sure?"

"Nope, but I don't need it."

"Haha, thanks."

"Are you gonna ever tell me how you busted your face and ribs?"

"I don't think I am."

Jared snorted with a laugh. "Must be one hell of a story. I'll have to see if I can find out through other means."

"Please don't."

The sound of a crying baby had Jared up and out of his seat. "I'm going to check on them."

"Text if you need me for anything."

Jared nodded as he left the room.

Watching him go, Cooper feared that Lizzie wasn't the only one becoming overly committed to the baby. The entire situation filled him with an unusual level of anxiety and concern for two people he loved more than most.

Cooper wandered outside and found his favorite goddess doing laps in the pool, wearing the white bikini that would forever be the thing of fantasies for him. He sat slowly and painfully at the shallow end, putting his feet in the water, hoping she'd notice him eventually.

While he waited, he watched her intently, noting her stroke seemed different today, as if maybe she was upset or something. He was so mesmerized by the way she ate up the distance between the two ends of the pool that when she finally popped up and saw him there, she took him by surprise.

"Stalker."

"Goddess."

She smiled. "You're forgiven."

"What's the matter?"

"Huh? Why do you ask that?"

"You were angry-swimming."

"That's not even a thing."

"Yes, it is, and you were doing it. Why?"

"Just working some stuff out."

"You want to talk about it?"

"Nope."

"You want to get lunch and go to the beach?"

"Yes, but only if I can drive."

Cooper grinned at her sassiness. "Jared gave me the keys to the Porsche, but I'll let you drive this time."

"Give me ten minutes to get my stuff."

"Sounds good."

She lifted herself out of the pool, the sun making the water on her lean, toned arms glisten like diamonds.

Now she had him waxing poetic about her arms. He'd learned about such things in a literature class in college, never suspecting he'd one day wax poetic about a woman. But Gigi Gibson was no average woman. As he watched her strut across the pool deck to the garage apartment, his mouth watered, and desire beat through him like a live wire.

CHAPTER 11

Cooper had never wanted any woman the way he wanted her—and not just because she was hotter than the sun. It was also because of the way she took no prisoners and blazed through life on her own terms, following her own rules. Before he'd met her, he'd had no idea how sexy those traits would be to him. Most of the women he'd met were far too concerned with the approval of others to blaze their own paths. Gigi didn't give a rat's ass what anyone thought of her, and he loved that about her.

When he went inside to get a beach towel and the sunscreen he'd bought before he came to the island, he was glad the baby had gone quiet, but there was no sign of Jared or Lizzie. He texted Jared. *Gone to the beach with Gigi. Let me know if you need me.*

Since she was driving, he left the keys to the Porsche on the kitchen counter. It was a relief not to have to use that car. He might never ask his brother to use it again after the other night. His shoulders, arms and hands still ached like a bitch, but not as badly as his ribs. Before he left the house, he popped a couple of painkillers and chased them with a full glass of water.

Outside, Gigi leaned against the car, checking her phone as she waited for him.

"Ready?" he asked.

"I was born ready."

"I'll bet you were," he said, grinning as he walked around to the passenger side, eyeing the low-slung car with trepidation. This was going to hurt. He lowered himself carefully into the passenger seat, holding his breath in anticipation of the blast of pain that left him panting and sweaty.

"Shit, Coop. Are you okay?"

"Yep. As long as I don't move or try to get into a sports car."

"God, that sucks."

"I'm fine. Anyway, back to what I was saying before. I bet you were hell on wheels from the minute you were born."

"Maybe."

"You don't know?"

She backed the white Mercedes out of the driveway. "No, I don't know."

"Oh."

"If I tell you my deep, dark secrets, it won't make things weird between us, will it?"

"I won't let it if you don't."

She drove for at least a mile before she spoke again. "I was born to a crack addict, which means I was born addicted."

Cooper blew out a deep breath. Wow.

"I was put into the foster system and don't really have much info on my life before I was adopted at four."

"The family who adopted you… They were good people?"

"They weren't cut out to be parents."

"How do you mean?"

"They were super-ambitious Hollywood types who were perfectly fine to leave the raising of their child to a progression of nannies. He was a producer, and she was a studio executive. I was about thirteen when I realized I was just a box they'd felt the need to check on their path to world domination. Get married. Check. Have a kid. Check. Take over the world. Check. They liked to stage elaborate photo shoots of the three of us, as if we were some sort of sweet little family when I hardly ever saw them except for when they decided they needed family time."

Cooper had no idea what to say.

"I first became interested in the law when I was fifteen and decided to sue for emancipation from them. I got tired of them wanting nothing to do with me until it suited their purposes."

"Did you win?"

"Hell yes, I won—with a financial settlement that allowed me to finish high school with my friends and get my own apartment."

"When you were fifteen."

"I was sixteen by the time it was finalized."

"So, you were on your own at sixteen."

"Yep, and I've never looked back. I became a lawyer so I could take care of myself financially and legally. I never wanted to be in another situation where I had to rely on other people to take care of things for me. I wanted to do it myself."

"I'm amazed, Gigi. You're incredible."

She shrugged. "You do what you have to."

"Have you ever seen your parents again?"

"Occasionally. I had no desire to be estranged from them. I just didn't want them telling me how to live my life when they had so little to do with me."

As they stopped at the deli in town to grab lunch, Cooper's heart ached for the young girl who'd had to grow up far too soon. He'd never been prouder of anyone than he was of her, except for maybe Jared. But as much as Jared had achieved, he'd done so with the safety net of a loving family to catch him if he fell. Gigi had already been on her own for thirteen years and had turned her life into a success story all by herself.

"Tell me the truth." She glanced at him when they were back in the car. "You're horrified to hear my shitty life story, right?" She laughed. "I don't even know why I told you. I never talk about any of it. I'm so thankful the press hasn't uncovered this stuff. My lawyer was thorough. It's buried pretty deep."

"I'm not horrified. I'm impressed. My biggest concern when I was fifteen was trying to hide my constant boners in school."

Gigi laughed hard. "I love that."

"It was a nightmare and the ultimate paradox. When you don't want boners, you have them all the time. When you're old, you have to take pills to get them. Why can't we store boners for when we need them later in life?"

"That is a question for the ages."

"I'd really like an answer. We need a storage facility for boners where you can bank them for later and withdraw as needed."

"Now that's a business idea that'd make you a billionaire."

"Boner Bank. I need to get that trademarked before someone steals my idea."

He loved the sound of her laughter.

"Will you have a drive-up window at the Boner Bank?"

"Hell yes, with one of those plastic tube things that shoots you out a boner any time you need one."

She laughed so hard, the car swerved out of the lane. "Thanks for the laugh. I needed that."

"I like when you laugh."

"I like people who make me laugh."

"What happened today?"

"What makes you think something happened?"

"The rage-swimming was my first clue. But then you told me stuff you said you don't tell just anyone, and that has me wondering what happened that has you thinking about the past."

She gave him an odd look that he could read by the way her brows arched over her sunglasses.

"What?"

"You're rather insightful for a boy your age."

"A boy," he said with a snort. "I'm *all* man, sweetheart. I'd be happy to prove that to you any time you'd like."

"After a pickup at the Boner Bank?"

"Nah, I'm still getting plenty of them all on my own. Such as whenever I come upon you in the pool in that white bikini. You're giving me a lifetime of spank-bank fantasies."

"Oh, Boner Bank and Spank Bank ought to go into business together."

Laughing, Cooper said, "That'd be one heck of a partnership." Thankful that the pain pills were starting to work, Cooper put his head back against the headrest and looked over at her. "I haven't forgotten my original question. What happened today?"

"Jordan found out she's pregnant," Gigi said, sighing. "I'm so happy for her."

"What else?"

"Nothing. That was it."

"No, there's more. You're happy for her, so why were you rage-swimming?"

Hesitantly, she said, "It's not rage so much as fear."

"Of what?"

She pulled into the town beach parking lot and took a spot at the far end, which was usually less crowded. After shutting off the engine, she kept her hands on the wheel as she stared at the water. "When you have no real family of your own, your family becomes the one you choose for yourself. Jordan and Nikki are my family. Their grandmother is mine." She swallowed. "They're making lives for themselves here, which means they'll be staying when I go back to LA."

Cooper began to get the picture. "Nothing says you have to be there if your family is here."

"I can't live on Gansett Island, Cooper."

"Why not? A thousand other people do it year-round. They seem to love it. Look at my brother and Lizzie."

"I'd go stark raving mad here year-round."

"Okay, so then live in LA part of the year and spend the summers here with your girls."

"I don't know."

"Are you going to tell me that the girl who sued her parents for emancipation at fifteen can't figure out a solution to this challenge? I refuse to believe that."

"When you put it that way, it does seem far less daunting."

"You'll work it out."

"Thanks for listening. It was an eventful half day at work, and I was still processing it while I was swimming."

"Is Jordan excited?" he asked as he got out of the car, took a second to catch his breath from the pain and then carried their beach chairs to the boardwalk.

He gestured to a spot several yards from the nearest group. "How's this?"

"Perfect. I don't want to people."

"I'm sure you do plenty of peopling in Los Angeles."

"I can't go anywhere anymore without being mobbed by paparazzi and fans, which I'm told is a good problem to have."

"Until it happens to you."

"Exactly, and you need security to leave your house. The drive-up window at Starbucks has become my best friend."

"We'll serve coffee at the Boner Bank for our female customers."

"So you're saying the ladies can't buy themselves a boner with no man attached, because if so, you're missing out on a crucial demographic."

"You make a good point."

"Hahaha, a good point. Nice pun."

"I'll see what I can *come up* with next."

"It's *hard* to think of a good pun."

"At the Boner Bank, we'll be all about the dick puns. I wish I'd had this idea in grad school. Imagine the fun I could've had with that as my business plan."

"Men everywhere would be *flooding* to your Boner Bank to drop off unneeded boners for use later on."

They laughed so hard, Cooper had tears in his eyes. "You're good at this."

"Everyone has their talents. My talents apparently include dick jokes. I get enough dick pics to stock your bank for years."

"Ew, do you?"

"Yep. I had to hire someone to manage my social media—and Jordan's—to deal with the dudes who think we want to see their junk. Among other things."

"Gross."

"You have no idea. Dick pics and prisoner mail. Apparently, that's how you know you've made it in Hollywood. That's why I pay someone to manage our social media."

"Good call." He handed her the salad with chicken she'd chosen at the deli and dug into his roast beef sandwich with mustard, horseradish, onions and hot peppers. As he devoured the first half, he realized the onions might've been a mistake, as he'd very much like to kiss her again as soon as possible. He picked them off the second half. "Thanks for telling me the things you shared earlier."

"Thanks for not making a big deal out of it."

"People usually do?"

"Most people don't know, but those who do feel 'so bad' for me, and I don't want that. I was raised in a mansion in Beverly Hills. A lot of people had it way worse than I did, especially the kids who spent their entire childhoods in foster care."

"Yes, I'm sure a lot of people had it worse, but your situation was no picnic."

"No, but I always had what I needed."

"Did you?"

She shrugged. "The important stuff. I don't dwell on any of it. That was years ago. I have a whole new life now."

"Which is going to change if Jordan permanently relocates here."

"Yeah, but hey, I've seen that coming for months now. She and the tall-as-fuck fire chief are madly in love, and it's not like he's going to suddenly quit his job and move to LA to live with her."

"Did you maybe kinda sorta hope that's what they'd do?"

"It was always a long shot, and it's fine. I want her to be happy. She deserves that after her nightmare marriage to Zane the dickhead."

"Was it as bad as the tabloids made it out to be?"

"It was way, way worse, especially the part where he came here and took Nikki and their grandmother hostage while we were in LA. That was one long-ass flight to get here."

"I meant to ask before how you managed to keep that quiet."

"We made that a condition of him being charged with lesser crimes in exchange for a serious stint in rehab. The last thing Jordan needed was another firestorm involving him. The incident in Charlotte was more than enough."

"I saw on Twitter that he asked his fans to leave her alone and took all the blame for the problems in their marriage."

"That was also condition of his deal, to call his lunatics off her. They were relentless toward her after *he* put *her* in the hospital in Charlotte."

"Sounds like a prince of a guy."

"He's an asshole, and I hope we never see him again. And when I tell you I'm happy she's with Mason, I mean it. He treats her like a queen, which is what she deserves."

"You deserve that, too."

"I don't need that. I can take care of myself. I don't need some man to make me feel complete."

"And she does?"

"No, but that's what she has with Mason. They're very cute together. I couldn't be happier for her."

"But you're sad for you."

"'Sad' is a big word. It's going to be an adjustment to be at home without her and Nikki. That's all."

"It's okay to be sad about it. You know that, right?"

"I don't need you to shrink me, Coop."

"That's not what I'm doing. I'm simply pointing out that the changes your friend is making are going to affect you, too, and it's okay to feel the way you do about that."

"I'll be okay. I'm like a cat. I always land on my feet." She jumped up. "Let's swim."

Cooper took a second to put their trash in the bag and tie it off so the seagulls wouldn't get it. Getting out of the beach chair was even more painful than the car, and by the time he made his way to the water, she was already out past the breaking waves. He moved carefully, turning his uninjured side toward the crashing waves, but even that hurt.

Worst time ever to be injured, he decided, with a woman like Gigi around. Under normal circumstances, he might swim out to join her, put his arms around her for a kiss. Under these circumstances, he didn't dare do anything more than stand in waist-deep water and hope she'd come to him.

When she seemed to realize he wasn't coming out any farther, she caught a wave that brought her right to where he stood.

She looked up at him, smiling. "What's up?"

"Not much. I was just standing here minding my own business until this sea nymph showed up in a white bikini. My day just got a whole lot better."

"Are your ribs hurting?"

"Like hell. I was afraid to go out any deeper."

"I'm sorry you're hurting."

"It'll feel better in a day or two. I hope." He held out a hand to her.

She looked up at him, her expression unreadable as she took his hand and stood.

Cooper put his arm around her as they walked out of the water and returned to their camp on the beach.

CHAPTER 12

This guy was not what she'd expected. For one thing, she could talk to him. Like really talk to him, about things she rarely talked to anyone about. She cringed when she recalled telling him about being born to a crack addict and landing in foster care. When was the last time she'd told anyone that story? It'd been years. So why had she told him?

She chalked it up to the emotional morning she'd had with Jordan, which had lowered her defenses.

He'd tuned right in to the fact that something was off with her, and rather than avoid it, he'd asked her about it and given her a forum to talk it out. Almost every other guy she'd ever dated would've rather had a root canal than *talk* about anything.

She liked him. More than she'd expected to. Not that it meant anything. They were hanging out. Having fun. It would never be anything more than that, so there was no sense getting worked up about it.

True love and happily ever after were for girls like Jordan and Nikki. Not for her. She wasn't wired that way. The thought of needing someone else so much that her happiness depended on him made her twitchy. Gigi didn't need anyone else to "complete" her. She'd been fine by herself for thirteen years, and she'd be fine by herself once she got back to LA.

If anyone was capable of going it alone, she was.

"I need to go help Jordan get ready for tonight," she said around three as she got up to shake the sand out of her towel. She extended a hand to help him up, wincing at the grimace that formed on his handsome face. "You okay?"

"Yep," he said, even as he broke into a sweat from the effort it took to stand.

She felt so bad that he was in that kind of pain. "Still want to come to the party tonight?"

"I'd love to, if you still want a date."

It was on the tip of her tongue to tell him it wasn't a date, but she kept the thought to herself. "Sure."

When they arrived back at Jared's, she waited for him to get out of the car.

"If I get a ride to Jordan's, can I hitch a ride home with you?" he asked.

"Of course."

"What's the dress code?"

"Super casual. Come any time after seven. I'll text the address." She kissed his cheek. "Thanks for lunch and the beach. I needed that today."

"It was fun. See you later."

As he started to walk toward the main house, she said, "Hey, Coop?"

He turned back, eyebrow raised over his aviator sunglasses. "Yeah?"

"Thanks for listening. Before. I appreciate it."

When he smiled, she felt the weirdest twinge of something in her chest. It was probably heartburn. "Any time."

She went upstairs to her apartment over the garage, rubbing the spot in her chest that felt weird while trying to remember if she had any Tums.

If not, she needed to get some when she went into town.

AT THE WAYFARER, General Manager Nikki Stokes was counting the days until Labor Day, when the high season would end, and sanity would return to her days. At least she hoped so. They had a robust off-season planned with numerous weddings and events, which was why she needed an event manager to help handle the details that had become too much for her to handle on her own.

Jaclyn, one of the college students who'd spent the summer working at the Wayfarer, came to Nikki's office. "Dara Watkins is here to see you."

"Would you mind bringing her in?"

"Sure, no problem."

"Thanks, Jaclyn." She and the other college kids would be heading back to school in the next week, leaving them shorthanded for the last two weeks of the summer season. Good times ahead.

Jaclyn returned with Dara, who was tall, Black and pretty with her hair up and wrapped in a funky headband. She wore a summer dress with a white denim jacket.

"Come in." Nikki walked around her cluttered desk to greet Dara with a handshake. "So nice to meet you. And thank you, Jaclyn."

"No problem."

Nikki shut the office door so they wouldn't be disturbed. "Can I get you anything? I've got cold water handy."

"I won't say no to that. I got the big idea to walk into town from the lighthouse, and the walk was farther than I expected."

Nikki got one of her bottles of water from the cooler bag she brought to work every day and handed it over to Dara.

"Thank you," Dara said, taking a drink.

"What's it like living at the lighthouse?"

"I love it so far."

"I heard you got here the day the power went out."

"Yes, it was like an hour after we arrived. Thankfully, Big Mac and Linda McCarthy came to our rescue and took us in until the power came back on."

"They're the best."

"They really are."

"Full disclosure—I'm engaged to his nephew Riley."

"Oh, okay. That's Kevin's son, right?"

"Yes, one of them. Finn is the other."

"I met Kevin, Chelsea and baby Summer while we were staying with them."

"She's a cutie. We're all crazy about her."

"I can see why."

"Can I ask you something totally unprofessional?"

Dara laughed. "Sure."

"What's the secret to your amazing cheekbones?"

"Genetics. My mother and grandmother had them, too."

"I'm seriously jealous."

"Every friend I've ever had has said the same thing."

"I can see why." Nikki reached for Dara's application and résumé. "I have another question."

"What's that?"

"You're an attorney. What do you want with an event job at the Wayfarer?"

"My husband and I are here for a year, and I'd like to stay busy."

"Did you check in with Dan Torrington? He has a law practice on the island. He could probably use help that would be more in your area of expertise."

"I'd rather manage events at the Wayfarer, if you can get past my lack of experience."

"I assume your other professional skills would be transferrable. Mostly, it's a lot of organization and attention to detail."

"Which is not that different from being a lawyer."

"Why do you want this job, Dara?"

"My husband and I lost our three-year-old son a year ago in an accident."

Nikki gasped. "I'm so sorry. I hadn't heard that."

"Thank you. I'm sort of glad that the whole town isn't talking about the sad parents in the lighthouse."

"No one is talking about that, at least not that I've heard."

"Well, that's a relief. One of the reasons the opportunity here was so appealing is that it gave us a fresh start with people who don't know about our terrible loss. But we both feel compelled to tell new people we meet. It's a conundrum."

"I can see how that would be. I'm glad you told me, and I'd love to have you on our team at the Wayfarer." She discussed the salary and benefits, which didn't include health insurance. "Is that going to work for you?"

"Yes, that's fine. We have it through my firm. They've been so good to us."

"I'm glad to hear that."

"I'm not sure how long we'll be here. A year at least. Beyond that, we're not making any plans."

"I'll take what I can get. This summer has whipped me, and there's no way I can do another one without event help. I'm also getting married in

November. We're doing it at the Chesterfield, but I'll probably need extra help around that time."

"It sounds fun."

"It can be, but it can also be chaotic at times. Being on an island means planning way ahead to get things here when we need them. It means improvising and rolling with all sorts of unforeseen challenges. Does it still sound fun?"

"It does."

"Good. I didn't mean to try to talk you out of it."

Dara laughed. "No worries. I loved planning my wedding. Helping other brides and grooms plan theirs would be fun."

"I'm glad you think so. After this crazy summer, I told Riley last night that eloping is looking better to me all the time."

"Don't do that. You'll never forget your wedding day. One of the best days of my life."

"We're looking forward to it."

"When would you like me to start?"

"Would tomorrow be too soon? We have a dozen weddings in September and October that I'm in no way ready for, and I could use the help right away."

"Tomorrow is fine."

"Let's say ten o'clock, and you can fill out all the new-employee paperwork then."

"Sounds good." Dara stood to leave and extended a hand to Nikki. "Thank you for taking a chance on me. I won't let you down."

Nikki shook her hand. "I'm delighted to have you on the team. I'll see you tomorrow."

"I'll be here."

When Dara opened the office door, Riley was there, his hand up like he was about to knock. Like always, the sight of him filled Nikki with the kind of happiness she hadn't known existed before she met him.

"Dara, meet my fiancé, Riley McCarthy. Riley, this is Dara Watkins, the new event manager."

"Oh, great to meet you," Riley said, shaking hands with Dara. "And thank you for taking the job. I've barely seen Nikki this summer."

"Happy to help," Dara said. "I'll see you tomorrow, Nikki."

Riley stepped aside to let her go by.

Nikki waved him into the office. "Shut the door." She went over to wrap her arms around him.

"Hello to you, too," he said, returning her embrace.

She breathed him in. "Happy to see you."

"Everything all right?"

"Dara was telling me how she and her husband lost their three-year-old son in an accident."

"I heard about that. My dad told me the little boy let himself out of the house and got hit by a car."

"Oh my God. That's so awful."

"It's so, so sad. Maybe the job will be good for her."

"I hope so. It'll certainly keep her busy." She looked up at him, thankful every day that she'd found him in this great big world and that she got to keep him forever. "I'm ready to get out of here, and I promised Jordan I'd come early. She wants to talk to me about something."

"Is she okay?"

"I think so. She's been the happiest I've ever seen her this summer with Mason. I can't imagine anything could be wrong between them."

"They're solid, babe. Anyone can see that. You're prewired to worry about her because of everything with the dickwad, but she's happy now."

"I know. I'm thankful every day for that and for Mason. They're perfect for each other."

"Now we just have to find someone perfect for Gigi, and all your girls will be set."

"Gigi will never settle down. That's not her groove."

"I heard she was out with Cooper James the other night. Jared's younger brother."

"Interesting. She didn't tell me."

"You can get the scoop tonight. I'm looking forward to it. We've both been working way too much this summer."

Nikki picked up the bag of work she'd packed to take home, even though the chance of her getting to it was slim to none. "No kidding. I'm so ready for Labor Day."

Riley waited for her to go out ahead of him and shut the door to her office. "How about I drive and bring you back in the morning?"

"I won't say no to ten extra minutes with my sexy fiancé."

"Do we have time for a nap before the party?"

Nikki checked her watch. If they got to Jordan's in an hour, that'd still be early. "I think we do."

"We want you *very well rested* for the party," he said, grabbing her ass as they walked out to his truck.

Time alone with Riley was her favorite thing in the world, but even with his arm around her and a night of friends and family to look forward to, Nikki couldn't shake the sadness she felt for Dara after hearing about how her son had died.

DARA CAME WALKING down the lane to the lighthouse two minutes after Oliver had arrived. He was immediately on guard for how she seemed as came closer to him and Maisy, the yellow Lab they'd brought to the island with them.

"How'd it go?" Oliver asked, relieved to see her smiling. Her smiles had been so rare in the last year that he celebrated every one of them.

"It went great. I got the job!"

"That's fantastic, babe. Congratulations." He hugged her and kissed her forehead. "I'm so happy for you."

"I'm happy for me, too. It sounds like so much fun, helping brides plan their weddings and overseeing birthday parties and other events."

"You'll be great at that."

"I hope so," she said, bending to give Maisy a kiss on her head. "It's a long way from the legal rat race, and the money isn't great."

"That's okay. We don't need as much as we used to. Living rent-free at the lighthouse for a year will help us get back on our feet."

After their son died, neither of them had been able to work for months. Rather than lose their former dream house to the bank, they'd sold it, paid off the mortgage and were living off the remaining proceeds. They'd agreed to use the money his grandparents had left him to seed Oliver's foray into trading, which was why he was so relieved to have Jared's help. They didn't have money to lose.

"How was your meeting with Jared?"

"It was great. Way better than I expected. He offered to meet with me weekly and be my mentor."

"That's amazing, Olly. You couldn't have a better mentor."

"I know. I couldn't believe when he offered that. I also met his younger brother, Cooper, who seems great."

"I'm happy for you. We both had an awesome day."

"That seems to be happening a lot since we got here." Every day was different on Gansett Island. The community had warmly welcomed them, inviting them to dinners and get-togethers and nights out to listen to live music that had their calendar full of engagements for the next few weeks. Life on Gansett was fun and relaxing, and with every passing day, he felt himself looking forward to each new experience rather than dreading having to get through another day.

Naturally, he felt guilty any time he had fun or experienced joy or happiness, knowing his beloved son would never again have any of those things.

"I like it here." Dara followed him inside and up the spiral staircase that led to the combined kitchen/living room. "I didn't expect to like it so much. I'm glad we came."

"I am, too. We needed something, and this place has a soothing vibe. Like you can't help but relax and breathe here."

"Yes, exactly. It doesn't hurt that the island is beautiful, and the people are so friendly and welcoming."

Oliver slipped an arm around her waist. In the last few weeks, they'd begun to reintroduce some basic affection into their once-passionate relationship. Being able to touch her again felt like coming home, even if they hadn't made love in more than a year. He was more optimistic than he'd been in a long time that they'd eventually get back to some semblance of normal, or whatever that was these days. "Do you still feel like going to Jordan and Mason's party?"

"I do. I really enjoyed meeting Jordan's twin sister, Nikki, who'll be my boss at the Wayfarer. She was nothing like I expected after watching Jordan's show. I figured she'd be a typical Hollywood type, like Jordan seems to be, but Nikki was nothing like that. She was lovely and so down-to-earth."

"Jordan is, too. You'll like her." Oliver had met Mason when he came to do an inspection at the lighthouse while Dara had been out to lunch with Linda McCarthy and some of her friends. Jordan had been with him, and he'd enjoyed talking to them both. They'd invited him to the dinner party that day.

"I suppose you can't believe anything you see on those reality shows."

"Probably not." He raised his hands to her shoulders and gazed into her warm brown eyes. "That smile looks good on you, sweetheart."

"Feels good, even if, you know..."

"I know." Even their best days were tinged with grief. "But we're doing better, aren't we?"

"Anything is better than we were." She looked up at him, seeming shy, which was another thing she'd never been with him before disaster struck. "I've missed you."

They'd existed together for an entire year as two ships that passed in the night, unable to share the terrible burden of grief. "I missed you every minute of every day. The whole time, I kept trying to find some way to reach you, but for the first time, I had no idea how. I was so lost without you, Dar."

"Same. I'm sorry. I could barely breathe. I didn't know how to include you in that."

He wrapped her up in a hug. "Don't apologize. We did the best we could."

She put her arms around him and returned the embrace. "Maybe, but this is better."

"Much better." Oliver couldn't stop the predictable physical reaction he'd had to her from the first time they met. He started to pull back. "Sorry."

She tightened her hold on him. "Don't go, Olly."

"Nowhere I'd rather be than holding you." He pressed his lips to her neck and breathed in the familiar scent of his love.

Her hands moved from his waist down to grip his ass and pull him in tighter against her.

Oliver bit back a groan. "Dara... Honey. Tell me what you want."

"You, Olly. I want you."

He'd waited so long to hear those words, all the while wondering if she'd ever want him again. It was all he could do not to weep from the sheer relief.

"Olly? Are you okay?"

"I'm better than I've been in a long time."

"Do you think we could, you know, spend some time together before the party?"

He'd come home from the meeting with Jared bursting with ideas and plans and research he wanted to do, but none of that mattered now that his wife was in his arms and telling him she wanted him. "There's nothing in this world I'd rather do."

He followed her up another winding staircase to the bedroom and bathroom that made up the lighthouse's top floor. He'd never lived anywhere more unique or special and couldn't miss the symbolism of the lighthouse illuminating their way back to each other.

"I just need a minute," Dara said, ducking into the bathroom.

Oliver unbuttoned his shirt and sat on the edge of the bed. In the past, he'd have been naked and already in bed when she joined him. This, however, felt like the first time all over again, even though their first time had been more than ten years ago. That felt like forever ago after everything that'd happened since then.

Neither of them was the same person they'd been before they lost Lewis. Figuring out who they were now—as individuals and a couple—was their primary goal for this year on Gansett.

Dara came out of the bathroom. She wore a robe and had let her hair down. As she approached him, he noticed she seemed shy and hesitant, two things she'd never been with him before.

He held out his hands to her, wanting her to feel welcome with him in every possible way.

She took his hands and stepped between his legs.

Oliver put his arms around her and pressed his face to her abdomen, closing his eyes against a rush of tears that took him by surprise. This was no time for tears, however. There'd been more than enough of them for any one lifetime. This was a time for looking ahead, for coming back together after a long winter of pain and sorrow. This was about the love of his life and finding the way forward together.

"Are you okay, Olly?" she asked softly.

"I am if you are."

"I feel… I don't know how to describe it. Better, I guess. A little better."

"I'm so glad to hear that."

"Do you feel better, too?"

"I do. Being here has been good. It's taken some of the pressure off."

"Yes, exactly. And I'm excited about my new job, even if it's a million miles from what I thought I'd be doing."

"Maybe you'll find something you love better than the law, which you'd stopped loving as much as you used to long before we lost Lewis." The long hours, endless demands and intense stress of trying to balance a high-pressure job with motherhood had taken a toll on her.

"True."

He pulled back, looked up at her and gave a gentle tug on the knot holding her robe together. The two sides fell apart, revealing the body that was as familiar to him as his own, albeit less curvy than she'd been before. They'd both had trouble eating for months after their loss.

Oliver kissed the soft skin on her belly while sliding his hands around her to cup her ass. "Sexiest girl I've ever seen," he said, as he always did, hoping the familiar refrain would make her laugh as usual.

It did. "Always the charmer, Oliver Watkins."

"I can't have my best girl thinking there's anyone better than her."

"You still think that? Even after everything?"

The vulnerability in her words tore at him. His Dara was never uncertain with him. "I'll think that for the rest of my life, until we're old and gray and wrinkled. You'll always be the sexiest girl I've ever seen."

To his dismay, her eyes filled with tears. "I'm so sorry, Olly. For everything. For working when I should've been with you and Lewis, for pushing you away after, for all of it."

"Don't be sorry, love. Neither of us was at our best after we lost our boy. All we can do now is look to the future and hope for better days ahead."

"Do you think there'll be better days ahead?"

"I'm sure of it."

"Thank you for pushing me to come here, to shake things up, to change our scenery. It's been good."

"Yes, it has, and it's getting better all the time," he said with a suggestive grin. "Come be with me, love. I've missed you that way, too."

He pulled off his shirt and sat back, waiting for her to join him. His heart nearly stopped when she dropped the robe on the floor before crawling into his outstretched arms. With her naked body pressed against his chest, he had to remind himself to go slow, to be gentle with her. This was no time for ravenous need. It was the time for tenderness.

Kissing her, holding her, making love to her was like coming home after a long, difficult journey. The desire they'd felt for each other from the beginning came back like it had never left.

"Phew," she said, breathing hard afterward. "We've still got it."

Oliver laughed. "We certainly do." He ran his hand from her breast to the curve of her hip and then back up, leaving her with goose bumps. "Just like always with the goose bumps."

"That's only ever happened with you."

"Don't remind me there were others."

"No one who mattered the way you do." Dara suddenly gasped. "Olly! We didn't use birth control!"

CHAPTER 13

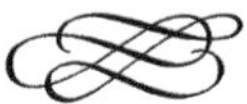

"Oh shit," Oliver said. "I never even thought of it. It's been so long since we needed it."

"I haven't gotten a shot in ages. Crap."

"Would it be terrible if we had another baby?"

"No, but… I just don't know if I can do it again." She gave a short laugh. "At the very least, we probably should've had a conversation about that beforehand."

"That would've killed the mood."

"Probably." She turned her head so she could see him. "What do we do now?"

He flattened his hand on her belly. "We keep doing it and see what happens?"

"Isn't that sort of like juggling with dynamite?"

"Nah. We were great parents, and we would be again."

"We were great parents until our son died on our watch."

"That was a tragic accident."

"I'm just so afraid that if we had another baby, I'd never be able to take a deep breath again for the rest of my life."

Oliver thought about that for a long moment before he replied. "The other day when I was at the marina for coffee with Big Mac and the guys, they were talking about Luke's wife, Sydney. From what I was able to piece together, she lost her first husband and two children in a drunk driving accident."

"Oh my goodness. That's awful."

"She and Luke have a baby daughter named Lily. Maybe she's someone you could talk to about this."

"I can't just ask some woman I've never met to tell me about her deepest grief."

"I've gotten to know Luke fairly well. Would you mind if I asked him how she might feel about it?"

"You're sure it wouldn't be weird to ask about something like that?"

"Everyone here is so nice. Luke is such a good guy. I can't imagine him being offended in any way by me asking the question. I mean, he was speaking rather freely about her losses in front of me the other day."

"True." Dara thought about it for a minute before she shifted her gaze to meet his. "I suppose it couldn't hurt to ask him. But please tell him to tell her there's no pressure."

"I will." He continued to caress her as they talked. "Does that mean we're on hold until we can address the birth control issue?"

"How would you feel about condoms? You know, just until we decide we really want to try."

He wrinkled his nose to tell her his true feelings on the topic. "I'll get some."

"My hero."

"Haha. Hardly."

"No, Olly, you are. I wouldn't still be here without you. Even when it seemed I was pushing you away, knowing you were still there made all the difference."

"Same here. I kept telling myself we'd survive it as long as we stuck together."

"Have we survived it?" she asked.

"We're in the process of surviving it, and we probably will be for the rest of our lives."

"Yes, I guess that's true. I just want you to know I'm thankful to be surviving it with you, even if it seemed at times that wasn't the case."

He gazed into her eyes. "I'm glad to be surviving it with you, too. After all, there's no one else in this world who loved him like we did."

"Except the grandparents."

"Yeah, they loved him, too."

"I feel like I let them down."

"You didn't," he said. "A terrible thing happened, but it was no one's fault. We did everything we could to keep him safe. I had the right to take a nap when I thought my son was safe in his room. You had the right to work. We were both in the house, and this still happened."

"That's what terrifies me about having another one. We did everything we could, and the worst still happened."

"You know what they always tell us in church. God has a plan, and we're just along for the ride?"

"Yeah."

"If we believe that, then we must also believe that nothing we did or didn't do would've changed the fact that Lewis was only supposed to be here for a short time."

Dara took a deep breath and released it slowly. "I hate that, but I suppose we have no choice but to accept it."

"And to accept that it's all out of our hands. Every damned bit of it. We're just along for the ride."

"That makes it a little easier to accept that there was nothing I could've done to change what happened."

"There wasn't. If you'd known he was in danger, you would've knocked walls down to get to him if that's what it took. You would've killed for him, Dar. And I would've, too. What more can anyone do than everything they can, even if it's not enough?"

"Nothing, I suppose." She looked at him the way she used to, with her heart in her eyes. "Do you want to have another baby?"

They'd been trying for a second child when Lewis died. "I'd love to be a dad again. It was my favorite thing, other than being your husband. But I only want that if you feel strong enough to handle the risk we'd be taking with two badly broken hearts."

"I feel stronger than I did, but I don't know if I'm there yet."

"Then we'll take it a step at a time until we're both ready," he said.

"And if we never get there?"

"Then we never get there."

"And you'd be okay with that?" she asked.

"I'd be okay with whatever you want. We were a good team for a lot of years before Lewis joined us."

"But we were better with him."

"He was pretty great."

After a long silence, Dara said, "Ask your friend Luke if his wife would be willing to talk."

"I'll do that tomorrow."

COOPER FELT like a lovesick fool because he couldn't wait to see Gigi after just a few hours away from her. As a professional player, it wasn't like him to count the hours until he could see someone. But she was different in every possible way. There was just something about her that did it for him, big-time.

Not that he was letting himself get carried away or anything. Whatever this was, it would be only a summer fling, if it even went that far. If he hadn't gotten injured, maybe they'd be hooking up by now. Or maybe that first date would've been the only one they had. Who knew? But counting the hours until he could see someone was certainly unprecedented for him.

"So yer Jared's baby brother, huh?" the cab driver asked.

"That's right."

"He's a real fine fellow, yer brother."

"Thank you. I like him."

"Doesn't let the success git to his head."

"No, he doesn't."

"How they making out with that baby girl?"

"Okay, but hoping to hear something from her mother."

"Tough spot the mother put 'em in."

"For sure. What did you say your name was?"

"Ned Saunders, at yer service."

"Nice to meet you, Ned. You seem to have the inside scoop on what goes on around here."

"I keep my eyes 'n ears open." He met Cooper's gaze in the rearview mirror. "Heard ya had some trouble out at the bluffs the other night."

Cooper winced. "Yeah."

Ned cackled with laughter. "Does yer brother know?"

"I don't think he knows the whole story, and I'd love to keep it that way."

"Won't hear it from me. How long you planning to stay?"

"Not sure yet. I'm working on a business idea that'd be situated here."

"What idea is that?"

"You promise you won't steal it?"

Ned snickered. "Shit, boy, I'm too old ta be startin' anythin' new. Got my hands full with what I already got, not ta mention a whole buncha grandkids underfoot these days."

"Driving the cab keeps you pretty busy, huh?"

"That and real estate. I buy 'em cheap, fix 'em up and sell 'em for a profit. Been doing it forty years or so now."

"Wow. That's amazing. Why do you still drive the cab?"

"I do that fer fun. I like ta meet new people. Tell me about yer idea."

Cooper gave him the lowdown on his plan to support the wedding industry on the island with party boats for bachelorette and bachelor parties.

"Yer gonna need a boatload of insurance."

"I got that covered."

"Ya got a full proposal?"

"I do."

"Wouldn't mind hearing more about it if ya wanna come by the marina one a these mornin's ta pitch it to us."

"Who is us?"

"Me and my buddies. We're kinda like a brain trust of sorts."

"Is that right?" Cooper asked, equal parts amused and intrigued. "What marina do you meet at?"

"McCarthy's. Is there any other?"

"I was going to speak to Mr. McCarthy about running my boats out of his place."

"Ya have ta talk ta Big Mac, Mac Junior and Luke Harris. Three a them own the joint."

"Good to know."

"Ya got any interest in real estate? Got a few places that need some work, but I'm so busy these days with the grandkids that I don't have much time to deal with 'em. Wouldn't mind having some help if yer interested."

"Seriously?"

"Yep. I'm gettin' old. Got other stuff I wanna be doin' than paintin' and shit."

"Would you be interested in a partner?"

Ned glanced in the mirror again, maybe gauging Cooper's level of sincerity. "Maybe."

Wow, you never knew who you might meet on Gansett Island. "If I stop by this meeting of the minds in the next few days, perhaps we could discuss this further?"

"Perhaps we could."

"I'll look forward to that, Ned." Cooper handed over a twenty as he noted the cars lining the road outside Mason's house, where Jordan had resided for most of the summer. Gigi said they'd never officially made the decision to live together. It'd just sort of happened. "Thanks for the ride."

Ned took the bill and started to make change.

"Keep the change. Coffee's on me at the marina."

"Sounds like a plan. Ya got a ride home later?"

"I do, thanks."

"Have a nice evenin'."

"You do the same. It was really nice to meet you."

"Likewise, young Cooper."

Cooper got out of the car at the end of Mason's driveway and walked toward the lights and voices, rehashing the conversation with Ned. Was the guy for real? He drove a cab for fun while making a fortune in real estate? If it was true, Cooper might've just gotten an extremely lucky break in his fledgling career, and one that didn't involve Jared.

Not that he didn't want to be in business with his brother. Anyone would want to be in business with Jared. But Cooper didn't want all the success he achieved in his life to be tied to his billionaire brother. He wanted to do some of it on his own, separate from Jared and the money he'd given him.

As he approached the gathering in the yard, his gaze immediately found Gigi standing with Jordan and her twin sister. All three women were stunning, but he saw only Gigi. She stood out like the rarest of diamonds. She wore a short white strapless thing that left miles of sexy skin on display, and her blonde hair fell in soft curly waves to her midback.

She dazzled him, making his heart beat funny and his hands feel sweaty. That never happened. When she looked up and saw him there, the smile that stretched across her face made him feel like a conquering hero returning from battle to find his love waiting for him.

His love.

Wow, man. Way to get ahead of yourself.

Gigi said something to Jordan and Nikki and then came to greet him with a hug. "How're you feeling?"

She smelled as good as she looked. "Much better now."

"Did you take something for the pain?"

"A while ago, but it's you that made me feel much better."

"What'd I do?" she asked, seeming perplexed.

"You smiled at me."

"That's all it takes?"

"Apparently so." He kept an arm around her, even though he was uncertain whether she'd want him to with her friends looking on.

Jordan and Nikki came to say hello. Though they were identical twins, Cooper spotted subtle differences.

"Glad you could come, Cooper. I'm Jordan, and this is my sister, Nikki. We met at the wedding."

Keeping his left arm around Gigi, he shook hands with them. "Right. Great to see you both again. I'm a huge fan of the show."

"Thank you," Jordan said. "That's always nice to hear."

"We're big fans of Gigi's, and you have your arm around her," Nikki said.

Whoa. These ladies didn't mess around. "I like Gigi. A lot."

"She likes you, too," Jordan said, "and she doesn't like *anyone*."

"That is not true," Gigi said. "I like you two. Most of the time."

"You have to like us," Jordan said. "We're family. You don't have to like him, and you do, which is headline news."

"Don't listen to them," Gigi said.

Cooper found her flustered state adorable and knew her just well enough to understand that it didn't happen very often.

"You're very handsome," Nikki said, giving him a critical once-over, "but I suppose you already know that."

"I, uh..."

"You don't have to respond to that," Gigi said with a pointed look for

Nikki. "Let's get you a drink." She took hold of Cooper's hand and led him out of the hornet's nest. "Sorry about that."

"Don't be. They love you and wanted to put me on notice. I get it."

"They're ridiculous. They know perfectly well that I can take care of myself."

"But isn't it nice to have others who care?"

She shrugged, as if it was no big deal to her that her two best friends would kill for her. What was that about?

"What do you want to drink?"

Noting the full bar, he said, "I'll do a vodka and soda with a twist of lime."

"How long ago did you take pain meds?"

"Right after the beach. I should be okay to have a drink or two since I'm not driving."

"All right, then." She made the drink and added the lime with a flourish. "There you are."

"Thank you. How are things here?"

"Good. Jordan didn't get a chance to tell Nikki the news before the party people showed up, so she asked us to hang out for a bit after. We're going to pretend she's telling us both at the same time."

"Because Nikki's feelings would be hurt that she's not the first to know?"

"We're not sure if they would be, so we're playing it safe. Twins are weird that way."

"Darling, introduce me to your deliciously handsome friend," a gorgeous older woman said as she approached them, drink in hand. She had short silver hair, bright blue eyes and wore a red floral blouse with white pants.

"Evelyn Hopper, grandmother extraordinaire to Jordan and Nikki—"

"And you," the woman said.

"And me," Gigi said with a soft smile that changed her entire demeanor. Interesting. "Meet Cooper James."

She took hold of his hand and gave it an affectionate squeeze. "It's *lovely* to meet you, young man. I had the great pleasure of meeting your brother and sister-in-law recently. They're good people."

"Yes, they are. It's great to meet you, too, Mrs. Hopper."

"Call me Evelyn. Mrs. Hopper makes me feel old."

"I'll do that, Evelyn."

"So you and our lovely Gigi have been spending time together. What're your intentions toward our girl?"

Cooper nearly swallowed his tongue. Intentions?

"Evelyn! Stop it!" To Cooper, she said, "Don't answer that."

"It's a perfectly reasonable question, Gabrielle."

Gigi groaned at Evelyn's use of her real name.

"Gabrielle, huh?" Cooper asked, raising a brow.

"Don't call me that if you expect me to answer."

"Ah, good to know."

"Back to my perfectly reasonable question," Evelyn said. "About your intentions, young man?"

"I, uh, I like Gigi very much and enjoy spending time with her."

"She's very special to us. We wouldn't want to see her hurt in any way."

"I understand." Cooper swallowed hard. "Ma'am."

"Excellent, now let's have some fun." Evelyn walked away to greet an older couple who'd just arrived.

"That was mortifying," Gigi said. "I'm sorry."

"Don't be sorry. They love you. I get it."

"They know I can take care of myself and don't need them hovering."

"Everyone needs someone watching their back."

"I don't."

Cooper had so many things he'd like to say in response to that, questions he'd like to ask, but this wasn't the time or the place. "Did Jordan get to tell Mason the news?"

"She did." Gigi glanced toward the happy couple.

The six-and-a-half-foot fire chief had Jordan tucked in close to him with an arm around her.

"The two of them haven't stopped smiling for one minute."

"So I guess he took the news well?"

"He's thrilled. They both are. He immediately popped the question, and she said yes."

"Good for them. And what about you?"

She whipped her head around to look directly at him. "What about me?"

"How are you feeling about it?"

"I'm happy for my friend."

"But?"

"No buts, so quit shrinking me. I'm fine. If she's happy, I'm happy. Trust me, no one deserves it more than she does after the hell of the last few years with Zane the asshole."

"Everyone deserves to be happy. Even you."

"I'm happy. Excuse me for a minute."

She walked away, leaving Cooper to wonder if he'd said the wrong thing, which was another thing he rarely worried about when it came to women. While most men complained they didn't speak the same language as women, Cooper had never had that problem. He got them. They got him.

But Gigi, she was different. She didn't wear her heart on her sleeve or give away her every thought or emotion the way most women did. She kept her feelings buried deep, and the more he got to know her, the more he wanted to know the secret to cracking the code to her well-guarded heart.

CHAPTER 14

He sees too much.

Gigi went inside to use the bathroom, locking the door to give herself a minute alone. What the hell was a twenty-four-year-old man-child who looked like him doing with all that insight? He rattled her. A smart woman who didn't like being *seen* by anyone would take a step back from a man like him.

Protecting herself had become an art form to Gigi, and Cooper was a threat to the life she'd created for herself. That life worked for her, and protecting it was a top priority.

But she liked how she felt when he was around, which was also a concern.

Men didn't get to her. She didn't let them.

Cooper could get to her, and she wasn't sure how she felt about that.

A knock sounded on the door.

"Let us in," Jordan said.

Groaning, Gigi opened the door. "What if I'd been peeing?"

"You aren't peeing," Nikki said. "What's wrong?"

Gigi rolled her eyes. "For fuck's sake. Nothing is wrong. Everything is great."

Jordan eyed her shrewdly. If anyone could see through Gigi's shit, Jordan could. "Something is bothering you. We both saw it earlier, and when you walked away from Cooper just now, we worried he said something to upset you."

"He didn't. He's lovely."

"Is that the problem?" Nikki said. "Do you like him?"

"Yes, I like him, or I wouldn't be hanging out with him."

"But do you *like him* like him?" Nikki asked.

"Huh?"

"She's asking if you have *feelings* for him," Jordan said.

Gigi stared at her as if she was crazy. "No, I don't have feelings for him. That's not my thing, and you know it."

The sisters exchanged grim glances.

Gigi's gaze traveled between them. "What the hell is wrong with you two?"

"We're just wondering if you're ever going to give a man a chance to care for you," Jordan said gently. "Ever since you broke up with jackass number two, you haven't let anyone get close, and we're just wondering why."

"Look, you guys, I'm so, so glad you're happy with Riley and Mason. I mean it. No one is happier for you than I am. But you know true love and all that is not my groove. It never will be."

"How do you know that?" Nikki asked. "You're only twenty-nine."

Gigi was filled with an odd sense of desperation, as if she were somehow fighting for her life, or some other dramatic thing. "I know how old I am, and I know how I'm wired. You're never going to see me settled down with one guy and half a dozen baby chicks. That's what you guys want. I've never wanted that."

"You haven't wanted it *yet*," Nikki said. "That doesn't mean you never will."

"Yes, it does. Love and all the nonsense that goes with it is not for me."

"How do you know that when you've never been in love?" Nikki asked.

"I just know it. Love is not for me."

"Gigi," Jordan said, looking stricken. "Don't say that."

"I get what you guys are trying to do, and I love you for it. I really do. But Cooper and I will never be anything more than a fun maybe-fling at the end of a nice summer on Gansett before I go back to my real life in

LA. Please don't go looking for something that isn't there. Now you need to get back to your guests, Jord."

Gigi pushed past them and nearly ran smack into Cooper, who was standing outside the door. Oh fuck. How much of that had he heard?

"Does it really take three of you to use the facilities?" he asked with a small smile.

She couldn't help but note the sadness in his eyes. *Fuck, fuck, fuck.* "You know how girls are."

"Yes, I do. Everything all right?"

"Sure. Let's go find seats at the table. They'll be serving dinner soon."

As she led the way out of the house, Gigi hoped she hadn't hurt his feelings by speaking the truth about them to Jordan and Nikki. Because there was no doubt he'd heard what she'd said.

"Listen," she said hesitantly when they were seated at the long teak table Jordan had bought for the yard earlier in the summer. "I don't know what you heard in there."

He rested his hand on top of hers. "We'll talk about that later."

Fuckity, fuck, fuck, *fuck*.

COOPER TRIED NOT to show her how deeply affected he was by what he'd heard her say. He hadn't intended to eavesdrop. He'd gone to check on her and had come upon the open door and the conversation that involved him.

What else should he have done but listen in?

His heart ached for her. Why in the world had a beautiful, smart, funny woman like her decided love wasn't for her? While his heart ached, his mind raced, picking over the things she'd shared about her past and wondering if the answers could be found in her chaotic childhood.

Caterers served a delicious dinner consisting of a wide variety of kabobs, rice, salad with coconut and a veggie dish that was one of the best things he'd ever tasted. As he took a bite of teriyaki shrimp, he tuned in to the conversation Mason was having with Big Mac and Linda McCarthy about the fencing being installed at the bluffs.

Too bad that hadn't been there the other night.

"You got hurt out there recently, didn't you, Cooper?" Big Mac asked.

"I did. My brother's car started to roll, and when I tried to stop it, I busted two ribs and made this mess on my face."

"You forgot the part where the car had been driven around the logs that keep cars from rolling toward the bluffs," Mason said with a smile.

"I knew you'd fill in the blanks in my story," Cooper said, grinning. "I'll never again do something so stupid in pursuit of the almighty selfie. I've learned my lesson. And please don't tell Jared how it happened, or I'll never get to drive his Porsche again."

"How much is it worth to ya?" Big Mac asked, laughing.

Another couple came strolling into the yard, holding hands.

"So sorry we're late," the man said.

"Come in," Jordan said, jumping up to welcome them. "Everyone, this is Oliver and Dara Watkins, our new lighthouse keepers."

Room was made for them at the table, plates full of food were delivered, and drink orders were taken.

"This is my kind of party," Oliver said. "Show up to immediate food and drink."

"We're glad you could make it," Mason said, reaching over Jordan to shake hands with Oliver.

"Thanks for the invite. Everyone here has been so friendly. Dara and I were just talking about that."

"Glad you're enjoying Gansett," Linda McCarthy said. "This place is special, and we love to see other people discovering that."

"We love it so far," Dara said.

"Let's raise a glass to Dara," Nikki said, "the new events manager at the Wayfarer."

"Hear, hear," Big Mac said. "Welcome to the team."

"Thank you for having me," Dara said. "I'm excited to get started."

As the conversation flowed in a number of different directions, including the upcoming Labor Day Weekend, off-season plans and the final weeks of shooting for the show, Cooper let his mind wander to how he wanted to play this situation with Gigi.

Growing up as the youngest of five older, accomplished siblings, Cooper had learned early on to work the system to his benefit. He'd used charm and sweetness to get what he wanted from family members and had deployed those same skills in his dating career. If people liked you, they were more willing to help you get what you wanted, whether it was a second bowl of ice cream after dinner or a night in the bed of a sexy woman.

Gigi liked him, so that gave him an advantage. However, he knew her well enough to know if he pushed her too hard that she'd push right back.

Hearing she didn't believe in love made him want her to fall in love with him so he could show her how great it could be.

The idea had shown up as a fully formed plan, ready for execution. With the show's shooting schedule winding down, he had a limited amount of time to sweep her off her feet, to show her that love wasn't something to be feared. He'd been in love once. In high school. He and Teagan had been sure their love would last forever, until they ended up at colleges two thousand miles apart and found out how painful first love could be when it ended.

Since then, he'd gone out of his way to keep his dealings with women closer to the surface and far from the heart of the matter.

But hearing Gigi say she didn't believe in love, hearing her friends confirm she'd never been in love... That made Cooper want to give her that experience.

Except, what would happen if they both developed deeper feelings and then went their separate ways? He'd be right back in the same mess he'd been in with Teagan, with Gigi living three thousand miles from him in Los Angeles.

It occurred to him that he hadn't done anything here on Gansett that couldn't be undone. So far, his party boat idea was just that—an idea. The conversation with Ned had been interesting, but so far, it was only talk. If this thing with Gigi turned into something more, there was no reason he couldn't go with her to LA and find a job out there. He had an MBA after all, and a last name that opened doors.

"Why are you so quiet?" Gigi asked him during a lull in her conversation with Jordan, Mason, Nikki, Riley, Riley's brother, Finn, and his fiancée, Chloe. People from the show were seated at the other end of the big table.

Their group of friends seemed tight, and Cooper found himself wanting to get to know the others better. Finn and Riley were great dudes, and despite Mason teasing him about the accident, Cooper liked him, too. "Just listening," he said in response to Gigi's inquiry.

"Are you mad?" she asked in a small voice that made him want to roar.

His Gigi didn't speak in a small voice. Nothing about her personality was small.

"Not at all." The others were so engaged in their conversation that they were able to speak somewhat privately even though they were surrounded by people.

"I'm sorry I was talking about you like that. I shouldn't have been."

He slipped an arm around her and kissed her temple. "It's fine. They're your girls. Of course you talk to them about everything."

"Still… I don't want you to think I talk about you like that."

"I want you to talk about me. It means you're interested."

"I, um… You know I like you."

"I do know that. And I like you."

"It's just that's all I'm capable of."

"I want you to do something for me," Cooper said, feeling as if he were at the edge of a high dive about to take a very big leap into the unknown.

"What?"

"I want you to not rule anything out." When she started to protest, he gently laid a finger over her lips. "Don't rule anything out."

"Cooper…"

"Hey, Gigi, what are you two whispering about over there?" Jordan asked.

"Wouldn't you like to know?" Gigi said.

"Yes, I would. That's why I asked."

"Mind your own business, darling," Evelyn said, "and leave Gigi alone."

"She never leaves me alone," Jordan retorted, sticking her tongue out at Gigi.

Gigi stuck hers out at Jordan.

"Now, that's more like it," Evelyn said. "These girls have been minding each other's business since they were little kids."

"How old were you all when you met?" Cooper asked.

"Second or third grade?" Gigi said.

"Third," Nikki said. "The year we all had the chicken pox. Remember that?"

"How could we forget?" Gigi asked.

"They all came down with it at the same time," Evelyn said, "so I kept them together at my house, figuring they'd be happier suffering together."

Cooper found it interesting that Gigi had stayed at Evelyn's when she was sick, rather than her own home. If his plan had any hope of working, he realized he needed a visit with Evelyn sometime when no one else was around. She would have insight into Gigi that could prove useful to Cooper.

What are you doing, man? Plotting and scheming to make her fall in love with you? Really?

As she tipped her head back to laugh at something Jordan had said, Cooper was struck once again by how incredibly lovely she was.

Cooper wanted to truly know her. He wanted to understand what made her tick. And he was starting to think he could love her. This was unprecedented territory for him, and he ought to be thinking about how he might extricate himself from this situation before it got complicated. That's what he'd do under normal circumstances.

But nothing about this was normal.

MUCH LATER, after most of the guests had left, Gigi and Cooper joined Evelyn, Jordan, Mason, Nikki, Riley, Finn and Chloe at the fire pit.

"So I've waited all night to hear this news you have," Nikki said to her sister. "Spill it."

Jordan, who was seated on Mason's lap, smiled at him as he held her even closer. "We're pregnant."

Nikki let out a shriek that had everyone else laughing. "I told you," she said to Riley. "Pay up."

"You bet on what it was?" Cooper asked.

"Hell yes."

"How much did she win?" Jordan asked.

"Fifty bucks," Riley said with a playful frown as he slapped a fifty into Nikki's outstretched hand.

"What did you think it was?"

"That you guys had eloped."

"I told him you'd never do that to me or Gram or Gigi," Nikki said. "We deserve to be there for your happy ending."

"You're right," Jordan said. "You do deserve to be there."

"We're going to find a time this winter, after your wedding, to get it done," Mason said. "Maybe we'll go somewhere warm."

"Sign me up for that," Evelyn said. "I'll even pay for it."

"You don't have to do that, Gram."

"I'm old. I can do what I want."

"I love when she plays that card to shut you guys down," Gigi said, laughing.

"She's playing that card a lot more often lately," Nikki said.

"I'm getting even older," Evelyn said. "I plan to get much worse before I depart."

"You're not departing," Jordan said. *"Ever."*

Gigi couldn't begin to imagine life without Evelyn Hopper telling them all what to do and how to live. The very thought of her leaving them was enough to turn Gigi's stomach.

Cooper reached over and took her hand in a smooth, subtle move that seemed well practiced.

In the past, she might've worried about her man of the moment wanting to talk later about something he'd overheard her saying about him. But Cooper had already set her mind at ease and let her know he wasn't angry. She appreciated he hadn't let it fester to the point that it ruined an otherwise lovely evening.

Nikki was so excited about Jordan's news, the two of them buzzing the way they did about weddings and showers and babies. Gigi felt truly separate from them for the first time in all the years the three of them had been a squad. Their lives were going in very different directions, and before too much longer, Jordan and Nikki would no longer be in her daily life.

The show would probably end with the season on Gansett, and Jordan would live happily ever after with Mason, while Nikki did the same with Riley. Finn and Chloe, who'd become friends during the summer they'd all spent together, were engaged and planning a spring wedding. Everyone around her was figuring out their shit.

She would go home and pick up the law practice she'd neglected somewhat during the years she'd appeared on Jordan's show. Maybe she'd take a closer look at some of the lucrative endorsement deals or business opportunities she'd been offered as the show skyrocketed in popularity. As a single woman with no family of her own, Gigi understood the importance of making as much money as she could while the iron was hot, so to speak, to ensure she'd have plenty for later in her life when the stardom faded, as it always did.

No matter what, she'd figure it out the way she had from the time she was a teenager, even if life without Jordan and Nikki at the center of it wouldn't be as much fun.

"Do you want to go?" Cooper asked.

"Sure. I'm ready if you are."

"I'm ready."

They said their goodbyes and headed for her car.

"You want me to drive?" he asked. "I quit drinking hours ago."

She handed him the keys. "Don't drive my baby off any cliffs."

"A guy has one close call at a cliff, and suddenly, he has a reputation."

"That's right, and we'll never let you forget it."

"Good to know." He held the passenger door of her white Mercedes coup and waited until she was settled.

"Nice manners, Mr. James."

"Why, thank you, Ms. Gibson."

When he was in the car, she turned to him. "How are you feeling?"

"Much better than I was earlier today. I've always bounced back fast from injuries and illness."

"You're lucky. We had a cameraman on the first season of the show who broke ribs in a motorcycle accident, and he was out for months."

"I broke my arm when I was twelve. I was only in a cast for three weeks. The doctors couldn't believe it was totally healed that fast."

"Wow. That is fast."

"And I was thankful because it happened on the last day of school. The last thing I wanted was to be in a cast all summer."

"Which hurt more? The ribs or the arm?"

"The ribs. Way worse at first, but it's dwindled to an ache at this point."

"I'm glad. I don't want to see you suffer like that."

"Aww, you like me."

"When did I say that?"

"Just now."

"When did I say the words 'I like you'?"

Cooper laughed. "You just said it again."

"You're hearing things, my friend."

"It's okay. I'm a very likable kind of guy. Ask anyone."

"I'll take your word for it."

"How're you feeling about Jordan and the baby and the weddings?"

"I'm fine."

She said that a little too quickly, if you asked him.

"Why wouldn't I be? My best friends are deliriously happy. It's nice to see."

"They seem like a nice group of people. I really like Finn and Riley."

"They're funny together. And you should see them with their older cousins. It's a full-on comedy show." Gigi paused for a brief moment. "I guess I'll be going to another wedding sometime soon."

"Is she staying on Gansett, then?"

"I suppose that was always going to be the case after she met Mason, who has a good job here."

"What about the show?"

"Nothing's been decided yet. Jordan isn't sure she wants to do any more of it, and it's really up to her. I'm just the sidekick."

"You're much more than that, Gigi. People watch that show as much for you as they do for her."

"I guess." After another pause, she said, "Don't mind me. I'm just in a weird place right now. I'll feel better when I get home to my real life."

The more he listened to her try to deflect the painful changes happening in her life, the more Cooper wanted to wrap his arms around Gigi and protect her from anything that could hurt her. Under her tough exterior, he suspected she was far more fragile than anyone suspected.

When they arrived back at Jared's, Cooper parked Gigi's car in the spot next to the Porsche and turned off the engine.

"You feel like swimming?" she asked.

If it meant more time with her, he was all in. "Sure."

"Meet you out there?"

"Sounds good."

CHAPTER 15

Gigi went up the stairs to her apartment over the garage while Cooper went inside Jared's house to change. When he entered through the slider to the kitchen, the first thing he heard was the baby crying. He noticed right away that she sounded different, almost frantic.

As he walked toward the noise, Jared came out of his bedroom, looking as stressed as Cooper had ever seen him.

"What's going on?" Cooper asked.

"We aren't sure. It's been like this for hours now. We're taking her to the clinic."

"Is there anything I can do?"

"No, thanks. Not sure when we'll be back."

"Text me when you know more, will you?"

"Yeah, I will. Poor Lizzie is a wreck."

Jared was, too, although Cooper kept that thought to himself. "I'm here if I can do anything at all."

"Thanks, Coop."

When Lizzie came out of the room, carrying the shrieking baby, Cooper's heart went out to both of them. Lizzie's face was streaked with tears.

"Sorry for the noise," she said to Cooper.

"Please don't apologize. I wish there was something I could do for you."

"Me, too. We'll see you in the morning. I hope."

They strapped the screaming baby into the car seat, which sat on the kitchen table. Jared carried the seat to Lizzie's SUV, and they left a minute later.

Cooper changed into swim trunks, grabbed a towel and headed out to the pool.

Gigi was already in the water. "So that was intense."

"Seriously. Jared said she's been crying like that for hours."

"I feel so bad for them, plunged into this situation with no idea what they're doing or whether the mother will come back for the baby."

"I don't know whether to wish for or against that."

"I know."

Cooper went down the stairs and into the heated pool. In an uninjured state, he might've dived into the deep end. But with his ribs feeling better, he didn't want to risk aggravating them, so he took it easy. "Where'd you learn to swim like an Olympian?"

Gigi snorted. "I'm hardly an Olympian."

"Maybe so, but you're a hell of a swimmer."

"High school swim team. It was my favorite thing."

"I bet you were a champion."

"I did okay."

"Did you think about pursuing it further?"

"Not really. After the emancipation, I had bigger concerns, such as feeding myself and financing college."

Cooper was rarely unsure of himself around women, but this woman defied all the norms. He moved closer to her, hoping he'd be welcome to do so. Under the water, he put his arms around her and brought her onto his lap. "I think you're incredible," he whispered in the second before he kissed her.

"Why?"

"So many reasons, it would take me a while to list them all."

"I've got time."

"Let's start with you choosing to support yourself as a teenager rather than have your wealthy family take care of you."

"They were never my family. I lived with them. That was it. Jordan, Nikki and Evelyn are my family."

"I know, and they love you very much."

She shrugged. "I guess."

"They do, Gigi. Anyone can see that. You're also brave, strong, resilient, sexy as all hell and a great friend to the people you care about."

"The list of people I care about is small."

"I know that, too, which makes me want to find a way into your inner circle."

She recoiled somewhat from that statement. "That's not going to happen, Cooper. I like you. I do, but this can never be more than whatever it is right now."

"Why not?"

"You already heard why not earlier. That's not who I am. You pay attention, which is an admirable quality in any guy, especially someone as young as you are. But please, *please* don't fall for me. Don't ruin a fun thing by trying to make it something it'll never be."

He wondered if she could hear the ache that came through in her every word. Did she have herself convinced that she was unlovable? Was that the problem? Because he'd like nothing more than to show her otherwise. As he kissed her again, he was fully aware that he could be setting himself up for something he'd studiously avoided since the painful breakup with Teagan—heartbreak.

The kiss spiraled quickly out of control as her arms tightened around his neck, and her tongue rubbed up against his. She wasn't kissing him like a woman who didn't want him. She kissed him like she wanted more, and he was happy to give it to her. His fingers dug into her ass as he tugged her in tight against his erection.

Gigi withdrew slowly from the kiss. "If I do this with you, I need to know you understand what it is—and what it isn't."

"I get it."

"I'd never want to hurt you."

"I appreciate that. Same goes."

"So."

"So."

"Want to go upstairs?" she asked.

"Yeah."

"Do you have condoms?"

"In the house."

"Why don't you go get them?"

Cooper couldn't believe this was actually going to happen. He was going to have sex with Gigi Gibson. In the time they'd spent together, he'd discovered there was so much more to her than the hysterically funny, sexy woman she portrayed on the show. She carried a well of hurt a mile deep, and all he seemed to want out of life since he met her was to make her happy and soothe the pain she carried deep inside.

He disentangled from her, got out of the pool and grabbed his towel to dry off before he went inside to grab the condoms he had in his shaving bag. Would bringing three seem overly optimistic? Cooper laughed at that thought and took a second to get himself together before he joined her.

This thing with her, which had started out as lighthearted fun, was quickly becoming much more than that for him. He'd heard what she said about not falling for her, and he took that to heart, but he was falling, nonetheless, and having sex with her was only going to make it "worse." In this case, worse had never been so good.

Yes, he was young, and yes, women had been a source of fun for him for most of his life, but never had he met anyone he could see himself being with for the long haul until he met Gigi. She'd be an endless source of excitement, mystery, confusion, laughter and desire. If someone had asked him before he met her what his perfect woman might be like, he couldn't have said. Now he knew that Gigi in all her maddening variations was his idea of the perfect woman.

Convincing her to give him a chance was going to be a daunting task, but he was more than up for it.

GIGI HOPED she wasn't making a huge mistake by inviting Cooper into her bed. He was a great guy, but his intensity concerned her. He looked at her as if he could see all the way through her to the junk she kept buried deep inside and off-limits to everyone. She didn't want him or anyone seeing that crap, which meant she needed to be extra careful around him.

His footsteps on the stairs announced his arrival. He came in wearing only swim trunks, with his muscular chest on full display. Deep, dark bruises marred the perfection that included light blond chest hair that went darker around the waistband of his trunks. The man was sexy, sweet and sincere, three things that were hard to find. So hard to find that she appreciated those qualities in him, but she absolutely refused to become attached to a man who'd soon be living three thousand miles from her.

She'd meant what she told him before. This could never be more than a late-summer fling. Now if only she could convince herself of that before it was too late.

He came right over to her, put his arms around her and picked up where they'd left off in the pool with hot, sexy kisses that made her head spin.

"I wish I could do something cool like sweep you off your feet and carry you to bed, but I'm afraid if I did that, I might not be able to do anything else."

"Save your strength, Tarzan. You're gonna need it."

"Am I panting? Drooling?"

Smiling, she took his hand and walked backward toward the bedroom. When they were standing by her bed, she gently ran her fingertips over the bruises on his side. "If it hurts too much, will you tell me?"

"Yeah, I'll tell you. But I'm fine. Never been better, in fact."

"Is that right?"

"Uh-huh."

Something in the way he looked at her put Gigi on alert that she might've made a huge mistake agreeing to sleep with him. An odd tingling sensation traveled down her spine as he touched her with reverence. She wanted to stop him, to remind him of what this was and what it *wasn't*, but she couldn't get words past the huge lump in her throat.

Sex wasn't about emotion. That bullshit was for other people. Sex was a physical release, and that was it. She needed to take control of this situation before it spiraled out of her control.

"Let me," she said, her hands on his chest.

"No." He dipped his head and kissed her neck, laying a path to her chest, where he quickly removed her bikini top and began to worship her breasts.

There was no other word to describe the way he tended to each one, making her squirm and ache from the sensuous torture. Cooper might be younger than her, but he clearly knew his way around the female body.

He was tender, sweet and demanding—all at the same time. She no sooner processed one thing than he was on to the next.

As he lowered her to the bed and gazed down at her, Gigi couldn't keep up, and holding on to any semblance of control seemed foolish considering how he played her body like a maestro. She'd had no idea that her belly button could be so sensitive or that hip bones could be erogenous zones.

He raised her legs to his shoulders and left hot kisses on her inner thigh.

"Cooper."

"Hmm?"

"I, uh..." Her brain went completely blank when his tongue connected with her clit. Holy. *Shit.* Gigi couldn't recall the last time she'd allowed a guy to do that to her. It was too intimate. She wanted to tell Cooper to stop, to move along to the main event, to get it over with so she could put her protective walls back in place to keep him from getting too close. But when a man had his face buried in your unmentionables, that was hardly the time to remind him that this was supposed to be just sex, not whatever *this* was.

Gigi was always, *always* in control. She never drank too much or did any kind of drugs that would leave her unprotected. The habit of self-protection was so deeply ingrained in her that she'd rarely had an orgasm with a man, preferring to fake them rather than let herself go there with someone else. Besides, she'd yet to meet a man who could give her a better orgasm than she could give herself.

Cooper seemed determined to be the exception.

He was in no particular rush as he used every tool in his arsenal to devastate her defenses. Fingers, tongue, lips worked together in a combination that had her making noises she'd never heard herself make before as he brought her to the very edge of release before backing off and starting over. He did it so effortlessly that she began to wonder just how much practice he'd had in how to make a woman lose her mind.

And as soon as she had that thought, she hated every woman he'd ever done this to before her with a wild, unreasonable fury.

Gigi Gibson didn't do jealousy, which was another unprecedented emotion on top of all the others that overwhelmed her one right after the other. She was about to insist he stop when the orgasm he'd been building broke so suddenly, it took her breath away. When she came back down from the incredible high and opened her eyes, he was perched above her, too sexy for his own good—and hers. His small, smug smile did wonders for his already sinfully handsome face, and as he pressed into her, Gigi winced from the tight fit.

Holy. *Hell.* The man was packing, and it should've come as no surprise to her that he knew just how to use his God-given gifts. Christ have mercy, he was going to be the death of her. And then he began to talk.

"You're so, so pretty, Gigi," he whispered as his lips skimmed over her tingling nipple. "Prettiest girl I ever met."

"No."

"Yes. And so, so sexy, you make my head spin."

He did the same for her, not that she could say so. Putting words to the crazy emotions he made her feel would be dangerous.

"You have the softest skin, the sweetest lips, and you taste like honey and strawberries."

Body wash, she wanted to say, but taking him into her body required every bit of concentration and focus as he pushed deeper than anyone had ever been. He seemed to touch the very heart of her, pushing her limits as she tried to accept and accommodate him.

"That's it," he said, moving carefully so he wouldn't hurt her. "Nice and easy."

"That thing ought to come with a warning," she said through gritted teeth.

He laughed as he used his fingertips to brush the hair back from her face. "Are you complaining?"

"I might be."

"We can't have that." He withdrew from her so suddenly that she gasped. Moving carefully, he turned so he was on his back and reached for her. "Come here."

Gigi sat up and got her first look at the huge cock that stretched almost to his belly button. Dear God. She hadn't expected *that.*

"Um, hello? Gigi?"

She'd had her share of sex, mostly meaningless encounters with men who exited her universe almost as quickly as they entered it. Even the two men—and that was using the word loosely—she'd been engaged to hadn't made her feel like he did. Sex like this, like she was having with Cooper, scared her. But she couldn't let him see that, or he'd want to fix it. That's who he was, and she didn't want him fixing her. She was fine the way she was.

Get your shit together, Gabrielle, her reliable inner voice demanded. *Stop letting this be more than it is. He's just a man, and soon enough, you'll never see him again.*

Why that thought made her sad was something she could think about when she didn't have him and his formidable penis to contend with.

She took the hand he offered and straddled him, settling on top of his hard cock.

As he ran his hands over her thighs and up her sides to cup her breasts, Cooper watched her in that way that made her feel far too *seen*. "What's the matter?"

"Huh? Nothing."

"You do this thing with your brows when you lie." He mimicked the expression. "Did you know that?"

"What? I'm not lying." Desperate to get things back on track, she raised herself up over King Kong cock and slid down on it, trying to take as much of it as she could. But even in this position, the struggle was real.

"Easy, sweet Gigi. We're in no rush. Take your time."

She was suddenly in a rush to get this done and to get him out of there before it was too late. But as she inched down on him, and he filled her to absolute capacity, she realized "too late" might've happened an hour ago.

CHAPTER 16

Something is wrong, Cooper thought. She was upset about something, and it'd happened since they'd been in her bedroom. "Do you want to stop?"

She looked up at him, seeming surprised. "What? No, I don't want to stop."

"Would you tell me if you did?"

"Yes, I'd tell you."

"It's okay, you know. If you've changed your mind." He wanted to tell himself to shut up. What man in his right mind said that when he had a goddess like her on top of him, halfway impaled on his cock?

"I haven't changed my mind about the fact that this weapon of yours ought to come with a warning."

Cooper laughed at the face she made, but then her internal muscles fluttered around his cock, and it took every ounce of control he could find not to lose it too soon. That couldn't happen. Not with her. He felt like he'd been rehearsing for this main event since his first time with Mindy Farthing ten years ago. Everything since then had been leading to this, to Gigi.

By the time she finally took all of him, he was sweating from the effort to hold back, to let her take the lead.

"Are you okay?" he asked.

"Ask me that tomorrow when I can't walk or sit."

"I'll carry you around."

She rolled her eyes. "You can barely move, let alone tote me around."

"I could tote you around if I had to." He squeezed her ass cheeks and gave a gentle push that took him deeper into her.

Her head fell back, and her mouth opened on a silent scream.

She was the sexiest fucking thing he'd ever seen, and Cooper knew he'd remember this moment for the rest of his life.

"Fuck me, Gigi," he whispered.

"I'm afraid to move."

"You're not afraid of anything."

Her eyes opened, and when her gaze collided with his, he realized that wasn't entirely true. For some reason, she was afraid of him, and he couldn't have that. "When we're done here, you're going to tell me why you seem upset."

"No, I'm not."

"Yes, you are."

"No."

"Yes."

She was magnificent. Her eyes flashed with annoyance even as her cheeks flushed with desire. She was a study in contrasts—funny, prickly, secretive, effortlessly sexy, insightful, loyal to the few people she loved and protective of herself and the tender heart that loved so few people. He desperately wanted to be one of them.

As he watched her, she began to move, probably trying to throw him off the scent of whatever was troubling her. Maybe she figured if she fucked his brains out, he might forget about that conversation he wanted to have with her after the fact.

He wouldn't forget, but *damn*, she knew how to move.

Watching her breasts bounce and her skin flush with heat as she rocked his world had him at the edge, clinging to control when she threw her head back and came.

Cooper was right there with her, his fingers sinking into her ass as he exploded inside her. Nothing in his life had ever been better than sex with Gigi.

When she would've disentangled herself from him right away, he stopped her by putting his arms around her and bringing her to rest on his chest. Exertion had them both breathing hard, and his heart beat so fast, he could hear the echo of it in his ears. Her internal muscles continued to contract around him, keeping his cock harder than it should've been after that grand finale.

"Wow," he said when he could speak again. "That was amazing."

"It can't happen again."

Stunned, he asked, "Why not?"

"Because. It just can't."

"Gigi."

She wriggled free of his arms and was up and off him so quickly, he had no time to prepare for the loss of her. The bathroom door closed with a loud slam.

What the fuck?

Cooper ran his hands through his hair and sat up slowly and painfully to find his shorts. He had put them back on and was sitting on the edge of her bed when she emerged from the bathroom ten minutes later, wearing a robe tied tight around her waist. "What's wrong?"

"Nothing."

"Save that bullshit for someone who doesn't see right through it."

Her eyes flashed with outrage. "Don't act like you know me so well, because you don't. So we fucked. So what? That doesn't suddenly give you *rights*."

Cooper was surprisingly hurt by her harsh words. "I'm not looking for rights. I'm just wondering what happened in the last half hour besides the fucking."

"Nothing happened. Nothing's going to happen. I told you that from the beginning, so please don't act like I'm changing the rules on you or something. Nothing has changed. You should go now."

Cooper sat frozen in place, staring at her for a full minute before he found the wherewithal to stand. "I don't know what you're so afraid of, Gigi, but it doesn't need to be me. I'd never hurt you."

"I know that."

"Then why—"

"This is *who I am*, Cooper."

She never blinked as she said those words, but her voice wavered ever so slightly. Just enough to let him know she wasn't as unemotional as she seemed as she kicked him out of her home.

Though he wasn't one to stay where he wasn't wanted, he couldn't leave her like this. He went to her, put his hands on her shoulders and gave a gentle squeeze. "I like you, Gigi. I like you more than I probably should. I understand that's not what you want, but I can't help how I feel. You've been through a lot in your life, had people disappoint you, so I get why you've learned not to let new people get too close. But you should know I don't give up easily, and I want to show you something different, something you maybe haven't had before now."

"Cooper—"

He kissed her softly. "Sleep well, sweet Gigi. I'll see you tomorrow."

"No, you won't."

He let her have the last word, but he hadn't even left her place before he was formulating his plan for tomorrow.

AT THE CLINIC, Jared paced the hallway outside the cubicle where Lizzie was with the baby, who hadn't stopped crying in what seemed like hours. They'd done everything they could think of to soothe her—fed her, changed her, rocked her. Nothing had helped. His nerves were shredded, and Lizzie's had to be, too, even if she never gave up on trying to pacify the baby.

Dr. David Lawrence approached him. He was tall with dark hair and wore a white coat and an exhausted expression. Summer on Gansett was rough on a number of island residents, including the clinic's only doctor. "So sorry to keep you waiting, Jared. We had a moped accident in town with multiple trauma patients that had to be stabilized before we could send them to the mainland."

"Those damned mopeds." Island residents hated them. Tourists loved them.

"You said it. I'd personally outlaw them if I could. We have a serious moped accident come through here at least once a week all summer long."

"Are the new patients expected to make it?"

"They are, but it'll be a rough recovery."

"Sorry to hear it."

"What's up with the little one?"

"I wish I knew. She's been inconsolable for hours. We weren't sure if it was normal or something to be concerned about. We have no idea what we're doing."

"I'm sure you're doing great. Let me take a look and see what we can do."

Jared followed David into the cubicle where Lizzie was standing, swaying back and forth in her latest attempt to calm the crying baby.

"Let's put her on the table," David said.

Lizzie did as he asked, placing the baby on her back on the table.

The baby wasn't having that. Her little face turned red, her hands curled into tight fists, and she screamed her head off.

Jared went to Lizzie and put his arm around her rigid shoulders. He hated seeing her so undone and wanted to rage at Jessie for doing this to them, even if he knew that wouldn't help anything.

David performed a thorough exam of the baby, who'd finally stopped screaming. Figured. "I suspect we might be dealing with gas. Her abdomen is rigid."

"What do we do about that?"

"I've got some drops we can give her to ease her discomfort. I'll be right back." He waited until Lizzie was there to make sure the baby couldn't fall off the table before he left the room.

"Gas," Lizzie said. "All this over gas. Who even knew that was a thing with babies?"

"Thankfully, David knew."

"Maybe this is a sign that we're not cut out for parenthood."

"It's not a sign, Lizzie. You're doing great with her. You can't be expected to know everything there is to know when you had a baby dumped in your lap. Most people have months to prepare themselves. You had minutes."

The baby sucked on her own fists as her body shuddered with sobs.

"She needs a name. Something we can call her besides 'the baby.'"

"We can't name her." With every passing second they spent with the baby, Jared felt more desperate to free them from this situation. Naming the baby would only drag them deeper into it.

"It wouldn't be an official name. Just something we call her while she's with us."

"Hopefully, she won't be with us for much longer." He felt cruel saying that, but he had to keep things real with her. The baby wasn't theirs, and he would remind her of that repeatedly if necessary. In a day or two, when Jessie realized the magnitude of what she'd done, she'd be back to collect her child. Jared was determined that neither he nor Lizzie would be decimated when that happened.

David returned and administered the drops to the baby, who lapped them up like they were candy. "That ought to give her some relief." He handed the baby to Lizzie and the bottle to Jared. "You can give them to her any time she seems uncomfortable. If that doesn't work, give me a call." He handed Jared a business card. "Any time, day or night."

"Thanks so much, Doc."

"No problem. Still no word from the mother?"

"Nothing," Jared said. "I know you have privacy rules and such, but if you have info on how to reach her, we'd sure appreciate any help you can provide."

"I'll take a look at the file and see what she gave us."

"If there's anything useful, and you'd be willing to contact Blaine, we'd be very appreciative. We're trying to hold out until she comes back, but eventually, Blaine will have to get more formally involved."

"I'll do whatever I can."

"Let's get her home and try to get some rest," Jared said, leading Lizzie from the room. "Thanks again for seeing us so late, David."

"Happy to help."

While Lizzie headed for the clinic's main door, Jared hung back to speak to David. "Please help us find her mother. We can't do this."

Since their infertility journey had begun in the clinic with him and Victoria sending them to the specialists on the mainland, David knew why Jared had said that.

"I understand, and I feel for you guys in this situation."

"Lizzie doesn't want to turn her over to Blaine and social services, but I feel like that's what we need to do for our own sanity."

"No one would blame you if you did that, Jared."

"My wife would never forgive me." As he had the car keys, he couldn't linger. "Thanks for anything you can do."

"Call if you need me."

"Will do. Thanks again." Jared headed for the main door and joined Lizzie outside. "How is she?"

"Already asleep. The poor thing wore herself out."

Jared unlocked the door and stood back to watch in awe as Lizzie buckled the sleeping baby into the car seat as if she'd been doing that sort of thing all her life.

They drove home in silence he'd never again take for granted. And while silence from the baby was welcome, silence between him and Lizzie was unusual and put him further on edge. "Are you okay?"

"Never better."

Jared had no idea what to say to that. He wanted to tell her he was sorry, but what was he sorry for? That her efforts to help someone else had landed them in an unfathomable situation?

"Just proves that no good deed goes unpunished," Lizzie added with a bitter edge to her tone that was so not like her.

"You can't stop trying to help people because this happened."

"Yes, I can. This is too much. For both of us. Tomorrow, I'll ask Blaine what our options are."

"Please don't do that because you think that's what I want."

"Isn't it?"

"I want Jessie to come back and take her baby."

"That's not going to happen."

"We don't know that yet."

"Yes, we do. She doesn't want to be found, or your guy would've found her by now."

"He's only been looking a couple of days."

"She's gone."

"People don't just disappear off the face of the earth, Lizzie. We'll find her."

"And what'll happen when we do? We can't make her come back for her child."

"No, but we could ask her if she wants to make this arrangement permanent."

Lizzie gasped and turned in her seat to stare at him. "Are you *serious?*"

"It's not as if we don't want a baby. We just don't want to fall in love with one we can't keep."

"Jared, don't even go down this road if you don't mean it."

"I mean it. If we can find Jessie, and she's willing to make it legal—airtight legal—then maybe we could keep her."

To his great dismay, she broke down into sobs that came from her very soul.

"Lizzie. What? What did I say?"

"I can't allow myself to even think about that possibility," she said between gut-wrenching sobs. "I already love her so much."

"I know you do, which is why I'm thinking about how we might make this work for all of us."

"We have to find her, Jared."

"I know, sweetheart. And we will."

"We have to find her before Blaine has no choice but to intervene. He knows we have an abandoned child living with us. Eventually, he'll need to get more involved."

"I know that, too." Jared tightened his grip on the wheel as anxiety had him wishing for a magic wand that could quickly solve this difficult and confounding situation. He would take a million and one business challenges to deal with over one abandoned baby who was quickly wrapping herself around their fragile hearts. "Try not to worry, sweetheart. Blaine is a friend. He'll work with us to the best of his ability. He knows she's in a good and caring home while we try to find her mother."

"I've got this knot of stress in my stomach that won't let up no matter what I do."

"Right there with you."

"I'm sorry I did this to us. You told me not to, and I should've listened to you."

"Don't say that," he said with a sigh. "The way you care for others in need is one of the things I love best about you."

"That's very kind of you to say, especially considering recent events, but I'm sorry that I didn't listen to you."

"No apology needed."

"Do you really think it's possible Jessie might let us keep her?"

"I don't know, Lizzie, and I sorta wish I hadn't mentioned that. I don't want your hopes up when it might not happen. She could show up tomorrow and want her back, and we'd have no choice but to turn her over."

"I wouldn't do that without Blaine's involvement."

"What do you mean?"

"She abandoned her child with *strangers*, Jared. If she wants her back, she ought to have to jump through some hoops so we know the baby will be well cared for."

"I hadn't thought of that."

"I won't just hand her over."

As this situation got ever more complicated, Jared could only hope it would end in a way that didn't leave his precious Lizzie heartbroken.

When they got home, Lizzie transferred the sleeping baby to the carriage they'd bought the last time they were in New York and had hoped to quickly become parents. Nothing had gone according to plan, and now a baby who didn't belong to them was sleeping in the carriage they'd bought for their own child.

What a fucked-up mess.

Lizzie rolled the carriage into the master suite and parked it next to her side of their bed while Jared took a hot shower, hoping it would help him cope with the stress that had him strung tighter than a drum. It didn't.

He went to the kitchen to pour himself a drink and ran into Cooper, who stood shirtless at the sink, downing a piece of cold pizza. "Holy shit," Jared said, shocked by the bruises on Cooper's side. "That looks evil."

"It doesn't hurt as bad as it did at first," Cooper said around a mouthful of pizza that he chased with a beer.

Ah, youth. Jared would be up all night with heartburn if he ate cold pizza at this hour. He poured some whiskey into a cocktail glass.

"How's the baby?"

"She's gassy."

"That's all it was?"

"Thankfully, yes."

"Wow, who even knew that was a thing?" Cooper asked.

"Not me or Lizzie. We had no clue."

"Anything new from the investigator?"

"Nope."

"Jeez, Jared. What the hell?"

"I don't know, but I'm going to get some sleep while I can." He started to walk away. "Forgot to ask how your night was."

"Fine. Good time at the party."

"Glad to hear it. See you in the morning."

"Hope you get some sleep."

"Me, too."

Jared returned to his room and closed the door. Lizzie was in bed, on her side facing him. Her face was red and her eyes puffy from crying. He downed most of the drink in one swallow and removed his clothes, leaving them in a pile on the floor that she would've gotten on him about tomorrow if they hadn't had a baby to care for.

Their former life already seemed like ages ago, and it'd been only a few days since Jared sat on the edge of the bed and pleaded with Lizzie to let someone else help the new mother.

"Come here, sweetheart," he said, reaching for her when he got into bed.

Lizzie moved closer to him, resting her head on his chest.

"Try not to worry," he whispered as he ran his hand over her back. "We're going to figure this out, and no matter what happens, we'll always have each other, okay?"

She nodded, but he felt her tears land on his chest, every one of them gutting him.

"Don't cry, sweet Lizzie. Please don't cry."

"Trying not to."

He held her tighter, wishing love was enough to solve every problem, because if it was, they wouldn't have a problem in the world.

CHAPTER 17

Cindy Lawry wasn't much for the bar scene, but with nothing else to do that evening, she'd found herself seated at the bar at the Beachcomber, listening to Niall Fitzgerald play his guitar and sing. Live music was a big thing on Gansett Island, and Cindy had loved the various bands and performers who'd come through the island that summer.

She'd enjoyed everything about spending time on the island that summer, especially having her mom, brothers Owen, John and Jeff and sisters Katie and Julia around. It'd been years since she'd lived close to that many of her family members, and she'd never lived near them without the specter of their violent, unpredictable father hanging over them.

Mark Lawry was in prison, where he belonged, and his family was finally free to enjoy their lives without him around to ruin everything.

John had apparently left his job as a police officer in Tennessee, although he wasn't talking about why. He and Jeff, a recent college graduate, were staying at the spacious new home their mom shared with her new husband, Charlie Grandchamp, while they figured out their next moves.

Cindy was filling in for Chloe Dennis as the stylist at the Curl Up and Dye salon while Chloe supervised the building of a day spa at the McCarthy's Gansett Island Hotel in North Harbor. Cindy wasn't sure what the off-season on Gansett would be like, but she was looking forward to finding out. The job at the salon was fun and busy, and she'd socked away some money this summer to help pay the rent in the winter when things slowed down.

With Julia basically living with her fiancé, Deacon Taylor, Cindy was going to need another roommate to help swing the rent. She hoped she could find someone, but feared that would be a difficult task with the summer ending and the seasonal jobs drying up for the winter.

"You need a refill?" Jace, the new bartender, asked. He had sleeve tattoos over bulging arm muscles and a gruff way about him. He was handsome in a bad-boy sort of way that had appealed to Cindy in the past. At this point in her life, however, she'd had enough of bad boys to last her a lifetime. All she wanted was to find a nice, boring guy who would never break her heart to settle down with and have some babies. Was that too much to ask?

Apparently so, because she hadn't found him yet.

Cindy realized she hadn't answered his question. "Sure, I'll take some more ice water. Thank you." She'd had a salad and a cup of chowder for dinner earlier, and thankfully, Jace didn't mind keeping her in ice water while she took up a seat at his bar and listened to Niall's music.

"He's great, huh?" Jace asked, nodding to Niall.

"He is. I could listen to him all night."

"You don't want anything stronger to drink?"

"Wish I could. Alcohol and migraines don't play nicely together."

"Ah, gotcha. That sucks."

"It really does."

"You get a lot of them?"

"Two or three a month, which is much less than the bad old days when it was one or two a week. My new meds help."

"Still, two or three a month is too many."

"True." She took a sip of her ice water and noted the lemon he'd added to give it some flavor. "I haven't seen you here before. Are you new?"

"Just started yesterday."

Providence, RI, was listed as his hometown under his name on his name tag. "It's late in the season to be starting a new job around here."

"So I hear, but the Beachcomber stays open year-round, and they were looking for someone who wanted to be here for the off-season. I guess that's not easy to find."

"What brings you to Gansett?"

"My sons live here."

"Oh, wow. How old are they?"

"Jackson is seven, and Kyle is six."

"Those are great ages. Do they live with your ex?"

"They did until she passed away last year, and their next-door neighbors stepped up to take them in."

"That was nice of them."

He nodded even as his cheek pulsed with tension. "Truth is, I wasn't around for a lot of years, so my ex did what she thought was best, you know?"

"Yeah," Cindy said, curious to know the rest of the story, but not willing to ask questions that were none of her business.

"What about you?" he asked, seeming eager to change the subject. "What brings you to Gansett?"

"My entire family seems to have ended up here in recent years. I came for a sibling's wedding and decided to stay for the summer."

"You got a big family?" As they talked, he wiped the bar and washed glasses.

"I'm one of seven."

"Whoa. That's a lot of siblings. Fun growing up that way?"

"At times." When their father had been around, it was a freaking nightmare, not that this handsome stranger needed to know that. "Do you have siblings?"

"Just a sister. She's older than me, has three kids and a nice husband. She did everything right."

Did that mean he'd done everything wrong?

Jace moved on to tend to other customers while Cindy contemplated the things he'd told her. He had kids he'd been out of touch with for quite some time, who were now living with friends, and a sister who'd done everything right. He'd seemed pained telling her his kids had gone to someone other than him when their mother died.

It was none of her business, of course, but she still wanted to know. Cindy possessed an innate curiosity about people and their stories. Sometimes she thought about writing, but work and life always seemed to get in the way of that lofty dream.

Over the next hour, Jace kept her in ice water while she listened Niall's music, and Jace tended to other customers.

Cindy hadn't intended to stick around all night, but she found herself still there at last call. "I should settle my tab," she said.

Jace produced her check and ran her credit card.

She added a ten-dollar tip and signed the slip. "Thanks for keeping me hydrated."

"My pleasure. Hope you'll come back to see me again."

"I'll do that." She got up from her stool and started to walk away.

"Hey, you never told me your name."

She turned back, smiling. "It's Cindy. Cindy Lawry."

"Nice to meet you, Cindy Lawry."

"You, too." She walked the short distance home with a smile on her face, feeling as if she'd made a new friend.

"WHAT DO you mean he's *living here now*?" Seamus O'Grady felt like his head was going to explode at any second.

"Janey heard from Libby at the Beachcomber that they'd hired a new bartender for the off-season and that his name is Jace Carson. She remembered that was the boys' father's name and thought we'd like to know he's on the island." Carolina paused before she looked up at her husband. "What do you suppose it means that he's here?"

"I have no earthly idea, but you can bet your ass I'm going to find out."

Seamus didn't sleep a wink that night as one dreadful scenario after another had him gripped with anxiety. Jace had agreed to leave the boys with Seamus and Carolina, where they'd been doing as well as could be expected after tragically losing their mother to cancer.

The four of them had become a family in the months since they'd lost Lisa, and the possibility of anything upsetting that, especially the boys' biological father deciding to move to their island, didn't bear consideration.

What did it mean that he had *moved* to Gansett?

That question plagued Seamus during that long night and had him at the front desk of the Beachcomber at seven in the morning asking where to find their new bartender.

"He lives in employee housing," the manager, Libby, said. "He's not in some kind of trouble, is he?"

"No, nothing like that." While the entire island community knew he and Carolina had taken in the boys, only their family and closest friends knew the boys' father had come back on the scene recently. "I just wanted to see him about something."

"He's in room seven out back. You know where it is, right?"

"I do. Thanks, Libby."

"Sure, no problem."

Seamus walked through the hotel and exited out the back door, crossing the crushed-shell driveway to the employee housing. Room seven was on the second floor. Seamus took the stairs two at a time and banged on the door. He waited a full minute before he started banging again.

The door flew open to reveal Jace, bare-chested, hair standing on end and a scowl on his face.

"What're you doing here?" Seamus asked.

"I was sleeping until you started making a racket."

"What're you doing on Gansett Island?"

"Working."

"You just suddenly decided to get a job here, of all places?"

"It wasn't sudden. After I saw the boys, I wanted to live closer to them so I could see them more often."

"And you made this decision without so much as a conversation with me? I thought we had an understanding, you and me."

"We did. We do. I'm not here to disrupt their lives or yours. I'd just like to see them once in a while."

"You could do that without moving here."

"It's easier if I live here."

"Tell me the truth... Is your endgame to try to get custody of them?"

"No."

"You swear to God? On their lives?"

"I swear to God on their lives that's not my plan."

Seamus took the first deep breath he'd had in hours. "It feels strange, you moving here with no word to me after I let you see them."

"It was a spur-of-the-moment decision when I saw the job opening at the Beachcomber."

"A simple text could've taken care of giving me a heads-up so I didn't have to hear through the grapevine that the boys' father had moved here."

"I'm sorry I didn't tell you. I should have." Jace propped an arm on the doorframe. "Ever since I saw them..."

"What?"

"I realized how much I miss them. I fucked up everything, you know? My marriage, my kids, my job. Everything. Since I got clean, I've been trying to make amends. I can't do that with Lisa, and I'll always regret that she died before I had the chance to make things right with her. But the boys... I still have a chance with them."

Seamus swallowed hard. "I don't know what you're expecting to happen."

"I don't expect anything except maybe the opportunity to see the boys whenever I can."

"You didn't have to move here for that to happen. I told you we'd let you see them."

"I've been looking for a fresh start. When I saw the bartending job opening at the Beachcomber, it felt like a sign."

"Aren't you in recovery?"

"Booze wasn't my drug of choice." Jace folded his arms. "Look, man, I get why you're wound up. You and your wife stepped up for the kids, and you don't want me or anyone else to upset their new life."

"They're doing really well." A lump of emotion suddenly appeared in his throat. "A lot better than they were when Lisa first passed."

"The last thing in the world I want to do is hurt them any more than I already have, even if they don't remember me hurting them in the past."

"That's good to know." Seamus looked the other man in the eye. "So where do we go from here?"

"That's up to you. I'm here, and I'd like to be as much a part of their lives as you and your wife see fit. I'm not looking to displace you as their father figure. I just want to be a friend to them. And you. If you'll have me."

Seamus felt himself relax ever so slightly. "Aye, I hear you. I'm just trying really hard not to feel threatened by you."

"I promise you don't need to be. I'm not playing any kind of game here. You have my word on that. I just..." He rubbed at the stubble on his jaw. "I wanted to be closer to them, but you're absolutely right that I should've talked to you about it first."

"I'm glad we agree on that." Seamus took a deep breath and let it out. "Carolina and I are having a clambake on Labor Day, in the afternoon, if you'd like to come by."

"I'd like that very much."

"I guess we'll see you then."

"Thank you, Seamus."

Seamus nodded. "No more surprises, okay?"

"I hear you. No more surprises."

Satisfied that they understood each other, Seamus went down the stairs, feeling much better than he had when he'd arrived. He pulled out his cell and called Carolina.

"Did you see him?"

"I did."

"And?"

Seamus conveyed the gist of their conversation to Carolina. "I invited him to come by on Labor Day, and now I'm realizing I probably should've talked to you about that first."

"It's fine. As long as he's not here hoping to wrestle custody from us, I can live with them seeing him occasionally."

"Aye," he said, sighing. "Me, too. I feel like I can breathe again for the first time since you told me last night what Janey had heard."

"Same."

"I never expected parenthood to be so..."

"Stressful?" she asked, laughing.

"Yeah. Stressful is a good word."

"It's that, but so many other things, too."

"Very true. Those boys and you, our little family... You're my whole world, Caro. Anything that threatens it makes me crazy."

"I understand. Believe me. I've been a little crazy myself since Janey told me that yesterday. It's funny because if you told me a couple of years ago that I'd be raising young children again at my age, I would've laughed. But now those boys are everything to me."

"Those boys are damned lucky to have you, Caro. We all are."

"Same to you, my love. Are you going to be able to function today?"

"I believe so," he said with a laugh. "He was nice about it all. Apologized for not giving me a heads-up he was coming out. I keep wanting to dislike him, but I find that difficult."

"I suppose it's better for everyone if we keep it cordial with him."

"Right you are, as usual. Well, I'd better get to the office. I'm on the ten o'clock boat, and I've got some paperwork waiting for me before that."

"Thanks for taking such good care of our family, Seamus. We love you."

"Love you, too, sweet Caro. With everything I am."

CHAPTER 18

Cooper was awake early, his mind racing with thoughts about Gigi. If he had to guess, he'd seen the last of her after last night. He didn't need to be a rocket scientist to figure out that her showing him the door ten seconds after her second orgasm wasn't a good sign of things to come. No pun intended.

He had to do something, because he'd meant it when he told her he really liked her. At first, he'd been dazzled by her, as anyone would be. But the more he'd gotten to know her, the more he'd liked who she was under the shiny Hollywood veneer. While replaying every minute they'd spent together, he kept coming back to one obvious idea: Evelyn. She'd known Gigi since she was a kid and was a surrogate grandmother to her. If anyone could give him insight into what made Gigi tick, Evelyn probably could.

However, it felt sort of underhanded to seek intel from someone close to her. The only reason he'd do it was because he felt like they might have something special if he could only figure out the secret handshake. Maybe Evelyn would refuse to see him or talk to him about Gigi, but he figured he had nothing to lose by trying.

After taking a shower, he got dressed in an NYU T-shirt and shorts and tiptoed out of his bedroom. Things were quiet in the house, which meant Jared, Lizzie and the baby were getting some much-needed sleep.

He left Jared a note to let him know he'd borrowed the car for a quick errand and would be back shortly.

With Jordan and Gigi shooting the final episodes this week and next, Cooper wasn't surprised to see that her car was already gone. As he started the Porsche, he prayed this outing in Jared's car would go better than the last one.

Cooper drove into town and picked up muffins and coffee at the bakery before heading to Eastward Look, hoping Evelyn could be charmed by baked goods. At Jordan's party, he'd talked to Evelyn about her gardens at the house, which were her pride and joy. She'd told him to come by some time to see them, so she wouldn't be surprised to see him.

As he drove into the long driveway at Eastward Look, he hoped he wasn't making a huge mistake with this mission. He'd feel things out with Evelyn before he said anything about Gigi.

Evelyn came to the door as he brought the car to a stop in the driveway. Her face lit up with a welcoming smile when she saw him. "This is a nice surprise."

"I was hoping I could get a tour of your legendary gardens, and I come bearing gifts."

"I love gifts—and gardens. Come in. I just made some coffee. Can I interest you in a cup?"

"I brought my own along with some fresh-baked muffins."

"How lovely."

Cooper took a seat at one of the barstools at the island and took the muffins out of the bag. "This kitchen is gorgeous."

"Oh, those look yummy," Evelyn said, cutting the coffee cake muffin in half while Cooper chose the chocolate chip. "My granddaughter Nikki and her fiancé, Riley, did it along with some help from his brother, Finn."

"They did a great job."

"They sure did. They're slowly bringing this old house back to life, and I couldn't be happier about it."

"Have you lived here long?"

"I've summered here for more than thirty years."

"It's a great spot to spend a summer."

"I couldn't agree more. The girls loved it so much when they were younger, and I'm thrilled to see them falling in love with the island as adults, too. Although I think they're more in love with Riley and Mason than they are with the island."

"The island has its selling points, too."

"It does. Is your brother enjoying living here year-round?"

"He loves it."

"I heard about what happened with the baby. How're they doing?"

"It's a minute-to-minute thing." He glanced at her. "Can you keep a secret?"

"I'm known as the vault to my granddaughters, who get annoyed when I won't tell them things they feel they have a right to know."

Cooper smiled because how could he not? She was awesome. "Jared and Lizzie have been trying to have a baby for quite some time. Their most recent round of IVF failed shortly before this happened."

"Oh dear. That makes them the worst possible people to be left with a newborn."

"Or the best. I suppose it depends on your perspective. But we're concerned about Lizzie getting attached. And Jared, too. It's kind of a mess."

"Sounds like it. What can be done?"

"Jared has an investigator looking for the mother on the mainland, and the police are involved, too."

"I don't know whether to hope they find her or that they don't."

"Same. It'd be cool if they could somehow keep the baby, but I bet that would be complicated, too."

"They'd have to find the mother to make that happen. Probably the father, too. I'll say a little prayer for your brother and his wife to ask for guidance for them in this situation."

"I'm sure they'd appreciate that. They need all the help they can get."

"It's interesting, isn't it, how people would look at someone like your brother and assume he doesn't have a problem in the world."

"Everyone has problems, even billionaires."

"That's the truth." Evelyn gave him a saucy side-eye. "So did you really come by to see my gardens?"

Cooper laughed. "Among other things. I wanted to talk to you about Gigi, but only if you're willing. I don't want to put you in an awkward position."

"Gigi is very dear to me. She's my third granddaughter, and I love her very much."

"She's becoming very dear to me, too."

"Is she?" Evelyn seemed intrigued. "I do so love to hear that. Our Gigi needs someone in her corner."

"She would tell you she doesn't need anyone in her corner, or anywhere else, for that matter."

"Yes, she would say that. But it's only because she's been on her own for such a long time. You know that, right?"

"She told me about her childhood."

Evelyn put her hand on Cooper's arm. "The fact that she told you her story is a huge, *huge* deal, Cooper. Hearing that makes me feel better about this conversation, because there's no way she would've done that if she didn't trust you."

Cooper waited to see if she'd say more.

"Come with me. Let's take a walk in the garden."

He got up to follow her out the back door.

On the way out, she grabbed an oversized sun hat. "You must always take good care of your skin and protect it from the sun."

"Yes, ma'am."

"You young people don't take us seriously when we tell you how you'll pay later for the foolishness of your youth."

"I believe you. My mother says the same thing. She bathed me in sunscreen when I was little."

"Good for her. I did the same with my girls, and they have gorgeous skin as a result." She hooked her arm through his. "But you're not here to talk about the sun. You want some insight into our Gigi so you can better understand her."

"Yes, but I wondered if I could ask you something first."

"Sure you can. I have a feeling we're going to be great friends."

"I'd like it if we were."

"What's your question?"

"Do you think it's possible she thinks she's unlovable?"

Evelyn's deep sigh said it all. "I think it's more than possible. In fact, I'm quite sure that's the case."

Hearing his suspicions confirmed made Cooper ache for what Gigi was denying herself.

Evelyn glanced his way. "I have to say I'm surprised at that level of insight from such a young man."

"My mother would tell you that my special gift has always been the ability to cut through the bullshit and get to the heart of a matter. I think it comes from being the much younger brother to four older siblings. I was forever trying to keep up with them, and I learned early to figure out their pain points."

"I'll bet you were one of their biggest pain points."

Cooper laughed. "I'm sure I was. You become very observant when you're trying to keep up with a bunch of overachievers."

As they strolled the grounds at Eastward Look, Evelyn pointed out her prized roses, hydrangeas and lilies, all of which were in full, fragrant bloom.

"Your property is gorgeous."

"Thank you. It's my happy place. Always has been since I lost my husband as a young woman and was left with a business to run and children to raise without my love."

"I'm so sorry you lost him."

"Thank you. I am, too. I miss him every day." She used clippers to cut some of the roses and held up a large pink one for Cooper to see. "This is how I see our Gigi, a rose of the first order, but with some thorns that she uses to keep herself safe."

"That's an apt description."

"She would literally do anything for me and my granddaughters. If we asked her to sell everything she had to bail us out of a jam, she'd do it in a red-hot second. But she would never, *ever* ask us for anything in return."

"She's struggling with Nikki and Jordan settling here."

"I wondered if she would be, especially after Jordan's news yesterday."

"She's thrilled for Jordan."

"Of course she is, but she's heartbroken for herself, even if she'd never say so."

"Yes."

"What is it that you want, Cooper?"

"I want Gigi."

"For now or for good?"

"I, um, well…"

Evelyn's delicate laugh reminded Cooper of the lovely sound wind chimes made. "That's the crux of the issue, my friend. Our Gigi is far too smart to risk her heart on someone who isn't sure what he wants."

"We haven't known each other that long."

"No, you haven't. And yet you're here looking for insight from one of her closest friends. What does that mean?"

"I'm not sure exactly."

"I think you need to figure that out before you ask anything of her."

"Is it possible to know—like, really *know*—another person is for you when you're my age?"

"I was twenty-two when I married my husband. I didn't have a single doubt that we'd be happy together for the rest of our lives—and we were. We had fifteen glorious years together."

"I'm so sorry, Evelyn."

"Thank you. Our wedding was fifty years ago this fall, and if he'd lived, I'm one hundred percent certain we'd still be going strong. So yes, it's possible to know at a young age that you've found your forever love. But it's also possible to make a big mess of things."

"I don't want to do that, especially with Gigi."

"You *can't* do that with her, Cooper. You absolutely cannot. She wants us all to think she's a tough-as-nails badass, but under her strong outer shell is the most fragile, delicate glass that shatters far too easily."

Her words struck Cooper like a fist to the chest, knocking the wind out of him for a second.

"There's nothing wrong with an end-of-summer fling," Evelyn said. "As long as everyone is on the same page. If you want more than that with her, you're going to have to step up big-time. You understand that, right?"

"I'm beginning to."

She handed him the bouquet of roses she'd clipped as they walked. "Take these home for Gigi, but only give them to her if you're prepared to make that step. Otherwise, I'd ask you to take a step *back* from her."

"That's the last thing I want to do."

"Then maybe you have your answer, hmm?"

A wild feeling unlike anything he'd experienced before came over him as he stood in Evelyn's garden, holding the bouquet of multicolored roses. His heart fluttered, and his knees felt a little weak.

"Are you all right?" Evelyn asked, looking at him with concern.

"I think I might be." He smiled as he leaned in to kiss her cheek. "I appreciate your wisdom and insight more than you'll ever know."

"I'm glad you came to me, Cooper, and I hope you'll come back again."

"I will for sure."

"Follow your heart, young man. You'll never be sorry if you do."

"I wish you were my grandmother."

Evelyn laughed. "I'm a grandmother to anyone who needs one."

"Consider yourself adopted."

She held out her arms to him, and he hugged her. "I hope you and our Gigi can make a go of it. I have a feeling you might be just what she needs."

"I'd like to be what she needs."

Evelyn's smile lit up her entire face. "I may be a silly old woman, but I find myself very excited for my sweet Gigi."

"You're not silly, and you're sure as hell not old."

"I do quite like you, young Cooper."

"I like you, too, Evelyn. Thank you very, very much."

"My pleasure, honey."

OLIVER WAITED until the morning meeting of the minds at McCarthy's Marina had mostly dispersed for the day before he went looking for Luke, who'd wandered out to the main pier to land a boater. As he tied the last of the lines around one of the pilings, Oliver said, "You make that look easy."

Luke turned to him, grinning. "It is easy when you've done it ten thousand times."

"I suppose so."

"Sometimes it's not easy. We were standing right about here when a drunk captain threw his boat into gear and pulled Big Mac off the pier a couple of years ago."

"Oh wow. Was he hurt?"

Luke grimaced as he nodded. "Pretty badly. Head injury, broken arm. Took him a long time to bounce back."

"That's scary shit."

"It was a very bad day, but thankfully, he's back to his old self now."

"He's a good dude."

"He's the best man I've ever known. I showed up here as a fatherless fourteen-year-old asking for a job. He gave me that and so much more."

"He and his wife have been wonderful to us since we arrived."

"That's how they are."

"All of you have been. We appreciate it."

"How are things at the lighthouse?"

"Better than they were when we first arrived."

"There's something about this place," Luke said, resting his arms on the piling and looking out over the vast Salt Pond.

The scents of seaweed, salt air, diesel fuel and fried food had become familiar to Oliver after spending part of every day at the marina.

"It cures a lot of ills," Luke continued. "Some people find it too slow, too sleepy, too boring, and it can be all those things. But if you take the time to look beyond that, you'll like what you see."

"I already do, and Dara does, as well. She's coming back to herself, if that makes sense."

"It does. I saw it with my own wife."

"I actually wanted to ask you about her," Oliver said haltingly. "I hope it's okay to say I heard about what happened to her first husband and children."

"It's okay."

"I wanted to ask if we might get them together, Dara and your wife, that is. Dara and I… We're, well, talking about maybe having another baby, and Dara, she's struggling a bit with the idea."

"Sydney would be happy to talk to her."

"She would? Really?"

Luke nodded. "She's very supportive of people who've been through things like what happened to her and to you." He gazed off at the pond again. "When Jenny Wilks came to live in the lighthouse, she was still reeling after losing her fiancé in the 9/11 attacks. It was years later, and Jenny would tell you she was still stuck in first gear. She's since become one of Syd's closest friends. Jenny's would-be sister-in-law, Erin, her late fiancé's twin sister, who was the lighthouse keeper after Jenny, is also one of Syd's good friends."

As Oliver listened to him, he realized there was a community of fellow travelers on Gansett. "Everyone has been through something," Oliver said.

"Some worse than others."

"Yes, for sure."

"Why don't you and Dara come for dinner tomorrow night?"

"I don't want to invite myself over."

"You didn't. I invited you."

"We'd love that, Luke. Thank you."

"Of course. That's what friends are for."

Before Oliver had lost his son, he would've said he had all the friends he needed. Since arriving on Gansett, he was learning a man could never have too many friends.

CHAPTER 19

"What the hell is wrong with you today?" Jordan asked Gigi after a grueling morning taking surfing lessons from a local pro while the cameras tracked their every move.

"Huh? Nothing's wrong with me."

"Do you know how hard it is to film witty dialogue when the other person in the scene has nothing to say?"

"I said stuff."

"Not enough, Gigi, and you know it. What's going on?"

"I'm just tired, and I suck at surfing."

"We both suck at surfing. That's the whole point. We're going to have to redo this entire morning because you wouldn't engage. And Mason doesn't even want me surfing now that we know I'm pregnant. I promised him I'd be super careful, so I don't want to have to do this again."

"We can redo my parts and splice them. You're all set." Gigi wanted to scream because redoing her parts would keep her on the island even longer. After last night, she wanted out of there as soon as possible. Today would be a perfect day to leave.

Matilda approached the two of them, loaded for bear. "That was terrible. We got jack."

"My fault," Gigi said, squirming inside the confining wet suit. "I'll make it up to you."

"You're damned right you will. I should fine you for your lackluster performance today."

"I'm not allowed to have one off day in an entire summer? Fuck that shit." Fuming, Gigi walked away and ignored Matilda's demand that she come back. She went straight to her car and had backed out of the parking space before the show runner could catch up to her. Fuck it all. Fuck everything. And mostly fuck Cooper James and his sweet tenderness and gorgeous face. He had no right to do this to her, to knock her so far off her game that she'd forgotten how to be funny.

Her *job* was to be funny, and she couldn't do that when her head was all over the place.

She was finished with him and this goddamned island and everyone who lived here. It was time for her to go home, where things made sense.

Except, for a little while longer, "home" was here on Gansett Island, right next door to the man who'd caused her to be so out of sorts. As she sped away from the day's location, she knew she was being a brat, but there was no way she could find her groove today, so she was doing everyone a favor by stepping away. She'd send a text to Matilda to apologize later and would be back to work in the morning with a new attitude.

The show had given Gigi something she'd never had before—serious financial security. Her law practice kept the lights on and allowed her to lease a gorgeous car to help sell herself as a Hollywood player, but the truth was that until Jordan had asked her to join the show and be her comic relief, Gigi hadn't had much of a financial safety net.

That safety net was one more reason to love Jordan. She'd known what it would mean to Gigi to have that cushion and had included her in the show. At the beginning, neither of them could've possibly known the show would be a runaway hit that would make them both into major celebrities with huge followings and all the associated nonsense that went with stardom.

One of those things was big-time endorsement deal offers that were waiting for both of them in LA. They were wanted for cosmetics, shapewear, swimsuits, liquor and cars, to name a few. In short, they had their pick of what they wanted to do and had put off making any decisions until the season on Gansett was in the can.

With the end of filming in sight, they'd be under pressure about that before much longer. And with Jordan expecting the Gansett fire chief's child, there was a very good chance that she wouldn't be going back to LA at all.

Now that she'd stormed off the location, Gigi was at a loss as to where to go. If she went back to Jared's, there was a chance she'd run into Cooper, and she didn't want to see him. Not now when she was feeling so raw about what'd happened between them last night. And just for the record, it wasn't at all like her to freak out about sex. To her, sex was transactional. Everyone got off and went home happy—most of the time, anyway. A lot of the guys she'd been with wouldn't know how to get a woman off if their life depended on it.

Cooper hadn't had that problem—or any other, for that matter. The man was a god in bed and out. That was the problem. She didn't want to have found the unicorn. That stuff was for other women, not her. She had no time or patience for all the crap that went along with men and relationships. Gigi didn't do relationships. The word gave her hives, for fuck's sake.

Relationship.

It was so pretentious and full of loaded guns pointing at vulnerable hearts. If you didn't get involved in *relationships*, you couldn't get your heart broken. That seemed rather simple to her in concept, but with her two closest friends settling into *relationships* that had *forever* stamped all over them, Gigi had tried to keep her scorn and contempt well hidden.

Just because her friends had found their forever loves didn't mean Gigi was suddenly interested in the same for herself.

And why in the hell was she even thinking about that shit?

It was all Cooper James's fault. If he had just done what he was supposed to do and gone through the motions with the usual wham-bam-thank-you-ma'am routine, none of this would be happening. She wouldn't be in trouble with Matilda—and probably Jordan, too—and she wouldn't be looking for a place to hide out so she could avoid running into *him*.

Why'd he have to do the whole sweet, tender routine? Why couldn't he be like every other guy who wanted to get his rocks off and to hell with what the woman wanted?

Ugh, she was furious with him! Yes, she was well aware that her anger was ridiculous. The man had given her multiple orgasms, after all, and that alone made him special. However, she didn't *want* him to be special.

She wanted him to be a late-summer fling with no strings attached. Wasn't that the very definition of the word *fling*?

After driving twice around the road that ran the perimeter of the island, she pulled into the parking lot at the bluffs—the scene of the crime, if you will—rolled the windows down and killed the engine. As the warm summer breeze blew through the car, she took a deep breath and let it out.

She was being completely foolish, and she knew it. But if she held on to the anger, she wouldn't do something stupid, like go find him for another round of unicorn sex.

"You are not doing that, Gabrielle. Do you hear me? You will not have sex with Cooper James ever again. That is my final word on the matter."

Enough of that madness, she thought, reaching for the cell phone she'd left in the car during filming, intending to send a message to Matilda. But then she saw one from Cooper, and like the idiot she was where he was concerned, she devoured his words.

Dear Gigi, last night was amazing. Completely and totally AMAZING. For me, anyway. I sort of get the feeling that you don't agree, and I think I might know why that is. You've been very vocal about what this is and what it isn't. I respect that. I respect you. We both have lives that take place far away from this island—and far away from each other. It would be easy to look at this thing between us as nothing more than two ships passing in the night on their way to bigger and better things. But here's the thing... I've never met ANYONE like you. And I'm not talking about the larger-than-life public persona that's Gigi Gibson. I'm talking about YOU, Gabrielle, the woman behind the flash. I think you're magnificent, and all I want is to spend as much time with you as I possibly can for as long as I possibly can. You make me laugh. You make me think. You make me want like I've never wanted before. You make me crazy. You make me happy. You have me reconsidering my life plan so it can include you. I'm sure this message is making you boiling mad because we weren't supposed to be about THIS. Trust me, I didn't want THIS either. But here we are. I'd like to bring you dinner tonight so we can talk. Would that be okay? I hope so, because I have so much more I want to say to you. Love, Cooper

Gigi wiped tears from her face and then reread the message two more times.

Love, Cooper. *Swoon.*

Gigi Gibson did not swoon over any man! But *this* man… Dear God, he was killing her.

Her phone chimed with another text from him. *PS, I can see that you've read my text, so now I'm just suffering. You don't want me to suffer, do you? Do you?*

Now she was laughing and crying. Goddamn him.

She started typing. *Goddamn you.*

After she sent the text, he replied with laughing emojis. *My heart can't take all this romance.*

This is NOT a romance.

Feels like it could be.

I don't do romance.

I know, but jeez, Gigi, maybe we ought to give it a try, just this once, to see what it's like?

No.

Yes.

No.

YES.

Cooper...

Gigi... I like you. I REALLY like you, and I want to be with you.

You're just a little boy. You don't know what you want. There, that ought to piss him off and get things back on track.

I think I proved to you last night that there's nothing little about me.

Goddamn him. *Goddamn you.*

More laughter emojis.

You're not taking me seriously, Gigi wrote.

I'm taking you more seriously than I've ever taken anyone.

You weren't supposed to do that.

I know, but...

I don't want this.

I know.

So???

Can I see you?

Gigi shook her head as she responded. *No! You're radioactive now.*

LOL, stop being silly. Me liking you isn't a threat. From what I hear, it can be the nicest thing to ever happen to a person. Just ask my brother and Lizzie, Jordan and Mason, Nikki and Riley, Finn and Chloe. Need I go on? They all seem pretty damned happy.

Gigi felt herself wavering. He was so damned tempting, and that was the problem. She didn't need someone to like her or care about her or whatever. She had her people. Someone like Cooper had the potential to ruin her, and she'd already clawed her way back from ruination once before. She didn't have it in her to do it again.

I can't. She typed and sent the two words before she could talk herself out of fending him off.

Yes, you can.

No, I really can't.

Why? Is it because you're afraid? I kind of am, too. I mean, I've never before said anything like what I said to you above. It feels like a huge risk to put myself out there, knowing you could stomp on my delicate heart with your stiletto heels and go on with your life as if I never happened. Something like this... It's risky for both of us, and to be honest, I never wanted it for myself until I saw my brother with Lizzie. What they have... It's something truly amazing, and it got me thinking about what it would be like to have that with someone special. But that was supposed to be in the far-off future, not now. Not when I have so many other things I need to do, like start my career and figure out where I'm going to live and stuff like that. So trust me, I get why you think you can't do this. It makes no sense. You live in LA. I live in NYC, or I do at least until Jared kicks me out of his apartment. I have no idea what's happening tomorrow, let alone months from now. But the thing is, I want you to help me figure out my life, and more than anything, I want you to be part of it. Will you be part of it, Gigi?

Again, he had her in tears. How did he *do* that to her? And what was wrong with her that she was allowing a smooth-talking stranger to tie her up in knots? "This isn't who you are, Gabrielle. You don't let guys get close enough to do this to you." A sob took her by surprise a second before the floodgates opened. "And you sure as hell don't do *this* over a guy. We are not that girl. We have never been that girl!"

Cooper James was making her into *that* girl, and she had no idea what to do about him.

When her phone rang, she almost declined the call without looking at the caller ID. But since she was currently AWOL from work, she decided to glance at the screen.

Jordan.

She took a deep breath and then answered the call, attempting to keep her breakdown hidden from her best friend. "Hey."

"Are you crying?"

Gigi wanted to laugh at how well Jordan knew her. "It's nothing. I'm handling it."

"Talk to me, Gigi. Tell me what's going on with you."

"It's really nothing. I swear."

"I call bullshit. You don't walk away from work or me without a word, and you sure as hell don't cry, so you'd better tell me what's going on before I start to get seriously upset. And in my delicate condition—"

"Oh, for fuck's sake, Jordan. Are you going to play the delicate-condition card for the next nine months?"

"As needed. What's wrong, Geeg?"

"It appears, much to my incredible dismay, I have man problems."

"Oh. My. *God.*" Jordan's high screech had Gigi holding the phone away from her ear. "What is going on?"

Resigned to having to talk about *it*, she said, "He's making a play for more than I'm willing to give."

"Come to my house. Right now." Jordan ended the call before Gigi could tell her she didn't want to come there.

Her phone buzzed with a text. *You'd better be on your way. I'm your client, and I need you immediately.*

"Goddamn everyone today," Gigi muttered as she reached for the visor to pull it down so she could check the damage in the mirror. "Ugh, you look like shit."

She didn't want to see anyone or talk to anyone, but Jordan would hunt her down if she didn't go to her.

I'm tracking your location, and your car hasn't moved. Do I need to come to you?

Ease up, bitch, I'm coming.

Hurry up.

Another text, this time from Cooper. *You're making me suffer.*

Gigi wanted to throw the phone out the window so no one could find her or talk to her or say things to her that could never be unheard, as much as she wished they could be. As she started the car and drove to Jordan, she strategized on how she could talk to Jordan about Cooper without giving too much away.

His words had opened a door she kept firmly shut, making her yearn for things that weren't meant for her. Gigi had learned to stay in her lane, to keep her circle small and to not want more than she deserved. The life she had now was a dream come true from where she started as an emancipated teenager struggling to survive.

She wasn't proud of some of the things she'd done to get by, but she'd scraped through, put herself through college and then law school and had a beautiful home, car and life that she owed to no one but herself. She'd done those things before the show happened to elevate her to another stratosphere financially, and she would always be proudest of those early accomplishments.

The last thing in the world she needed was a man to threaten everything she'd worked so hard to achieve. No matter how successful she became, she never stopped feeling as if she was still suspended on a high wire without a net to catch her if she tripped and fell. Tripping and falling was not an option.

Because Gansett Island was so damned tiny, she arrived at Jordan's within minutes and pulled into the driveway, parking off to the side so she could leave quickly if need be. Gigi always had an exit plan and never allowed herself to be blocked in. She needed to remember that strategy when it came to dealing with Cooper and his campaign to turn their fling into something more.

Thankfully, Mason's fire department SUV wasn't there, so she wouldn't have to deal with seeing her best friend's happily ever after playing out in living, breathing color. She couldn't handle that right now.

Jordan stood at the door, waiting for her. "You look like shit."

"Thank you. I know."

Jordan opened the screen door and gestured for Gigi to get inside. "You want a drink?"

"Yes, I do." She also never drank during the day. That was one of her cardinal rules that she'd never broken until radioactive Cooper upped the ante.

Her best friend gave Gigi a curious look as she made her a vodka and soda with a twist of lime. Jordan kept Grey Goose, soda and limes on hand for Gigi, who accepted the drink from her and took a deep gulp as she recalled making her favorite drink for Cooper last night. Ugh, there he was again.

"What happened?" Jordan asked.

"It's nothing."

"Try that bullshit with someone who doesn't know you better than anyone. What. *Happened?* And don't say *nothing*."

Gigi brought the drink with her when she took a seat on the sofa. "I slept with Cooper."

Jordan came to sit next to her, holding the thermal cup full of ice water that she took with her everywhere she went. "Okay…"

Gigi told herself she wouldn't squirm under the glare of Jordan's intense stare. "It was just, you know…"

Jordan gasped. "It was good. Really good."

Gigi shrugged. "I guess."

"What else?"

"What do you mean what else? Isn't that enough?"

"That's not enough to cause this." Jordan waved her hand in front of Gigi's face. "You wouldn't be puffy and splotchy from crying if that's all it was."

Damn her. This was why Gigi never should've bothered to make friends. They saw too much. "He said some stuff and whatever. It's not going to happen."

"What did he say?"

"Stuff."

"What stuff?"

"He texted me—"

Jordan lunged for the phone and had it out of Gigi's hand before she could anticipate her plan. Normally, Gigi would've tackled her to get it back, but Jordan was pregnant, so she didn't do that. But she wanted to. Damn it, why had she given Jordan the code to her phone? Because Jordan had the code to Gigi's life and vice versa.

As her friend read Cooper's texts, her eyes darting back and forth, Gigi took another big drink from her glass and wished she could swig straight from the vodka bottle.

"Holy shit, Gigi."

"Stop with that. It's no big deal."

"Yes, it is. It's a massive, big deal, or you wouldn't have been crying—or day drinking."

"It's not a big deal. He caught me at a weird moment when I'm running on three hours of sleep."

Jordan started typing on Gigi's phone, and only because she was sleep-deprived did it take her a second to realize she shouldn't be letting that happen. "What're you doing?"

"Responding to the poor guy."

Pregnancy or not, Gigi lunged for the phone and succeeded in spilling the last of her drink and the ice all over Jordan, who never flinched as she held the phone out of reach to finish her text. "What the hell are you saying to him?"

"I'm telling him you'd love to see him to discuss this further."

"Oh my God! I'm going to stab you!"

"No, you aren't. You're going to pull yourself together and talk to him like the adult you are."

"No, I'm not. I can't see him again."

"I have to go to the bathroom. Stay right there."

Gigi slumped into the sofa and then realized Jordan had taken the phone with her. "I'm coming in there after my phone!"

"Oh damn, turns out I have to poop."

Gigi would've laughed if the whole thing hadn't been so absurd. Too bad they weren't filming this for the show. Matilda would love it. "If you're ruining my life in there, I'm going to dump you as a client and a friend."

"Can't hear you!" Jordan came out a few minutes later. "Phew, pregnancy poops are smelly! Mason is going to kick me out of here at this rate."

"You're so full of shit."

"Literally."

"Give me my phone."

"Oh snap, I left it in there by accident. Up to you if you want to risk going after it. Mason would advise you not to."

Gigi rolled her eyes. "That man loves you so much, I'm sure he thinks your poo smells like roses."

Jordan cracked up laughing as she returned to her seat on the sofa. "I don't think he's that far gone."

"Yes, he is. I have to get going. Get my phone."

"Nah, I need you to hang with me for a bit because I'm feeling sort of weird, and Mason is at work."

"Weird how?"

"Just strange."

"Like, good-pregnant strange or bad-pregnant strange?"

"I'm not sure yet."

"Do we need to go to the clinic?"

"It's nothing like that. Yet, anyway. But I don't want to be alone."

"We shouldn't just sit here and wait to see what's going to happen. You need to be seen at the clinic. Victoria will know if it's something you need to worry about."

"I'm afraid it might just be heartburn, and I'd be so embarrassed to go to the clinic for that."

"Is there something you can take?"

"I had a Tums. Waiting to see if it'll work." She burped for effect. "Ah, that felt good."

"What exactly is it that Mason sees in you, anyway?"

"I have no idea, but whatever it is, I hope he keeps seeing it forever. It's a really nice thing, you know, to have someone who's all yours forever."

"How do you know it's forever?"

"Sometimes you just know."

"In all fairness, you thought Brendan would be forever."

"I never had the faith in him or our relationship that I do in Mason. It's an entirely different thing from what I had with him."

"How is it different?"

Jordan appeared to give that some serious thought. "It's deeper. We talk about *everything*. He's taken the time to really know me and understand me. He knows me better in a few months than Brendan did in years, because he *wants* to know me that way. I talk to him about things I never talk about with anyone else. Like the custody shit, and I find that talking to him about it gives the whole thing less power over me than it's had in the past. By sharing that pain with him, it's like he takes on some of it for me. If that makes sense. And he's been amazing since we heard our father died. I was more upset about that than I expected to be, but having Mason there to go through it with me somehow made it easier."

As she listened to Jordan, a lump of emotion lodged in her throat. She'd expected Jordan to say something like *he's a god in bed*, or *he makes me come like a firecracker*. Both those things were probably true in addition to the other lovely things Mason had given her. Gigi had been around long enough to know that for Jordan to talk about the custody battle she and her sister had endured, mostly at the hands of their recently deceased father, was a big deal.

It was an equally big deal that you told Cooper about your crack-addict mother, the foster care and the absentee parents you emancipated from as a teenager. Gigi wanted to tell her inner voice to shut the hell up, but she couldn't deny the truth. It had been a momentous thing for her to share that stuff with Cooper. And why exactly had she done that, anyway? Because he was easy to talk to, and that made her want to share things about herself with him that she never shared with anyone, even the two men she'd been briefly engaged to. If she'd been alone, that thought might've made her groan. That was all the more reason to keep her distance.

He was dangerous.

And then he appeared in Jordan's doorway, looking inside, seeking her out with the intense gaze that seemed to see right through her. And were those roses he was holding?

"You total bitch," she whispered to Jordan.

"Someday you'll thank me."

"Today is not that day."

CHAPTER 20

"Cooper, come in," Jordan said. "I was just leaving to do some, uh, errands. Won't be back for *hours*. Mason is working late. The place is all yours." As she walked by Cooper, Jordan squeezed his arm, letting him know she was firmly on Team Cooper.

Worst best friend *ever*.

The screen door slammed shut behind Jordan. A few seconds later, her car started, and the tires crunched over the crushed shells as she backed out of the driveway, probably on her way to Eastward Look, where she'd nap the afternoon away. In the meantime, Gigi was left alone with the one man she had planned never to be alone with again.

Jordan had figured that out and had taken matters into her own hands.

"She sent that text telling me to meet you here, not you," he said.

"Ding, ding, ding. Tell him what he's won, Johnny."

"I'll go," he said.

"It's okay. You can stay." Despite her fierce desire to protect herself from whatever this was shaping up to be, she couldn't bear to hurt him. Not to mention that being willing to leave, if that was what she wanted him to do, earned him major points.

He came farther into the room, put the bundle of roses he'd brought on the kitchen counter and rested his hands on the back of a chair. "Would I have heard from you if Jordan hadn't texted me?"

"No."

"Ouch."

"I'm sorry. It's not you. It's me."

"Didn't they make a movie with that title?"

"Maybe, but in this case, it's true. You want things I'm not capable of giving you."

"What things do I want?"

"A commitment. A *relationship*." She wrinkled her nose as she said the dreaded word. "Emotions that don't exist in me."

He came around the chair and took a seat, resting his elbows on his knees and leaning toward her. "You know what makes me so damned sad?"

She really didn't want to know because it made her sad to know something was making him sad. "What?"

"The way you sell yourself so short."

"I don't do that."

"Yes, you do. You think you have nothing to give me or anyone, so you act as if this sort of thing could never happen for you."

His insight made her angry. How dare he have her so figured out? No one got to see that much of her, so why did this man, five years her junior, have to be so fucking astute? How was that even fair? She needed to be very, very careful. In the kindest way possible, she said, "It's not that I think it can't happen for me, it's that I don't *want* it to. Can you see the difference?"

"Yes, I can see the difference, but how do you know you don't want it when you've never had it?"

"I'm almost thirty years old, Coop. I've seen a lot of things in my life. I know what I want and what I don't, and it wouldn't be fair to a nice guy like you to let you get involved with someone like me—"

"Someone like you. What does that mean?"

"I'm damaged, Cooper! I don't have the same emotions other people have. You deserve someone who can truly care for you the way you deserve to be cared for, and that person is not me." Her chin quivered and her eyes filled, infuriating her. She was always in control of herself and her emotions, except, it seemed, when Cooper James was around.

He moved to sit next to her on the sofa and put his arm around her, drawing her in close to him. As he kissed the top of her head, he said,

"You're not damaged. You've had some stuff happen, some painful stuff that'll always be part of who you are, but you're beautiful and sweet and funny and so worthy of love."

Gigi was going to lose it if he kept that up. She tried to pull free of him, but he only held her closer.

"You have no reason to be afraid of me."

"I have every reason to be afraid of you."

"Nah."

"Yah."

He tipped her chin up to receive the sweetest, softest, least demanding kiss of her life that somehow managed to say everything without a single word being spoken.

"We shouldn't," she said.

"We should. We really, really should."

He kissed her again, and somehow, she ended up underneath him, with her arms and legs wrapped around his body and the heat of his hard cock pressed tight against her core. "I want you to listen to me, okay?" His lips were soft against her neck as he kissed his way to her ear. "I will never do anything to hurt you. I promise. I want only to make you happy, to make you smile, to make you laugh." Rocking against her, he added, "To make you come. You're safe with me, Gigi. I swear on the lives of everyone I love that you can count on me to be there for you no matter what happens, if only you'll let me be."

The words *I can't* were on the tip of her tongue, but unfortunately, her tongue was very busy fending off his, so she never got a chance to say them out loud even as they echoed loudly in her mind. With her fingers buried in his hair and her hand inside the back of his shorts, she wasn't exactly sending the "game off" signal that she'd intended. Rather, this was feeling extremely "game on."

"Cooper," she said, gasping as she broke the kiss. "Wait. I'm not sure I should…"

"You should, Gigi. You really should, because everyone deserves to have someone who loves them more than anyone else does."

"And that's what you want? To love me more than anyone else?"

"Yeah, I think that's what I want."

"Forever?"

"I sure as hell hope it lasts forever."

"How can you know you want that when you're not even twenty-five yet?"

"I'll be twenty-five in September. Will that make me qualified to possibly care about you forever?"

"This is all just *preposterous*!"

"What is? The fact that I'm offering you something real and potentially life-changing for both of us, or you being so afraid of getting hurt that you refuse to take a chance?"

She shoved at his chest. "Get off of me."

He pulled back and let her sit up.

She pressed her back into the corner of Jordan's sofa—or was it Mason's sofa?—and wrapped her arms around her knees.

"I'm sorry," he said. "I shouldn't have said that."

"Why not? It's true. I mean, what other reason could there possibly be for any woman with a heartbeat not to want what you're offering? You've probably had to beat women away with a stick your entire life."

"There was never an actual stick involved."

"Quit being cute. You're pissing me off."

His smile lit up his gorgeous eyes and filled her with a feeling of breathless, giddy joy that was entirely new to her. Of course, her first thought was to push back, to not let it flourish. But the feeling was too big to be denied.

"You're beautiful, even when you're pissed off."

"How do you see this working? Not that I'm saying yes to any of your craziness. I'm asking hypothetically."

"I'm glad you asked, because I've given that a lot of thought. I'd like to move forward with my party boat business here on Gansett, but that's a summertime gig. What if we lived here in the summer and in LA the rest of the year? That way, you'd get built-in time with Jordan, Nikki and Evelyn every summer."

Her heart hammered in her chest. He made it sound so easy, so possible. "And what would you do the rest of the year?"

"I'd manage my portfolio—and yours, if you'd like."

"Wow, you've got it all figured out."

"Not all of it, but it's a start."

Gigi looked at him for a long moment, gathering her thoughts and her defenses. "This is happening too fast for me."

"Okay."

"What does that mean? 'Okay.'"

"It means just what you think. If it's too fast for you, we'll slow it down and take our time. We've got some time before you're heading back to LA. We can see where we are when it's time for you to leave."

"What about what I said earlier, how I don't want this for myself?"

"I heard you, but here's my thought on that. You've never had this, so how do you know you don't want it?"

"Are you sure you went to business school and not law school?"

"Very sure," he said, chuckling.

"You have an answer for everything. It's annoying."

"I aim to annoy you with my answers for a very long time to come, but only if that's what you want, too. I have no desire to force myself on you, Gigi. And I mean that. If you tell me right now to go away, I will. I'll hate that, but I'll go." He tilted his head. "You want me to go?"

Yes, go away so I don't have to deal with any of this. The words burned at the tip of her tongue, but she couldn't make herself say something that would hurt him. "No, I don't want you to go."

"Had to think about that for a minute, huh?"

"Don't push your luck."

His sexy smile was positively lethal. "So now that you've decided to keep me around for a while, what do you want to do?"

"As you well know, I hardly slept last night. I'm tired."

"You want to go home and take a nap?"

"Like an actual nap with sleeping?"

"What other kind is there?" he asked, feigning confusion.

Gigi rolled her eyes. "No nudity."

"I suppose I can live with that, but it'll be a terrible hardship."

"Then let's go."

"Don't forget your roses. I picked them for you."

"Thank you."

"You're welcome."

She grabbed her phone from the bathroom and the gorgeous bundle of roses from the kitchen, followed him out of Jordan's house and locked the door. Jordan had told her that most people didn't lock their houses on Gansett, but Mason always did now that Jordan lived with him. He never knew when some crackpot would come looking for her, and he wanted Jordan to be safe.

The first time Jordan had told her that, Gigi had thought how nice it must be to have someone who cares so much about you that he started locking his house to keep you safe. But it hadn't occurred to her to want that for herself. Then along came Cooper James to turn things upside down.

Despite his sweet words and assurances, Gigi was still skeptical that they could turn a summer fling into something lasting. However, she was willing to give him a chance to show her what might be possible, which was a massive leap for her.

As the scent of the roses filled her senses, she only hoped she wouldn't regret it.

COOPER DROVE HOME to Jared's, reminding himself it was way too soon for a victory celebration. But she hadn't sent him away, and that was definitely a victory. When he'd gotten the text from Gigi to come to Jordan's ASAP, he'd initially been concerned that something was wrong. When he'd seen how shocked Gigi was to see him there, he'd quickly realized she hadn't sent the text. Jordan had intervened, and he'd be forever thankful to her. Who knew if he ever would've seen Gigi again if Jordan hadn't gotten involved?

He owed her a dozen roses and a huge thank-you.

It was also interesting to realize that by getting involved, Jordan was signaling her approval of him for Gigi, which would matter to her. Despite her bravado and devil-may-care attitude, Gigi loved the family she'd created for herself with Jordan, Nikki and Evelyn, and their opinions mattered to her.

He would need to be patient with her and show her, one hour at a time, one day at a time, that she could have faith in him.

His cell phone rang, and he took the call from Jared on the Bluetooth. "What's up?"

"Did you pair your phone to my Bluetooth by any chance?"

Cooper held back a laugh at Jared's indignant tone. "Maybe. Maybe not. What's up?"

"Lizzie wants to know if you'll be home for dinner. She's making kabobs."

"That sounds good. Can I bring a friend?"

"Sure. Which friend?"

"Gigi."

"No problem. So you guys are, like, seeing each other?"

Cooper glanced in the rearview mirror to make sure she was still behind him. "We are, and I'm hoping it'll be more than just a summer fling."

"Is that right?"

"It is."

"That's a big move for a little boy like you."

"Shut up with the 'little boy' shit. I'm a grown man, in case you didn't get that memo."

Jared laughed. "You'll always be a little boy to me."

In the background, Cooper could hear the baby crying. "Any word from the investigator?"

"He might have a lead. We're hopeful."

Cooper could hear the exhaustion and stress in Jared's voice. "I should be making dinner for you guys, not the other way around."

"It's fine. Lizzie says we have to get back to some semblance of normal, and she loves to cook. It'll relieve some stress for her."

"I wish there was something I could do for you guys besides hope you find Jessie."

"We appreciate you sticking around. It's nice to have the company."

"I'm going to hang with Gigi this afternoon, but if you need anything, call me."

"Will do. Where's my car?"

"Pulling into your driveway right now. I'll bring you the keys."

"Gee, thanks. That's awfully good of you."

"Glad to be of service."

Jared laughed. "Keep the comic relief coming. We need it."

"How's Lizzie?"

"She's amazing. She is barely sleeping, but she's so damned serene, as if she's been preparing for this her whole life."

"God, Jared, what're we going to do if you have to give the baby back to Jessie?"

"I have no idea. I can't even think about it."

Cooper's stomach hurt at the thought of that kind of agony descending upon Lizzie and Jared.

"I'm not sure what's worse, fearing that or living in this awful limbo of not knowing what's going to happen."

"They both suck."

"Yep," Jared said with a sigh.

As Cooper pulled up to the garage, Jared came outside.

Cooper handed him the keys, and in a spontaneous moment, he hugged his brother. "Wish there was something more I could do."

Jared patted Cooper on the back. "This helps. Thanks."

"Any word from Q?"

"Nothing other than they got to Ireland okay."

"Lucky dog."

"Took him a long time to take the plunge. I hope they enjoy every minute of their honeymoon."

"I'm sure they will."

Gigi drove in and parked next to the Porsche. "How's it going, Jared?" she asked when she got out of the car.

"About the same. Still looking for Jessie and taking care of the baby in the meantime."

"I give you guys all the credit for what you're doing."

"We're doing what anyone would."

"That's not true," Gigi said, a fierce edge to her tone. "Most people would've turned the baby over to the system. You're not most people."

"Thanks," Jared said with a weary sigh. "You guys have a nice afternoon. I'll see you at dinner."

Gigi glanced at Cooper.

"They invited us."

"Shouldn't *we* be making *them* dinner?"

"That's what I said, too, but Jared said Lizzie wants to do it."

"What can we bring?"

"Not a thing. I did a grocery run this morning and picked up wine. We're all set."

"Thanks for having us," Cooper said.

"We're looking forward to some adult time."

"Sounds fun," Cooper said.

"I'd better go check on Lizzie. See you in a bit."

As he walked away, Cooper noted the unusual curve of his brother's shoulders as he held up the weight of the world.

"I feel so bad for them to be put in this situation," Gigi said as she led the way upstairs to her place.

"I do, too. It's awful and wonderful at the same time."

"I need a shower. Make yourself comfortable."

Cooper followed her into the bedroom and pulled his T-shirt over his head and then dropped his shorts.

"Wait a second. I said no nudity."

"If I keep my boxers on, that's not nude."

"This," she said, waving her hand at him, "is too close to nude for comfort."

"Don't worry. I won't let you have your wicked way with me. This is sleep only. Go take your shower. I'll be waiting for you."

She let out an aggravated sound and slammed the bathroom door behind her.

God, he loved her, and yes, he knew that was crazy, but how could anyone not love her? She was amazing and funny and sweet and so wounded that she didn't even know how to let someone love her. He was determined to show her something so good, she'd want to keep him around forever.

They could be happy together. He knew that. How he knew it, he couldn't say. It was one of those things that just *was*. It couldn't be explained or rationalized or easily described in words. All he knew for sure was he needed to be with her. If he could make that happen, the rest would fall into place, or so he hoped.

Ten minutes later, she got into the other side of the bed, wearing a long T-shirt that landed midthigh, leaving the rest of her legs on display.

"Is snuggling allowed in this nap?" Cooper asked.

"Absolutely not."

"Oh, come on. That's not fair. I agreed to your no-nudity clause, but you never said anything about snuggling."

"That's for couples. We're still a fling."

"No, we're not. You gave me a promotion earlier to boyfriend status."

She looked over at him, eyes flashing with anger, and he'd never wanted her more. "*When* did I do that?"

"When you didn't kick me out."

"How does that make you my boyfriend?"

He rolled onto his side and moved closer to her. "If you didn't want me around, you would've kicked me out."

"I was sparing your feelings. That's the only reason I let you stay."

"Are you sure about that?" he asked, placing his hand on her abdomen.

She tried to push it away, but he stayed firm.

"Don't. No touching."

"Yes, touching." He slid his hand from her belly to her leg and dipped under the hem of her T-shirt.

"Cooper..."

"Shhh, just relax and get some rest."

"How am I supposed to rest when you're doing *that*?"

She'd broken out into goose bumps that gave him tremendous satisfaction.

"What am I doing?" He ran his fingertips up her inner thigh, intentionally avoiding touching her anywhere she'd deemed off-limits.

She squirmed, trying to get closer to his hand, but he denied her. "Cooper."

"Yes, Gigi?"

"Knock it off."

"You still haven't told me what I need to knock off."

"Touching me without touching me where I want you to."

"You told me I couldn't!"

"Since when do you listen to me? I told you to go away, and here you are, mostly naked in my bed!"

"You're sending some seriously mixed signals. Do you want me to touch you or not? And if you do, you need to say so, because I don't touch without permission."

"I want you to touch me."

"Where?"

"Everywhere."

"I thought you wanted to sleep."

"I'll do that after you touch me, and go easy, because that big thing of yours made me sore."

Cooper rocked with silent laughter. "You're a piece of work, Gigi Gibson."

"Believe it or not, I've heard that a few times before."

"I believe it."

CHAPTER 21

Cooper continued to stroke her inner thighs with the lightest possible touch that was driving her crazy—and he knew that because she growled at him. "Patience."

"Got none."

"Get some."

"You're pissing me off again."

"I have a feeling you'll forgive me."

"I won't."

He kissed her neck. "Yes, you will."

"Hey, Coop?"

"Yes, Gigi?"

"You're not, you know, selling me a bag of bullshit, are you?" she asked, her voice and expression so vulnerable, she broke his heart.

He used his free hand to brush the hair back from her face. "No, sweetheart. I swear to God, I'll never tell you anything other than the truth." Kissing her as softly as he possibly could, he said, "And the truth is, I'm crazy about you. I was before I ever met you, and then I found out you're even more than I could've ever dreamed."

She blinked back tears that made him ache because he knew tears weren't her thing.

He kissed both her cheeks and the tip of her nose before returning to her lips as his fingers moved up her leg to find she was bare under the T-shirt. The discovery made him hard as a rock, but this wasn't about him. It was about showing her that he meant what he'd said, that he wanted her for more than just the surface things.

Earning her trust and her love would be the greatest challenge of his life, and keeping her happy would be his greatest pleasure. "I feel like we could set the world on fire together, you and me."

She arched her back, trying to get closer to his fingers between her legs.

"Easy, baby," he said. "Nice and easy."

A sound came from her that might've been a sob.

Cooper kissed her softly. "Just relax and let me love you."

"I can't let you love me."

"Yes, you can."

She shook her head.

He nodded and kissed her again as he slipped his fingers inside her heat.

She held on to him so tightly, it made his ribs hurt, but he didn't care. He wanted her to hold on to him as tightly as she could for as long as possible.

Cooper took her on a sweet, easy ride, teasing her until she was begging him to finish what he'd started, but he was in no rush.

"Cooper… please."

"Tell me what you want."

"You know what I want!"

"You'll get everything you want, but you have to have some faith in me."

"I do, or you wouldn't be here. Again."

He was wise enough to know that her admitting such a thing was a huge win for his campaign to convince her that not only was she worthy and deserving of love, but she was also able to give it back.

"You're the devil," she said, gasping as he took her almost to the point of explosion before backing off again.

Laughing, he moved carefully so as not to aggravate ribs that were finally feeling a little better and replaced his fingers with his tongue.

"Jesus H. Shitballs," she said as he sucked on her clit and pushed two fingers inside her, curling them to hit her G-spot.

He had her hovering on the brink when he stopped.

"Cooper!"

"Are you going to give me a chance, Gigi?"

"Isn't that what I'm doing right now?"

"A real chance, the kind where risks are taken, and two lives come together to make one that works for both of us?"

"I have to answer that before you'll let me come?" she asked, squirming against the fingers he had buried deep inside her.

"Yeah, you do."

"This is sexual blackmail!"

"Call it what you will. Answer the question. Are we going to do this?" He withdrew his fingers almost completely and then drove them back inside her, taking care not to hurt her after she'd told him she was sore from last night.

"I wish you would do it, for fuck's sake."

Cooper laughed. "I will. As soon as you give me what I want, I'll give you what you want."

"If this is the kind of boyfriend you're going to be, I've got a rabbit that doesn't talk back to me."

"Can your rabbit do this?" He twirled his tongue around her clit before sucking on the tight nub of nerves and making her cry out. "Can it do this?" He withdrew his fingers and pushed one into her anus before she had the opportunity to anticipate his intentions. "How about this?" He buried his tongue inside her and went for it, making her come so hard, she nearly broke the finger he had buried in her ass. "Now, as I was saying…" He kept his finger inside her while he waited for her to recover. "Are you going to give me a chance?"

"You've got your finger up my ass. I believe that means I'm giving you a chance."

Cooper laughed so hard, he had tears in his eyes. "Gigi, I really think I could love you."

"I've warned you that's not a good idea, but you won't listen to reason."

"I think it's quite possibly the best idea I'll ever have in my entire life."

"It's your funeral." She squirmed, trying to break free of him. "Now get your finger out of there. Right now."

He dipped his head, pressed his tongue to her clit and pushed his finger deeper into her. "Not until you give me a second one."

. . .

"THIS FEELS WEIRD," Dara said to Oliver as they drove to Luke and Syd's for dinner. "They don't even know us, and they invited us to dinner."

"He knows me. I see him every day."

"It still feels weird."

"Don't let it. You know how the people are here. Everyone has been so welcoming and kind to us. Luke is one of the nicest guys you'll ever meet. I'm sure his wife is great, too."

Dara had become accustomed to just about everything feeling strange since she lost her son, so it shouldn't come as a surprise to her that socializing with people she didn't know would be awkward. Since they'd come to Gansett, she'd tried to go with the island flow, as Oliver called it, meeting lots of new people who hadn't known them before they lost Lewis.

There was relief in that.

Everyone didn't look at her like she was a walking tragedy the way they did at home.

"Tell me more about your first day at the Wayfarer. What did they have you doing?"

"Nikki gave me three weddings to work on, all of them happening next spring and summer. I set up Zoom meetings with the brides to get acquainted and to go over the details for each of them."

"That sounds like so much fun, getting to work with couples on the happiest day of their lives."

"I'm looking forward to really digging in. The big challenge is that everything has to be ordered way in advance so it gets here in time. Nikki has a very impressive system in place with vendors and lead times."

"I never gave much thought to the challenges of island life until we came here. Big Mac's son-in-law Joe owns the ferry company, and Big Mac always has stories about things coming and going. They send a special ferry twice a week in-season to bring gas over. No passengers allowed on that one."

"It's all very interesting indeed. Nikki said the family has been doing a community Thanksgiving at the marina the last few years, but it's gotten so big, they want to move it to the Wayfarer. Since she's getting married that weekend, she's putting me in charge of that, the Christmas meal they want to add this year and a New Year's Eve party for the island's year-round residents."

"So the off-season will be busy for you."

"Looks that way."

"I'm happy to see you taking this on, Dar. I think it'll be good for you."

"I think so, too. Like you said, it's a challenge, but nothing like what work used to be like. I'm not ready to go back to that life any time soon, so this feels perfect for now."

"What if we decide we never want to leave this place? What if the Wayfarer turns out to be a job you love, and my day trading provides a sustainable income?"

"I guess then we'll figure out how to make this a permanent move."

"You'd be up for that?"

She shrugged. "I'm taking life one day at a time these days. That's all I'm capable of."

"I'm glad to hear you say you might consider staying. I feel more at home here in a few days than I have anywhere I've ever lived. I love the morning meeting at the marina and the friendly people and the gorgeous scenery and the adventure of living on an isolated island. I love it all." He looked over at her. "But I only love it if you do, too."

"I like it a lot. I feel like I can breathe here. Do I want to stay forever? I'm not sure yet, but I wouldn't rule it out."

"We probably ought to experience winter before we fall in love with the place, huh?"

Dara laughed, which was another thing that happened more often lately. "True." With the windows down, she turned her face into the last of the day's warm sunshine. Peace had been an elusive thing over the last year, but it had shown up occasionally since they'd come to Gansett. If nothing else, she and Oliver were finding their way back to each other, and for that, she would always be thankful.

For many dark months, she'd wondered if their once-blissful marriage was going to be a secondary loss. It seemed now like maybe they had gotten through the worst of it and were slowly but surely finding a new normal. That simply hadn't been possible at home. Why? She couldn't say, but she wasn't asking any questions. She was thankful for any peace she could find.

Luke and Syd lived in a ranch house right at the coast.

"Wow, what a spot this is," Oliver said as they stepped out of the SUV to the start of what would be a spectacular sunset.

"I inherited it from my mom," a handsome dark-haired man said when he came out to greet them. "She died young, so it was just me here until I got lucky and convinced Syd to spend the rest of her life with me."

"It's amazing." Oliver shook his friend's hand. "You must have people beating down the door wanting to take it off your hands."

"At least six offers a year, but I say no to every one of them." He gestured to a barn a few hundred feet from the driveway. "That's where I restore the boats."

"By the way, Luke, this is Dara. Dara, meet Luke."

"It's so nice to meet you," Luke said. "Oliver talks about you so much, I feel like we already know each other."

"Same. Thank you for making him part of your morning meeting. He loves it."

"We love having him."

"I forgot to tell you, Dara, that Luke does incredible restoration work. He did Big Mac's boats."

"They're gorgeous," Dara said.

"Thanks. I enjoy the work and the satisfaction of seeing something old and broken brought back to life."

She found that an apt metaphor for her current state of mind. "Thank you for having us tonight. I hope Oliver didn't invite himself."

Luke laughed. "Not at all. We're thrilled to have some adult time. Our daughter, Lily, is on the move these days, and she runs us ragged."

"I remember that stage," Dara said wistfully.

"She's keeping us hopping. Come in." Luke led the way down a lighted sidewalk to the door. "You're okay with dogs, right?"

"Yes, we have one," Oliver said. "Ours is a yellow Lab named Maisy."

"Oliver and Dara, meet Buddy and Lily. We should get him and Maisy together for a play date."

"Maisy would love that," Dara said.

When Luke bent to scoop the baby off the floor, she let out a screech of protest. "Now that she can get herself around, she doesn't want anyone helping her." Luke put her back down, and Lily crawled away at lightning speed.

"Holy crap, she's fast," Oliver said.

"We think she's going to be an Olympic sprinter," a gorgeous redheaded woman said as she joined them. "Hi, I'm Syd. It's so lovely to meet you both." She shook their hands and ushered them into a warm, cozy kitchen that was open to the family room, where Lily was playing with her toys. "Quick, she's occupied, so let me get you something to drink."

"We brought wine," Oliver said, offering the bag containing bottles of red and white.

"Awesome, thank you. I have a bottle of Chardonnay open."

"I'll have that, please," Dara said. "Olly will want the red."

"Coming right up. Let's go out to the deck. It's a beautiful night."

"I'll get the princess down for the night and join you in a few," Luke said.

"Bring her out to say good night to Mommy."

"Will do."

Dara and Oliver followed Sydney to a gorgeous outdoor space that had lights strung overhead and a fire pit in the corner.

"What an amazing deck," Dara said while Sydney tended to food on the grill. "It's right out of a magazine."

Sydney gestured for them to help themselves to the cheese plate on the table. "Aw, thanks. I'm a decorator, and according to Luke, he never knows what he's going to come home to. I'm always futzing with this place."

"I can see why," Dara said. Sydney's warm, welcoming personality had put her immediately at ease. "It's the most beautiful spot I've seen yet on the island, and that's saying something."

"Luke grew up here with his mom, and after she died, he had to really hustle to be able to keep the place. The taxes alone were killer. That's how he got into restoring boats. It gave him a year-round income when the marina was closed for the off-season."

"I'm glad he was able to hang on to it," Oliver said. "It's quite something."

"You should've seen the bachelor pad I walked into when we first got back together," Syd said, rolling her eyes. "Those windows there?" She pointed to the corner of the house. "They were a *wall*! How tragic is that?"

"Very tragic indeed," Dara said, laughing.

"Is she telling you about my bachelor pad?" Luke asked when he came out with Lily. His eyes were alight with amusement and affection for his wife. "I was waiting for her to get here to tell me everything that was wrong with it."

"He had beach chairs and a grill out here," Sydney said. "You can't make this stuff up."

"And yet she loves me anyway," Luke said, leaning in to give Lily to her mother.

Sydney hugged and kissed Lily. "Sleep tight, my sweet girl, and be good for Daddy. Say good night to our friends Oliver and Dara."

"Nnnn," Lily said.

"It's a start," Syd said, laughing. "Night-night, baby. Mama loves you."

"Night, Lily," Dara and Oliver said together.

"Be right back," Luke said as he took the little one inside.

"He's such a great dad," Syd said. "He does bedtime every night."

"I did, too," Oliver said. "It was my favorite time of day with Lewis."

"I'm so, so sorry you lost him," Sydney said. "I wish there was something more I could say than that, but as I know all too well, there's nothing anyone can say to take the pain away."

"No, there isn't," Dara said. "And people just don't understand. They think we ought to be 'better' by now."

"I hate to tell you, but 'better' is going to be a lifetime effort."

"I've begun to realize that." It was, Dara thought, such a relief to speak to someone who understood. "I was very sorry to hear about what happened to you, too."

"Thank you. It's been a few years now, and the ache isn't as sharp as it was at first, but it's always there, a part of who I am now. I'm thinking all the time about what Max and Malena would be up to these days and what my husband, Seth, would be doing. All three of them were always on the move, so I like to think of them still like that, together in the afterlife."

"That's a nice way to think of them," Dara said, dabbing at the tears that filled her eyes. "I've asked my late grandparents and Oliver's to take care of Lewis until we get there. I've pictured them taking him on picnics and having him for sleepovers."

"I'm sure they're taking very good care of him." Syd took Dara's hand and gave it a squeeze. "I'm so glad Luke invited you over. I've been planning to come see you at the lighthouse."

"I'm glad he invited us, too, even though I was worried about whether it was appropriate to bring our tragedy into your home, especially after what you've survived."

"After I lost my family, I was supported by so many people. Some I'd known for years, and others came to me because they'd been where I was and knew how to help in a way my longtime friends and family didn't. When I look back at that time, it's the people who were strangers to me—then—who made the biggest impact. Since then, I try to pay that forward to people going through similar things, because I know how much it meant to me to have that support. My door is always open to you, Dara—and Oliver. If you're having a bad day, come see me. I get it, and I'll always be happy to listen, to talk, to hug you or whatever you need."

Dara couldn't resist the need to hug her new friend. "That means so much to me. You'll never know. People reached out to me after we lost Lewis, but I was too broken to let them in. I think I'm ready now for the kind of support you're offering."

"It's always here. We'll exchange phone numbers, too, and I'll introduce you to my friends Jenny and Erin. They lost Toby in 9/11. He was Jenny's fiancé and Erin's twin brother. They get it, and we've been a huge source of support to each other."

"The people here are almost too good to be true," Dara said.

"We're not, though. Most of us are to the point in our lives where we've lived, loved, lost and survived. There's a sisterhood and brotherhood in that. And there's something healing about this place, which is why the town requires letters from the new lighthouse keepers. They're looking for people who'll benefit from what this place can do."

"It's working for us," Oliver said. "We both feel like we're coming back to life and to each other since we've been here."

"I'm so glad to hear that."

"One of the things I wanted to ask you," Dara said hesitantly, "is how you found the courage to have another child. But if that's too personal, I totally understand."

"I'm an open book, Dara. You can honestly ask me anything, and I'll always tell you the truth as I see it. And that's a good question. It was hard for me for a long time to imagine ever finding the nerve to try again, not to mention I'd had a tubal ligation after Malena was born, so that had to be reversed. We had no way to know whether it would work, and we decided to just roll the dice and see what happened. Luke also helped me to see that I've probably had my great tragedy, and I should be home free from now on." Sydney frowned, and the expression changed her entire demeanor. "But, of course, I found out it doesn't work that way."

"What do you mean?"

"Earlier this summer, I made a terrible mistake while in the car with Lily and ended up hitting the accelerator rather than the brake, which sent us off the pier at the marina and into the water."

"Oh my God!" Dara said. "But you were both all right?"

"Thankfully, Luke, Big Mac, Mason and Blaine were able to get us out, but it was the longest ten minutes of my entire life."

"Thank goodness neither of you was hurt."

"Yes, for sure, but my nerves were wrecked for weeks. I'm doing better now, but it was a sobering reminder of what can happen in a heartbeat."

"That's the part that has me paralyzed with indecision. Olly and I… We did everything right with Lewis. We never let him out of our sight. We had him in swim lessons as an infant. And still, the worst possible thing happened."

"I felt that way about my kids, too. I was the safety mom, always reminding them to be careful and to watch out for things that could hurt them. In the end, there was nothing I could've done to prevent what happened to them. Took me a lot of years, and a *lot* of therapy, to be able to say there was nothing I could've done, and there was nothing *you* could've done to stop what happened to Lewis."

"I wish I hadn't been working on a Sunday," Dara said.

"And I wish I hadn't fallen asleep watching football," Oliver added.

"There was nothing either of you could've done to prevent an accident. That's what it was. An *accident*. And by their very definition, accidents are things that shouldn't have happened. I'm not sure if you believe in fate or higher powers or anything like that, but I do. I believe there's a grand plan for all of us, and we're just along for the ride. Believing that helps me to understand there was nothing I could've done to save my family."

"I believe that, too, or at least I always had until we lost Lewis," Dara said. "Now I'm not sure what I believe, but I'm trying to get back to my faith along with everything else that was once important to me."

"The best advice I was given after my loss was to accept that I was spared for a reason. I think that reason was for me to come back here, to rekindle an old flame with Luke and to have Lily. I've come to believe this life, the one I'm leading now, was the one that was meant to be, but that doesn't take anything away from the life I had with Seth and the kids. It's hard to explain that to people who haven't lived through what we have."

Dara felt like Sydney was speaking directly to her battered soul. "You'll never know what it means to me to talk to someone who truly understands."

"I do know. I really do. I'll always be sorry you had to lose your sweet boy for our paths to cross, but we can never have too many friends."

"Thank you, Syd. Thank you so much."

Luke came back out a few minutes later and, after checking the grill, declared dinner ready.

"And Mommy's off duty, so it's wine o'clock," Syd said, throwing her hands in the air.

Dara laughed and followed her inside to help finish the dinner preparations while thinking about the advice Syd had given her. She was still here for a reason, and though she'd yet to figure out what that reason was, at least she was back to working, functioning and connecting with Oliver, not to mention breathing easier than she had since that dreadful day.

She'd take the progress where she could find it and appreciated Sydney's generous offer of friendship.

CHAPTER 22

When Gigi was in eighth grade, her class took a trip to the Grand Canyon. She and her classmates had prepared for the trip for months, but when the day of departure finally arrived, Gigi found out her parents never submitted the permission slip or paid the fee, so she couldn't go on the trip. She'd been absolutely devastated. That was the first time Evelyn Hopper stepped up for her, marching into Gigi's so-called mother's office to demand she sign the permission slip. Evelyn had also paid for Gigi to go on the trip and had made a scene at the school that'd resulted in Gigi boarding the bus minutes before it was due to leave.

Evelyn had saved the day, and Gigi had never forgotten what Evelyn had done for her or how amazing the Grand Canyon was.

Why was she thinking of that now, as the late-afternoon sun streamed into her bedroom? Cooper was out cold next to her, his arm across her middle, anchoring her to him. As she watched him sleep, she realized why she'd thought of the field trip. She'd dreamed about falling off the side of the Grand Canyon. The familiar dream had shown up occasionally after that trip to remind her not to get too close to the edge.

With Cooper, she'd already fallen into the canyon, so it was a bit late for warnings. She'd allowed him liberties no one else had ever taken with her, although "allowed" was a stretch. He'd done it without asking, and she'd loved it. Just remembering the way he'd played her body like a virtuoso had her tingling with desire.

This wasn't good. It wasn't good at all. The kind of entanglement he wanted was the last freaking thing she needed. So why was he still there?

That was a very good question and one she had no clear answer to.

She liked him. More than she'd expected to, if she were being honest. Yes, he was young, but he was what people sometimes referred to as an old soul. He was wise beyond his years and seemed genuine in his feelings for her. But how could anyone know for sure what another person felt? Was she supposed to stake her own happiness and future on the assurances of a man she'd known for such a short time?

The situation they were in lent itself to urgency. She would finish filming soon and was due to head home to LA. He was here for a short time before he went back to his life in New York. That was why everything felt so immediate and intense.

"Why are you staring at me?"

The low rumble of his voice startled her. "How can you tell I'm staring at you if your eyes are closed?"

"I can feel it."

"You can't feel someone looking at you."

"In this case, I can. It's like hot pokers burning into my skin."

Gigi didn't want to laugh, but how could she not? "You're so dramatic."

"Not really." He pulled her in closer to him so her breasts were pressed to his chest. And where exactly had her T-shirt gone? His hand curved around her breast, his thumb teasing her nipple. "What were you thinking about when you were staring at me?"

"The Grand Canyon."

"Huh. If you'd asked me to guess, I never would've said that."

"What would you have said?"

"That you were trying to figure out how to get me out of your bed and out of your life without hurting my feelings."

"That's not what I was thinking!"

"Liar," he said on a low chuckle. "It's okay. You can tell me the truth."

"I dream about my eighth-grade trip to the Grand Canyon once in a while, usually when I'm about to do something risky."

"What does the Grand Canyon have to do with risk?"

"I dream I've fallen into the canyon. I always wake up right before I hit the bottom."

"What do you think that means?"

"That I need to prevent the fall in the first place so I don't have to hit the bottom."

He kissed her and held her even tighter. "I'd jump in front of you so you could land on me."

"What if you were the reason I was about to crash?"

"I won't be."

"How can you possibly know that?"

"Because I already know I'd put myself between you and anything that could hurt you."

She sighed deeply. "Cooper, you can't be saying this stuff."

"Why?"

"I already told you why. It's preposterous."

"What's preposterous is you thinking there's no way someone could have real, genuine feelings for you."

"I don't think that."

"Yes, you do."

She poked him in the gut before she remembered he was injured. "Sorry. I shouldn't have done that because of your ribs, but otherwise, you deserved it."

"My ribs are fine. I'm aching in different places now."

"I told you I'd return the favor earlier."

"That's not where I'm aching, although he's always interested in you."

"What hurts now?"

"My heart feels a little achy because there's this beautiful woman I like so much, but I'm having trouble convincing her to give me a real chance to make her happy."

"Maybe you should be snuggling up to her rather than me, then. Won't she be mad that you're nekkid in a bed with another woman and doing unspeakable things to her?"

He rocked with silent laughter that made her smile. One thing she would say for him was he was fun to be with. "I did unspeakable things to you?"

"You know you did!"

"Was that untouched territory?"

"I'm not telling you."

Cooper pinched her nipple, tightly enough to get her attention. "Tell me."

"I don't want to."

He pinched a little tighter.

"Cooper! Stop!"

"Tell me."

"Fine. Yes. It's untouched. Or it was before you took liberties no one gave you permission to take."

"You loved it."

"How do you know that?"

"You nearly broke my finger when you came."

"Oh my God! I cannot believe you said that!"

"Why not? It's true." He held out his hand so they could both see it. "I probably have a bruise. Is there a bruise?"

"I'm going to kill you."

"No, you're not. You like me too much to kill me."

"No, I don't."

"Yes, you do." Her low growl made him laugh again. "You're funny, Gigi."

"And you're a pain in my butt, Cooper."

"Literally."

Laughter burst from every part of her. She laughed so hard, she couldn't breathe, before she remembered she didn't want to be encouraging him.

And then he was on top of her, gazing down at her with those eyes that seemed to see through to the very heart of her. How'd he do that? "Don't you see how good this is, Gigi? How good we are together?"

She saw it, and it scared the shit out of her.

"I want you to do something for me."

"I already let you be mostly nekkid in my bed, among *other* things."

"And I appreciate those things, but I want more than that. I want you to give me a real chance to show you I can make you happy if you let me. Can you do that, Gigi?"

Her heart was in her throat, because God, she wanted to. She wanted to take that chance so badly. Licking lips that had gone dry, she looked up at him and found that all signs of humor were gone, and he was dead serious. "I'm afraid we're getting carried away, that we're making this into something it isn't."

"I'm not doing that. I swear to you. I've had flings and girlfriends. A lot of girlfriends, in fact. This is different."

"How is it different?"

"I've never in my life asked anyone to give me a chance to make them happy. I've never once tried to picture how my life and hers might come together to make our life. I've never wanted anyone the way I want you." He pressed his hard cock against her core. "And not just in bed. I want to hear all your funny commentary and hold you when you're sad about your best friend moving on to something that doesn't include you. I want to hear about your clients, and I want to be your plus-one at everything. It's *different,* Gigi."

She closed her eyes and drew in a deep breath. "I don't want this."

"I know. You've said as much."

"But..."

"What?"

"You... You're..."

Cooper tilted his head, seeming to hold his breath, waiting to hear what she had to say.

If she said what she wanted to say to him, the words couldn't be taken back. She licked her lips again. "It's different for me, too. With you..."

He kissed her with a desperation she hadn't seen from him before then, as if his life—and maybe hers—depended upon this kiss and these halting steps toward something significant.

"You won't be sorry," he whispered against her lips. "I swear to God, you'll never be sorry you took a chance on me."

She could only hope that would be true.

LIZZIE MOVED AROUND THE KITCHEN, preparing dinner with the baby in a sling Abby McCarthy had sent over that kept the baby snug against Lizzie's chest. She hummed a random tune while she chopped vegetables for the kabobs, while Jared tended to the marinated chicken and beef on the grill.

"This is how it could be," she whispered to the baby. "The three of us together forever, getting ready to have friends over for dinner."

In her mind, she'd given the baby a name: Violet. Or Vi for short. Only because a child shouldn't be almost a week old and not have a name. Her attachment to the baby already ran deep and was getting deeper by the minute. Lizzie couldn't find the wherewithal to care that she was probably heading for the worst kind of broken heart.

In her rational mind, Lizzie knew Jessie would come back for the baby or make other arrangements for her, and Lizzie would have to give her up. In her irrational mind, she was already planning the baby girl's first birthday party and dreaming of the mother-daughter things they might do together, such as tea at the Plaza in New York, along with stops at FAO Schwarz and the American Girl store.

She couldn't wait to do everything fun with her little girl.

Lizzie would no sooner have that sort of thought when the black cloud of doom would descend once again to remind her the baby strapped to her chest didn't belong to her and might be taken from her at any moment. Every time Jared's phone rang, Lizzie held her breath, waiting to hear if this was going to be the call from Jessie that would force her to give baby Vi back to her mother.

No, Lizzie wanted to cry. *I'm her mother. I'm the one who's fed her and changed her and bathed her and rocked her to sleep and walked the floor with her for hours when she was fussy.*

Jared came in from the patio, carrying a platter with grilled meat. His instructions had been to cook it until it was about half done. Then she would add the veggies and put the skewers together. "Want me to take her so you can do your thing?"

Lizzie's immediate, visceral reaction was to say no and put her arms around the baby so neither he nor anyone could take her. But she couldn't do that. Jared was already worried about how attached she'd gotten. She couldn't let him see just how far gone she was over the baby who'd turned her life upside down in the span of a few momentous days. "Sure," Lizzie said reluctantly.

She unwrapped the sling and handed the baby over to him, her heart melting at the sight of Jared holding the little one in his big strong arms.

His phone rang, stopping Lizzie's heart as usual. Turning so his back was to her, he said, "Can you get that out of my pocket for me?"

Lizzie pulled the phone from his pocket and handed it to him, noting the investigator's name on the caller ID.

"Hey, Mike. What's up?" Jared listened for a full minute while Lizzie died inside the way she did every time he talked to the man who was trying to find Jessie. "Did she say anything?"

Oh God. Had he found her?

"All right. Keep me posted. Great job." Jared ended the call and put the phone on the counter. "He found her."

"Wh-where?"

"New Bedford. I guess that's where she's from, and he tracked her to her grandmother's house. She's agreed to talk to him in the morning, but because he doesn't trust her not to bolt, he's staked out at the house."

Lizzie felt like she was going to be sick, so she sat at the kitchen table and focused on trying to get oxygen to lungs that felt constricted.

"It's good news that he found her."

She wanted to agree with him, but couldn't.

"Sweetheart, look at me."

Lizzie forced herself to meet his gaze.

"We knew this wasn't forever."

Lizzie shook her head almost involuntarily as everything in her rejected that statement.

"Please don't do this."

Her hands were shaking so hard, she had to tuck them under her legs so he wouldn't see them shake. "I would like for you to ask Mike to ask her if we might keep her. Permanently."

"Lizzie… The baby is Jessie's. We can't just come right out and ask her to give us her baby."

"Why not? She already did! What's wrong with asking her if we can make the arrangement legal? It would be like… like surrogacy, only after the fact. Don't tell me we can't work something out with her."

"And what do we do in a month or three months or six months when she changes her mind and wants her back?"

"We make it so she can't do that. If she signs her over to us, it's permanent. Of course we'd let Jessie visit and see her, and I'd send her pictures, but the custody arrangement would be forever. Don't act like this can't work. You're the one who suggested it in the first place."

Jared took a deep breath and let it out. "Let me call Dan and see what he says."

Lizzie's heart surged from the depths of despair to the heights of joy in one second, leaving her feeling as if she'd had the wind knocked out of her.

"But please, Lizzie. Please don't get your hopes up until we know what our options are."

Lizzie didn't tell him her hopes were already as high as the sky and heading for outer space. She reached for the baby and held her close, praying with all her might that they could work something out. Because losing her wasn't an option anymore.

"Put it on speaker so I can hear him, too," Lizzie said.

Jared put through the call to Dan Torrington.

"Hey, Jared," Dan said when he answered. "How's it going?"

"Pretty well. Thanks for taking my call so late in the day, Dan."

While Jared detailed the latest in the situation for Dan, Lizzie got up, put the baby back in the sling and forced herself to finish making dinner, while trying to get her hands to stop shaking. When Jared got to the part about Lizzie's idea to propose a custody arrangement to Jessie, Lizzie turned toward Jared. "Is something like that legally possible, Dan?"

"Anything is possible if all parties agree to it."

"In that case," Jared said, "I have a huge ask. Could you draft something for us tonight that our investigator could propose to Jessie tomorrow?"

"I have a boilerplate custody agreement I could adapt for this. It wouldn't be a big deal to get that done tonight, but I just wonder if the mother is in the right frame of mind to sign something like that, and we'd need information about who the father is, too, because he'd be required to sign as well."

Lizzie's spirits plummeted again.

"I have no information about her state of mind or who the father is, but I can have Mike talk to her and get a sense of what she's thinking. Our only request is if she and the father sign over their rights to us, they need to understand it's a permanent arrangement. They can't come back in a year or two or whatever and ask for her back."

"The agreement they'd sign would be airtight on those points," Dan said. "The most important thing right now is to pitch the idea to her and ask about the father. I'll draft something your guy can give to her to consider."

"If Jessie is agreeable to this idea, we'd like to get this taken care of sooner rather than later. Every day that the baby spends with us only raises the stakes. For both of us."

When Jared said that, Lizzie's heart expanded with love for her husband as she realized she wasn't the only one who'd fallen for the sweet baby girl.

"I understand. I'll get right on it for you."

"Thanks so much, Dan. We appreciate your help."

"Glad to do it. I'll call you later."

Jared ended that call and put through another to Mike, all the while holding Lizzie's gaze.

Her husband had never been sexier to her than he was since she realized he wanted this every bit as much as she did. "Lizzie and I have spoken to our attorney, and we'd like to offer Jessie a custody arrangement that would keep the baby with us if that's what she wants and if the child's father is also amenable. We'll have something for you to present to her in the morning." After listening for a minute, Jared nodded. "That sounds good. Thanks again, Mike."

Jared ended the call and put the phone on the counter. "He said someone from his office can print out the agreement Dan writes up and bring it to him in the morning to present to her."

"How are you feeling about this?" Lizzie asked him as she swayed back and forth, which helped to keep the baby sleeping.

"I hope we're not setting ourselves up for disaster."

"Maybe we are, but I'd rather try than always wonder what might've been if only we had."

"I've said it before, and I'll say it again—you're the strongest, gutsiest person I've ever known."

"No, I'm not. I feel like a bowl of Jell-O on the inside. My heart is racing, and I can barely breathe at the thought of us possibly getting to keep her—or possibly having to give her back to Jessie."

"We're going to have to find a way to chill until tomorrow, when we'll know more."

"How exactly are we supposed to do that?"

Cooper picked that moment to come into the kitchen with Gigi. He stopped short at the sight of Jared and Lizzie standing in what probably appeared to be tense poses. "What's wrong?"

"Nothing," Jared said. "Yet. We found Jessie."

"Oh. Isn't that, like, a good thing?"

"Yes and no." Jared updated Cooper on the latest development.

"Whoa." Cooper looked from Jared to Lizzie and then back to Jared. "So, you guys might get to keep her?"

"We're not letting ourselves go there until Mike speaks to Jessie tomorrow. But we're making the offer."

"Holy crap," Cooper said. "That's exciting and terrifying."

"All at the same time," Lizzie said, keeping her arms wrapped around the baby as if that could somehow stop anything bad from happening. She was never going to survive having to give her up. That much she knew for certain.

"What can we do for you?" Gigi asked.

"Keep us entertained?" Lizzie said. "Help us keep our minds off it for a few hours?"

"That we can do," Cooper said.

They pitched in to help finish the meal prep and enjoyed a delightful dinner at the table on the patio. Vi slept through everything until they were finishing dinner.

Lizzie handed her to Jared while she went inside to prepare a bottle. A week ago tonight, Lizzie hadn't known she existed, and now the baby girl was the center of her life. Along with Jared, of course. While the bottle heated, she took a deep breath and let it out slowly. By this time tomorrow, they'd know whether Jessie would agree to a permanent arrangement.

Then the child's father would have to be located.

They were a long way from home free in this situation, but they were closer than they'd been this time yesterday.

Jared came into the kitchen carrying Vi, who was squalling with outrage. "I told her the bottle was coming, but it wasn't fast enough for her."

Lizzie tested the temperature of the formula on her inner arm and then handed the bottle to Jared. "Here you go, my sweet girl."

The baby latched on, sucking greedily while Jared and Lizzie watched over her in stunned amazement that anything could be as beautiful as she was.

"We're going to get to keep her," Lizzie whispered. "I know it in my heart." She looked up at her husband, met his intense gaze and shared the thing she'd kept to herself until then. "You're going to think I'm even crazier than usual when I tell you the minute I saw her at the clinic, I knew she was meant to be ours."

"You… You *what?*"

"I knew, Jared. I knew it here." She flattened her hand over her heart. "I couldn't have known that Jessie would leave her with us and take off, but I knew she was our child. I don't know how I knew that. I just did."

"Lizzie…"

"I know. I know. It's insane, but I can only tell you how I felt." She offered a shy smile. "I was afraid to tell you that before now when you've been so upset about this."

"I've only been upset about the potential for you to be hurt. That's all."

"What about you?" She reached up to caress his face. "Don't try to tell me you haven't lost your heart to her, too."

"I have. For sure. I mean, look at her. She's so perfect. But I never want anything to hurt you, and that's why I've urged proceeding with caution."

"I know, and I love you for always trying to protect me—sometimes from myself."

"I'll always protect you from things that can hurt you." He kissed the top of the baby's soft head. "Even little bits like her."

"She's not going to hurt me. She's going to make my life—and yours—complete."

"God, I hope so, Lizzie."

"It's going to be okay. Trust me."

Jared glanced out the window to the table, where Cooper was sitting as close to Gigi as he could get and not be on her lap. "We should get back to our guests."

"They're doing a good job of entertaining themselves."

"I think he really likes her. Like, seriously likes her."

"He does. For sure."

"I hope she's not going to crush him."

"I have a good feeling about them, too. They might be just what the other one needs."

CHAPTER 23

"How much longer until we can go back to bed?" Cooper asked as he placed strategic kisses on Gigi's neck. Since she'd agreed to give him a real chance, he'd been higher than he'd ever been in his entire life. All he wanted was her, and he wanted her with a ferocity that was all new to him.

His phone, which was lying on the table, lit up with a text he ignored. What did he care about texts when he was breathing in the most intoxicating scent in the entire world?

"Who's Lacey?" Gigi asked.

Oh shit. "A friend in New York." He kept kissing her even as she leaned away from him.

"She's feeling needy and wants you to come service her."

Fuck. That was the last thing he needed two hours after he'd finally convinced Gigi to take a chance with him. "She's an ex. We dated years ago, and I haven't seen her in ages. Now get back over here where I can reach you."

"How many Laceys are out there waiting for you to return to New York?"

"There's no one waiting for me."

"That's what you think. They're probably staked outside your place waiting for you with signs that say Find Cooper and He's All Mine."

Cooper gave her a lighthearted bop on the head. "You're silly."

"Am I? I bet there are hundreds of Laceys blowing up your phone morning, noon and night."

"The only so-called Lacey I want to hear from is my California Girl, and she knows it." He kissed her softly, aware that Jared and Lizzie could return at any moment.

"If we, you know, try to make something of this, there couldn't be anyone else, Cooper. That's kind of a hard line for me."

"I can't believe you think you even have to say that. I don't want anyone but you. From the second I saw you swimming in my brother's pool in that white bikini, before I even knew who you were, I wanted you. I wanted to know you, and now that I do, I want to know more. I want to know everything there is to know."

"Why me and not one of the thousands of Laceys?"

Smiling at how the number kept going up, he said, "All I can tell you is something happened with you that's never happened to me before."

"What does it feel like?"

He wondered if she felt as vulnerable as she looked when she asked him that. "Remember the first time you got high?"

"I've never gotten high."

Cooper pulled back, stunned. "Seriously?"

"Very seriously. No safety net, Cooper. I didn't have the luxury of doing the stupid shit other kids did. I had to support myself while going to college and law school. I had no time for pot or bullshit."

"Have I mentioned lately that I think you're amazing?"

She rolled her eyes. "Anyway, the first time you got high..."

"Let me preface this by saying I've mostly left my pot-smoking habit in the past, but the first time, you feel like you've lifted off in a hot-air balloon, and everything is just quiet and peaceful and perfect. That's how I feel with you, along with this extra feeling right here." He put his hand over his heart. "It's this breathless, lighter-than-air happy thing that has me counting the minutes until I can see you again and not thinking of anything but you when I'm with you. Everything about it is different from anything I've felt before. I'm not sure if that makes any sense, but—"

She surprised the crap out of him when she leaned in to kiss him. "It's the loveliest thing anyone has ever said to me."

"I mean it, Gigi. I swear to God. I mean it."

"I know, and I'm trying to wrap my head around it."

"Take your time, sweetheart. I'm not going anywhere without you."

"Break it up, lovers," Jared said loudly as he and Lizzie returned to the patio. Jared carried a tray, while Lizzie held the baby monitor she'd had overnighted to the island and a big glass of wine. "Dessert is served. Lizzie made shortcake from scratch to go with fresh strawberries and homemade whipped cream."

"So not only are you the nicest, kindest person in the universe, you're also Wonder Woman," Gigi said. "Juggling a baby and making homemade shortcake and whipped cream. I bow down in awe."

Lizzie giggled. "Oh stop. It was fun to do something normal. I love to cook."

"And I love to eat," Jared said, "which is one of many reasons we're a match made in heaven."

"You two are cute," Gigi said, taking a sip of her vodka cocktail.

"Funny, we were saying the same about you two when we were spying on you from the kitchen," Lizzie said.

"We have big news," Cooper said, grinning at Gigi, who once again rolled her eyes at him.

"What big news?" Jared asked.

"The stunningly beautiful, incredibly funny, sexy, take-no-prisoners Gabrielle Gibson has agreed to give me a chance to show her that I make for an excellent boyfriend when I put my mind to it."

"Wow," Jared said, seeming genuinely stunned. "That's big news indeed."

"Tell me the truth," Gigi said. "Am I a fool to give a player like him a chance?"

"Not at all," Jared said. "Cooper is one of the good guys. He's smart, loyal, fun, funny, dedicated, hardworking. He'd be one of the first people I'd want in my foxhole when shit goes sideways, and he's been one of my best friends since the time he could first walk and talk."

Cooper was so stunned by Jared's effusiveness that he could only stare at his older brother as he tried to process everything he'd said.

"What?" Jared said, laughing at Cooper's amazement. "None of that is news to you."

"I've just, uh, never heard you say all that before."

"I mean every word of it. Anyone would be incredibly lucky to have you as a boyfriend, not that anyone has ever truly test-driven that word with you."

"Now we're getting to the heart of the matter," Gigi said, laughing. "Do tell, Jared."

"Shut up, Jared," Cooper said, glaring at his brother.

"You can't shut up right when things are getting interesting," Gigi said, smiling at Cooper. "I want to hear all about the *millions* of Laceys in his life."

"Oh, Lacey," Jared said. "She was one of the crazy ones, right?"

"Jared! Stop!"

"Don't you dare stop now," Gigi said. "How many are we talking? Hundreds? Thousands?"

Jared laughed as he glanced at Cooper, who stared daggers at him. "Let me just say that my baby brother has always been popular with the ladies, but I've never seen him as interested in one as he is in you."

Cooper let out the breath he'd been holding. He should've known Jared would have his back. He always did.

"He's truly one of the good ones, Gigi," Jared said. "I believe it's safe to have faith in anything he's promised you."

"That's good to know. He talks a big game, your brother."

"It's not a game," Cooper said, his expression as dead serious as it had ever been. "Nothing about this is a game to me."

"That's good to know."

Cooper couldn't wait to be alone with her again so he could show her just how dead serious he was about her.

GIGI WAS STILL REELING from the public declaration Cooper had made in front of his brother and sister-in-law. It had become clear to her that he wasn't saying what she wanted to hear, but rather, speaking his truth. He was falling for her, and she was falling right back. That scared the shit out of her as someone who went out of her way to save her limited pool of true love and affection for the three people she knew for certain would never hurt her.

Although, she had to admit that she'd come to truly love Riley and Mason, too, as well as Finn and Chloe, all of whom had become close friends during this summer on Gansett. They would never be on the same level as Nikki, Jordan and Evelyn, but all of them had made Gigi feel welcome in their tight circle, and that meant so much to her.

And now there was Cooper, Jared and Lizzie, too.

That was a lot of people for a girl like her to care about, Gigi thought as she led Cooper up the stairs to her place after Jared and Lizzie had gone to get some sleep while they could. Not that either of them would get much sleep tonight with such a big day coming up for them tomorrow.

"What do you think will happen with the baby?" Gigi asked Coop.

"Jessie will take their offer."

"You sound so confident when they're anything but."

"I got to know Jessie a little bit when she was here, and I could tell she had no idea what to do with a baby. She left her with Lizzie because she knew Lizzie would take good care of her."

"I hope you're right. They'll be heartbroken if she wants her back."

"I have a good feeling that things will work out well for them and their little girl." He turned and drew her into his arms. "And for us."

"You really believe that?"

"I do. I just need to get you on board."

"I'm coming around. It's just… It's hard for me. I'm used to going it alone, and I like it that way."

"I understand that, and I respect you so much for what you've accomplished all on your own."

"It wasn't entirely on my own. Evelyn has had my back from the beginning. She helped me a lot."

"Still, you're not used to relying on someone else or allowing yourself to feel things that have the power to hurt you."

"No, I'm not used to any of that."

"Do you think you could get used to it? Eventually?"

"Maybe."

His smile lit up his sinfully handsome face, which was handsome even with road rash marring it. One benefit to having him around so much was that she got to look at his gorgeous face, eyes and smile any time she wanted. That was something she could get used to very easily. He led her into her bedroom, helped her out of the dress she'd worn to dinner and ran his hands over her with a reverence that was also new to her. Men didn't revere her. They pawed her, took what they could get and left.

Cooper wasn't like that. Every time they were together this way, he treated her as if she was the most precious thing in his life, and that was another thing she could get used to. If she allowed herself to go there. Even as he helped her into bed, stripped out of his own clothes and got in next to her, Gigi was aware of an invisible wall that remained firmly erected between them that would allow him to get only so close.

As long as that wall remained in place, she felt safe, even as he held her as close to him as he could get her, their legs intertwined as he stared at her for the longest time.

"What?"

"Nothing. I like to look at you."

She screwed up her face and made the silliest expression she could come up with.

Cooper laughed. "Even still. You're gorgeous."

"You're delusional."

"I must be, because even when you try to make yourself ugly, it doesn't work." He placed his hand on her face and caressed her cheek with his thumb.

The way he looked at her made her feel bubbly inside, as if she'd swallowed a gallon of champagne. And when he kissed her, all the agitation that was so much a part of who she was seemed to disappear. He was making a believer of her, and she wasn't sure whether to be elated or terrified.

The man certainly knew his way around a woman's body. She suspected he'd had a ton of practice, but if all that practice was preparing him for her, she supposed she could live with it.

"Why are you thinking so hard?"

"Huh?"

"You get that bump right here," he said, kissing between her brows, "when you're overthinking something."

Gigi sighed with the realization that she'd never stood a chance against him. There was absolutely no point resisting him or his certainty that the two of them were meant to be. He'd made a believer out of her.

"Cooper."

He was kissing her neck and making her shiver. "Hmm?"

"I need to tell you something."

"I'm listening."

"It's important."

Raising his head, he met her gaze. "What's up?"

She placed both hands on his face and felt his late-day whiskers poking her palms.

"Just tell me, sweetheart. Whatever it is, I promise I want to hear it."

"If you… If you break my heart, I'll never recover from it."

"Aw, babe. That's the last thing I'd ever do. If you take this chance with me, I swear to you, I'll take very good care of you and your fragile heart."

"That's good to know."

"I mean it, Gigi. I'd be so happy to have you in my life, I'd do everything I could to keep you there."

"You've given me a lot to think about."

"While you think," he said, drawing her nipple into his mouth, "I can come up with lots of ways we can have all kinds of fun together."

God, the man was good at that, and *that*. He was unreasonably good at *that* and had her hovering on the edge of release with the least amount of effort ever expended by man or toy. *How* did he do that?

"Are you still sore?" he asked.

"Not like I was."

"Hold that thought." He got up to find his shorts and retrieve a condom.

As he stood by the bed with that huge erection stretching past his belly button, Gigi said, "Hey, Coop?"

"Yes, ma'am?"

"I'm on birth control, and I'm clean. If you are, too, then I guess we don't really need the condom."

Staring at her, seeming stunned, he said, "If I heard you correctly, you're saying we don't need this?" He held up the foil packet.

"That's what I said," she replied, trying not to giggle at his reaction.

"I, um, you might want to, we might want to, uh, you know, take the edge off before we do that, or it'll be over before it begins."

Gigi rose to her knees and made her way to the edge of the bed, grasping his cock in a tight grip. "You need me to take the edge off like this?"

His Adam's apple bobbed in his throat as he nodded. "That works."

"Would this work better?" Gigi asked as she bent to take him into her mouth.

He sucked in a sharp deep breath. "That'd work *faster*."

She held back the laugh so she could focus on his pleasure.

"Shit, Gigi, you're making my legs shake." He buried his fingers in her hair and held on tight as he moved in time to the rhythm she set. "Geeeeeg... Ah, God... You'd better stop unless you want..."

She sucked hard and rubbed her tongue against the shaft.

He exploded, his entire body shaking with the force of his release.

Pleased with herself, she released him slowly, going for ultimate effect that made him tremble some more. "Is the edge off now?"

"I'm demolished."

She leaned forward and placed gentle kisses on the ugly bruises on his ribs, aching for the pain the injuries had caused him.

He wrapped his arms around her and kissed the top of her head. "That was the best I've ever had."

"Out of how many?"

"Shut up," he said, laughing.

"No, really. Are we talking a baseball team or the crowd that comes to the game? Probably the latter."

Laughing, he gave her a gentle push that had her flopping onto her back, her breasts bouncing as she landed. He came down on top of her and kissed her hard. "You think you're so funny."

"I know I'm funny, and millions of people agree with me." She'd never had this kind of fun with a man. That much she knew for certain.

"I knew there was a diva hiding inside you, what with all those millions of fans hanging on your every word. How could you not be?"

"I'm not a diva!" She pinched his ass. "Take that back!"

Cooper cracked up. "Touched a nerve, did I?"

"Yes! I'm a lawyer, not a diva."

"Uh, sweetheart, I hate to be the bearer of bad news, but you're not just a lawyer anymore. You're a huge star with a massive fan base, and I'd like to apply for the position of number one fan." As he said that, he nudged her with his reawakened erection.

That's what she got for tangling with a younger guy who still had stamina. "I'll take that under consideration."

"Will you take this under consideration, too?" he asked as he pushed into her.

At first, her body wasn't having it, and she almost told him to stop.

"Relax, sweetheart, we'll go nice and slow."

"Easy for you to say relax when you're not the one being impaled by a billy club."

Cooper faltered as he lost it laughing. "Don't make me laugh. You'll mess with my concentration."

"I won't make you laugh if you don't tell me to relax when you're coming at me with that gigantic *thing*."

"I'm hurt on behalf of my gigantic thing."

"Tell me the truth. It was the entire stadium, right?"

"Stop talking."

"Make me."

He kissed her with unleashed desire as he worked his way into her slowly but surely, until she was out of her mind, lost to him in every possible way as he owned her body, heart and soul. Even a jaded soul like hers could recognize that everything about this—and him—was special.

All she could do was hold on to him as he took her on the wildest ride of her life that ended with an orgasm for the ages. As she screamed from the pleasure, she was thankful for air-conditioning and closed windows, or they'd be giving Jared and Lizzie one hell of a show.

"Give me another one," he whispered.

Gigi laughed and then moaned as he slammed into her again, letting her know he wasn't joking. And damn if the telltale signs of reawakened desire didn't set her entire body on fire for more of his special brand of magic. "Cooper." She arched into him.

"Yes, Gigi, like that. Take it all."

God, what choice did she have but to take everything he had to give her, and as she tripped over the edge of the Grand Canyon into something big and scary, she couldn't find anything to stop the fall.

CHAPTER 24

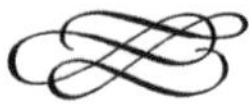

Cindy told herself she was going to the Beachcomber for the music, but if she was being truthful, she hoped to see Jace again. She felt silly to be halfway crushing on a tattooed bartender with a rough edge to him, but she hadn't stopped thinking about him since the other night.

While laid low with a migraine the night before, she'd stared up at the ceiling in her dark bedroom and wondered what his story was, and that had brought her back to a stool at his bar for dinner.

"Hey, beautiful." That charming smile had probably made many a pair of panties go damp. "Good to see you."

"You, too."

He poured an ice water and added a flourish of lemon.

"Thank you." She appreciated that he didn't seem to resent her for taking a place at his bar from someone who'd run up a big tab. "Anything good on the specials menu tonight?"

"As a matter of fact," he said, producing a printed page, "the natives are raving about the seafood casserole."

Cindy read the description of the dish and nearly drooled. "Sign me up."

"Baked potato, fries or rice?"

"I'll take the fries, even though I should have the rice."

"Fries for the pretty lady. Cole slaw, side salad or veggie medley?"

Cindy felt her cheeks flush at the compliment, which was mortifying. "Slaw, please, and tartar sauce on the side?"

"You got it. Coming right up."

As he went to put her order into the computer, she watched him covertly. His muscles bulged under his uniform shirt as he worked on the computer. When he glanced at her, he caught her watching him and smiled. "No allergies to shellfish, right?"

"Nope. All good."

"Excellent."

While she enjoyed her ice water and Niall's always-entertaining music, she watched Jace move around the bar. He offered every customer a friendly welcome and fast service that indicated seasoned experience behind a bar. He laughed easily, and his friendliness had his tip jar filling up fast.

Cindy played a game of gin rummy with her new friend, Piper Bennett, who was helping Laura at the Surf. Their game ended prematurely when Piper was called back to work to deal with a crisis at the front desk.

"Is this seat taken?"

Cindy was surprised to see her brother John, who'd been keeping a low profile since he'd arrived on the island a couple of weeks ago. "All yours, brother."

"How're you feeling? Mom said you had a migraine yesterday."

"Better today than last night, which was rough. The new meds help to keep them from being multiday events."

"That's good. I remember how bad they were when we were all at home."

"And how Dad never wanted to hear I was sick."

"'Get up and shake it off,' he'd say. The asshole."

"Such an asshole, who's exactly where he belongs." The relief of retired General Mark Lawry being in prison and permanently out of their lives was something his seven children were still coming to terms with months after he pleaded guilty to assaulting their mother. Thankfully, she was now happily remarried to the wonderful Charlie Grandchamp.

"Have you talked to Katie?" he asked.

"Earlier in the week."

"How's she doing? I've been afraid to ask."

"A little better. She's hoping to go back to work next week."

"I wonder why miscarriages happen the way they do."

"I suppose it's the universe's way of saying that particular baby wasn't meant to be. She and Shane can try again in a couple of months."

"You're sure she's all right?"

"Shane is taking good care of her, and Mom and Julia have been there every day. I took food, and Laura did, too. She's holding up okay."

"I never want anything to hurt any of you guys after what we've already put up with."

"We feel the same about you, you know."

Jace came back to their end of the bar and took a measuring look at John, who had blond hair and blue eyes and favored their older brother Owen. Was it her imagination, or did Jace seem annoyed to see her sitting with a man? "Jace, this is my brother John. John, this is Jace."

The two men shook hands.

"Good to meet you," Jace said, smiling since she said the word *brother*. "What can I get you to drink?"

"What've you got on tap?"

After Jace gave him the rundown, John said, "A Sam Summer, please."

"Coming right up. Are you eating?"

"Sure."

Jace handed him the menu and the list of specials and then went to get his beer.

"I'm having the seafood casserole that's on the specials list. Jace says people are loving it."

"Jace says that, huh? He didn't seem too happy to see you chatting with me."

"Don't be silly. I just met him the other night."

"He likes you."

"Stop it."

John nudged her. "You're blushing."

"Go away."

Her brother laughed, which was a welcome sight. He'd been in a deep funk since he'd come home for their mother's wedding to Charlie.

"Nice to hear you laugh," Cindy said. "We've been worried about you."

His smile immediately faded. "Sorry about that."

"What's going on with you? And don't you need to get back to work?" He was a police officer in Tennessee and had said something about an issue with a superior officer. But Cindy hadn't heard any more than that.

Jace returned with John's beer.

"Thanks. I'll have the same order as my sister."

"With fries, slaw and tartar sauce?"

"Yes, please."

"You got it. Want me to bring them out together?"

"That'd be good," Cindy said. "Thanks, Jace."

"Anything for you," Jace said with a wink and a smile.

"I rest my case," John said.

"He probably says that stuff to everyone. Check out his tip jar. Charm pays."

"He likes *you*."

Hearing her brother confirm what she already suspected made Cindy feel like she'd been dropped off the steep side of a roller coaster. "Enough about me. Let's talk about you."

"I'd rather talk about you," he said glumly.

"I've got nothing to say. You, on the other hand, haven't been yourself since you got here, and the fact that you're not in a big rush to get back to work tells me something's up."

"Yeah, something's up." He sipped from his beer and shredded the cocktail napkin into confetti. "I was, um, seeing someone I worked with, and it ended badly."

"I'm so sorry. Do you want to talk about it?"

"Not really, but I, um, quit the department."

Cindy was shocked by that news. John had loved that job. "*For real?* It was that bad?"

"It was with my sergeant. One of us had to go, and it wasn't going to be him."

Him.

"Oh, I, um… I hadn't realized."

"That's because I went to great lengths to keep my private life off the general's radar. You've heard his hateful rants about 'fags' and how they're ruining everything."

"You dated women. A lot of women."

"To keep him off the scent."

"God, John. I'm so sorry you had to go through that."

"We all went through something horrible at his hands. Why should I be any different?"

"True." Cindy sipped her water as she tried to process what her brother had told her. "You quit your job, though. What about your pension?"

"I get to keep a portion of it, which I'll invest. I'll figure it out. I couldn't stay there after people found out about us, and it turned into a BFD. I was afraid he was going to kill me."

"You really worried about that?"

"He was so angry that people found out about us. I think he thought I told someone, which I didn't. I never would've done that to either of us."

"So how did they find out?"

"That's a good question. I think he told someone and then tried to blame it on me."

"That's screwed up."

"Yep, and now here I am out of a job and a relationship all at the same time."

She put her arm around him. "I'm *so* sorry that happened to you, Johnny."

He leaned into her embrace. "Thanks, sis. I'll be okay. I've got some money saved, and Mom and Charlie told me to stay as long as I need to. I'll figure something out."

Jace returned bearing plates he put in front of them. "Clams casino, specialty of the house."

"Uh, we didn't order that," Cindy said, glancing at her brother.

"It's on me," Jace said with the charming smile that made her heart beat a little faster. "Enjoy."

"He *likes* you," John said the second Jace moved on to other customers.

"Shut up and eat your clams."

John's laughter rang through the bar. "Cindy's got a boyfriend," he said in a singsong voice, "and may I say, he's a *fine*-looking man."

Yes, he certainly is, Cindy thought. What did it mean that he was treating her—and her brother—to something special off the menu?

. . .

GIGI WOKE to a text to her and Jordan from Matilda. *Rise and shine, ladies! I need a meeting with you two this morning at nine to discuss the final episode. Please come alone to my hotel. This meeting is just for the three of us, and I'll provide breakfast. Thanks!*

Jordan replied a minute later. *Why does she have to be so chipper in the morning? It's annoying.*

Seriously annoying, Gigi said.

Matilda responded with laughing emojis. *I can hear you two! Get your asses out of bed and get to work!*

Gigi groaned and started to carefully extricate herself from the tight hold Cooper had on her. She usually hated when guys slept all over her, but she didn't seem to mind it with him.

All her usual rules had gone out the window since she met him, and with shooting coming to a close, she needed to get back to normal, whatever that was these days.

She managed to get out of bed without waking him and took a long, hot shower to clear her mind and body of thoughts of the man who'd rocked her world three times during the night. But when she emerged from the shower twenty minutes later, she was still thinking about him, still reeling, still reliving every second with him and still trying to believe she might get to keep him. Despite the seismic shift that had occurred yesterday, a big part of her still refused to believe something this good could last forever.

"Why you up so early?" Cooper asked, his eyes still closed.

"Got a meeting with the producer. Don't you have your thing with the McCarthys this morning?" He was pitching his business idea to Big Mac McCarthy, Luke Harris and Kara Torrington at the marina.

"Uh-huh. It's in an hour."

"You'd better get moving."

"Only takes me a minute to get ready."

Gigi got dressed in a sleeveless white dress and wedge sandals. "I'm coming back in my next life as a man."

"That'd be tragic, sweetheart."

Her heart ached in a way it hadn't in years, since the dreadful months that led up to her taking the extraordinary step to emancipate from the only "family" she'd ever had. It had been easier to go it alone ever since then. That had worked for her until Cooper came along and offered her things she had no business being tempted to accept. But oh, how he tempted her in every possible way.

"You want to come to the surprise party for Chloe's thirtieth tonight at the Wayfarer?" Cooper asked, sitting up now in bed and checking his phone.

"I'll have to see what Matilda wants with us and whether we're working tonight."

"Let me know?"

"Sure. I'll try."

She glanced his way and caught him frowning as he stared at her intently.

"What's wrong?" he asked.

"Huh? Nothing."

"Don't lie to me, Gigi. You're all closed off and sealed up this morning. What happened?"

You happened, she wanted to scream at him. "Nothing happened. I'm just annoyed that Matilda called me out of bed to come to some unscheduled bullshit meeting." She twirled her damp hair into an updo and captured it with a small clip.

"And that's all it is?"

"Of course," she said, turning to face him with a smile even as her heart continued to ache like a bastard with fear. She hated fear. It made her feel weak and pathetic. "What else would it be?" Before she left the bedroom, she went to the bedside table to get her phone off the charger.

Cooper reached out a hand to her.

Gigi was almost afraid to touch him. She put her hand in his.

"Last night was amazing," he said, kissing the back of her hand. "Let's do that again soon, okay?"

"Sure." She had to get out of there and away from him before she shattered into a million pieces that could never be put back together into the person she'd been before he found her in his brother's pool. "Gotta go. Matilda gets pissed when we keep her waiting."

"Let me know about the party," he said, pressing his lips to the back of her hand one more time.

"I will."

He released her hand, but continued to watch her in that knowing, all-seeing way of his that made her feel naked even when she was fully dressed.

As she headed out of the apartment, she hoped the coffee was good at Matilda's hotel, because Gigi needed a good strong kick in the pants to keep her from doing something really stupid, like falling in love with Cooper James.

She's a goddamned liar, Cooper thought as he watched Gigi leave, fully aware that at some point, she'd retreated behind her wall and was looking for a way to end this thing with him. Maybe not today or tomorrow, but soon. What the hell had happened between her third screaming orgasm and that show she'd just put on for him?

Cooper sat on her bed, picking over every second of last night, trying to find the moment when things had gone wrong. But the only thing he remembered was pure bliss, and he had no doubt whatsoever that she'd experienced the same thing.

That was probably the issue. Too much of a good thing made Gigi skittish. She wasn't accustomed to someone stepping up for her and offering to be her safety net under the emotional high-wire act she performed so effortlessly. She was so used to needing nothing and no one that she had no idea how to let him in.

He ached for her.

And he loved her.

Maybe it was too soon, but he couldn't deny that the feelings he had for her were bigger than anything he'd known before. He'd certainly done his share of "research," so he knew different when he saw it and felt it. Despite all his serial dating, he'd always hoped he'd find that one special person he could spend a lifetime with. Until Gigi, he hadn't met anyone who'd come close to reaching the high bar he'd set for a lifetime companion.

He wanted a woman he could laugh with, someone he could be entirely himself with, someone who did it for him in bed and who he could build something lasting with. Gigi checked every one of his boxes and others that hadn't been on his list until he met her.

His ribs hurt right along with his heart as he hauled himself up, got dressed, made her bed and left to see what was new with Jared and

Lizzie's situation while he tried to figure out what to do about his own problem.

Cooper walked into the kitchen, where Jared and Lizzie were seated with the baby in Lizzie's arms as they stared at Jared's phone, seemingly trying to will it to ring. "I'd ask how it's going, but I can see you're waiting to hear."

"Mike is meeting with Jessie now, and we're dying a slow, painful death waiting to hear from him," Jared said.

At some point, his brother had become as invested in the baby as Lizzie was, Cooper thought. He prayed to God and every higher power there ever was that they got to keep the baby. "Is there anything I can do for you?"

"I wish there was," Jared said. "Isn't your meeting with Mr. McCarthy this morning?"

Cooper reached his hand out to the baby, and his heart melted when she held on tight to his index finger. "It is. I'm going to shower and change." The baby let out a squawk of protest when Cooper reclaimed his finger. She was so damned cute. "Keep me posted on what you hear from Mike?"

"Yeah, we will," Jared said.

Cooper was concerned about the way Lizzie sat staring off into space as if she needed to escape from the reality unfolding in front of her. He couldn't blame her. He could hardly bear it for her.

He showered and changed into khaki shorts and a polo shirt in deference to the island's casual atmosphere. For the first time since he was injured, he shaved, avoiding the parts of his face that were still healing. It was still a mess, but not as much of a mess as it had been a few days ago. When he was ready, he gathered the proposal he'd put together and flipped through it one last time, even though he knew every word in it by heart. This plan had dominated his life over the last two years, and now it was show time.

Cooper returned to the kitchen, where things were exactly as he'd left them half an hour ago.

"You want to take the car?" Jared asked.

"Do you mind?"

"Not as long as you don't go anywhere near the bluffs."

Cooper stopped short at that. "How did you hear about that?"

"What does it matter?" Jared asked with a cocky grin. "I've told you before that your obsession with selfies was going to get you killed."

"I think I've officially been cured of my obsession."

"In that case, you can take the car, son."

"Thanks, Dad." Cooper grinned at his brother as he grabbed the keys off the counter.

"Good luck at the marina. They're great people to get into business with."

"Appreciate your help in arranging the meeting."

"No problem."

"Text me if anything changes here, okay?"

"Will do."

Cooper squeezed Lizzie's shoulder as he walked by her on the way out. He was worried about her and how this situation was affecting her.

CHAPTER 25

The drive to the marina took ten minutes. Cooper chose a parking space on the street before the more crowded marina parking lot, hoping the car would be safer there. He should've known it would only be a matter of time before Jared learned the details of what'd happened at the bluffs. It was a wonder he let him borrow the car again after hearing what he'd done. But his older brother had always been forgiving where Cooper was concerned, and he considered himself blessed to have Jared in his life.

He loved his other siblings, too, but was closest to Jared. Quinn had been away in the military from the time Cooper was very young, so he'd gotten to know him well only in the last few years since his brother retired, and his sisters had both been married for more than ten years. As the much younger brother to all of them, Cooper had struggled to connect with the others until he, too, was an adult, and they'd stopped treating him like a baby.

Cooper was a full-grown man and determined to succeed in business and in life. When he'd come to Gansett, he'd been focused only on the business side of that equation. But since he met Gigi, his plans had expanded to include her. If only he could convince her to include him in her plans. That was a challenge for later. For now, he had to keep his wits about him to pitch his business idea to Mr. McCarthy and the others.

He'd been working toward this moment for two years, and as he walked toward the open garage doors Mr. McCarthy had told him to look for, he took a deep breath to calm the fluttering nerves in his belly. He recognized Big Mac McCarthy right away from the wedding. He was sitting at a picnic table with a group of guys, laughing and talking over coffee and doughnuts. The smell of fried dough made Cooper's mouth water.

"Hey, Coop," Big Mac said, standing. "Good to see you again."

Cooper shook his outstretched hand. "You, too."

"I'd know you anywhere. You look like both your brothers."

"Only much younger and far more handsome," Cooper said, making them laugh.

Laughter, he'd learned, opened a lot of doors when dealing with other people.

"You might remember these characters from Quinn and Mallory's wedding. This is my partner Luke Harris, my best friend Ned Saunders and my brother Frankie."

"Good to see you all again," Cooper said, shaking hands with each of the men.

"Good ta see ya, too," Ned said.

"We're waiting for Kara, but she should be here soon," Big Mac said. "The poor gal is dealing with horrible morning sickness."

"Sorry to hear it."

"She's usually better by nine, so she'll be along soon. My son Mac is our other partner, and he's sorry to miss meeting you. As you know, he's still in Providence with his wife and newborn daughters."

"How're the babies doing?"

"Excellent. We're hearing they might come home at the end of the week."

"That's very good news."

"Speaking of babies," Luke said, "has your brother heard anything from the mother of the baby staying with them?"

"The investigator Jared hired found her. We're waiting to hear about next steps." He'd keep the rest of the story private until Jared and Lizzie got an answer to their proposal.

"Let's get you a coffee and some doughnuts before we get started."

"I won't say no to either."

Ten minutes later, he was settled at the picnic table with a coffee and a new plate of freshly made sugar doughnuts.

"Holy crap, that's good," he said of his first bite of doughnut.

"Specialty of the house," Big Mac said with a grin. "I swear they're what bring in most of our repeat customers each season."

"The atmosphere is pretty cool, too," Cooper said.

"We like it," Big Mac replied. "I read over the proposal you emailed last week, and I really like your idea a lot."

"Oh, good. That's nice to hear."

"I have some concerns, though. Chiefly, the combination of boats and alcohol can be worrisome."

"Yes, I agree, and that's why we'd institute a three-drink limit for each customer by offering tickets that they can redeem. Once they're out of tickets, they're out of drinks."

"What do you do about people who show up already loaded?" Luke asked.

"We're going to breathalyze everyone, and we retain the right to deny passage to anyone who's impaired."

Luke nodded, seeming satisfied by that reply. "If we allow you to dock your boats here, we'd want to be released from any liability."

"Understood," Cooper said.

"I'm here," a pretty redheaded woman said. "Sorry I'm late."

A handsome dark-haired man followed her. Something about him was familiar to Cooper.

"I'm Kara Torrington," she said. "This is my husband, Dan."

Ah, right. The world-famous attorney was known for freeing unjustly incarcerated people. Cooper shook their hands. "It's great to meet you both."

"Have a seat, honey," Dan said. "I'll order your smoothie."

"Thank you." Kara sat on the end of the picnic bench. "Particularly rough morning. This kid had better be worth it."

Big Mac laughed. "He or she will be. I promise."

"I'm gonna hold you to that. What'd I miss?"

"We were talking to Cooper about liability, booze and boating."

"Ah, yes, an often-lethal combination."

"He has a good plan for addressing it using drink tickets to limit consumption on the boats."

"I talked to my brothers about providing the boats, and they're interested in helping you out." She placed a business card on the table. "You can reach out to my brother Kieran, and he'll work with you to get what you need."

"This is awesome," Cooper said. "Thanks, Kara."

"No problem." She turned ghostly white and then green before she bolted from the table, running for the ladies' room.

"Something I said?" Cooper asked, grimacing.

"Happens like that just about every day," Luke said. "She thinks it's over, but it never is."

Dan came out of the restaurant carrying a takeout cup and straw along with a bag. He stopped short when he noticed Kara was missing. "Again?" he asked.

Big Mac used his thumb to point to the ladies' room.

"My poor baby mama," Dan said, sighing. "She's really suffering." He seemed torn about whether he should go after her, but took the seat she'd abandoned and helped himself to a doughnut. "I have to eat when she's not looking."

"I hope she feels better soon," Cooper said.

"Me, too," Dan said. "I can't bear it."

"It's always hardest on the fathers," Big Mac said gravely.

The other guys busted up laughing.

"I read your proposal," Dan said to Cooper between bites of his second doughnut. "You need a massive liability waiver. I can take care of that for you, if you'd like."

"Uh, yeah," Cooper said, stunned to have an attorney of Dan's caliber willing to help his fledgling business. "That'd be awesome."

"We'll sew it up tight so there're no loopholes."

"I'd appreciate that. So, it sounds like I've got the boats I need, and the legalities will be handled. I guess all that's left is whether you gentlemen are willing to lease me dock space next summer."

Big Mac glanced at Luke, who nodded.

"We'd be happy to," Big Mac said. "I also wanted to let you know that we're working on some wedding package deals and thought your business might make for a good fit."

"How so?" Cooper asked, intrigued.

"We also own the Wayfarer, and we're booking for next season's weddings, as well as planning the renovation of a former alpaca farm that we're going to use for smaller, more intimate weddings. We're putting together some packages that would include bridal party massages at our new spa that'll open next season at the hotel up the hill, along with reduced rates on hotel rooms and reduced dockage for wedding party guests who bring their boats over. It's a way to combine all our businesses into one big deal. Your bachelorette/bachelor party boats would be a nice addition to the package. We've also got the Curl Up and Dye salon on board to do wedding party hair and makeup and the Naughty and Nice shop to provide wedding night attire."

Cooper couldn't believe the way this was coming together or how savvy a businessman Big Mac McCarthy was. "I'd love to be part of your package deals."

"Perfect. I'll put you in contact with Nikki Stokes, the general manager at the Wayfarer. The packages were her idea, and she's putting together the details."

"That's great. I already know Nikki."

Dan stared at the ladies' room door. "Should I check on her?"

"Would she want you to?" Big Mac asked.

Dan shook his head. "She refuses to let me see her puke."

"Then I'd sit tight until she's done."

"I hate this," Dan said.

"It's tough to watch the one we love suffering," Big Mac said.

His words struck home for Cooper. He was watching the one he loved suffer through the possibility of falling in love for the first time. If only he could figure out how to help her understand how good they could be together. His phone chimed with a text from Jared.

Heard from Mike. He talked to Jessie, pitched our idea. She wants a few days to think about it.

Ugh.

"Crap," Dan said, making Cooper realize he'd been copied on the text.

"Speaking of unbearable," Cooper said.

"No kidding."

"Everything all right, gentlemen?" Big Mac asked.

"Just a development with Jared, Lizzie and the baby they're caring for," Cooper said. "We hope everything will be okay."

It had to be. It just had to be.

. . .

Jared was losing his mind. How were they supposed to wait *a couple more days* for an answer from Jessie? What did she have to think about? She'd dumped her newborn with them almost a week ago and hadn't so much as checked on her since then. If she thought they'd be returning the baby to her like nothing had happened, she was delusional.

If Jessie wanted her back, she'd have to deal with Blaine and social services first. How could they be sure Jessie intended to care for the child without some sort of formal review?

He stood at the edge of his property, looking out over the ocean crashing on the rocks below, wishing there was some way to resolve this hellish situation immediately.

Lizzie slipped her arms around his waist and rested her head on his back. The baby monitor dangled from her index finger.

Jared put his hand on top of hers. "I'm sorry this is so stressful, sweetheart. I'd hoped we'd have it resolved today."

"I'm the one who should be sorry. I brought this stress into our lives."

"You were trying to help someone in need. It's not your fault she dumped the baby with us and ran."

"She's had time and space to think, so I guess it's only natural she's reconsidering what she did."

"It's not fair to us for her to jerk us around this way."

"No, it isn't, but no matter what happens, we'll be okay because we have each other."

Jared pulled away from her, but only so he could turn toward her. Then he put his arms around her and held her tight. "How do you do that?"

"Do what?"

"Find that inner calm or whatever it is that makes it so you know what I need to hear?"

"I'm not sure how I do it, but the one thing I know for certain is we won't let this—or anything—break us."

"No, we won't."

"If we don't get to keep her, I'll be really sad because I already love her. But I promise either way, I'll be all right if you are."

"I am if you are." Jared held her close as tears burned his eyes. He couldn't remember the last time he'd felt like he might cry. Wait, yes, he could. It was after their last attempt at having a baby had failed. His cell phone rang, and he pulled back from the hug to retrieve it from his pocket and put it on speaker. "It's Mike." Lizzie kept her hands on his hips as he looped one arm around her. "Hey, Mike."

"Jessie called. She'd like to talk to you about a private adoption."

Lizzie let out a whimper.

Jared held her even tighter. "You have a copy of the temporary custody agreement to give her, right?"

"Already done, and I told her you'd cover the cost of her getting an attorney to walk her through the adoption process. She appreciated that. I set her up with an attorney friend of mine, and they're meeting in the morning to go over the details."

"And the father?"

"It was a one-night stand during a party, and she doesn't know his name and doesn't want to know his name. She was pretty adamant that he's not in the picture and isn't going to be. I think that's a big part of why this was so traumatic for her. She made a mistake and ended up with a baby."

"Thanks for your help with this, Mike." Jared was so overwhelmed, he could barely speak. They were going to be parents.

"Don't celebrate until the paperwork is signed," Mike said. "She could still change her mind."

"I hear you."

"I'll be back to you in the morning, hopefully with more good news."

"We'll be waiting for your call."

"Hang in there. We're close to getting this done."

"Thanks again." Jared ended the call and leaned his forehead against Lizzie's. "This might be happening."

She looked at him with barely contained joy and tears in her eyes. "I can't believe it."

"You heard what Mike said, though, about not celebrating yet."

"I'm already celebrating. Jessie knows this is the right thing to do for her little girl, and Dan wrote the agreement so she can visit her. It's the best possible solution."

Jared drew in a deep breath. "I'm afraid to get excited."

"I have a good feeling about this, and you know how my feelings are."

"They're always spot-on." He hesitated before he said, "She needs a name."

"Violet. We'll call her Vi."

"I love that. Could her middle name be Catherine, for my favorite grandmother?"

"Yes, of course. Violet Catherine James. It's a beautiful name for a beautiful girl."

"Our beautiful girl."

They hugged each other as tightly as they ever had, and when they pulled apart, both were in tears.

Lizzie reached up to brush his away. "We did it, Jared. Not the way we thought we would, but we did it just the same. I have to believe this was how it was meant to be."

"It does feel fated somehow, for sure. Thank goodness for you and your great big heart that can't help but get involved when you see someone in need. You brought Vi into our lives, and she's going to bring us so much joy."

"I can't wait to tell everyone the news."

"We have to wait until it's official."

"I know, but still... I can't wait."

With his hand cupping her cheek, he kissed her, thrilled to see her happier than she'd ever been. "I can't wait either. For everything."

CHAPTER 26

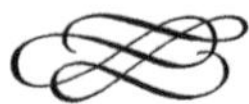

Jordan was late, and Matilda was getting pissed. "Where is she?" Matilda asked Gigi, checking her watch for the twentieth time in as many minutes. Every one of her short dark hairs was in perfect order and her makeup as flawless as ever. You could take the girl out of Hollywood, but the glam had come with her to Gansett. They were seated on the porch of her hotel with a splendid view of the Salt Pond, but Gigi was fairly certain Matilda hadn't even noticed the view.

"On her way."

"I said nine o'clock."

"You gave us an hour's notice. She might've been busy doing something."

"Like her firefighter?"

"Perhaps," Gigi said, cracking a grin. "They are rather insatiable."

"What's he going to do without her when she goes home to LA?"

The question astounded Gigi. Did Matilda honestly think Jordan was going to leave Mason to go home to LA? If so, she hadn't been paying attention. "No idea," she said, keeping her reply intentionally vague. It wasn't up to her to break the news to Matilda that Jordan had probably permanently relocated to Gansett Island.

"Well, I hope she gets here soon. We've got a lot to discuss."

As she sipped her second cup of coffee, Gigi was curious about what Matilda wanted to talk about, but her thoughts kept wandering to Cooper and how his meeting was going. He'd put so much work into his proposal. She hoped it was well received by the people he wanted to partner with. And she hoped Jared and Lizzie would get some good news about the baby before too much longer. They had to be stuck in purgatory waiting to hear from the baby's mother.

"Did you hear what I said?" Matilda asked.

"Oh, sorry, what?"

"I asked if you've reviewed the endorsement offers you've both received in the last couple of weeks."

"Not yet."

"What're you waiting for, Gigi? The two of you are sitting on a gold mine, and you need to strike while the iron is hot."

"We'll worry about that when we're done shooting the season."

"Those offers have shelf lives. You need to get on it."

Normally, Gigi didn't sit on stuff like that. She got shit done for herself and her clients, but since she'd come to Gansett, her sense of urgency had faded into an odd state of relaxation that had seriously messed with her mojo. It was time to go home, in more ways than one.

Jordan came rushing in five minutes later, full of apologies. "I'm so sorry I'm late."

"Where've you been?" Matilda asked.

"I had something I needed to take care of first thing, and time got away from me. Won't happen again."

Yes, it will, Gigi thought as she tried not to laugh at Jordan's bullshit. Judging by the freshly fucked look of her friend, Gigi concluded that the thing she'd had *to take care of first thing* had been Mason. Good for her.

"Now that you're both here, we have a lot to talk about," Matilda said. "First and foremost is the final episode of the season and how we want to leave things. We want to make sure the viewers are clamoring for next season the second this one ends."

"Ah, about that," Jordan said. "I don't think there's going to be another season."

Matilda stared at her as if Jordan had just said the sun was purple. "You're not serious. You two are sitting on the most popular show on cable. You don't walk away when you're number one, Jordan."

"Maybe it's not done, but that's what I want. I'm in love with Mason. We're expecting a baby and getting married, and we're going to live here. I'm going to keep working as the part-time activities director at the senior center and raise a family with the man I love."

Gigi had known it was coming, but to hear Jordan say it out loud was still a blow. Life as they'd known it in LA was over, and Gigi would be going home alone.

One thing Gigi could say for certain was that Jordan was doing the right thing for herself.

They'd shot a memorable episode with Jordan and Gigi entertaining the seniors for this season, and Gigi was looking forward to seeing that one put together. It'd been touching and hilarious at the same time. Jordan had a deft touch with the elderly population, and they adored her. Mason adored her, too. He loved her the way Jordan deserved to be loved, and no one was happier for her than Gigi, even if her heart broke at the thought of living so far from her best friend—and her best friend's sister.

They'd had a good run, but the time had come for them to live their lives separately. It would take a while for Gigi to get used to being without Jordan and Nikki, but she'd survive. She always did.

"What do you have to say about this, Gigi?" Matilda asked.

"It's her show. I'm just the sidekick."

"You're much more than that, and you know it," Jordan said. "I don't mean to mess things up for you, but I can't leave Mason. I won't leave him, especially now that we're expecting."

"Congratulations on the baby," Matilda said. "That's exciting news indeed, but none of this has to spell the end of the show. You two are magic together on camera, and I have to believe there's a way to continue with everyone getting what they want. One of the main reasons I wanted to see you both this morning is the network has prepared a major offer for three more seasons."

Matilda handed them each a sheet of paper that spelled out the terms of the multimillion-dollar deal that put Gigi's salary on the same level as Jordan's for the first time.

Jordan glanced at Gigi, seeming to gauge her reaction.

"You're the boss," Gigi said to her friend.

"I just don't know," Jordan said, seeming torn. "I love making the show with you both, but my life is here now. I'm not going back to LA. I've spoken to a Realtor there about putting my house on the market."

That news had Gigi struggling to swallow the huge lump that suddenly appeared in her throat. This was really happening. Jordan was staying on Gansett.

Stop being an emotional fool, Gigi told herself. *You knew that already. Yeah, but I hadn't heard her say it out loud.*

"I get what you're saying," Matilda said, "and I understand your desire to make a life here with Mason, but surely there has to be some sort of happy medium. Gansett's high season is the summer, so we can film in LA in the winter."

"Mason is the year-round fire chief on Gansett, Matilda. He can't come and go as he pleases."

Matilda sat back in her chair, seeming stunned. "You've both worked so hard to get to this point, Jordan. You're a big star in your own right, completely separate from Zane."

"Don't mention his name in our presence," Gigi said harshly.

"I'm sorry to bring him up, but we both know that's how this started, through your connection to him. But it's gone so far beyond that now."

"We're going to need some time to talk about this," Jordan said.

"That's the thing. We don't have a lot of time. If the show is over, we have one episode left to shoot to wrap things up. If it's not over, we need to figure out how we're going to leave them hungry for more. The plane is coming next Tuesday to pick us up to go home, which means we've got this week to shoot our final episode of the season. I'm going to need you two to tell me later today what you decide so we can end the season on the proper note."

Matilda signed the check the waiter had left on the table, took the receipt for her expense account and stood. "Here's the script for the first two-thirds of the final episode." She put two copies of the document on the table. "The last third is contingent on whatever you guys decide to do. I'll leave you to discuss it, and I hope you make the right decision. Opportunities like what you're being offered don't come along every day in this business. You have a real chance to build your show into an even bigger hit than it already is. I'll be looking forward to hearing from you soon as whatever you decide will need to be written ahead of shooting the last episode."

After she walked away, neither Gigi nor Jordan said anything for a full five minutes as they pondered what she'd said.

"So," Gigi finally said, "how's your day going?"

"It started out great, but now? I don't know."

"While Matilda was talking, I had an idea I wanted to run by you. Hear me out before you say no."

"Okay..."

"What if Mason was able to somehow take a three-month leave of absence in the off-season so we could film the show in LA or some other location, and he could be with you and the baby?"

"I doubt he'd go for that. His career is important to him, too."

"I know, but he'd tell you himself it's dead around here in the winter, and it probably wouldn't be a big deal for him to turn the department over to a deputy during those months."

"I'd hate to even ask him for that."

"He'd hate for you to give up a huge opportunity that could set you both up for life without even asking him about the possibility."

"You want to keep going, then?"

"Only if we can find a way to make it work for both of us. I'm fine with stopping now or keeping it going."

"I want you to have the financial safety net. I'm sure the crew would be thrilled to have guaranteed employment for a few more years, too."

"I'm good. I've been very frugal with what we've already made, and I've got my practice and a bunch of endorsement offers—as do you."

"But this kind of money would make life easier for you forever. I want that for you."

"Not if it messes up things for you with Mason. That's got to come first."

"What about Cooper?"

Gigi nearly recoiled from the question. "What about him?"

"Doesn't he factor into the decision for you?"

"Of course he doesn't. I just met him." Feeling immediately disloyal to him, she said, "I like him. He's a nice guy, and he's been very sweet to me. But it's just a fling."

"Who are you trying to convince of that? Me or yourself?"

"Could we please get back on track and figure out what the hell we're going to do about Matilda and the offer?"

"I liked filming on location," Jordan said.

"You like banging your brains out with the tall-as-fuck fire chief."

"I like that, too, but I enjoyed doing something other than predictable LA nonsense."

"I did, too. So if we continue, we pick some other place to explore and get to know for a few months, like Santa Fe or Phoenix or somewhere warm in the winter."

"I'd be down for that if I could come back here for the summers," Jordan said. "You think Matilda and the crew would go for shooting on location again?"

"They want three more seasons of job security, and they need us to make that happen, so I suppose they'd go along with whatever we decide. You need to talk to Mason before we do anything else."

"I guess so," Jordan said with a sigh. "You're sure he won't hate me for asking this of him?"

"I'm sure he loves you more than anything, even his job."

"He's so excited about the baby. I've never seen him this happy about anything."

"He's excited about a life with you. Talk to him. Tell him what Matilda is offering and figure out if you guys can make it work. If you can't, there's no point in talking about it anymore, and we'll end the show with this last episode."

"And you won't hate me if that's what I decide?"

Again, Gigi rolled her eyes. "Mason's not the only one who'll love you forever."

Jordan's eyes filled with tears as she put her hand on top of Gigi's. "Same goes. Forever."

Jordan would never know how much hearing that meant to Gigi. Everything had changed this summer, but some things—the most important things—had stayed the same.

"I'll talk to him and let you know."

"Talk fast. She wants an answer later today."

"I'm on it—and PS, you should talk to Cooper about it, too, because the man is crazy about you and deserves to know about this."

"I'll think about it."

"Don't mess it up with him, Geeg. I have a feeling you'd regret that forever."

Gigi was afraid her friend was right about that.

JORDAN LEFT THE MCCARTHYS' hotel in North Harbor and drove to the public safety building in town, hoping to catch Mason in his office between emergency calls. He was so busy this time of year that he came home exhausted after twelve-hour shifts that had him running straight out. They were counting the days until Labor Day, when things would calm down for both of them.

She'd been looking forward to finishing the show and had expected it to end with the final episode of this current season. The massive offer for three more seasons had thrown a wrench in her plans to nest with Mason and their baby on Gansett for the foreseeable future.

Her sister was there and about to marry Riley McCarthy. Jordan had made fantastic new friends, like Chloe and Finn, Kevin and Chelsea and too many others to name. Every day, there was something fun to do with people she genuinely loved to be around, including the seniors she worked with a few hours a week.

In addition, Evelyn had extended her stay into the fall, and Jordan was thrilled to have her grandmother nearby at this exciting time in her life.

Jordan didn't want to be anywhere but right here.

Except, Matilda was right. The offer from the network behind the show was the kind of money that would provide financial security for the rest of their lives. They'd be crazy to turn it down, especially since filming the show with Gigi was so much fun. All they had to do was be themselves in front of the camera. People seemed to love the two of them being themselves together, thus the network's offer. The offer also meant they were liking what they were seeing of the season they had just about finished filming on Gansett.

Jordan had wondered how that would go when she'd suggested filming there so she could be with Mason for the summer. Apparently, the magic had transferred from LA to a tiny, remote island off the coast of Rhode Island, or there wouldn't have been an offer for more.

Mason's department SUV was parked in his spot outside the public safety building, which was a relief. She needed to have this conversation with him before she lost the nerve to make such an audacious suggestion to him. Part of her still wondered if she had the right to even ask him such a thing. But he'd made her feel confident in their relationship, and she carried that confidence with her when she went inside and asked the officer at the reception desk if she could see the fire chief.

After making a call to Mason's office, the young man said, "He said to go right in, Ms. Stokes."

"It's Jordan."

The young man blushed. "Oh, well, I love your show."

"Thanks so much for watching."

Mason stood in the doorway to his office, watching her come toward him with the greedy look of love that still took her by surprise after months together. He was so tall and muscular that he nearly filled the doorway completely. "This is a nice surprise."

"I'm glad you think so."

Mason sent her in ahead of him and shut the door. "Young Officer Quigley will never forget Jordan Stokes smiling at him."

"Oh hush."

"My girl has that effect on most mortal men." He took her by the hand and brought her down on his lap after he sat in one of his visitor chairs. "What brings you by?"

"I'm sorry to interrupt your workday."

"You can interrupt my workday any time you want. That's the benefit of being the boss." He placed a big hand over her abdomen and kissed her as if he hadn't seen her in months, when he'd woken her with sublime morning lovemaking that'd made her late for her meeting with Matilda. "How's my baby mama doing?"

"Better now that she's back with her baby daddy."

"It was a long two hours apart."

Jordan smiled at his silliness. "We're ridiculous."

"Ridiculous never felt so good. What did Matilda want?"

"She wanted to go over the last episode of the season and to know if this is the end of a season or the show."

"What'd you tell her?"

"Well, she complicated the decision with a massive offer for three more seasons from the network."

"Wow. That's amazing, sweetheart. Congratulations."

"We didn't take it."

His brows furrowed adorably. "Why not?"

She gave him a *you know why* look. "Our life is here. The show was supposed to end after this season. That was always the plan."

"But now you have this offer, and you shouldn't say no to it, especially because of me."

"Why else would I say no to it? I want to be with you, and your job is here."

"Jordan, we should at least talk about this before you turn down an amazing opportunity."

"We are talking about it." She looked at the gorgeous face that had become the center of her life in a few short months. "Gigi had an idea."

"I'm almost afraid to ask."

Jordan laughed at how he said that. Mason had learned to be wary of the hijinks she and Gigi got up to together.

"What's this idea of hers?"

"This is a huge what-if scenario, and I want you to say no if it's preposterous. Will you promise me you'll tell me the truth?"

"Always. Lay it on me."

"What if you were to take a leave of absence from work in the winter so we could film the show on location and still be together?" Her heart beat erratically as she waited to hear what he would say.

"I'm not entirely sure I could, but if I can, I'd do it in a second."

"You would? Really?"

"To spend the winter somewhere with you and the baby and get a huge break from work at the same time? Hell yes, I would."

"In case I haven't told you yet today, I love you."

"I love you, too, and I want you to have everything you want. If you want to keep filming the show, then that's what you'll do. We'll figure out the rest."

"I can't be away from you for months, Mason. That won't work."

"Let me talk to the mayor and see what he says. I could leave Dermott in charge for the winter. He'd love the responsibility, and it would be good for him to learn the ropes of being in charge."

"Thank you for even considering this. I know how much your work means to you."

"Nothing in this world means more to me than you and our little peanut."

Thankful for the love of such an incredible man, she kissed him and leaned her forehead against his. “Matilda wants an answer later today.”

“Of course she does,” Mason said with his usual disdain for Matilda’s unreasonable requests.

“How we end this season is contingent upon whether there’ll be more of the show, so that’s the reason for the urgency.”

“I get it, sweetheart. I’ll talk to the mayor and let you know what he says.”

“I know how much you enjoy talking to him.”

Mason laughed at that. Mayor Upton annoyed the living shit out of Mason and Blaine. “I’ll take one for the team for you.”

CHAPTER 27

Gigi left the hotel and drove straight to her favorite hidden beach on the island's west side. She took her beach chair from the trunk and found a spot in the shade under an overhang of rocks. Chloe had told her about this place weeks ago, and it had since become Gigi's go-to place when she needed to be alone.

She flipped through the script that Matilda had given them for the final episode. People were often surprised to learn how much of the show was scripted by the team of writers who helped to bring structure to each episode. The two of them were encouraged to add their own flair to whatever the writers came up with, and that flair was where they found the sweet spot that made the show so popular.

Suddenly, tears filled her eyes and threatened to spill down her cheeks at the thought of leaving Gansett next Tuesday. Tears infuriated Gigi. They were for weak people, and she wasn't weak. She prided herself on being the strongest person she knew, and she refused to let one summer change everything about who she was.

Jordan liked her with Cooper, saw something different in her when she was with him, and Gigi couldn't deny that she felt the same thing. But that didn't mean she had to turn her entire life upside down to accommodate him.

You wouldn't have to, her inner voice said. *He's already told you he'll go wherever you want to be in the off-season as long as he can come back to Gansett to run his business next summer. And you wouldn't hate coming back here every summer, where Jordan, Nikki and Evelyn are.*

Everything in her yearned for a life that looked just like the one he'd suggested for them, if only she could make herself take the extraordinary risk that'd be required to let him all the way in.

"Hey, is this seat taken?" Chloe asked as she parked her chair next to Gigi's.

Appalled to have nearly been caught weeping over a man, Gigi rallied with a smile for the exotically beautiful Chloe Dennis. "It is now."

"Sorry to barge in on your peace and quiet. I had an hour free and came right here."

"I'm glad you did."

"You guys aren't filming today?"

Gigi shook her head. "We finish the season over the next few days."

"Oh wow. That was quick, although I'm sure it didn't feel quick to you guys."

"The summer went by fast."

"It always does. The winter is endless, and the summer just flies."

"How're you feeling?"

Chloe had recently suffered a serious flare-up of her rheumatoid arthritis that had put her out of commission for days—the same days that the power had failed on the island.

"I'm much better than I was. Thanks for asking."

"I hate that you suffer like that."

"It truly sucks, but it sucks less than it did before I had Finn to take care of me."

"It's sweet of him to do that."

"It really is, and it was hard for me to allow him to do it at first, until I realized a man like him doesn't do anything he doesn't want to do. You know?"

"Yeah," Gigi said, thinking of Cooper, who could certainly be categorized the same way. "I know what you mean."

"How's it going with Cooper?"

"Does the whole island know we've been seeing each other, or does it just seem that way?"

"When you nearly roll a Porsche off the bluffs on your first date, word tends to get around."

Gigi groaned. "That was all his fault. He wanted a selfie with me and the car."

"The man is only human, and you're Gigi Gibson."

"Oh hush," Gigi said.

Laughing, Chloe said, "The poor guy is crazy about you. Anyone can see that."

"He's a nice guy."

"Yes, he is, and they can be hard to find. Just ask me. I spent years looking for one before I gave up, convinced they were all a bunch of dogs. Then Finn McCarthy stepped into my salon and showed me there're still a few good ones in this world."

"I'm happy for you that you found him—or he found you."

"I'm happy we found each other." Chloe glanced at her, seeming tentative all of a sudden. "I hope you don't mind that I know a little of your story."

Gigi shrugged, accustomed now to people knowing things about her that she would've preferred to keep private. But celebrity didn't work that way. "I'm an open book."

"I was a product of the foster system, too. My father killed my mother and then himself."

"Oh my God, Chloe. I'm so sorry."

"Thanks, but it was a lifetime ago. It doesn't define me. Not anymore."

Gigi's mind raced as she tried to process what Chloe had told her.

"I'm only telling you this because I understand the spot you're in with Cooper."

Gigi was almost afraid to ask. "What spot is that?"

"You like him—a lot—but you're not sure you have it in you to take a chance on what he has the potential to be to you."

Staring at Chloe, she said, "How do you know that?"

"Because I've been right where you are. Not that long ago, in fact. I tried really hard to resist what was happening with Finn. I'd taken care of myself for so long that I'd forgotten how to let someone else in."

Gigi understood that all too well.

"Plus, I'm dealing with this damned RA situation that could seriously impact my future—and his—and I tried to talk him out of loving me."

"What did he do?"

"He kept showing up and proving to me over and over again that I could put my faith in him, and he'd never let me down. He proved that in a big way during this latest flare-up. He was a rock."

"I'm happy for you that you guys managed to work things out. Anyone can see he's crazy about you."

"We can see the same with your Cooper."

"He's not my Cooper!"

"Isn't he, though, Gigi?" Chloe asked, her tone gentle.

The question broke something inside Gigi, leaving her raw and unprotected against the feelings she had for him.

"You don't want it. I get that better than anyone else ever could. I realized I was projecting the bullshit from my past onto Finn, expecting him to be like my dad was, which was totally fucked up and unfair to him. He's nothing like my dad, and he's never going to be anything other than what he is—perfect for me."

Freaking tears spilled down Gigi's cheeks, despite her fierce desire to contain them and the emotions causing them.

Chloe put her hand on top of Gigi's. "I totally get it, Gigi. I really do."

Gigi turned her hand up to lightly clasp Chloe's. Her knuckles were red and swollen and painful looking.

"It's a big risk when you come from what we do to take a chance on people."

"I spent most of my life in a gilded mansion in Beverly Hills," Gigi said. "You had it much harder than I did."

"I heard how you emancipated from your adopted parents, which probably means not everything in that Beverly Hills mansion was gilded."

"No, it wasn't."

"Then I assume you're very much in the same spot I was in when Finn was demanding entry to my heart and my life, and all those walls I'd erected to keep out threats to the life I'd built for myself were crumbling as if they were made of sand."

Chloe's words struck at the heart of Gigi's dilemma where Cooper was concerned. "I always thought my walls were built of concrete and rebar, but since I met him, I'm discovering otherwise."

Chloe's laughter echoed through their little encampment under the rocks. "It's shocking to realize how easily they can climb over and get inside, isn't it?"

"Shocking and a bit horrifying."

Smiling, Chloe said, "It's only shocking and horrifying at first. Once you get past the initial jolt, it's actually quite lovely to have someone who has your back through all of life's ups and downs." She touched the stunning diamond pendant that hung around her neck on a gorgeous chain. "Finn is the best thing to ever happen to me. I've never been happier until I allowed myself to let him make me happy."

Chloe's words resonated with Gigi. *Until I allowed myself to let him make me happy.* "I'm glad it worked out so well for you guys."

"I am, too, and he says he's never been happier, too, which is just as important to me as my own happiness." She shrugged as if she hadn't described life-changing developments. "When it's right, it's right."

Gigi felt like her brain would explode from all the thoughts competing for her attention. So many thoughts, emotions and concerns as her summer on Gansett came to a close. "Thanks for sharing that with me, Chloe. I appreciate your insight."

"I've discovered that when you're happy like I am with Finn, you want everyone else you care about to find their happiness."

Hearing that Chloe cared about her had Gigi's emotions stirring again. What was it with this place and these people? She'd never been such an emotional waste case in her life, even during all the crap with her parents. She'd powered through like she hadn't a care in the world, but this...

Jordan was right. Chloe was right. This, with Cooper... This was different.

Her phone chimed with a text from him. *How was the meeting with Matilda? Mine went great—better than I could've expected. Can't wait to tell you about it. You going with me tonight?*

"Are you guys coming to my surprise party tonight?"

Stunned, Gigi looked at Chloe, who laughed. "Finn sucks at surprises. He's given it away about six times in the last two days."

"But you'll act surprised tonight?"

"Of course I will. I'd never ruin his fun."

Gigi wanted to be there for her new friend, and she wanted another night with Cooper, even if she was aware that every minute she spent with him would make it that much harder to leave when the plane arrived to pick her up next Tuesday.

Meeting was interesting. Decisions to be made. Can't wait to hear about yours. I'd love to go to Chloe's party. Be home shortly.

I'll be here.

Three simple words that said so much: *I'll be here.*

She had a few days left to decide if she was going to take a chance on him or stick to the safe route. But the more she thought about it, the less the safe route appealed to her. Nothing appealed to her as much as he did.

LATER THAT NIGHT, wrapped up in Cooper's arms on the Wayfarer dance floor as he softly sang along to Owen Lawry's rendition of "God Only Knows," Gigi understood she was in much deeper with him than she'd previously acknowledged. Him singing, "God only knows what I'd be without you," to her had her mind racing with scenarios and implications and dread.

She had to go back to LA, where things made sense to her. Nothing made sense on Gansett Island. It was like she'd become someone totally foreign to herself in three short months on the tiny island in the middle of the ocean. How was it possible for twenty-nine years to be wiped out by three short months and a few weeks with a guy who said and did all the right things?

Finn had gone overboard with food and drinks and music. Chloe was glowing with happiness as she danced with her fiancé. Things had worked out well for her friend. She was one of the lucky ones. Gigi had never been one of the lucky ones.

"How do you know this song?" Gigi asked Cooper, desperate for a reprieve from her own thoughts.

"It's my mother's favorite. I was weaned on *Pet Sounds*."

"What the heck is *Pet Sounds*?"

"Only one of the most iconic albums of all times. Beach Boys, circa 1966, and thank God we had this conversation before you meet her, or my mom might not approve of you for me."

"She won't approve anyway."

Cooper drew back from her and looked down, his expression full of confusion. "Why in the world would you say that?"

"Along with the rest of the world, she's watched me act the fool on TV for the last couple of years. She'll probably think you could do better."

"You haven't acted the fool. You've made a lot of people laugh and entertained them with your antics."

"It's silly."

"It's *fun*. You should be proud of what you and Jordan have created."

"I am. Sort of."

He took her by the hand and led her from the dance floor to the veranda that looked out over the beach.

"This is one hell of a spot the McCarthys have here," she said as she took in the view that was magnificent, even at night.

"It sure is. Now why don't you tell me what's wrong, and once again, I have to say don't tell me it's nothing, because you haven't been yourself since you got home earlier."

"And you know me well enough to say that?"

"I do, yes."

Gigi folded her arms across her chest, as if that could fortify defenses that were nonexistent when he looked at her in that particular knowing way. "I'm leaving Tuesday."

His eyes went wide. "As in this coming Tuesday?"

She nodded.

"Why so soon?"

"We finish shooting on Monday, and the network is sending a plane to pick everyone up."

"So, you don't *have* to leave on Tuesday. You're *choosing* to leave on Tuesday."

"My job is done here. I have a ride home. I'm going."

"Okay."

"Okay. Can we go back to the party now?"

"Sure."

As they walked back inside, Jordan and Mason were coming in through the main entrance. Jordan made a beeline for Gigi, hugging her tightly while Cooper stopped to talk to Finn. "The mayor said *yes* to Mason taking a three-month leave of absence in the winter! We can keep making the show!"

"That's great, Jord. I'm happy for you."

"I'm happy for *us*, Geeg. Three more seasons to be together and have fun while making enough money to be set for life. This is the best day ever!"

"What're you girls freaking out about?" Nikki asked as she joined them.

"We were offered a big fat deal to do the show for three more years, and we just found out that the mayor is going to let Mason take a three-month leave of absence in the winters so we can film then."

"That's great news, you guys," Nikki said, hugging them both. "You've worked so hard. I'm proud of you."

"You'll come to wherever we are to make an appearance, right?" Jordan asked her twin.

Their most popular episodes included Jordan's identical twin.

"Of course," Nik said. "Sign me up."

"Everything's falling into place," Jordan said, her smile as big as Gigi had ever seen it. "One more episode to film for this season, and then we're on vacation until January!"

"I'm not on vacation, diva," Gigi said. "I've got a law practice to get back to." She'd had two associates running the office in her absence, but it was time to get back to reality. "I'm leaving Tuesday."

"What? *Why?* You don't have to go yet."

"Yes, I do." She needed to get out of there while she still could. Gigi glanced to her right, where Cooper was with Riley, Finn and some other guys Gigi didn't know. He was laughing and talking to them, but his troubled gaze was fixed on her.

Jordan and Nikki hooked their arms through hers and made off with her.

CHAPTER 28

"Um, okay, what is happening?" Gigi asked as they perp-walked her into Nikki's office and closed the door.

"An intervention," Jordan said, arms crossed, eyes narrowed. "What're you doing?"

"I don't understand the question."

"Why are you *leaving* when you have a great guy who's crazy about you and clearly wants more with you?" Jordan asked.

"I'm leaving because I don't live here."

"You're self-employed, Gigi," Nikki said. "You don't have to leave the second shooting ends. What's another week or two after three months?"

Another week or two would make it so she couldn't leave him. She had to go now while she still could. She shook her head. "I have to go."

"You're running away from him," Jordan said.

"No, I'm going back to my real life. This place is a fantasy."

"It feels pretty damned real to me," Nikki said.

"And to me," Jordan added. "He's in love with you."

"No, he isn't. He's in love with the idea of me."

Jordan shook her head. "He sees the real you, and he loves the real you."

Feeling more desperate to escape this intervention with every passing second, Gigi laughed. "You're so in love with being in love, you think you're seeing it everywhere you look. Cooper and I are friends. It was a *fling*. That's it."

"Who you trying to convince, G?" Nikki asked softly. "Us or yourself?"

"You guys are insane! I've known him a couple of weeks. People don't change their lives or their plans for someone they just met."

Nikki raised her hand. "I did."

Jordan raised hers. "Me, too."

"It's different for you guys. You want hearts and flowers and happily ever after. I'm not wired that way."

"You think we were wired that way after living through the worst divorce and custody battle in recorded history?" Nikki asked. "Things were tough for you growing up, but don't forget how rough it was for us, too. If we can take a chance on hearts and flowers and happily ever after, why can't you?"

"Because I don't *want* it. I like my life the way it is—uncomplicated and unencumbered. That's what works for me."

"For now," Jordan said. "But that life is going to look very different without us in LA, isn't it?"

Oh, low blow. Gigi's chest ached, and that goddamned lump lodged in her throat again. "I'll be fine."

"You didn't ask for our opinion," Nikki said, "but I think you're going to regret running away from what this could be with Cooper."

"Maybe so, but I'll survive. I always do. Can I go now?"

"Don't do something you're going to regret, Geeg," Nikki said gently. "Cooper is a great guy who genuinely cares about you. Let him."

If she didn't get out of there right away, she was going to break down in front of them, and that couldn't happen. "I hear you, and I love you both, but I'm leaving." Blinking back tears, she turned to leave the room and crashed right into Cooper's broad chest.

He wrapped his arms around her, and she lost it all over him, shaking with sobs and choking on that damned lump that had settled permanently in her throat, or so it seemed.

"Hey," he said, "what's this?"

Gigi couldn't speak, and anyone who knew her well would say that was a rare thing. She gave herself five lovely minutes of being comforted by him while she breathed in the scent she'd forever associate with him. "I have to go."

"I'll take you home."

"No, I have to *go,* Cooper. This, with you… I can't do it. I just can't. I'm sorry." She pulled herself free of him and got the hell out of there while she still could. Half running, half walking, she made it to the ferry landing in a matter of minutes and jumped into the first cab she saw. "Can you please take me to the James estate?"

"Sure thing," the driver said. "Y'all right, doll?"

"I will be. Eventually."

"Ya wanna talk about it?" he asked, looking at her in the mirror with kind eyes.

"No, but thank you for asking."

"My missus and I, we love yer show. You and Jordan are a hoot."

"Thank you so much," Gigi said, wiping away tears.

"I read somewheres that the funniest people are the ones who feel things the deepest, or somethin' like that."

His kind words had more tears flooding her eyes.

"I met yer friend Cooper. Seems like a real nice young man."

"He is." Gigi held back a sob that wanted out right now. How did he know about her and Cooper?

"Tough to say goodbye to someone special like that."

She nodded, hoping he could see her in the mirror.

"I'm sorry. You said ya didn't want to talk about it, and here I am prattling on. But can I tell ya a little story 'bout myself?"

"Sure," Gigi said, wiping away more tears.

"I met a gal right here on Gansett Island round about thirty-three or so years ago. Fell madly in love, the kinda thing you never recover from, ya know?"

She was starting to know all too well. "What happened?"

"She married someone else."

Gigi was heartbroken for him. "Oh no."

"Yeah, it was pretty rough for a long time. They had a coupla little girls, and I had ta watch her walk around town with an unhappy look on her pretty face. I knew he wasn't treatin' her right, but what could I do? She'd made her choice. Then one day, he up and left on the boat and never came back."

"He left her with two little girls?"

"Yep."

"What did you do?"

"Nothin' I could do but watch from a distance."

"That must've been so hard."

"It was tough cuz I still loved her and woulda stepped up for her and her girls, but ya know what kept me from doin' that?"

"What?" Gigi asked, riveted by his story.

"My own foolish pride and a whole lotta fear. I coulda had it all with her and those sweet girls years ago, but I was too afraid ta try. Ya have any idea what I missed out on?"

Gigi shook her head, not sure what to say.

"Everythin'," he said softly. "That lovely gal and I are married now cuz I finally worked up the courage to do what I shoulda done years ago, and now… Now I finally have it all when I coulda had it decades ago. Those little girls are grown women now, and they've made me a grandpa seven times over. I have *everything* now, doll. Every single thing I coulda had way back when, if only I coulda found the courage."

Gigi wept silently in the back seat, moved beyond reason by his sweet story.

He pulled the station wagon into Jared's driveway and put the engine in Park before he turned to her, handing her a tissue. "Don't have regrets, sweetheart."

She took the tissue from him and used it to dry her eyes. "I'm so happy things worked out for you and your wife."

"I am, too. Never been happier in my whole damned life. I have a feeling things are gonna work out the way they're supposed ta for you, too."

Gigi opened the case that housed her wallet and phone and held out a twenty.

"Yer money's no good here, sweetheart. Happy to have the chance to meetcha and have a chat."

"What's your name?"

"Ned Saunders."

"Thank you, Ned, for the ride and the chat."

"A pleasure, doll."

Gigi got out of the car and walked up the dark driveway to her apartment over the garage.

Ned put the high beams on to light her way and waited until she was at her door before he tooted and drove away.

His wife and daughters were lucky to have a man like him in their lives, even if it had taken years for them to find their way to each other.

Some people got lucky. Others didn't. That was how the world worked, and Gigi had always been a realist who didn't let herself get caught up in the fantasy of happily ever after that other women pursued so relentlessly. Marriage and children and white picket fences... That life wasn't for her, and she'd known that all along.

Now that she'd ended things with Cooper, she could focus on getting back to reality.

"SHE BROKE UP WITH ME," Cooper told Nikki and Jordan when they joined him in the hallway outside Nikki's office.

"No way," Jordan said. "She did not."

"Ah, yes, she did." The ache that started in his heart had overtaken every part of him as he'd watched her run away from him as if her life depended on getting as far from him as she could get.

"She's afraid," Nikki said. "She's learned the hard way that she can't trust anyone except the very small circle of friends she allows to get close to her."

"I've tried in every way I can think of to let her know she can trust me."

"Now, you're going to have to take a step back and wait for her to come to you," Jordan said.

"Except she won't."

"No," Jordan said, "I think she will, but she has to believe it was her decision, not something that was forced on her in any way."

"So what am I supposed to do in the meantime?" Cooper asked, desperate for insight from Gigi's two closest friends.

"Wait and hope," Jordan said. "Give her the space to figure out for herself that you're what she wants."

"And if she doesn't?"

"Then I guess it wasn't meant to be, but I don't think that's what will happen."

Cooper wished he shared Jordan's certainty.

"Jordan is right," Nikki said. "You have to let her go for now and give her the space to think and breathe and make her own decision. She knows what you want. Let her figure out what she wants."

He'd go mad waiting and hoping for her to come around, but the sisters knew her better than anyone, so he'd try to take their advice.

"Let me ask you this," Nikki said. "Was she crying when she said it was over?"

"Yeah." Her tears had wrecked him. "Big-time."

"Gigi doesn't cry," Jordan said. "Like, ever."

"If she was crying as she ended things with you," Nikki said, "it's because she cares too much about you and isn't sure what to do about it. I completely agree with Jordan's plan for you to chill and give her time to come around on her own."

"Thanks for the advice. I appreciate it."

"In case you haven't noticed," Jordan said, smiling, "we're on Team Cooper. We're rooting for you guys to figure things out."

"Means a lot to me that her two closest friends want us to be together."

"She's happy with you," Nikki said. "Anyone can see that. The problem for her is she doesn't know what it's like to be truly happy, so she's resisting it out of fear of everything going bad and ruining the life she's created for herself."

"Strangely enough, I get that," Cooper said. "All I want to do is make her happy. I already told her I'd never hurt her or let her go if she takes a chance on me."

"It's freaking her out that she can't find any good reason *not* to take that chance," Jordan said. "She feels things so deeply, and she's been burned by that in the past, starting with the parents who couldn't have cared less about her even as they said all the right things and two idiots who convinced her they were madly in love with her when they were only in love with themselves. She's learned to be wary when people make big promises."

"I mean every word I've ever said to her."

"And she knows that." Nikki squeezed Cooper's arm. "Now give her the time to decide for herself that she wants you in her life."

Cooper heard what they were saying and even agreed with their advice, but how in the world would he find the patience to stay away from her when he wanted her more than he'd ever wanted anything or anyone?

He hung out at the Wayfarer until the party wound down shortly before midnight.

Chloe hugged and kissed everyone, thanking them for helping her turn thirty in style before she left with Finn.

Cooper drove home by himself, which wasn't how he'd expected this evening to end. After parking in Jared's driveway, he glanced up at Gigi's apartment, which was dark. He walked toward the house and noticed a spark of light on the pool deck. "Jared?"

"Yep. Join me for a smoke, brother?"

Though he desperately wanted to be alone with his thoughts, Cooper walked toward his brother and took the seat next to him, along with the cigar and lighter Jared handed him.

"Any news from the mainland?" Cooper asked when he'd lit the cigar and taken a few puffs.

"Looks like my wife and I are going to be parents by this time tomorrow."

Though the statement was delivered in a low-key manner, Jared's elation came through in every word. "That's great, Jared. I'm so happy for you guys."

"Thanks. Nothing's signed yet, but it's looking good. Jessie has acknowledged that she's not equipped to give the baby what she needs. We've agreed to an open adoption that would allow her regular visitation."

"Seems like a best-case scenario."

"We think so. Now we just have to hold our breath until tomorrow, when Jessie signs the agreement. Then a judge has to sign off on it, which will take a couple of months, during which she can change her mind. So we're not entirely home free, but closer than we were."

"Cripes, that's stressful."

"Yeah, but in the end, we get a daughter out of it. Violet Catherine James, who'll be called Vi."

"That's beautiful."

"Couldn't help but notice you came home alone."

"Yeah. Gigi broke up with me."

"Really? Didn't see that coming."

"Neither did I. They finish filming on Monday and are scheduled to go back to LA on Tuesday. Jordan and Nikki say she's freaking out about the summer ending as this thing with me has become more serious than expected. They say I need to give her space to come around on her own."

"What do you think of that?"

"They know her better than anyone."

"Waiting and hoping puts you in a tough spot."

"Yeah, it sucks."

"I remember what that's like. The weeks after I thought Lizzie turned down my proposal were among the worst of my life. I thought I was never going to see her again."

"I can't picture one of you without the other."

"Now, but there was a time when that was hardly assured. This stuff is hard, bro, and for some people, it's damned near impossible for them to take the leap and keep the faith."

"That's the problem Gigi's having. She's had a lot of hard knocks, so she's super cautious."

"She hasn't been with you."

"That's part of the problem."

"I agree with the advice Jordan and Nikki gave you. Take a step back, and let her come to you. If it's meant to be, she'll be back."

"And if it isn't?"

"Then you're going to experience serious heartache, and it's gonna suck."

"Already does, and this just happened two hours ago."

"Hang in there, bud. I'm sure you've done all you can to show her how it could be between you guys, and if that's what she wants, she'll be back."

"I hope so."

"I do, too, but I have to say, it's good to know you're mortal after all."

"Haha, very funny. I've been waiting for you to remind me I had this coming."

Jared's low chuckle made Cooper smile for the first time in hours. "How'd the meeting go with the McCarthys?"

"Better than expected." He told Jared about the wedding package deals the family was thinking about offering and how his business could be included.

"That's awesome. You can't pay for that kind of free publicity."

"I know, and Mr. McCarthy's friend Ned Saunders talked to me about getting involved in some real estate investments, too. Apparently, that's been his main hustle for forty years, and he's looking to take a step back and spend more time with his family. He needs someone who might be interested in stepping into that game."

"That's an incredible opportunity, Coop. He's made a fortune buying and selling houses on the island."

"I find that funny since he drives a cab."

"He does that for fun." Jared took a puff of the cigar. "So your day didn't totally suck."

"The first half was pretty awesome."

"Hang in there, brother. Gigi knows by now that you're a good guy. Give her time to think about it, and try to have some faith."

He'd give her the space she needed even as he worried he might've lost her forever.

CHAPTER 29

Gigi threw herself into filming the season's last episode, during which they revealed that Jordan was expecting her first child. They planned to keep that news under wraps until the episode aired later in the year. Over the course of the episode, they revisited some of their favorite spots on the island, including the bluffs, the beach and the ferry landing, where they had learned how to drive one of the massive ferries.

The final scenes were set to be filmed Monday afternoon at Eastward Look, Jordan and Nikki's childhood summer home.

Nikki and Riley would make an appearance, as would Evelyn, Finn and Chloe, who were super excited to be on TV.

It's not all it's cracked up to be, Gigi wanted to tell them.

Wanting a second opinion, she'd had Dan Torrington take a look at the offer the network had made her to appear in three more seasons, and he'd agreed with her own assessment and declared it legally sound. She and Jordan were due to sign the new deal at the end of filming today.

As her days and hours on Gansett ticked down to single digits, she'd tried her best not to think about Cooper or what he was doing or how he was feeling or anything about him. When she let her thoughts venture in his direction, she hurt like she never had before, which made her feel like the biggest kind of fool.

How in the world had she ended up with such strong feelings for a man she'd met so recently? She didn't know how, but she couldn't deny the feelings were big and getting bigger with every day that went by without him in it.

Matilda came to find her under the portable tent the production team had erected to keep them out of the sun between takes. "I was hoping for a second with you. Mason has a surprise planned for Jordan that we're going to capture on film, so when you see him coming, step back if you would."

"Sure, I can do that. What kind of surprise is he planning?"

"I'm not sure. He only asked if he could interrupt filming for a couple of minutes and if we'd do him the favor of getting it on video."

Was he going to propose again, this time for the cameras?

Oh God, he was.

Gigi couldn't breathe over the emotions that overwhelmed her—happiness for Jordan and Mason and despair for herself that made her feel stupid and immature. Her friend was getting married, not dying from a dreaded illness.

Get it together, she told herself. *And PS, you could have the same kind of happiness she's found with Mason if you could only get out of your own way. Shut up. No, you shut up.*

They were called back a few minutes later to begin shooting the final scene, which would culminate on the lawn of the home Jordan and Nikki had run to the minute school ended every summer. Most of their best childhood memories had occurred here, and as they sat in Adirondack chairs reminiscing with Nikki and Evelyn, Mason came striding onto the lawn, wearing his fire department uniform.

He was the tallest son of a gun Gigi had ever met, and he loved her friend with his whole heart and soul.

Jordan's back was to Mason, so she didn't see him coming until he was right on top of them. She gasped with surprise when she saw him there. "What're you doing here?"

"Ladies, could I please have a moment alone with Jordan?"

"Of course," Evelyn said, beaming.

If he was going to formally propose, he'd probably asked Evelyn's permission first, because he was that kind of guy.

"Wait, we're filming here," Jordan said.

"This will only take a second."

Gigi, Nikki and Evelyn stepped out of the shot and gave Mason the spotlight.

He dropped to one knee in front of Jordan.

Her hands covered her mouth as her eyes flooded with tears.

Gigi could barely see through her own tears.

Mason took hold of Jordan's hand and kissed the back of it. "Hi there."

Jordan laughed through her tears. "How's it going?"

"Never better than since I met you. This has been the most beautiful summer of my life, and it's all because of you. I'd given up on ever finding true love until I found you right here at Eastward Look. Granted, you weren't at your best that night."

"Near-death experiences will do that to a girl. Thanks for saving me, by the way."

"Best thing I ever did was save you so you could save me right back. Jordan Stokes, love of my life, will you do me the immense honor of being my wife?"

"Yes," Jordan said, leaning into the bear hug he wrapped her in.

He pulled back to kiss her as he slid a ring onto her left hand. "If you don't like the ring, we can swap it out for another one."

"I love the ring. I love you, and I can't wait to marry you."

They kissed again before Mason looked up at Matilda. "Did you get that?"

"We got it," Matilda said, dabbing at tears.

"Are we allowed to hug them now?" Nikki asked.

"Go for it," Matilda said, signaling to the cameraman to keep rolling.

They hugged, drank the sparkling cider Evelyn had ready in deference to Mason who was a recovering alcoholic and Jordan who was pregnant, and celebrated the happy couple as their season on Gansett came to a triumphant end.

When Gigi drove home alone after the celebratory dinner Evelyn had prepared for the family and the crew, she wanted to call Cooper and tell him all about it. But she couldn't do that. It wouldn't be fair to call him after she'd ended things with him.

He'd respected her wishes and kept his distance over the last couple of days.

She'd seen him once, sitting by the pool with Lizzie and the baby, but otherwise, she hadn't had any contact with him.

When she got back to the house, she went upstairs to her apartment and spent the rest of the night packing to leave the island at ten o'clock the next morning. She'd hired a guy to deliver her car to the dock to be shipped home at the end of the week, and with the car loaded and her bags packed, there was nothing left to do but go to bed and stare up at the ceiling, reliving every minute she'd spent with Cooper as tears slid down her cheeks.

The fucking tears hadn't quit since she'd called things off with him.

It'd been the right thing to do. She still believed that, but damn, it hurt.

The night passed with excruciating slowness as she tried to keep herself from walking across the yard to him.

But she'd made her decision, and now she had to live with it.

She got out of bed at eight, stripped the sheets and put them in the washing machine with the towels and other linens. Lizzie had told her to start the wash, and she'd finish it. Their new tenant was due to arrive in September, and life would go on for all of them as if Gigi had never been there.

By the time she carried her bags down the stairs to the cab she'd called, Gigi was ready to take it all back if only she could have five more minutes with Cooper before she never saw him again.

Ned Saunders greeted her with a warm smile. "Nice ta see ya again, doll."

"You, too, Ned."

"Heading back to La-La Land, are ya?"

"Home sweet home." Even as she said the words, she acknowledged that nowhere on earth had ever felt more like home to her than this ridiculous little island did after spending the best summer of her life there.

She'd seen Jared and Lizzie the day before, celebrated the news about baby Vi joining their family, said her thank-yous for having her and goodbye. Jared and Lizzie had promised to visit the next time they were in LA. She hadn't seen Cooper, and none of them had mentioned him.

Leaving without saying goodbye to him felt wrong but necessary.

If she saw him for even a second, she'd never leave.

She got in the back seat of Ned's car and shut the door, refusing to look back. Keeping her gaze firmly fixed on the future had kept her moving forward all her life, and that's what she'd do now, too.

COOPER WATCHED her leave from the living room window, astounded by how much it hurt to realize she was leaving without saying goodbye to him.

But what did he expect? She'd told him from the start that their relationship was nothing more than a fling. That's all it had been to her. He was the one who'd let it get out of control. That was on him, and now he had to go on without her.

He'd given her room to breathe, and she'd made her decision.

But, God, it hurt to watch her go.

"Did she leave?" Jared asked.

"Yeah, just now."

"I'm sorry, Coop."

"It's okay," he said, although nothing about this was okay. "I'm going to sit by the pool and get some work done."

"Let me know if you need anything."

The one thing he needed was the only thing his billionaire brother couldn't get for him. The irony of that might've made him laugh if it didn't hurt so fucking bad. He took his laptop to the pool and gave his portfolio some attention for the first time in days, losing himself in the work so he wouldn't be tempted to chase after her like a pathetic, lovesick fool.

A short time later, a sleek Learjet took off from the airport and went right over the house, taking the woman he loved with it. His heart sank as he watched the plane climb out over the island. She was gone. It was over. And now he had to figure out how to live without her.

Half an hour later, he was forcing himself to focus on the work so he wouldn't howl from the pain of losing her. He was deep in the weeds of charts, graphs, prospectuses and trades when a car pulled into the driveway.

Cooper forced himself to keep his eyes on the screen until the click of heels and the unmistakable scent of his love surrounded him in a cloud of sensation that had him finally looking up. As he blinked at the sight of

Gigi dragging a full set of Louis Vuitton luggage onto Jared's pool deck into focus, he couldn't believe what he was seeing.

"Funniest thing happened at the airport," she said.

He was afraid to so much as breathe, let alone speak. But as he studied her one-of-a-kind face, he saw the ravages the last few days had taken on her in the swollen eyes, the dark circles under them and the unusually pale cheeks.

"I realized I'd left the most important thing in my life behind, and I had to come back to get it. I had to come back to get you, Cooper."

"I saw the plane leave. I thought you were gone."

"I couldn't bring myself to go."

He put his laptop on the chair next to his and held out a hand to her.

She took his hand and let him draw her down onto the lounge with him. "I'm sorry, Coop."

"Don't apologize. You had to come around to this in your own way and your own time." He put his arms around her, and when she snuggled into his embrace, he was able to breathe for the first time in days. "Have you come around to it? To me and us?"

"I think I have."

"I need you to be sure, sweetheart, because the last couple of days were hell."

"I'm sorry I put you through that."

"You're not apologizing, remember?" He tipped her chin up so he could kiss her. "There's something I never got the chance to tell you before you dumped me."

She cringed at his choice of words. "What's that?"

"I love you, Gabrielle Gigi Gibson."

"I love you, too, Coop. I really do, and that's why I freaked out. I don't know how to do this."

"This is a first for me, too. How about we figure it out together?"

"I'd love that." She rested her head on his chest and let out a deep sigh. "You were right here, and I was right there, and I missed you so much."

He stroked her hair and rubbed her back. Now that he was allowed to touch her again, he would never stop. "I missed you, too."

"Cooper, will you come home to LA with me this winter and possibly on location to shoot the show from somewhere cool, and then bring me back to this magical place next summer to start your business on Gansett while I hang with my girls?"

"I'd love nothing more than to live that life with you, sweetheart."

"Then that's what we'll do."

He hugged her tightly. "That's what we'll do."

EPILOGUE

"Have you heard from Jordan since she and Mason got officially engaged?" Cooper asked Gigi much later that night when they were in her bed in the apartment she'd taken ownership of again for a few more days. Jared and Lizzie were so glad she'd come back for Cooper, they told her to stay as long as she'd like.

"I haven't talked to her since their big day. They've gone deep undercover. I heard he even took some emergency leave from work."

"Good for them," Cooper said, chuckling. "And good for us." He turned so he was on top of her, gazing down at her as he slid into her for round two. "I haven't forgotten that I owe you dinner at the Beachcomber to make up for our disastrous first date."

"Our first date was the best first date I've ever had."

"Was it?"

She nodded as she wrapped her arms around him. "And as for dinner, I find myself on something called a vacation. People tell me they're fun and that you can do anything you want, such as go to dinner at the Beachcomber with your boyfriend."

"I love being your boyfriend," he said, kissing her before resting his forehead against hers. "Tell me again."

"I love you, Cooper."

"I love you, too, Gigi. We're going to have it all. Every single freaking thing in this world, we're going to have it."

"You make me believe anything is possible."

"It is as long as we have each other. Thanks for coming back for me."

"I have a feeling that's going to turn out to be the smartest thing I ever did."

JARED WENT LOOKING for Lizzie and found her gazing down at their daughter. They had a *daughter*. Jessie had signed the temporary custody agreement, and Dan had begun the official adoption proceedings. Pending court approval, they'd be adopting Violet and raising her as their own.

Dan had warned them that Jessie could change her mind until the adoption was final, but Jessie had assured them she wouldn't be changing her mind. She'd apologized profusely for leaving the baby with them the way she had in the first place, but Lizzie had told her things happen for a reason. She'd been so calm and reasonable when Jared was losing his shit over the way this had happened.

He was a dad to a sweet little girl.

They were a family.

"You need some rest, love," he whispered, placing his hands on Lizzie's shoulders.

"I just want to stare at her and never blink."

"She'll still be here in the morning."

"You promise?"

"I promise."

She ran her fingers gently over the baby's cheek and then let him lead her to bed. "How long do you think it'll be before I believe this actually happened?"

"It might take a while, but we'll get there."

"We have a *daughter,* Jared."

"Yes, we do," he said, amused by the wonder in her voice as he held her close. "And Gigi came back for Cooper."

"Thank goodness for that. I've never seen him so low as he was after she ended things with him."

"I know. I was worried about what would become of him."

"I think they're going to be very happy together."

"I think so, too, but let's talk about how happy we are."

"I've never been happier. Thank you for putting up with me and my craziness and the stray babies and all of it."

"I love you and your craziness more than anything."

"It's amazing, isn't it, that you and I came back together right here, and now Cooper and Gigi have, too."

"It's this place. It's magic. I've thought so from the first time I ever came here, and the proof keeps piling up." He pulled her closer to him and kissed her. "How about you and me and Vi keep making magic for the rest of our lives?"

"I'm down with that."

MCCARTHY, PARTY OF SEVEN

A GANSETT ISLAND SHORT STORY

Big Mac McCarthy drove Mac and Maddie's SUV off the ferry in Point Judith and headed for Women & Infants Hospital in Providence to pick up his son, daughter-in-law and newborn baby granddaughters.

"I can't wait to see those babies again," Big Mac's wife, Linda, said. They'd taken clothes and other supplies to the kids a few days after the babies' dramatic birth, but hadn't been back again since, as they were helping to care for the couple's other three kids at home.

"I can't either. I'm so thankful they're strong enough to go home."

The babies had been released from the hospital two days ago and had stayed at Frank's house in Providence until the doctors declared them ready to return to Gansett.

Mac had called the night before and told them Maddie was nervous about bringing the twins to a remote island. Big Mac had tried to assure his son that with Dr. David Lawrence and nurse practitioners Victoria Stevens and Katie McCarthy close by, the girls would be perfectly safe on the island. They also had Life Flight helicopters in cases of emergency, but he prayed to God they'd never again need one of them for his family.

His daughter Janey and daughter-in-law Maddie had both been evacuated by chopper in recent years, and that was enough for one lifetime.

"What're you thinking about?" Linda asked.

"Life Flight helicopters and how I'm glad we have them if we need them."

"The twins will be fine, or the doctors never would've released them to go home to Gansett. Plus, David and Victoria have been in consultation with the doctors in Providence. It'll all be fine." The babies had one last checkup with the doctors at the hospital that morning, and they'd be picking them up from there.

Mac had ordered an Uber with car seats to get them to Frank's and then back to the hospital that morning.

Big Mac and Linda navigated heavy beach traffic that stretched the one-hour ride into an hour and a half. At the hospital, they retrieved the seat portion of the infant car seats and brought them inside.

Linda had texted Mac that they were close, and he said he was waiting for them in the lobby.

He hugged them both and took the seats from his parents. "Thanks for this, guys, and for helping with the other three these last two weeks."

Big Mac noted that his handsome son looked happy and tired.

"We've had the best time with them, and Kelsey was a huge help, too," Linda said. "They can't wait to meet their baby sisters. Even Thomas is excited."

Mac laughed at that news.

Thomas had expressed annoyance at the arrival of two more baby sisters when the one he already had was such a nuisance.

"How's Maddie holding up?" Big Mac asked, even though they'd gotten regular reports on her and the babies over the last two weeks.

"She's tired, but glad to know she'll never be pregnant again."

"That is a good feeling," Linda said. "To know you're done with that part of your life and can settle in to enjoy the rest."

"She's got me scheduled for the big V in early September," Mac said glumly as they rode the elevator to the pediatrician's office.

"You'll survive, son," Big Mac said, thinking of his own vasectomy years ago after Janey was born, and they'd decided five kids were enough. Little did they know there was a sixth one waiting to be discovered in Mallory, who'd found him when she was nearly forty after her mother died. Now Mallory was such a big part of their family, it was like she'd always been there.

They found Maddie in an exam room, holding one of the girls while the doctor examined the other one.

She smiled at her in-laws. "Here they are," she said to the girls. "It's time to go home."

"Emma and Evie passed their exams with flying colors this morning," Maddie said.

"Green light to head home to the island," the doctor said. "They're doing great."

Mac and Maddie loaded the babies into the car seats like the experts they'd become with three previous children.

Twenty minutes later, they had babies, diaper bags and suitcases loaded in the SUV that Big Mac drove south on 95 while the kids rode in back with the babies.

"You girls are getting the best chauffer ever on your ride home," Mac told the babies. "Grandpa Big Mac is the best of the best."

Big Mac smiled at hearing those words from his beloved son. The only thing in the world that truly mattered to him was that his family was happy, healthy and safe. Everything else paled in comparison to those priorities. He couldn't wait to watch those little girls, their siblings and cousins grow up and to spoil them rotten the way a grandfather was supposed to.

Their friend Seamus O'Grady was waiting at the ferry landing for them to arrive and came over to stick his head in the window to get a first look at the new babies. "They're gorgeous," Seamus declared. "Joe said to tell you he's thankful they look like their mother."

"Haha," Mac said. "Very funny."

"Don't shoot the messenger." Seamus gestured for Big Mac to back the SUV onto the ferry. "VIPs coming through, people."

The crew members working on the pier jumped to attention to see to the boss's orders.

"Nice to know people," Big Mac said when he had the car parked on the boat.

They unloaded the babies in their seats and carried them upstairs for the one-hour passage to the island. People they knew from the island came by to say hello, which made the voyage pass quickly. As they pulled into port, Big Mac saw Ned and Francine with Thomas, Hailey and baby

Mac. They had balloons and flowers and a big sign that said Welcome Home, Emma and Evie!

"The babies have a welcoming committee," Big Mac said to Linda, pointing to the others on the pier.

"Mac and Maddie will be so glad to see the kids."

"Let's wait and let them find out they're here when they come off the boat."

They loaded the car seats back into the SUV, and as they rolled off the ferry, Maddie let out a happy cry at the sight of her other three children and her parents.

Big Mac pulled into a parking space so the family could be reunited.

Mac and Maddie got out of the car and caught Thomas and Hailey as they ran to them.

Baby Mac let out a loud screech at the sight of his mother.

Maddie took him from Francine and hugged him tight. "We missed you guys so much!"

"We missed you, too," Thomas said. "Hailey was naughty the whole time you were gone."

"Now, Thomas," Francine said. "What did we say about being a tattletale?"

"Well, she *was* naughty," Thomas said.

"Business as usual around here, I see," Mac said as he hugged his eldest son.

"Can we see the babies?" Thomas asked.

"Sure, come take a peek, but remember to be very quiet and gentle with them."

Thomas climbed up into the car himself while Mac lifted Hailey and Mac for a look at their new baby sisters.

"What do you think?" Mac asked them.

"They're tiny," Thomas said, "like Mac was."

"They will be for a while, but they'll be running around before we know it."

"Great," Thomas said. "That's just what I need."

"Babies," Hailey said.

"Yes, those are your baby sisters," Mac told his little girl. "We need to get them home, so you go with Grandma Francine and Grandpa Ned, and we'll follow you, okay?"

Hailey held on tighter to her daddy as if she was afraid he'd leave again if she let go.

"We'll be right behind you, sweet girl," Mac said as he turned her over to Ned.

They got back in the SUV and headed for Sweet Meadow Farm Road.

"The first time I saw this house," Maddie said, "I never suspected I'd need every one of the bedrooms."

"I knew we'd need them," Mac said.

"Sure you did," Maddie said, laughing.

"We have *five* kids."

"In restaurants, you're now the McCarthy family, party of seven," Big Mac said.

"They'll all be in college before we ever take them to a restaurant," Mac said.

Big Mac smiled at Linda. "Remember how we said that, too?"

"I remember all too well, and it went by in a flash. Enjoy every minute of it, you two. You won't believe how soon you'll be empty nesters."

"That seems like a lifetime from now," Maddie said.

"You'll be shocked at how fast it goes by," Big Mac said.

"We've already seen that with Thomas," Mac said. "How is he already *six?*"

"And full of beans," Linda said.

"We wouldn't have him any other way," Mac said.

Big Mac could tell his son was thrilled to be home and to have his family under one roof for the first time. He and Linda made dinner, helped get the three older kids bathed and ready for bed and read them the required three stories before they headed home, promising to be back to help out tomorrow.

"I'm spent," Big Mac said. "How can three little people run two experienced grannies ragged?"

"Speak for yourself. I'm as fresh and perky as I was first thing this morning."

"Sure you are," he said, laughing.

"My back is killing me from hauling baby Mac around. He's a chunk all of a sudden."

"He's growing like a weed, just like this family of ours." Within a year, they'd have fourteen grandchildren, including the new twins and Adam and Abby's quads. Evan and Grace and Grant and Stephanie had joked about feeling like slackers because they were expecting "only" one baby each.

"We're going to need a spreadsheet to remember all the birthdays," Linda said.

"It's a good 'problem' to have."

"It sure is. I was thinking earlier today about the first time I ever came here, the day after we met when you wanted to show me the marina you'd just bought."

"Ah, yes," he said, chuckling. "The ferries were canceled, and we had to spend the night in the spider room."

Linda cringed and shuddered the way she did every time he mentioned the spider room.

"I was lucky you ever talked to me again after that," he said, smiling at the memory.

"Oh please. You had me so hooked on you after twenty-four hours together, I would've followed you anywhere you wanted to go."

"That's all it took, huh? Twenty-four hours?"

"I think it was more like twelve."

Big Mac barked out a laugh. "It took about twelve seconds for me to set my sights on you."

"I love thinking about those early days and all the days that've come since then."

"I do, too. We couldn't ask for more than all six of our kids happily married, fourteen grandchildren here or on the way and all of them living close enough to spoil any time we want. And when the baby boom settles down a bit, we'll get back to traveling."

"I'm with you, sport."

Big Mac parked the truck in the driveway of the "White House," the name locals had given their home overlooking North Harbor, and leaned across the center console to kiss his bride. "That was—and is—all I need to hear."

WHILE MADDIE TENDED to fussy babies, Mac checked in with the older three, starting with baby Mac, who was halfway asleep in his crib, and then Hailey, who was already out cold, before ending up in Thomas's room. "Move over. I'm coming in."

He'd missed his son's husky giggle and the way he followed Mac around with hero-like worship. Thomas had been nine months old when Mac met Maddie. He'd formed an instant bond with the little boy, who was now his son. "I heard you were very helpful with baby Mac while we were away."

"He's so cute and funny. I like helping with him."

"And you like pushing your sister's buttons."

"What buttons does she have?"

"It's a figure of speech."

"What does that mean?"

"It's another way of saying you like to annoy her."

"She annoys me! Why'd you have to get me two more baby sisters? There's more of them than there are of us. And Mac is still too little to help me fight them."

"You're not going to fight them. You're going to love them."

"Someday, maybe, but right now, they're just a pain."

Mac had to bite his lip to keep from laughing. Sometimes he had to remind himself that he was the parent now and no longer one of the kids.

"I wish Connor hadn't died," Thomas said.

The reminder of the baby they'd lost sent a jolt of shock through Mac. "I do, too, buddy, but if he'd lived, we might not have Mac."

"Why not?" Thomas asked, his soft blond brows furrowing with confusion.

"I'll explain how that works when you're older, okay?"

"Why is there so much secret stuff I can't know until I'm older?"

"Because you need to be older to understand it. I promise I'll tell you all the important secret stuff when you're ready."

"How will you know when I'm ready?"

Mac kissed the boy's forehead. "I'll know. I was once a six-year-old boy with lots of questions myself."

"You were never little like me!"

"Yes, I was!"

Thomas cracked up laughing. "Nuh-uh."

"Uh-huh. Now go to sleep so you'll grow up to be big and strong like Daddy." Mac flexed his muscles to make his point.

"I'm glad you're my daddy."

How could five little words nearly bring him to tears? "Being your daddy, and Hailey, Mac, Emma and Evie's daddy, is my favorite thing in the whole wide world."

"But mostly you like being my dad, right?" Thomas asked with a sly smile.

"You'll never get me to admit that." Mac was endlessly amused by him and could never admit that he'd always have an extra-special place in his heart for the boy who'd first made him a dad. "I'll see you in the morning."

"You guys will be here, right?"

"We'll be here, buddy."

He left Thomas's room and returned to the master where Maddie was breastfeeding one of the twins while the other slept on the bed next to her. Breastfeeding twins was an Olympic event, and Maddie was a gold medalist. She made it look easy when it was anything but and had joked that her overly large breasts were finally coming in handy.

"Can I get you anything?" he asked.

"If you could hand me my water, that'd be great."

Mac walked into the room, retrieved her thermal cup of ice water off the bedside table and handed it to her.

"My hero," she said, smiling up at him.

"Sure, I am. I'm the reason you're breastfeeding twins."

"That's definitely all your fault, but they sure are beautiful."

"Yes, they are. They look just like their gorgeous mother, and thank goodness for that."

"I see you in them, too. Evie does this thing with her lips when she's annoyed that reminds me of you."

Mac glanced at the yellow bracelet on the baby Maddie was feeding. Yellow for Emma, pink for Evie. Mac sat on the edge of the bed, wanting to tell her what Thomas had said about Connor, but not wanting to upset her on what had been a great day for their family. "I've never felt more useless than I have since I've watched you feed twins."

"You're not useless," Maddie said. "Don't say that. You've been so much help with everything."

"You're the rock star, love. You amaze me with how you take everything in stride, even twin newborns."

"Twin newborns with you are easier than single motherhood was with Thomas. Everything is easier when we do it together."

"I can't wait until we can do it together again," he said, waggling his brows as he leaned in to kiss her.

"Not until the snip."

"Stop talking about that. You're hurting his feelings."

Maddie's laughter disturbed Emma, who wailed indignantly and woke up her sister. "Look what you and your thing have done now."

"I'm offended on behalf of my thing." Mac picked up Evie while Maddie tended to Emma.

"You and your thing will be just fine."

"I'll be just fine as long as I have you and our kids."

"I'd say at this point, you're stuck with us."

"Thank God for that." With five of his children sleeping under his roof and a sixth one forever in his heart, Mac McCarthy Jr. considered himself the luckiest man on Gansett Island.

THANK you for reading *Temptation After Dark*! I hope you loved Cooper and Gigi's story as well as the chance to catch up with some of our other friends on Gansett Island. For those of you who guessed that Jace and Cindy are next up—you are correct! I'm very much looking forward to writing their story and to moving things forward for the rest of the Lawry siblings in book 25, *Resilience After Dark*. I think that's the perfect title to sum up two people who've survived the rough stuff and are now in a place to reap the rewards of true love. I can't believe we're heading for book 25! It's so exciting to see Gansett Island going strong, ten years after *Maid for Love* was released—and with no end in sight!

If you'd like to chat about *Temptation* with other readers, join the reader group at *facebook.com/groups/temptationafterdark*. You can also join the Gansett Island Reader Group at *facebook.com/groups/McCarthySeries* to keep up with all the series news.

Thank you to the wonderful team that supports me behind the scenes: Julie Cupp, Lisa Cafferty, Jean Mello, Andrea Buschell and Ashley Lopez. A shoutout to Diane Lugar, the Gansett Island cover designer, and to my beta readers Anne Woodall and Kara Conrad. Thanks to my editors Linda Ingmanson and Joyce Lamb as well as Dan, Emily and Jake.

Huge thanks to my Gansett Island Series beta readers: Judy, Marianne, Mona, Jennifer, Andi, Jennifer, Julianne, Betty, Doreen, Betty, Melanie, Michelle, Jaime, Kelly and Gwen. Once again, you all saved my bacon with your great catches on the final draft of *Temptation*!

And finally, a huge thanks to the readers who have embraced the Gansett Island for the last decade. Looking forward to much more to come!

Xoxo

Marie

ALSO BY MARIE FORCE

Contemporary Romances Available from Marie Force

The Gansett Island Series

Book 1: Maid for Love *(Mac & Maddie)*

Book 2: Fool for Love *(Joe & Janey)*

Book 3: Ready for Love *(Luke & Sydney)*

Book 4: Falling for Love *(Grant & Stephanie)*

Book 5: Hoping for Love *(Evan & Grace)*

Book 6: Season for Love *(Owen & Laura)*

Book 7: Longing for Love *(Blaine & Tiffany)*

Book 8: Waiting for Love *(Adam & Abby)*

Book 9: Time for Love *(David & Daisy)*

Book 10: Meant for Love *(Jenny & Alex)*

Book 10.5: Chance for Love, *A Gansett Island Novella (Jared & Lizzie)*

Book 11: Gansett After Dark *(Owen & Laura)*

Book 12: Kisses After Dark *(Shane & Katie)*

Book 13: Love After Dark *(Paul & Hope)*

Book 14: Celebration After Dark *(Big Mac & Linda)*

Book 15: Desire After Dark *(Slim & Erin)*

Book 16: Light After Dark *(Mallory & Quinn)*

Book 17: Victoria & Shannon (Episode 1)

Book 18: Kevin & Chelsea (Episode 2)

A Gansett Island Christmas Novella

Book 19: Mine After Dark *(Riley & Nikki)*

Book 20: Yours After Dark *(Finn & Chloe)*

Book 21: Trouble After Dark *(Deacon & Julia)*

Book 22: Rescue After Dark *(Mason & Jordan)*

Book 23: Blackout After Dark *(Full Cast)*

Book 24: Temptation After Dark *(Gigi & Cooper)*

Book 25: Resilience After Dark *(Jace & Cindy)*

The Green Mountain Series

Book 1: All You Need Is Love *(Will & Cameron)*

Book 2: I Want to Hold Your Hand *(Nolan & Hannah)*

Book 3: I Saw Her Standing There *(Colton & Lucy)*

Book 4: And I Love Her *(Hunter & Megan)*

Novella: You'll Be Mine *(Will & Cam's Wedding)*

Book 5: It's Only Love *(Gavin & Ella)*

Book 6: Ain't She Sweet *(Tyler & Charlotte)*

The Butler, Vermont Series

(Continuation of Green Mountain)

Book 1: Every Little Thing *(Grayson & Emma)*

Book 2: Can't Buy Me Love *(Mary & Patrick)*

Book 3: Here Comes the Sun (*Wade & Mia)*

Book 4: Till There Was You *(Lucas & Dani)*

Book 5: All My Loving *(Landon & Amanda)*

Book 6: Let It Be *(Lincoln & Molly)*

Book 7: Come Together *(Noah & Brianna)*

Book 8: Here, There & Everywhere *(Izzy & Cabot)*

The Quantum Series

Book 1: Virtuous *(Flynn & Natalie)*

Book 2: Valorous *(Flynn & Natalie)*

Book 3: Victorious *(Flynn & Natalie)*

Book 4: Rapturous *(Addie & Hayden)*

Book 5: Ravenous *(Jasper & Ellie)*

Book 6: Delirious *(Kristian & Aileen)*

Book 7: Outrageous *(Emmett & Leah)*

Book 8: Famous *(Marlowe & Sebastian)*

The Treading Water Series

Book 1: Treading Water

Book 2: Marking Time

Book 3: Starting Over

Book 4: Coming Home

Book 5: Finding Forever

The Wild Widows Series—a Fatal Series Spin-Off

Book 1: Someone Like You

The Miami Nights Series

Book 1: How Much I Feel *(Carmen & Jason)*

Book 2: How Much I Care *(Maria & Austin)*

Book 3: How Much I Love *(Dee's story)*

Single Titles

Five Years Gone

One Year Home

Sex Machine

Sex God

Georgia on My Mind

True North

The Fall

The Wreck

Love at First Flight

Everyone Loves a Hero

Line of Scrimmage

Romantic Suspense Novels Available from Marie Force

The Fatal Series

One Night With You, *A Fatal Series Prequel Novella*

Book 1: Fatal Affair

Book 2: Fatal Justice

Book 3: Fatal Consequences

Book 3.5: Fatal Destiny, *the Wedding Novella*

Book 4: Fatal Flaw

Book 5: Fatal Deception

Book 6: Fatal Mistake

Book 7: Fatal Jeopardy

Book 8: Fatal Scandal

Book 9: Fatal Frenzy

Book 10: Fatal Identity

Book 11: Fatal Threat

Book 12: Fatal Chaos

Book 13: Fatal Invasion

Book 14: Fatal Reckoning

Book 15: Fatal Accusation

Book 16: Fatal Fraud

Sam and Nick's Story Continues....

Book 1: State of Affairs

Book 2: State of Grace

Historical Romance Available from Marie Force

The Gilded Series

Book 1: Duchess by Deception

Book 2: Deceived by Desire

ABOUT THE AUTHOR

Marie Force is the *New York Times* bestselling author of contemporary romance, romantic suspense and erotic romance. Her series include Fatal, First Family, Gansett Island, Butler Vermont, Quantum, Treading Water, Miami Nights and Wild Widows.

Her books have sold more than 10 million copies worldwide, have been translated into more than a dozen languages and have appeared on the *New York Times* bestseller more than 30 times. She is also a *USA Today* and *Wall Street Journal* bestseller, as well as a Spiegel bestseller in Germany.

Her goals in life are simple—to finish raising two happy, healthy, productive young adults, to keep writing books for as long as she possibly can and to never be on a flight that makes the news.

Join Marie's mailing list on her website at marieforce.com for news about new books and upcoming appearances in your area. Follow her on Facebook at www.Facebook.com/MarieForceAuthor and on Instagram at *www.instagram.com/marieforceauthor/*. Contact Marie at *marie@marieforce.com*.

Milton Keynes UK
Ingram Content Group UK Ltd.
UKHW020116030823
426179UK00005B/102